AND THE TEST STARTS ... NOW

Stooping down in his pressure suit, Pappy picked his rifle up by its long barrel from where it rested against the rough wall of his hastily excavated foxhole. His rifle. The Ueys would have semis and full-autos, maybe even small cannon or rockets. Real military weapons.

He and the other Loonies had paintball guns.

They were very *good* paintball guns, of course. Unlike their Earth-bound toy brethren, these were tools, with the range and accuracy to mark potential mining targets people like Morgan found, sometimes from as far as a kilometer away. She and KC were supposedly two of Hadley's best shots, but there hadn't been time for Pappy to give them a full field test before they'd been hustled out here to stand between the dome and the enemy advance.

"It's dust over there, all right," Morgan confirmed. "About three hundred forty meters out. Doesn't look like a meteor strike. I guess they're here. I know that particular dust pool. Give them another fifty meters, and I should be able to tell if it's one tank or more."

One tank or more. Terrific. Pappy hissed out a silent sigh. Apparently, his team's field test was starting now.

m "Foxhole"
imothy Zahn

LUNA

TRAVIS S. TAYLOR
TIMOTHY ZAHN
MICHAEL Z. WILLIAMSON
KACEY EZELL
JOSH HAYES

BAEN

BATTLE LUNA

Battle Luna copyright © 2020 by Travis S. Taylor, Timothy Zahn, Michael Z. Williamson, Kacey Ezell & Josh Hayes

Additional copyright information: Preface and The Rules copyright © 2020 by Travis S. Taylor; "Foxhole" copyright © 2020 by Timothy Zahn; "Under the Hill" copyright © 2020 by Michael Z. Williamson; "Moondog" copyright © 2020 by Kacey Ezell; "The Mimic" copyright © 2020 by Travis S. Taylor; *"Mama's Express"* copyright © 2020 by Travis S. Taylor; "Lunar Fury" copyright © 2020 by Josh Hayes; "The Battle of North Dome" copyright © 2020 by Travis S. Taylor.

A Baen Books Original

Baen Publishing Enterprises
P.O. Box 1403
Riverdale, NY 10471
www.baen.com

ISBN: 978-1-9821-2543-1

Cover art by Dave Seeley
Maps by Joy Freeman

First printing, July 2020
First mass market printing, June 2021

Distributed by Simon & Schuster
1230 Avenue of the Americas
New York, NY 10020

Library of Congress Control Number: 2020018055

Printed in the United States of America

10 9 8 7 6 5 4 3 2 1

CONTENTS

⊕

PREFACE

The idea for this book came about during a panel discussion that I was moderator for at a science fiction convention. It was LibertyCon in Chattanooga, Tennessee, in July of 2014. The panel was something along the lines of "Space Warfare: What would war in space really be like?" On this panel were, from the far left facing the crowd, Timothy Zahn, Dr. Charles E. Gannon, John Ringo, and then myself, Dr. Travis S. Taylor.

Now if you have never seen a panel with any of these particular individuals you must understand that each of us, well, we are self-proclaimed experts in most all matters regarding military science fiction, science fiction, future science, military science, blowing stuff up, world building, world killing, lightsaber construction, lightsaber destruction, faster-than-light space travel, slower-than-light space travel, alien invasions, invading alien worlds, graphic violence, blowing stuff up (we're so good at that one I decided to say it twice), and in particularly we are all excellent at sitting on panels and taking control of them for our own individual nefarious public relations purposes. In other words, moderators hate us because they can't keep us between the ditches.

Lucky for me I was appointed moderator of this mixed herd of rancor monsters, space bugs, crabpus, and Posleen godkings. I have known most of these fellows since I started science fiction and I realized a long time ago that you can lead the crabpus to water, but there is nothing stopping the mutated-looking mixture of giant octopus and crab claws from turning around and snapping you in half, chewing you up, and then defecating you out over a large alien cliff. So, I did the best thing I could think of when it came to moderating such a crew. I pretty much let them talk about whatever the hell they wanted to and interrupted every so often reminding them that we were supposed to be talking about war in space and how different or the same it might be.

Then, finally, an idea popped into my head. Tim Zahn seemed to catch on to it almost as soon as I came up with it. I interrupted the panel mid-sentence; I forget who was talking but I'll bet you a dime to a Death Star that it was Ringo.

"Alright, I have an idea. We're going to do a real-time simulation," I interrupted. "Tim, you and I have Ringo and Chuck surrounded." We actually did as they were sitting between us.

"You're gonna need more forces, Doc," Ringo laughed.

"So, here's the deal," I continued. "Ringo and Chuck's team are holding Fort Tranquility Base on the Moon. Tim and I have you surrounded with an equal-sized force. We'll be Blue Force and y'all can be Red Force. Now we also must assume that we will get no reinforcements for, let us say, three days or so. John, Chuck, how does Red Team hold the fort? Tim, how does our Blue Team take it?"

"Ah! I like this." Tim smiled with a very intrigued look on his face. He could do this, I was certain. After all, he was wearing all black, they'd never see him coming. "What level of weapons can I have? Rayguns? Transporters? Lightsabers?"

"Good question, Tim. Okay, we need some rules," I responded as I realized that my LibertyCon mug was completely empty of whatever it was I was drinking at the time. Hey, it was a con; I'd been talking all day; I was thirsty. "Already established no reinforcements for three days. We'll say that is our level of space travel. It is modern, assuming we still had a space program worth its weight in anything. Also, we can allow for better space suits. We've been on the Moon long enough to build a fort there so our suits and buggies and similar infrastructure should be better than we have now but only in a 'we've built more of them so they fit better and work better' way and not in a 'we invented unobtainium and impervium' kind of way. Bullets, missiles, bombs, and no rayguns other than laser systems we already have, but we can allow them to be half the size and twice the power output, maybe. No new energy sources. How's that?"

For the most part they all agreed. I could tell Tim wanted more details on the weapons, but before I could get more out John jumped in doing the two-gun mojo.

"I want claymores," he said. "Before we were attacked we put them all around the facility creating a perimeter of death."

"Hmm." I thought about that for a second. "Do you have any established satellites for recon, comms, GPS, etcetera, in orbit around the Moon?"

"I would think we would if we had established a base there already," Chuck added.

"Great! Then the first thing I plan to do is set off every single one of those mines as soon as I can. With no atmosphere on the Moon to slow the shrapnel down you're going to be launching small chunks into orbit. That should do wonders for knocking out your eyes and ears in orbit above." I smiled triumphantly.

"No atmosphere and less gravity certainly changes how we think about this." Tim was contemplating his first move. "Recoil might be an issue also. We need a list of weapons that would be safe to use in the lunar environment."

"What is our building made of?" Ringo asked. "I mean, is it a tin can or rock?"

"Let's say it has been there a year or two and it was made using lunar materials fashioned into something like concrete. You could do sandbags or, I guess, lunar regolith bags," I answered.

"Okay. Rock and sandbags." John seemed to be okay with that. "Military forts have been made out of that stuff for millennia so this isn't anything new to worry about."

The panel went on like this for almost an hour and when it was done neither team had held or captured a damned thing. We were still arguing about the things we had and/or could use. I pointed out to the group that this would make a great idea for an anthology where we set up the rules of the engagement and then we each wrote our own version of the battle just to study where this could take us. We all got excited about it. Think about it. Not only would it be a fun story, but this is Pentagon simulation and DARPA think-tank kind of stuff. It would be cool.

So, I immediately chased down Toni Weisskopf, God Empress, of Baen Books and told her of the idea. She agreed that it sounded fun.

"But, Toni, I'd like to have the experts in military SF that we could get anyway on this anthology. Who would that be? I mean, David Drake and David Weber are likely to be contracted up and busy. I'd like to get Mike Williamson, perhaps."

"Mad Mike would be good," she said. "But this isn't really the Davids' thing. I think with the addition of Mike you four really are the nuts-and-bolts science fiction military experts in the business."

"Aw shucks, ma'am." I didn't really say that, but I thought it. What I did say was, "Okay, then. The five of us do a twenty-thousand-word short story of our own take on Battle Luna. Ringo came up with the name. What do you think?"

"Who's going to write up the rules?" she asked.

"Well, Tim had some ideas?"

"Great! Tim it is. You write up an intro and Tim writes up the rules. Then each of you write up a version of the battle. Then you edit it and we've got ourselves a book," she said.

So, here it is. Battle Luna. But alas, along the way I somehow managed to let Ringo and Gannon slip out of the herd of space bugs, rancors, Posleen godkings, and crabpus. Chuck was too contracted up and Ringo got busy killing zombies to no avail. What I did do was get Mike Williamson on board and two new writers that I really enjoyed working with on the project. I think you'll like them as well. Hope you enjoy reading it as much as we did writing it.

I'd also like to point out that the story concept has morphed and evolved over time. We decided to add some more SF to the plot and I added a bit of "revolution" as in American Revolution to the backstory. So, what we ended up with was a *Battle Luna* rich with specific battles, events, and an overarching story of a Free Luna! One day in the not-too-distant future there might be thirteen colonies on the Moon ranging from tourist to mining to manufacturing to science colonies. And one day, the governments of the Earth are very likely to want to overly tax those colonies based on the goods they generate, the infrastructure needs they have, and whatever other money is to be made there. Anywhere fortunes can be made, government will eventually want a piece of it—a big piece of it. And this is likely what might happen under such circumstances. It is certainly what has happened in the past and as we all know history is like a Mandelbrot set in time repeating itself over and over and over with slight variations here and there. But hey, that's what makes humanity interesting, ain't it? That said, let's go to the Moon. And LET'S GET IT ON!

THE RULES

＋

Added here is a bit of a back-and-forth between Tim and me about what our rules would be from the start. And as typical between us, we started out with rules and great intentions and then ended up doing whatever the Hell we wanted to.

Okay Tim, here we go. As we discussed at the con, let's keep the tech to what we have now plus no more than 20–50 years with no new physics breakthroughs. We should maybe have a list of 10 to 20 weapons that we can choose from. Perhaps we allow each author to develop one device/weapon/tool themselves for originality if they desire. But the rule on that weapon is that it can't be new physics just new engineering.

I'll start up on an introduction chapter to introduce the Red and Blue teams and the story behind the engagement which Ringo and I already brainstormed. The general premise is that the Red Team is holding the base. They took a team of scientists there to test a new type of energy source. Let's say it is a quantum vacuum energy collector, but they moved the experiments to the Moon because small—very, very small— tests on Earth went really wrong and blew up multiple city blocks with a microchip-sized experiment. So these guys were being altruistic and cautious.

Big note from hindsight here: We didn't use any of that stuff from the above paragraph. Tim actually came up with a much better idea called the Mimic. You'll see as you read through.

But, the Blue Team fears they are building a WMD to wipe out an entire continent or more. And even if it is just a new energy source it would destabilize the market and change the balance of power on Earth. So, neither team is good or bad. They are just Red and Blue. There should be heroes on both sides as well as baddies. Also, I think we should allow it to be permissible to set off the device as a doomsday alternative to keep it out of the enemy hands. This, of course, is a last-ditch effort that would kill everybody Red and Blue.

Okay, everyone feel free to chime in on this and/or start writing. Let's get the dialog open and the writing started.

The writing then started and it took us nearly four years to get to the end of this book. And it looks a lot different from the proposed evolution in the paragraphs above. But that's okay, I like how it turned out. I hope you will as well!

FOXHOLE

✛

by Timothy Zahn

"I wonder how many of the people up there hate us."

Papillon "Pappy" MacLeod—who disliked his given name so much that even the sarky nickname "Pappy" he'd been saddled with had come as something of a relief—turned from his contemplation of the half-Earth hovering ominously over the lunar surface and looked across at the foxhole twenty meters to his left at the other end of his comm cable. The cables were a little awkward, but under the circumstances no one wanted to be caught gabbing over a radio, not even a theoretically secure one. "Excuse me?" he asked.

"I was just wondering how many Earthers hate us," KC Devereux repeated.

"Odd question," Pappy said, peering across the rocky ground. KC had always liked rolling verbal grenades into the middle of conversations. But this was hardly the time or place for such antics.

Still, from what he could see of KC's expression through his helmet faceplate, that didn't seem to have been the big French Canadian's goal anyway. "Any reason in particular you're bringing that up right now?"

"I saw a new CNN poll this morning," KC said meditatively. His eyes, Pappy saw, were fixed on the hovering half-Earth. "It said eighty percent thought the Moon wasn't worth the time and money United Earth is pouring into us. Eighty percent comes to about five and a half billion. That's an awful lot of hate."

"I wouldn't worry about it," Pappy soothed. "CNN likes to claim they speak for the whole world, but no one believes that, not even them. It's probably only a couple hundred million who hate us. The rest don't even know we exist. Or care."

"Thanks, Pappy," KC said drily. "That makes me feel *so* much better."

"They'll know soon enough," Morgan Lee murmured from the foxhole twenty meters to Pappy's right. Her voice was thoughtful and a bit distant. *Inscrutable*, Pappy might have characterized it if that term wasn't pompously frowned upon by Earthers in regards to Asians like Morgan. "They'll care, too. Eventually."

"Right," KC said. "*The shot heard 'round the world. The high drama of the century.*"

"Pun intended?" Pappy asked.

"Pun intended," KC confirmed. "Heard 'round *their* world, of course, not ours. Can't hear anything in a vacuum."

"It's supposed to be metaphorical," Morgan said. "I wouldn't worry about the poll, either. If you know how to tweak the questions, you can make a poll give whatever answers you want."

"They're fattening us up for the slaughter," Pappy added. "The minute that first shot is fired—by either side—we're the ones who'll get blamed for starting the war."

"With seriously edited recordings, no doubt," KC said darkly. "Pretty hard to blame us when the Ueys are blowing up domes and slaughtering people."

"Hey, if we weren't so damn stubborn about paying our fair share of the taxes that keep us going they wouldn't have to teach us a lesson," Pappy said. "See? See how easy it is? Even easier than writing slanted polls."

"They're not going to blow up any domes," Morgan said.

"And what share of taxes are they talking about?" KC retorted. "The tariffs—the prices they're paying for our metals—hey, *we're* the ones getting robbed, not them."

"And when you're in charge of CNN and the rest of the media, you can explain that to the world," Pappy said. "Good luck. Even just speaking the word *economics* is usually enough to make people's eyes glaze over."

"Yeah," KC growled. "Too bad economics is what drives everything else. Suppose I'm preaching to the choir, though."

"Well, that *is* what accountants do," Pappy agreed.

"Understand economics?" KC asked. "Or glaze over people's eyes?"

"Both," Pappy said, trying to put a little lightness in his tone. Neither of his two companions had ever been in combat before, and he could feel their tension and bubbling fears.

Not that Pappy himself was exactly immune from that.

In the fifteen years he'd been with the British SAS, until the leg injury that had ultimately turned him into a Luna Colonies accountant, he'd seen action on three different continents. He was well aware of the role adrenaline and fear played in combat readiness, and how to find that fine line where they stopped being assets and became liabilities.

But that had been a long time ago, and under vastly different circumstances. On Earth he'd had his mates at his sides, and even when the plan went sideways—and plans always went at least a little sideways—he knew what he was doing and how his weapons and gear functioned.

But no one had ever fought a war on the Moon.

The reports from Tranquility said the Ueys had brought rifles with them. That was fine, as far as it went. Modern cartridges had enough oxygen mixed in with the propellant to make them function in vacuum.

But did the soldiers know how to use them? The reports had suggested that the invasion force had landed, unloaded their improvised tanks from the transports and loaded up the troops, and headed immediately toward the various domes. Certainly there'd been no indication of the soldiers being put through any target practice.

Charging in without proper training was typical of Uey forces, of course. They were cocky S.O.B.s at the best of times. More importantly, if the rumors were to be believed, the United Earth leadership had leaped into this whole thing way faster than they should have.

The rumors.

Mentally, Pappy shook his head. As former military he knew a lot about rumors. They were like motor oil: a lubricant for social interactions that could spill out into the air at the slightest opportunity, and typically got pretty much everywhere. Their reliability, according to his own private tally, ran to maybe sixty percent with at least a whiff or two of truth, twenty percent with enough truth to make them worth listening to, and less than one percent that were spot on.

By all logic, the Mimic rumors he'd been hearing for the past month should be well within the forty percent that were a hundred percent make-believe. But at the same time, the United Earth response was far out of proportion to the Lunar Colonies' threats to withhold metal shipments until a more equable profit-sharing scheme could be worked out. *Someone* down there apparently believed in the Mimic, and that someone had troops, transports, and firepower at his disposal.

And the Loonies had nothing.

They had no soldiers. No weapons. No fighting vehicles. No experience. The *shot heard 'round the world* metaphor might be the current darling of the fringe news media, but at least the American Colonies had had muskets and had known how to use them.

They'd had allies, too, eventually. Sadly, Lafayette and his buddies wouldn't be coming this time around. France was as much a part of United Earth as everyone else.

It was going to be a slaughter. Everyone knew it. Or rather, it would be as much of a slaughter as Earth decided to make it. Morgan's rose-eyed trust in Uey restraint notwithstanding, there was no reason they couldn't blow one of Luna's colony domes just to prove they were serious.

Certainly the mass drivers the Council had scrambled to set up as anti-spacecraft weapons weren't much of a counterthreat. They were designed to throw metal canisters across large distances as an aid to ore transport, and no matter how much jury-rigging the techs did to the programming they were always going to be slow and ponderous and utterly incapable of targeting something moving past at even a moderate rate of speed.

Granted, if a Uey attacker insisted on flying straight at its target dome before unloading his bomb, a mass driver might have a chance of taking it down. But any pilot who did something that stupid deserved to be shot down anyway.

But then, the Ueys didn't have to take even that small risk. The mountains and ridges around most of the domes meant their mass-driver defenses couldn't throw at anything running at ground level. With troops and tanks, the Ueys could simply roll up to the colonies' front doors.

Which led to Pappy and his companions.

Pappy turned to look behind them. *The Freeway*, the people of Hadley Dome called it: the doglegged, more or less level approach to the dome wending its way through the jagged ridges of the Rima Fresnel, the fields of scree, and other hazards to ground transportation. It was the only lane big enough for the Ueys' tanks, at least according to Tranquility's description, so if they decided to hit Hadley, this was the route they would have to take.

He grimaced. *If*, hell. *When*. There was no point in bringing all these men to Luna and not making as much noise and fury as possible. Even if they decided to start with some of the other domes, sooner or later they would come to Hadley.

"Is that dust?" KC asked suddenly. "Pappy, is that dust over there?"

Sooner or later; and apparently, sooner. "Where?"

"Just past the end of the Cross-eye," KC said. "Morgan, you might not be able to see it from your angle."

"Wait a second," Pappy said, frowning out into the distance. He'd never heard of any formation near Hadley called the Cross-eye. "Past the end of the *what*?"

"Sorry—the end of Waffle Ridge," KC said. "*Cross-eye*'s what miners call that kind of formation."

"No, I can see it," Morgan said, bending over her compact rangefinder scope. It was the best scope in Hadley, and given that geosurveyors used that kind of gear all the time, it made sense that it had been assigned to her.

Still, it made Pappy's fingers itch that it was on the edge of her foxhole and not attached to his rifle.

His rifle.

Stooping down, Pappy picked it up by its long barrel from where it rested against the rough wall of his hastily excavated foxhole. His rifle. The Ueys would have semis and full-autos, maybe even small cannon or rockets. Real military weapons.

He and the other Loonies had paintball guns.

They were very *good* paintball guns, of course. Unlike their Earth-bound toy brethren, these were tools, with the range and accuracy to mark potential mining targets people like Morgan found, sometimes from as far as a kilometer away. She and KC were supposedly two of

Hadley's best shots, but there hadn't been time for Pappy to give them a full field test before they'd been hustled out here to stand between the dome and the Uey advance.

"It's dust, all right," Morgan confirmed. "About three hundred forty meters out. Doesn't look like a meteor strike. I guess they're here."

Pappy hissed out a silent sigh. Apparently, his team's field test was starting now. "Okay," he said as calmly as he could. "KC, give Hadley a heads-up. Morgan, any idea what size party they're bringing?"

"Not really," Morgan said. "But I know that particular dust pool. Give them another fifty meters, and I should be able to tell if it's one tank or more."

One tank or more. Terrific. "Keep watching," Pappy ordered. "KC, keep Hadley updated."

"Right." Across to Pappy's left, KC unplugged their local comm cable from his suit's junction box and plugged in the one that slithered down the ground behind him and disappeared into the dogleg that led back to Hadley Dome. Radio communications on Luna were encrypted for privacy, but no one seriously believed the Ueys couldn't decrypt them if they wanted to badly enough. Wired communications were awkward and fragile, but it was the only way to maintain at least a modicum of secrecy.

Pappy lowered his eyes to the meager collection of equipment in his foxhole. He had his paintball gun, complete with an improvised and highly inadequate scope, and two spare canisters of ammo. At the back of the teardrop-shaped hole was his catapult, also hastily constructed, with a cylinder a shade smaller than a standard oxy tank that was filled with a combination of propellant and vacuum cement. Beside the catapult was a suit repair kit and two spare oxygen tanks, plus some replacement struts and a small welding torch in case the catapult broke while there was still time to repair it.

And propped up against the side wall was a coil of monofilament line, two hundred meters long and half a ton test.

He eyed the monofil with a mixture of frustration and regret. There were so many things a clever soldier could do with high-stress thread. So many things he'd wanted to do with it. But the Ueys had moved faster than anyone had expected, and he'd hadn't had time to rig even half the traps and snares he'd hoped to create before he and the others had been ordered back to their foxholes.

He'd argued about it at the time, but Hadley had insisted. In hindsight, given that the Ueys were apparently here, it was probably just as well they'd pulled back.

He gave his equipment one last scan, reflexively memorizing positions in case he had to grab for something without looking, then turned back to the front. Hadley was supposedly throwing together more equipment for the upcoming battle, but it wasn't going to get here before the Ueys did. He could only hope that the haste of the Ueys' advance meant they were just as ill equipped as the Loonies.

To his left, KC again swapped out his comm cables. "Okay, Hadley's cranking up the mass drivers in case they try a sky assault," he said. "Spotters aren't showing anything flying in the area, but that could change at any minute."

"Did they say anything about our Uey tanks?" Pappy asked.

"I asked, but they can't see anything out here," KC said. "Too much stuff in the way."

"Anything from the rest of the perimeter?"

"Nothing they thought worth telling us."

"There won't be," Morgan said.

"Won't be what?" Pappy asked. "Sky assaults or other perimeter movement?"

"Neither," Morgan said. "They're not going to try walking soldiers over the ranges until they try the tanks first, and this is the only route wide enough."

"Unless they drop something into the dome first," KC said. "Even if they don't want to start off with mass slaughter, they could drop a javelin or something into the entry foyer. That probably wouldn't hurt anyone, but would prove they could do it."

"They won't," Morgan said. "They can't risk damaging Hadley or any of the other domes."

"That's the second time you've said that," Pappy commented, eyeing her. "Seems to me that KC's got a point. Bombing an enemy's capital is a traditional way to prove it's not invulnerable. And a javelin or a few rounds of small-gauge cannon fire would seal so fast that we wouldn't even lose much air."

"It's—" Morgan broke off. "I just don't think they want the bad publicity, that's all."

"Uh-*huh*," KC said knowingly. "With eighty percent of the public already on the Ueys' side? Come on, Morgan. You know something, don't you?"

There was a long pause. "I'm sorry," she said at last. "I can't talk about it."

"You can't talk about the Mimic?" Pappy suggested.

She shot him a hooded look. "I said I can't talk about it."

"Come on, Morgan," Pappy cajoled. "We've all heard the rumors. Hell, we've all heard the *name*. If we're going to die out here, I'd like to know it's not just because United Earth is stiffing us on chromium prices."

"You'll know when everyone else does," Morgan said firmly, turning back to her scope. "All right. I'm calling it a single tank. Could be something smaller leading it, though. Maybe a runabout?"

Pappy turned back to his own scope. To him, the dust looked exactly the way it had before, with no reason to call it a single tank or a pair of them. Or a herd of elephants, for that matter.

But Morgan was the expert. "So a tank, plus an outrider," he said.

"Or no outrider, but a couple of soldiers," KC put in. "There they are, just coming around Waffle."

Pappy shifted the direction of his scope. All he could see from his angle was the ridge itself. But if the Ueys were coming in from the right, as the dust cloud suggested, then KC would see them first. "You say there are two of them?"

"Two in front," KC said. "Might be more behind them. They've got some kind of—I don't know. Long sticks or something. Don't look like rifles."

And then, coming around the ridge, there they were.

There were two of them, just as KC had said, dressed in some strange hybrid of Uey spacesuit and Uey body armor. The spacesuit was the base garment, the same type the United Earth administrators used at their bases at

Tranquility and Hippalus. The same type, moreover, that the Loonies themselves had originally been saddled with before they'd made some sorely needed improvements. On top of the suits each of the two soldiers was wearing a heavy-looking torso vest, a slightly cheaper-looking version of the kind of armor Pappy had worn in the SAS. They had long-barreled machine pistols belted at their hips, probably modified MP5s or some knockoff.

Mentally, Pappy shook his head. Body armor was all well and good; but with a helmet faceplate the size of a serving platter as an alternative target, all a torso vest really accomplished was to add weight, throw off balance, and encourage headshots.

Which could be a serious problem for the soldier inside. Modern spacesuits were self-sealing, and depending on how sophisticated a biomed kit you put in was, even chest wounds were reasonably survivable if the victim could be moved into a pressurized facility fast enough. But a round through the faceplate and anywhere into the skull was a probable lights-out. The Ueys were just damn lucky that the Loonies didn't have any real guns.

And as for the long sticks they were carrying...

"You're right, those aren't rifles," he told KC. "They're mine detectors."

KC made a long, rude noise. "*Mine detectors?* On the *Moon?* Oh, that's just too funny."

"No argument here," Pappy agreed with the first breath of humor he'd felt all day. Between the micrometeors, the condensate needles, and the various mascons, the Moon was riddled with bits of relatively pure metal. If the detectors were set at a high enough sensitivity level, the soldiers could be out there for hours.

The real irony being that the meager weaponry Pappy and the others had available contained virtually no metal at all.

"And look how they're walking," KC said. "See that? They're just *walking*."

"I see it," Pappy said. Walking—one foot in front of the other—instead of doing the little kangaroo hops that every Loonie quickly learned was the best way to get around.

"They can't have been here more than two days," KC continued, a new hint of hope in his voice. "Maybe less."

"Tranquility said the ones they saw seemed to know what they were doing," Morgan pointed out.

"Maybe all the competent ones went somewhere else," KC said. "Maybe we got the runts of the litter. If they really don't know what they're doing, it could be the Winter War all over again."

"The *what*?" Morgan asked.

"The Winter War," KC said, his voice slipping into what Pappy had heard the other miners privately refer to as his professor mode. "Back in 1939 the Soviets rolled into Finland with an eye toward creating a buffer zone in case Leningrad came under attack. They had the numbers and the guns, but they had no idea what they were doing. They didn't know how to fight in snowy forests, their winter clothing was ridiculously inadequate, and their olive-drab tanks and khaki uniforms stuck out in the snow like marker paint."

"They'd also lost most of their officer corps in Stalin's 1937 purge," Pappy murmured. Over a century later, the lessons and tactics of the Winter War were still part of the SAS curriculum.

"Don't know about the Uey officers, but that's the Uey forces, all right," KC said. "Charging onto our turf with no idea what they're doing."

"Maybe," Pappy said. "You *do* know the Finns lost that war, right?"

"But they held out for a hell of a long time," KC countered. "I'm just saying we're starting out with the same home-court advantage the Finns did. And it'll be a hell of a lot harder for the Ueys to bring in more troops than it was for the Russians."

"Maybe," Pappy said, pitching his voice for caution. Enthusiasm and confidence were necessary. Overconfidence could get you killed. "Morgan, you got them yet?"

"The minesweepers, yes," Morgan confirmed. "The tank should be visible any minute. You should probably get your bombs ready."

"Right," Pappy said. "One at a time. I'll load mine first; KC, keep an eye on them. Give me a shout if they do anything."

He dropped into a squat, feeling a small and slightly irrational sense of relief as he temporarily left the enemy's line of fire—small, because he would eventually have to stand up again; irrational, because there *were* such things as mortars. A small hop took him to the rear of his foxhole and his catapult.

The device was hardly a work of art. Still, for all the hasty welds and obvious scrap-heap sourcing of some of the bracing gear, it seemed functional enough. Its grooved ramp was about a meter long, its launch angle adjustable with a hand crank, and was coated with solid lubricant that would send the projectile on its way unhindered. The driving force was provided by a tank of compressed nitrogen, which fed into an intermediate chamber for more precise gauging of launch speed and power, and had a dual nozzle that could also take one of Pappy's spare oxy tanks in a pinch. A printout of launch angles, compression levels, and range had been attached to the back near the compression gauge where it could be quickly consulted. Pappy had seen better, but he'd also seen far worse.

It was the projectiles themselves that concerned him.

He picked up the canister. While it was about the same size and shape as an oxy tank, it was considerably heavier. Heavy enough that he probably would have strained his back if he tried lifting it in Earth gravity. The shell was one of the many ceramics that the Loonies used in building, encased in one of the fracture webs miners like KC used to break off and fragment particularly useful rock outcroppings. Inside, mixed with some kind of propellant, was compressed vacuum cement of the sort used to repair damaged domes, vehicle frames, and pretty much anything else that didn't need to move.

Which, of course, was the whole point of using it here. *If* it worked.

"Morgan, you worked with the people who put these things together, right?" he asked.

"Not really," she said. "But a friend of mine did, and I saw her report."

"And they tested everything, right?"

"They tested all the components," she said. "But they

couldn't do a field test. There isn't a vacuum chamber big enough."

"You're joking, right?" Pappy growled. "The whole damn *Moon* is a vacuum chamber."

"Which the Ueys are watching like hawks."

Pappy winced. "Of course they are," he said. "Stupid of me."

"Don't worry, they'll work," Morgan assured him. "They worked fine in the simulations."

"You want to know what we called simulations in the SAS?"

"Probably not."

"More soldiers," KC said. "Three—whoa. You seeing that?"

"I'm seeing it," Pappy said grimly.

Three more soldiers had appeared around the ridge, walking abreast about twenty meters behind the minesweepers. Unlike those first two, though, this group had their MP5s up and ready in hand. Also unlike the first pair, they held clear plastic riot shields in front of them, rectangles about a meter wide and a meter and a half long.

"Uh-oh," Morgan murmured.

"Agreed," Pappy said. The key to their strategy was to blind the Ueys with paintball rounds into their faceplates and viewports. With those shields in hand, they could take a lot of paint before their vision was even slightly impaired.

"Don't worry about it," KC said. "We've got other fish to fry, like you Brits say."

"We never say that."

"Well, you should," KC said. "Wait just a second . . . let 'em come around the ridge . . ."

And then, there it was, rolling around Waffle Ridge: the Uey tank.

At first glance it didn't look like much. It was a Dunsland 400-series, rolling along on eight sets of sponge-rubber, independently axled tires. The body was about fifteen meters long and three high, with a submarine-style sail/conning tower rising from the main body a couple of meters behind the bow. The driver would be there, along with the observation and navigational gear.

Dunslands had been the workhorse vehicle early in Luna's history, the first group of them shipping when there were only three domes instead of the current thirteen. But over the years, as the flaws in the design and operating systems had become apparent, they'd been phased out and replaced by vehicles of the Loonies' own design. The few Dunslands still in service had mostly been converted to hauling ore in places where mass drivers weren't practical.

A point that hadn't been lost on KC. "Look at that," he said scornfully. "We're being attacked by museum pieces."

"Probably all they had down there they could grab," Pappy said. "They haven't needed to make rovers for us since the Quatermass II debuted."

"I'm surprised they didn't just commandeer some of ours," Morgan murmured.

"What, and have them delivered with sabotage and booby traps already in place?" Pappy shook his head. "They're not *that* stupid."

"At least they picked a wheeled rover instead of a

tracked one," KC said. "That could have been awkward. But you see up there on the sail? Those are the fish I was talking about."

"I see them," Pappy acknowledged. On both sides of the Dunsland's sail the Ueys had welded one-man personnel cages, where watchful soldiers stood with Kord 9P150 light machine guns swivel-mounted on the front rims of their cages. Neither man carried a sidearm that he could see, but both had spare 150-round canisters secured to their utility webbing. Like the minesweepers and the shieldbearers, both were wearing torso vests.

But unlike the shieldbearers, their faceplates were presented nakedly to the sun and the harsh lunar environment.

And to the Loonies' paintguns.

"So I'm thinking we go for those sail gunners first," KC said. "Then the Dunsland's viewports, then the minesweepers. How's that sound?"

"Let's do the minesweepers before the viewports," Pappy said. "We don't want the Dunsland stopping short just because the driver can't see. By that same token, Morgan, they might speed up when the shooting starts, so be ready."

"Got it," Morgan said. "Looks like they're going to hug the Waffle."

Pappy nodded. They would have seen the other side of the ridge on their approach, confirmed that no one was lurking there, and now they would hug this side of the low ridge to guard against any last-minute attacks along that flank. "Just bear in mind that they could suddenly go into a zigzag if their commander smells a rat."

"I'll be ready," Morgan assured him.

"Are we done talking yet?" KC said. The earlier amusement was gone from his voice, leaving just the original stress behind. Maybe he'd taken a good look at those Kord 9P150 machine guns.

"Almost ready," Pappy soothed. "Let's let them get just a little closer. When I give the word, you take the minesweepers, I'll take the machine gunners."

"Got it."

Moving slowly and carefully, Pappy set his paintgun's barrel on the edge of the foxhole, leaning down so he could look through his scope. He'd made sure the team's spacesuits were painted with the best lunar-rock camo Hadley's artists and geologists could come up with, and their faceplates had been done up in a crosshatch that should provide similar protection without interfering too much with their vision.

But the guns themselves were too narrow for proper silhouette-breaking methods, and while they'd been painted to match the local whites and grays the result was far from perfect. Given time, Pappy could have worked up some kind of shroud to do the trick, but time had been of the essence. Additional refinements would have to wait for Round Two.

Assuming, of course, the citizens of Hadley Dome survived Round One. Right now, that was still up in the air.

The Dunsland and its escorts were moving closer. Pappy peered through his scope, lining up the crosshairs on the left-hand machine gunner, reminding himself firmly that he'd already pre-ranged the scope for exactly this distance. Lunar drop was considerably less than on Earth, and of course there was no windage to worry about. All of that made targeting much simpler.

But the Dunsland *was* two hundred meters away. At that distance, even a space-suit faceplate was a damn small target, not to mention the shot he was actually going for.

He took a quick moment to check his partners. To his left, KC was peering through his scope, his gloved finger resting on the trigger. To his right, Morgan was likewise watching the Ueys' approach.

Unlike her companions, though, her hands were nowhere near her gun's trigger. Instead, she was balancing a small relay box on her left palm, its protective cover open, her right forefinger resting on one of the two toggle switches inside.

It was the one piece of this plan that absolutely depended on a functioning radio, and Pappy sent up a quick prayer that the Ueys weren't jamming all Loonie transmissions just for the hell of it.

He turned his attention back to his own scope. Almost time . . . almost . . .

Time. "Fire," he said quietly. Holding his breath, he gently squeezed the trigger. There was a brief kick against his shoulder, hardly even noticeable through the heavy material and air pressure of his suit . . .

And a sudden blossom of red exploded across his view.

Not onto the machine gunner's faceplate. Faceplates were the obvious target, and even an untrained miner like KC could hit *that.* Former SAS elites, on the other hand, should be held to higher standards.

And so Pappy watched in satisfaction as the thick red

paint hit, congealed, and—hopefully—jammed the firing mechanism of the machine gunner's Kord. The rest of the paint spattered harmlessly across the gunner's torso.

"Got him!" KC crowed.

"Great," Pappy said. The scope image abruptly blurred as the soldier swung his weapon around—"Now *duck*!"

Leaving his gun stretched out across the ground, Pappy bent his knees and dropped down out of sight. Just in time; a fraction of a second later the ground around his foxhole began exploding with dust and rock chips as the Ueys opened fire.

It was a curious sensation, watching the barrage take place without even a breath of an accompanying *bang-bang-bang*. His own shot hadn't been so jarring, gut-level speaking—paintball guns were pretty quiet even on Earth, and it had been easy to get used to the loss of that small *chuff* up here. But Kords and MP5s were horrendously noisy things, and all the three-shot bursts popping soundlessly around him gave him the eerie sensation of suddenly having been struck deaf.

Which made Morgan's sudden voice in his ear both jarring and a welcome relief. "Here they come," she called. "Pappy? They're almost there."

"Yeah, I'm here," Pappy said. Bracing himself, he eased carefully up again. The potshots were still coming, though the sheer ferocity of that initial response had faded as the Ueys apparently decided they were wasting ammo. It was a risk to show himself, but he needed to see this.

He made it back to viewing height without anyone putting a round through his helmet. Getting a grip on his gun, he refocused the scope on his earlier target.

One glance at the soldier fumbling with the Kord's firing mechanism was all he needed to confirm that the paintball had at least temporarily put the weapon out of action. Smiling to himself, he lowered the scope to the tank's front wheels.

The Dunsland had sped up, just as he'd warned it might, and was lumbering toward the innocent-looking crack in the ground where he and Morgan had set their trap. "Okay, get ready," he said. He and Morgan had examined the undercarriages of every vehicle that fit the description of Tranquility's observers, and he had no doubt that Morgan could do this without any help from him. But he'd been in enough high-pressure situations to know that having someone standing beside you, even figuratively, was an immense psychological help. The Dunsland rolled over the crack...

At Morgan's electronic command, the crack erupted into a spray of compressed nitrogen and multiple coils of monofilament line. Even as the cloud of gas dissipated the tank rolled squarely into the floating loops, its motion tangling them around the wheels, the axles, and into every angle and nook of the driving motors.

And with an abruptness that would probably have been accompanied by an ear-wrenching screech if the vehicle had been on pavement on Earth, the Dunsland ground to a halt.

"We got it," Morgan breathed, sounding immensely relieved and vaguely surprised. "It worked—"

She broke off as another volley of gunfire spattered silently around the foxholes. "*Down*," Pappy ordered as he again ducked.

This time, though, a single salvo seemed to be all the Ueys were willing to spend. The bullets stopped flying; carefully, Pappy raised his head.

His hope, between the paintballs and the monofil coils, had been to stop the Uey advance. For the moment, at least, they'd succeeded. The two minesweepers were heading back toward the Dunsland, one of them leading the other by the hand. The rearmost turned his head slightly, and Pappy could see the bright red splotch from KC's paintball neatly covering his faceplate. The machine gunner whose Kord Pappy had disabled was still trying to clear it, while his partner on the other side of the sail kept his weapon trained on the foxhole area. Even through the bulky suits there was a stiffness to their stances that showed their frustration and anger. The three shieldbearers had also retreated a few paces and were now standing shoulder to shoulder a few meters in front of the Dunsland, also facing their Loonie opponents. The Dunsland's rear side hatch had swung open, and a half dozen more Ueys were climbing awkwardly out onto the surface. Like the shieldbearers, they carried MP5s at their sides; unlike those other troops, they were carrying tools instead of shields.

"Are those wire cutters?" KC asked.

"Yes," Morgan confirmed. She did something with her scope, probably zooming in a bit more. "A couple of them have small torches, too."

Pappy smiled tightly. For all the good that would do them. From the strength of the monofil the Ueys clearly assumed it was wire, and were preparing their counter accordingly.

Only the stuff now wrapped tightly around their axles

was probably too thin for standard wire cutters, and the synthetic material had a melting point that was almost certainly higher than that of the tank's driving gear. Most Loonies had had experience with the stuff getting where it wasn't wanted, and knew the only efficient way to deal with it was a specifically designed solvent.

But like most things about Luna and the Loonies, the people who ran United Earth didn't have a clue about that.

"Looks like I'm up," KC said briskly. "Pappy?"

"Go," Pappy said. "But watch yourself—the man with the working machine gun looks seriously annoyed. Morgan? What's his range?"

"One hundred eighty-three meters," Morgan said.

"One-eighty-three, got it." KC ducked out of sight.

The newcomers from the back of the tank were clustered around the front now, working no doubt industriously at the snarled axles. Pappy shifted his scope to the shieldbearers, still holding their ground in front of the tank, then at the machine gunners standing vigil above.

Should he try to lob in a few more paintballs while KC finished getting his bomb ready? There was no point in shooting at the shieldbearers—their shields were being held high enough to protect their faceplates. The repair crew, for the most part, had their backs to him, and were furthermore blocking any shot into the axle mechanism. He didn't know if the paint would do anything to the heavier-duty gear there, but with the monofil in place there was no point in wasting ammo. Besides which, every shot he or the others took risked the Ueys zooming in on their exact locations.

But that remaining machine gunner was a tempting target, and well worth the risk of exposure. The soldier had his Kord leveled, which unfortunately put the firing mechanism out of Pappy's reach, and in the man's current semicrouch his shoulder and left arm were partially blocking his faceplate.

Still, most of the faceplate was visible. It was worth the risk, Pappy decided. Especially as it would provide some distraction until KC was ready—

"Bombs away!"

Pappy looked over just as the cylinder blasted out of KC's foxhole, arcing its leisurely way toward the tank.

And that was that. When the bomb hit the ground by the wheels and blasted its cargo of cement into the drive mechanism, the Ueys might as well kiss the Dunsland goodbye and start walking. The only question would be whether they would walk toward Hadley Dome and try to attack on foot or else retreat back to wherever their local staging area was for this operation. The canister hit the top of its arc and started back down.

In perfect unison, the three shieldbearers jumped straight up, still shoulder to shoulder, the edges of their shields pressed together. They rose higher, their momentum and timing moving them directly into the cylinder's path.

And as Pappy watched in disbelief and chagrin, their shields intercepted the bomb. There was a burst of foamy white liquid as the canister exploded—

And then the Ueys were floating back down to the surface. Their shields were now cemented solidly together, with the handful of stray tendrils that had flowed over the shield tops sticking rigidly out into space like frozen octopus legs. One tendril, thicker than the others, had managed to stay liquid long enough to attach itself to the shoulder of the Uey on the end.

The shields had been rendered mostly useless. One of the soldiers would similarly be at minimal performance until he could get the cement off his suit.

But the Dunsland—the immobilizing of which had been whole reason for the bombs in the first place—had escaped unscathed.

"Well, *damn*," KC growled. "How the hell did they know we had vac-cement bombs?"

"I doubt they did," Pappy said. "The plan was just for them to block *anything* we threw at them."

"Including real bombs?"

Pappy nodded. "Including real bombs."

"Damn idiots," KC muttered. "They could have died right there."

"They're soldiers," Pappy said soberly. "That's what soldiers do."

There was a moment of silence. Across by the Dunsland, the three men and their—now—single shield were heading around the rear of the tank. One of them was trying to bounce, but the other two still insisted on using their awkward walk and the third gave up after a couple of steps and went back to doing it their way. "So it's back to paintballs?" KC asked.

"At least until they clear out the monofil," Pappy said, peering through his scope. Somewhere during the confusion the machine gunner he'd paintballed had disappeared from his cage, presumably going back inside where he could work on his Kord with fingers instead of gauntlets.

The other guard was still standing ready, though. He would be the first target, Pappy decided, followed by the Dunsland's own viewports. As long as the vehicle was stalled, he might as well keep it that way as long as possible.

"Hold it," Morgan said suddenly. "More company, coming around the Dunsland's right side."

Pappy scowled as he shifted his scope that direction. More company, and more shields. Three more shieldbearers had appeared from the rear hatch, moving briskly toward the front to take their cemented comrades' positions.

"Damn," KC muttered. "I was hoping to get another shot at the wheels."

"We still might," Pappy said, frowning at the untangling group by the wheels. They seemed to be having a conversation of sorts. Which, judging by some of the hand gestures, was becoming a little heated.

Morgan had noticed it, too. "What do you think they're arguing about?" she asked uneasily. "Maybe whether to give up on the Dunsland and just go in on foot?"

"Will that get them what they want?" Pappy asked.

Morgan threw him a quick frown. "What?"

"The Mimic," he said pointedly. "Can they get it out of Hadley without the Dunsland?"

"Who needs their Dunsland?" KC scoffed. "There are ten other vehicles that size in there they could commandeer."

"And risk getting out in the middle of nowhere when

the Loonies' sabotage catches up with them?" Pappy shook his head. "*I* sure as hell wouldn't take that risk with a borrowed vehicle. So; Morgan?"

"I can't tell you, Pappy," she said, her voice tight.

"You have to," Pappy insisted. "I need to know what I'm working with. I need to know the parameters. I need to know what I've got in the way of bargaining position if it comes to that."

"*Bargaining?*" KC asked. "Who says we're going to bargain with them?"

"If it comes to that," Pappy repeated. "Morgan?"

"Hold that thought, Pappy," KC said. "They're up to something."

Pappy looked back at the Dunsland. The Ueys had finished their discussion and four of the six headed back toward the rear hatch. They met the replacement shieldbearers halfway along the side and the two groups passed each other. "Giving up so soon?" he murmured.

"Probably decided to try something else," Morgan said. "Maybe acids or a different type of cutter."

"Or they're just going to get more guns," KC muttered.

"They need the Dunsland to move the Mimic," Pappy said. "Right, Morgan?"

She didn't answer. "Fine," Pappy growled. "Either way, this is our chance."

"Our chance for what?" KC muttered.

"To take the bastards down for good," Pappy said, frowning. KC's tone had suddenly taken a nosedive. "You okay, KC?"

"Oh, sure," KC said. He didn't sound especially okay. "My brain just caught up with me, that's all. They've got machine guns. They've got soldiers. We've got paintballs. What the *hell* are we doing?"

"Our job," Pappy said firmly. "So they've got numbers. We've got brains." He nodded toward the Dunsland. "Let's give them another cement bomb."

"Okay." There was a hollow-sounding hiss as KC took a deep breath. "So where do the brains come in?"

"Right now," Pappy said. "Morgan, get your catapult ready. As soon as that new batch of shieldbearers are in position between us and them, lob your bomb at the tank."

"They'll just block it again," Morgan warned.

"Yep," Pappy agreed. "And once they've done that, while they're floating back down, I'll throw *my* bomb. They won't be able to react, and hopefully no one else will have time to, either."

The last word was barely out of his mouth when the remaining machine gunner abruptly opened fire again.

Reflexively, Pappy ducked his head, only then noticing that the rounds weren't coming anywhere near his foxhole. Instead, the entire salvo seemed to be going in KC's direction.

But not at his foxhole. Instead, the bullets were blasting into the steep-faced rock stack on KC's far side, splintering them into stone chips and sending them spinning into the sky in lazy arcs.

"Too late, Bozo," KC said sarcastically, lifting a one-fingered salute toward the Ueys even as he prudently ducked his head below ground level. "I already used my bomb. And you're a lousy shot, too."

Pappy caught his breath as he suddenly understood.

"KC—*down!*" he snapped. "He's not missing. He's trying for a ricochet!"

KC snarled a curse. "Son of a *bi*—"

The word disintegrated into a grunt of pain. "Aahh!"

And to Pappy's horror he saw twin puffs of expanding air drift up out of the other foxhole. "KC?" he snapped.

There was nothing but a low moan. "KC?" he called again. The Uey machine gunner was still firing into the rock stack. "*Report*, soldier."

"Yeah," KC said. It was more a curse than a word. "Yeah. Okay. Got me."

"How bad?" Pappy asked. He couldn't see any more leaking air, but that didn't necessarily mean anything. Even autoseal could only do so much, and it was entirely possible that the ricochet had dug a hole big enough that the suit would have no choice but to close off the affected area. In that case, one of KC's limbs or a large section of his torso could already be exposed to vacuum. "Where are you hit?"

"I don't think it's too bad," KC said through clenched teeth. "Shoulder—hurts like hell. And I think he got my helmet, too."

Pappy mouthed a curse. "Okay, hang on," he said, unplugging his direct line to KC. He started to unplug Morgan's as well—"Morgan, I need cover fire," he said. "On three, start firing at anything over there with a faceplate, starting with that S.O.B. with the machine gun. And for God's sake, keep your head down."

"If I keep my head down, I'm not going to be able to hit anything," she warned.

"I don't care if you hit him," Pappy said. "I just need him too busy to shoot at me. One, two, *three.*"

He yanked out her comm cable, put his hands on the edge of his foxhole, and with a convulsive push launched himself out onto the surface. Keeping as low as he could, his skin crawling with anticipation of the bullet that was surely on its way, he crossed the open ground in a handful of short kangaroo bounces and jumped into KC's foxhole.

And nearly landed on the other man. KC was sprawled on the bottom of the hole, twitching, his left hand over his shoulder as if he was trying to pat himself on the back. Pappy managed to find two open spaces for his feet as he fell and landed in a crouch straddling the other man's torso.

KC had been hit, all right. The bright orange of fresh autoseal showed where a bullet had cut through his back on an angle and eventually penetrated somewhere in the vicinity of his right shoulder blade. Another, more worrisome spot of orange showed on the back of his helmet. It was less angled than the one on his back, indicating it had gone in at a steeper angle.

Steep enough, and traveling fast enough, to penetrate KC's skull? Because if it had, the man was in serious trouble.

Pappy took a deep breath. First things first. Yanking open his emergency kit, he pulled out a set of patches and carefully spread them out over the two tears. The med readout jack was on the front of KC's suit, momentarily out of reach. Pappy double-checked both patches, then leaned forward and pressed his helmet against KC's. "Can you hear me?" he called.

"Yeah," KC's voice came back, distant and tinny. "How's it look back there?"

"Stable," Pappy said. "How about in there? Are you bleeding?"

"Don't know. Haven't checked."

Pappy blinked. "Say again?"

"Of *course* I'm damn bleeding," KC bit out. "I've got a *bullet* in my back, you idiot. Hurts like hell."

"Okay, hang on." Digging another comm cable from his kit, Pappy plugged them together. "Can you hear me better now?"

"Yeah, fine."

"I'm here, too," Morgan added. "How does he look?"

"That's what we're going to find out," Pappy said. "What about our friends out there?"

"I emptied most of my first magazine at them," Morgan said. "They stopped shooting, so I did, too."

"Are they coming toward us?"

"No, they're still sticking close to the Dunsland," she said. "The four who went inside are back, though, and all six are working on the wheels again."

So the Ueys still hadn't gotten the axles unsnarled. That should buy them at least a little more time. "Keep watching," he said. "KC, we're going to roll you up onto your left side—nice and easy—and get a look at your med readout."

"Sure," KC said. "You know, I might have popped a painkiller. I don't really remember."

"If you don't remember, you probably did," Pappy said. The side effects of the painkillers they packed into Loonie suits were well known and just a bit spooky. "I'll check. Okay; nice and easy."

"I think my head might be bleeding, too," KC

continued. Already the pain was fading from his voice and being replaced by a sort of dreaminess. "I've got some blood dripping on my faceplate."

"Got it," Pappy said, wincing. Dripping was probably okay, at least for the short term. Gushing or pouring would be very, very bad. "Just relax. I'll do this." Between the lower gravity and the inherent padding effects of the suit itself, he got KC on his side with a minimum of effort on his part and only a few vague comments of discomfort on KC's.

SAS doctrine trained you to be prepared for the worst. In this case, fortunately, it wasn't as bad as Pappy had feared. The med display indicated a small-caliber bullet lodged below KC's right shoulder blade and a shallow furrow across the back of his head. Neither was immediately life threatening, but both needed attention.

"Pappy?" Morgan called hesitantly. "How is he?"

"He'll be okay," Pappy assured her, falling back on the standard low-information answer for when you didn't want people to worry. KC's comm cable back to Hadley Dome was hanging down the back of the foxhole, over the catapult. Pappy plugged it into his suit and cut KC and Morgan out of the circuit. "Eagle Four to Hadley," he called. "We have a man down; repeat, man down. We need that MASH truck, stat."

There was no answer. "Hadley, this is Eagle Four," he repeated, louder this time. "Hadley, please respond."

"This is Hadley Control," a harried voice came back. "Who is this?"

"Eagle Four," Pappy said. "Where the hell were you?"

"Sorry, Eagle, sorry," the other said, sounding even more harried. "Lot of stuff happening. I was just—I'm running the whole periphery comm. All six Eagles."

A cold feeling settled in on the back of Pappy's neck. "Are there other attacks going on? Where?"

"No, no, no other attacks," the controller said hastily. "Someone spotted a drone, and there was a big discussion on whether we should shoot it down."

"You didn't, I hope," Pappy said. The drone had probably been sent for the express purpose of drawing fire from Hadley's defenses so the Ueys could see exactly what they were facing. As a general rule, the longer an enemy could be kept guessing, the better.

"No, no," the controller said. "It just took a while to decide."

"Yeah," Pappy said through clenched teeth. Decision gridlock was bad enough among trained and experienced military people. Throwing complete amateurs into the mix just exacerbated the problem.

But he'd better get used to it. Aside from a few ex-military like Pappy himself, amateurs were all the Loonies had.

"*If* you've got that sorted out, we have a man down," he growled. A burst of gunfire spattered on the ground around the foxhole, and he crouched a little lower, giving KC a quick look to make sure he hadn't taken another ricochet. "Two bullet injuries, one of them a headshot. Get that MASH truck rolling."

"Oh, God," the controller gasped. "Who got—I mean how bad—?"

"Bad enough that we need the MASH truck," Pappy

cut him off impatiently. This clown put the most garrulous SAS controller to complete and utter shame. "Transfer me to the truck and I'll give them the details."

"I can do that," the controller said. "What about the Uey tank? Devereux said there was a Dunsland 406 rigged out as a tank?"

"Yeah, and we're working on it," Pappy said. "Get the truck moving so I can get off the comm and work on it some more."

"It's not disabled?"

Pappy glared at the mountains hiding Hadley Dome from sight. What the *hell* was this? "No, it's not disabled. Does that matter?"

"Oh, God," the controller muttered. "I'm so sorry, Eagle Four. I can't send the truck until the Dunsland's been disabled."

Pappy felt his mouth drop open. "*What?*"

"Orders," the controller said, sounding completely miserable now. "Command says we can't send the truck when there's a chance it'll be destroyed. It's the only one we've got. We can't afford to lose it."

Pappy took a deep breath. Strategically, he could see, it made sense. Assets, balance, and costs were all part of military analysis, and in the long run a fully equipped rolling medical facility was far more valuable than a single soldier's life.

But KC was part of *his* team, damn it. He was Pappy's responsibility, and there was no way in hell the man was going to slowly bleed out just because someone sitting in a climate-controlled office had put together a spreadsheet. "Fine," he ground out. "Just get it warmed up and the crew inside. I'll call you when it's safe for them to come out in the sunshine."

He yanked out the cable without waiting for a response and linked KC and Morgan back in. "Okay, they're coming," he said. "How you holding up, KC?"

"Okay," KC said, with the muddled tone that showed the painkillers were going full force. "Listen, I don't think . . . I'm still getting drips running down my neck. You sure the press-patch is working?"

Pappy winced. The suits had an inner layer that was supposed to swell up against broken bones or sprained joints, immobilizing them long enough for a trip to the nearest dome and a proper med facility. But whether the system could put the necessary pressure in a small enough spot to stop a bleeder was a big unknown.

And the helmets didn't have that, at least not above neck level. The graze on KC's skull was going to keep bleeding until they could get him out of that suit and onto a treatment table.

Which left him two options. He could disable the Dunsland so the rice-counters in Hadley would send the MASH truck, or he could carry KC back to the dome on his own.

He lifted his head cautiously to eyeball level. And whichever one he picked, he needed to do it fast. If the enthusiastic action by the Dunsland's front wheels was any indication, they were getting close to unsnarling the monofil. Any minute now the vehicle would be on its way again, with nothing to stop it except him and Morgan.

He frowned. The tank had come in right beside Waffle Ridge, as a guard against flank attack. It had been brought to its forced halt about twenty meters along the ridge, too far for a sneak attack from the rear even if most of the Ueys were working at the front.

But KC had called Waffle a *cross-eye*. Pappy hadn't known the name was used for that particular ridge, but he *had* heard the term before. Maybe. "KC, why did you call Waffle Ridge the cross-eye?" he asked.

"What?" KC muttered. "Oh. 'Cause it's frangible rock. Look at it cross-eyed and it comes right down on you. Hate that."

"Don't blame you," Pappy said, studying the ridge and the surrounding terrain. Waffle Ridge ran all the way along their current right flank, passing within ten meters of Morgan's foxhole. It was just as steep there as it was by the Dunsland, but he could see a couple of potential hop spots that might get him to the top.

It would be tricky. It would also possibly get him shot, unless the Ueys were trying to be reasonable. But right now, it was all he had. "Okay," he said, crouching down and picking up one of KC's spare oxy tanks. "Morgan, get one of your oxy tanks and point the valve toward the Dunsland. When I give the word, crank it open and try to blow as much dust off the ground as you can. I'll do the same over here." *Somehow*, he added silently to himself as he looked around the foxhole. He could hardly hold the tank while he was scrambling madly to get over Waffle Ridge.

"What are you going to do?" Morgan asked.

"They won't send the MASH truck until the Uey tank's been disabled," Pappy said. "So I'm going to."

"How?"

"You just concentrate on making as much dust in front of us as you can," Pappy said, looking back at the catapult. The contraptions were heavy and unwieldly, and it had taken all three of them to get them into the foxholes in the first place. But if he could get it up onto the rim and brace it . . .

"I'll do that," KC wheezed.

And to Pappy's amazement, the other levered himself up off the foxhole floor. He took a moment to balance himself, then gestured to the tank in Pappy's hands. "Get it up there," he said, "and I'll hold it."

"You sure?" Pappy asked.

"Beats waiting forever for the bus," KC said. "Get going before they start moving again."

"Okay," Pappy said. He manhandled the tank up onto the rim and pointed the nozzle toward the ground in front of them. There was a dust-filled depression five meters out that should do the trick. "Morgan?"

"Ready," she said. "Be careful."

"I will." Pappy helped KC into position, then ducked down again and grabbed another oxy tank and the cutting torch from KC's catapult-repair equipment. "On three," he said, standing upright again and peering toward the Dunsland. Of all the soldiers, only the machine gunner seemed to have his full attention pointed in their direction. "One, two, *three*." He twisted the valve wide open.

He'd expected the escaping gas to blow the dust into a fine mist. Instead, the whole puddle exploded into a roiling tornado-like swirl of powder and rock chips. Pappy bounded out of the foxhole, the spare oxy tank cradled in his arms, and set off in short, quick hops toward the ridge. He passed his foxhole, briefly coming into a partial clear, then disappeared behind another dust cloud as he bounced behind Morgan's position. She was doing an even better job than KC, systematically sweeping her oxy tank back and forth to create an entire wall of dust that reached from the edge of Pappy's own foxhole all the way to Waffle Ridge. Pappy reached the ridge, bent his knees, and leaped as high up along the side as he could, landing on a slab of rock jutting out from the rest of the slope.

And flailed for balance as the slab promptly broke off beneath him.

Frangible, KC had said. *Damn rotten balsa wood*, he might have warned.

The first casualty was Pappy's left knee—the one on his bad leg, naturally—as it banged against the remains of the ledge hard enough to be felt through the suit. The second casualty was the oxy tank, which went flying as Pappy scrambled for handholds. He managed to hang onto the cutting torch as he regained his balance, found another even more marginal bit of footing, and leaped again. Two more jumps from equally fragile footholds and he was finally at the top.

He caught a slender spire and redirected himself over the sharp-edged crest. The footing on the other side was even more treacherous, and this time the torch also went flying as he grabbed at everything available in an effort to slow himself down. He succeeded, mostly, and landed on the ground with a jolt. For a moment he crouched there, wincing at the sharp pain in his knee and watching for signs that the Ueys might have spotted him. He had no idea how high Morgan's dust cloud had gone, but there was a fair chance he'd come out of its protection before he cleared the crest.

But whether they'd spotted him or not, he still had the initiative. Retrieving the torch, he got back to his feet and started hopping toward the Ueys.

He'd made note of the distinct rock pattern at the top of the ridge beside the tank, and while rock patterns didn't always look the same from different angles this one was unique enough to show when he arrived. Unlike the spot by the foxholes, the slope here was somewhat gentler, and he was able to climb it with a minimum of trouble and no false steps. He reached the crest and eased his helmet over for a look.

It was quickly apparent that the Ueys hadn't caught his mountain goat act. The scene was exactly as he'd left it, with two trios of shieldbearers standing guard against anything thrown from the Loonie side of the arena, two machine gunners in their cages—apparently the one had managed to get his Kord cleaned enough to function again, or else had had a spare—and the rest of the team working at getting the monofil out of the front axles.

He felt his lip twist as that first bit belatedly registered. *Two* trios of shieldbearers. There had been only one such team when he'd set off a few minutes ago.

And that was going to pretty much ruin his plan of throwing two vac cement bombs in rapid succession. If the Ueys were on their toes, two teams meant they'd be able to intercept both of them.

Still, if Pappy did his job here, the bombs might not be necessary. He eased his head up far enough to see the tank's rear axles, noted the corresponding spot below him on the ridge, and lowered himself out of view. Moving as quickly as he could, he worked his way sideways to that place.

As he'd already discovered to his detriment, the ridge was largely composed of loose and breakable rock. About a meter below the crest he found a conveniently placed indentation. It wasn't quite big enough, but by extending his air hose to its fullest length he was able to use the bottom of his oxy tank to hammer out enough rock to make the hole big enough for what he needed.

On Earth he would never have gotten away with something like that—the racket of metal on rock would have brought the enemy down on him in double-quick time. But here, in the near vacuum of Luna, the Ueys on the far side of the ridge wouldn't hear a thing.

And best of all, odds were that that potential weakness hadn't even occurred to them. Maybe there was something to KC's Winter War analogy, after all.

Of course, like everything else in warfare, Luna's vacuum was a two-edged sword. Now that Pappy had silently gouged out his hole, he needed something to fill it with. And with the loss of his extra oxygen tank, there was only one option.

According to the specs, a modern spacesuit held enough air on its own to keep its wearer alive for ten minutes if heavily active and half an hour if completely passive. Pappy wasn't sure exactly where in that range he would end up, but probably dangerously close to the front. Taking a few deep breaths, he jammed the tank into the hole in the rock, wedged the torch underneath it and locked it on, and unfastened the hose. Then, with the ominous sense of a timer counting down in his head, he bounced his way down to ground level and headed back toward the Loonie foxholes.

Every couple of hops he glanced back to see what was happening with his pressure bomb. On the fourth such glance, he saw the oxy tank explode, blowing the top of the ridge into a vertical avalanche and raining slow-falling rocks across the whole area.

Probably none of them would be close enough to give Pappy any trouble. Just the same, he turned his attention forward again and picked up his pace. Flying rocks or furious Ueys aside, his air was still running out.

The spot where he'd first crossed the ridge, at least, was obvious from the scattering of freshly broken rock at the base. He took a moment to visually pick out his route, and started up.

Luck, recent experience, and the fact that he now had both hands free combined to get him up the rock wall without falling. He peered over the top, confirmed that the ground below him was clear, and started down.

And lost his balance completely as the top of the ridge beside him splintered in a spattering of gunfire.

He tried to catch himself as he toppled toward the ground, or at least slow his fall. But the useful handholds were few and far between, and in the end his efforts didn't make much difference in his impact speed. But he did at least manage to turn himself upright, enabling himself to land on his feet instead of his side or back.

Which turned out not to be much of a gain. His bad left leg, freshly stressed by the earlier thump against his knee, collapsed under him as he hit the ground, sending him toppling into a bouncing impact on his left side.

He had rolled over onto his stomach and was starting to push himself back to his feet when another burst of chips blasted from the ground just in front of him. He dropped back to the ground, spun around onto his right side, and looked behind him.

Just in time to see the soldier who'd apparently followed him back from the Dunsland topple backward off the ridge, his flailing gun the last thing to disappear from sight. Pappy rolled back onto his stomach and again started to push himself back up.

And once again dropped flat as a second explosion of rock chips erupted from the ground in front of him.

Damn, damn, double damn. Pappy pressed himself as close to the ground as he could, cursing as another bunch of chips and dust popped from the ground along his path. He'd assumed from the Ueys' previous behavior that they had orders either to go easy on the Loonies or to conserve ammo; maybe both. Clearly, those orders had now gone by the boards. Whatever his oxy-tank bomb had done, it had apparently made a nice mess of things.

Another burst of chips. Still, at least they weren't mad enough to open up with full-auto. The machine gunner chipping away at the lunar landscape was limiting his attacks to single shots and three-shot bursts.

Pappy frowned. Unless the gunner wasn't mad at all. Unless this was part of a deliberate, carefully coordinated strategy.

But to what end? He had Pappy pinned down, but that still left KC and Morgan free and clear. Granted, aside from two more cement bombs the Loonies didn't have any real weaponry, but the Ueys didn't necessarily know that.

Unless...

Carefully, Pappy eased up onto his left side and looked back over his shoulder at the spot where the Uey had opened fire before losing his balance and falling backward. Eyeballing the vector for his fire...

Pappy hissed between his teeth. From that vantage point, not only could the soldier pin down Pappy, but he also had a clear shot into Morgan's foxhole. There should be enough space along the side for her to be safe from direct fire, but there would be no way she could make any countermoves from that position. Both of them would be sitting ducks.

And the remaining member of their group, KC, was already injured and half out of action. A little more judicious gunfire from their two gunners, and the Ueys would be able to clear the Dunsland and roll into Hadley Dome at their leisure, with their three opponents unable to do anything but watch helplessly as they drove past.

Or rather, two of them would watch helplessly. Pappy himself would be long dead. He wondered if the soldier on the ridge had noticed his lack of oxy tank before losing his footing. Or, if he'd noticed, if he cared.

Mentally, Pappy shook his head. Irrelevant. What was relevant was that he was about to die, and Morgan was about to come under attack, and without a direct-line cable there was no way he could communicate with her or otherwise make plans without the Ueys having a front-row eavesdropping seat.

Another shot, well wide of the mark. Still, Pappy couldn't stay here forever. He started moving forward, noting with distant annoyance that the standard SAS elbow-and-knee crawl didn't work nearly as well in lunar gravity, where it had a distinct tendency to make him bounce. He got about a meter when there was another shot, this one a triple, just in front of him.

And with that, there was no longer a choice. A shot that close strongly suggested the Ueys were losing patience; and if it was a choice between getting shot and suffocating, he might as well go with the shot. Lunging up to his feet, keeping his attention on the machine gunners on the Dunsland, he leaned forward and bounded toward Morgan's foxhole.

Out of the corner of his eye he spotted something moving in his direction from Morgan's direction. Reflexively, he dodged sideways, fighting to keep from losing his balance as he snapped his attention back that way.

It was a cable—a comm cable—snaking gracefully toward him. He grabbed it, his eyes tracking it back to Morgan's foxhole. She was standing mostly upright, her helmet partially exposed, either oblivious to the machine gunners or else ignoring them, her faceplate turned toward Pappy, her paintball gun gripped in her hand but pointed toward the sky. Pappy gave another bounce, fumbling the comm cable jack into his suit—

"*Get down!*" she snapped.

It was the first time Pappy had ever heard Morgan use that tone. But he knew how to respond to it. Even as he bent his knees for his next hop he froze his legs in place, letting himself topple to the ground onto his outstretched hands.

Or tried to. To his consternation, his elbows buckled unexpectedly under the impact, dropping him flat on his face and stomach. He blinked with disbelief...

And suddenly realized he was gasping for breath, his lungs burning, his muscles twitching as he rushed toward the limit of his air supply. Something flew out of the foxhole ahead, arcing over his head. He grabbed for a rocky protuberance, but discovered his fingers wouldn't close solidly around it. There was another motion in front of him, something bigger this time, but he couldn't tell what it was through the sudden sparkling glitter sprinkling across his vision.

A shadow passed over the rock he was trying to grab, plunging it into darkness. The darkness and the sparkling made it nearly impossible to see, but he couldn't remember why he wanted it in the first place. He tried again anyway, forcing his fingers to close...

Without warning, a flood of cool air washed over him.

He inhaled deeply, aware that he was panting again, only this time actually clearing out his lungs. The sparkling in his vision faded away, the pounding in his ears diminished—

"—Pappy?"

"Yeah," he managed. His voice sounded like something coming from a frog pond. "Yeah."

"Come on." Someone—the big shadow from earlier— *Morgan?*—grabbed his arm and dragged him toward the nearby foxhole. Pappy pressed a hand against the ground, trying to help by pushing himself along as he felt strength starting to flow back into the weakened muscles.

And then, abruptly, he remembered.

He twisted half over, nearly breaking Morgan's grip on his arm in the process, and looked behind him. The Uey soldier who'd followed him must surely have recovered from his fall and scaled the ridge again.

He had. He was there now, along with a companion who hadn't shown himself earlier. Both of them were leaning half over the crest, their long-barreled pistols gripped in their hands.

Both of them glued solidly to each other and the rock of the ridge by a cake-frosting spatter of glistening white from a vac cement bomb. Which, Pappy realized now, must have been the smaller shadow that had passed over him while he was suffocating.

And then he and Morgan were at the edge of the foxhole, and Morgan was shoving him over the rim. Pappy managed to catch the edge with one hand and turn himself around to land on his feet. Morgan was right behind him.

He'd just dropped below the level of the surface when another burst of gunfire spattered across the ground and ricocheted off the foxhole's rear wall.

"You okay?" Morgan asked, breathing a little heavily herself. "What the hell were you thinking?"

"I needed to slow them down," Pappy said. His breathing was nearly back to normal now. Amazing what a fresh oxy tank could do for a man. "Did it work?"

"If you mean did it drop a pile of rocks against the back of the Dunsland, yes, it worked great," Morgan said, a little sourly. "If you mean did it make the Ueys mad, oh yeah, definitely. If you mean did it immobilize the Dunsland, no, it didn't. It looks like a bunch of the rock landed on both sides of the left rear wheel, but they're already working on clearing it away."

"Yeah." Pappy gave himself another couple of lungsful of air, then eased his head carefully up over the edge of the foxhole. He confirmed that the two men on the ridge were still safely cemented in place, then turned his attention to the Dunsland.

For all the anger Morgan had referenced, the Ueys still had their priorities in place. Much as they would probably love to send another team to perforate Pappy's team in their foxholes, the important part was to get the Dunsland free to roll into Hadley and grab this Mimic thing nobody wanted to talk about.

His radio crackled. "Hello, Hadley Dome Defense Commander," an accented voice came in his ear. "This is Colonel Chakarvarti of the United Earth Command. Please respond."

Pappy looked at Morgan. "Is he talking to *us*?"

"He must be trying to reach Lieutenant Sassou," Morgan said doubtfully. "I don't know if he's listening to radios right now, though."

Pappy thought back to his brief conversation with the man at Hadley Control. "Or if anyone else is, either."

"Hadley Defense Commander?" Chakarvarti prompted.

Pappy gazed out at the Dunsland and the soldiers working like busy little ants around it. With Morgan having used her cement bomb to pin down two of the Ueys—quite literally—they had only one bomb left, which was currently lying twenty meters away in Pappy's foxhole. Aside from that they had cable, cutting torches, oxy tanks, and paintball guns.

And that was it. No real weapons, and no defenses beyond a couple more of the monofil traps that had briefly derailed the Uey advance. Within an hour or two, unless Pappy could pull something out of his hat, the enemy would be rolling unopposed into Hadley.

When all else failed—or when you needed to play for time—a good soldier could always fall back on talking or Psy Ops. Pappy checked his radio display, found out the frequency Chakarvarti was using, and keyed his transmitter to it. "This is Papillon MacLeod," he announced. "Where are you, Colonel?"

"Greetings," Chakarvarti said. "I'm a bit surprised by your question. My rangefinder puts me approximately a hundred sixty-two meters from your line of foxholes."

"You're running the Dunsland?" Pappy asked, frowning. "I'm surprised."

"How so?"

"Full colonels don't usually lead the charge themselves," Pappy said. "Normally a lieutenant would be a more proper commander for what's essentially a mechanized platoon."

"Agreed," Chakarvarti said. "But in this case, United Earth Command was hesitant to share the true nature of this mission with anyone but trusted senior officers."

"What mission would that be?" Pappy asked. "The complete subjugation of the Lunar Colonies?"

"I think you know what the mission is," Chakarvarti said. "And the true pot of gold at the end of the rainbow."

"You've got the accent wrong," Pappy said, feeling his lip twist as he studied the Uey position. He'd hoped that the need to clear out the rock pile pinning the Dunsland in place would have Chakarvarti ordering every spare hand to that task. But the colonel was clearly still wary of the Loonies' cement bombs, and had left both three-man shield teams in place to guard against more such attacks.

"Excuse me?"

"I'm British, not Irish," Pappy said. "No leprechauns or pots of gold." Not that the second shieldbearer team was even necessary. Not anymore. With Morgan's bomb gone, Pappy's earlier idea of lobbing two of them in rapid succession was already over and done with.

Unless . . .

He keyed off the radio. "Morgan, is there any chance we can aim our catapult high enough for plunging fire?"

"What's that?"

"You give the bomb enough of an upward vector that it lofts over the shieldbearers," Pappy explained, frowning at her catapult. "Like at a sixty- or seventy-degree launch angle. I'm not seeing any way to do that."

"There isn't one," she said. "They're not designed for anything higher than forty-five. I guess no one thought we'd need anything higher than that."

"Or else they didn't want one of us accidentally firing it straight up and dropping it back on top of us," Pappy growled. So much for that idea.

Chakarvarti was talking again, and Pappy keyed his transmitter. "Sorry; what was that?"

"I said I didn't mean to insult your heritage," the

colonel said. "I assumed the pot of gold at the end of the rainbow had entered more common usage."

"It has," Pappy acknowledged. "Just wanted to clear up any misconceptions as to who you were talking to."

"Oh, no misconceptions at all," Chakarvarti assured him. "Former Sergeant Papillon MacLeod of His Majesty's Special Air Service 'A' Squadron Mobility Troop. Joined September 2027; discharged February 2042 after the Birmingham insurgency left you with a permanently damaged left leg. Joined the Lunar Colonies fifteen months later as an accountant. An *accountant*? Really?"

"I also work with inventory and acquisition," Pappy said, his gut twisting as a hundred half-buried memories came flooding to the service, threatening his composure and focus. Probably the reason Chakarvarti had brought up the Birmingham disaster in the first place. "None of it requires much walking around."

"And no one's shooting at you," Chakarvarti said. "At least, no one was until now. Speaking of which, I believe one of your team has been injured. If you're willing, I can offer him help."

The knot in Pappy's stomach tightened another half turn. "He's hardly injured. A couple of scratches, that's all."

"I'm glad to hear that," Chakarvarti said. "Still, I don't see anyone from Hadley Colony rushing to his aid. We, on the other hand, have a fully equipped first-aid setup here."

"In your Dunsland that's currently going nowhere?"

"The operative word being *currently*," Chakarvarti said. "Your rock slide was most impressive, but all it accomplished was to block that wheel and axle. Once we clear away the rubble we'll once again be free to advance."

"Maybe," Pappy said. "The work would probably go faster if you put more people on it."

Chakarvarti gave a low chuckle. "You mean draw off our advance line? No, thank you. Those adhesive bombs of yours are extremely effective. What is the material inside, if I may ask?"

"He's stalling," Morgan murmured in Pappy's ear.

Pappy keyed off his transmitter. "I know," he told her. "Watch the ridge—he may be trying to move in more flankers."

"What do I do if I see any?"

"Paintball the crap out of them." He keyed his transmitter again. "It's a vacuum cement we use for emergency repairs," he said. "Very tough stuff. You can repair dome damage with it."

"Very tough indeed," Chakarvarti agreed. "I'm surprised you haven't tried marketing it on Earth."

"We might have," Pappy said. "I really don't know. Could be the Council decided running the gauntlet of environmental vetting wasn't worth the effort. Chemicals leaching into the groundwater or confusing aphids isn't exactly a problem up here."

"Definitely not," Chakarvarti said. "But I'd like to return to your wounded soldier. I presume you're aware how quickly a man can bleed to death in a spacesuit. If you bring him to me I personally guarantee on my honor to deal with his injuries and to treat him fairly and justly."

"As a prisoner of war?"

"*Are* we at war?" Chakarvarti countered. "After all, the

presence of insurgents in Birmingham didn't mean the entire city was at war with the United Kingdom."

With a conscious effort, Pappy unclenched his teeth. Chakarvarti was really pulling out all the stops on this one. "They're hardly equivalent situations."

"Aren't they? The insurgents used guns and explosives, just as you did. That alone violates the most recent agreements between the Lunar Colonies and United Earth."

A movement to Pappy's right caught his eye, and he turned just in time to see a helmeted head drop back out of sight behind the ridge as Morgan's paintball spattered a splash of bright red onto the nearby rock. "Damn," she muttered.

"Keep firing," Pappy ordered, stifling a curse of his own as he again cut off his transmitter. And his own gun was stuck in the next foxhole, across twenty meters of open ground.

No choice, though—he had to risk it. "And keep an eye on the whole ridge," he added. "That one might have been a feint. I'm going to get my gun."

"Pappy—"

Morgan's protest was cut off as he yanked out the cable, bent his knees, and bounded out of her foxhole. Leaning forward, he bounded off across the ground as fast as he could, his muscles tensed in anticipation of the machine-gun bullets that could tear into him at any moment.

But if the Ueys attacked, none of the shots came near enough for him to spot. He dropped into his foxhole with a puff of relief and scooped up his paintball gun with one hand and the cable to Morgan with the other. He spun around toward her, his eyes sweeping the ridge for attackers as he plugged in the cable. No one was in sight, but there were two more fresh paintball splotches. "Morgan?"

"You were right—he was a feint," she said. "Two more tried coming up at—"

"Yeah, yeah, I see the marks," Pappy cut her off, scanning the ridge. No one yet. Reaching down blindly, he snared the comm cable to KC and plugged it in. "KC? How are you holding up?"

"I'm fine," KC gritted out. "Look—those two Ueys Morgan plastered? I think they're—"

"*Damn* it," Pappy snarled as it suddenly clicked. How the hell hadn't he caught that himself? Oxy starvation, or just damn mental rust? "Morgan—listen—those Ueys you pinned earlier are spotting for the others. We have to blind them—"

"No, no, wait," KC interrupted. "Not yet. Give me a second."

"What?" Pappy asked, frowning. KC's breathing changed subtly, indicating some activity. But Pappy didn't dare turn around to see what he was doing. "KC?"

"Okay," KC said. "Get ready to blind the Ueys—you'll know when."

The last word was cut off as KC unplugged his cable. Pappy swore under his breath, his eyes flicking between the spotters and the rest of the ridge, berating himself for not seeing it sooner.

A second later he jerked in surprise as KC bounced past him into view, bounding toward the ridge with a big wrench in one hand and the knife from his tool kit in the other. Raising the knife high, he charged toward the ridge.

Grinning tightly with sudden understanding, Pappy sent a blinding barrage of paintballs into each of the trapped Uey soldiers' faceplates.

"Pappy?" Morgan gasped as KC bounded past her.

"Keep watching," Pappy said, keying his transmitter again. "Chakarvarti—for the love of God—get your men back!" he barked. "Get them back *now*! He's gone off the rails."

"What are you talking about?" Chakarvarti demanded. But Pappy could hear the sudden wary confusion in his voice.

"The pain meds," Pappy said tightly. "They have side effects in an oxy-rich atmosphere."

"Is that a *knife*?"

"You want this war to start with United Earth gunning down a wounded, half-insane man?" Pappy snarled. "With *you* gunning down a wounded, half-insane man? Pull them *back*, damn it."

KC reached the ridge and started bounding his way up. Pappy held his breath, his own less than stellar attempt to climb the crumbling rock flashing to mind.

But KC was a miner, and had had far more experience with this kind of thing. He hit the first set of footholds like a gymnast sticking a landing, and even as one of them began to crumble he was on his way up to the second. He passed the two blinded Ueys, reached the top and balanced there for a second . . .

And then, dropped his arms suddenly to his sides and started sliding back down the slope.

Morgan gasped. "Pappy—?"

Pappy keyed off his transmitter. "Hold on," he cautioned. KC looked like he was simply falling, but Pappy could see the subtle but deliberate shifting of hands and feet to slow his descent. He reached the ground and collapsed onto his back, his knife and wrench bouncing a couple of times off the rock before they came to a halt.

At his side, invisible from the Ueys' position, his fingers curled toward his palm and his thumb stuck briefly up.

Pappy puffed out a brief sigh of relief. *Talking or Psy Ops.* He once again keyed his transmitter. "Chakarvarti? You there?"

"I'm here," the colonel said. "I've pulled back my troops. Is he all right?"

"I don't know," Pappy said. "You going to let me go get him and bring him back to my foxhole?"

There was a brief hesitation as Chakarvarti probably ran United Earth's orders through his mind. But apparently the thought of his name plastered unflatteringly across the next century's worth of history texts tipped the balance. "Go," he said. "But if you try to escape or attack, we *will* shoot you down."

"Thanks." Unplugging his cable, Pappy heaved himself cautiously over the lip of his foxhole. If Chakarvarti was going to be an unprincipled bastard, this was his chance.

But the Ueys held their fire as he hopped over to KC. Leaving the wrench and knife where they were, he got the man up into his arms. "Though history might well say that your bombs were the true start of this war," Chakarvarti continued as Pappy made his way back to his foxhole.

"You mean the cement bombs?" Pappy asked. "Hardly a lethal weapon."

"I mean the bomb you used to bring down the top of the ridge."

"That wasn't a bomb," Pappy said. "Just an oxygen tank with a torch wedged under it to heat it past the pressure-stress margin. And you already said no one was hurt, right?"

"I didn't say that."

"*Was* anyone hurt?"

Another pause. "Not directly," Chakarvarti said, a little grudgingly. "But that cement could be a problem. It's already torn at least one man's outer suit layer."

"You were probably trying to brute-force it off him," Pappy said, easing KC into the foxhole and climbing in after him. "Hang on a second—I need to check his med display."

He cut his transmitter and plugged in KC's cable. "Nice job, KC," he said. "How are you doing?"

"You tell me," KC said, his voice distant. "You're the one looking at the display."

"Yes—silly of me," Pappy said, feeling his eyes narrow. KC's vitals were okay, but as Pappy had feared the suit wasn't doing a very good job of stopping the bleeding. It was slow, but not showing any signs of stopping. He had to get that MASH truck here, and fast.

"Sergeant MacLeod?"

Pappy switched on again. "He's stable," he told Chakarvarti. "Still bleeding, though."

"I've offered our assistance," the colonel reminded him. "That offer still stands."

"Yeah, I'll take it under advisement," Pappy said. "As to your own little problem, as I was saying, you can't just force the cement. You have to be a bit more inventive."

"How?"

"I have no idea what you've got in there," Pappy pointed out. "Even if I did, I'm hardly a materials expert."

"Could you at least offer some suggestions?"

"Sure," Pappy said. "First suggestion: pack up and get back to the Tranquility Transfer Station. Second suggestion: get in your ship, head back to Earth, and don't come back."

Chakarvarti chuckled. "That's three suggestions, actually. Five, counting your two first. Come now, Sergeant, let's be reasonable. We're just the pawns in a much bigger game, you and I. There's really no need for us to be at each other's throats. On the contrary, this is the perfect opportunity for us to show both of our worlds that we can behave like civilized men. You have wounded; I have disabled. We can help each other, and in the process perhaps defuse this whole unfortunate situation."

"I already told you how to defuse it," Pappy reminded him. "United Earth is the aggressor here. We're just defending our territory."

"*Your* territory?" Chakarvarti retorted, his calm demeanor cracking a bit. "As I read the numbers, you're still nearly eighty percent subsidized by United Earth. If we withdrew our support, you'd starve inside of six months."

"Oh, I doubt that," Pappy said. "I'm an accountant, remember? I know how Geneva is cooking those numbers. Throw in the lopsided tariff and taxation arrangements you've saddled us with, and those numbers shift dramatically."

"But not enough," Chakarvarti said. "Interesting, though, that you should bring up money. In particular, the *shot heard 'round the world* analogy is especially relevant when you consider the history of the phrase. It was, after all, the rich American landowners who sent the poor colonists out to fight and die. Very much like the situation here."

"We don't really have landowners here," Pappy said. "Not much on the land worth having."

"Not at all," Chakarvarti said. "There are all the metals and other resources. But I was thinking more about how Luna's rich and powerful are the ones holding the Mimic. I doubt they're sharing its largesse with the rest of you."

Pappy felt his ears prick up. "I have no idea what you're talking about."

"Really?" Chakarvarti made a tsking sound. "Then you make my point for me. Your masters haven't even told you what they've sent you out here to die for?"

"Not a clue," Pappy said. If Morgan couldn't—or wouldn't—let them in on the big secret, maybe Colonel Chakarvarti would be more obliging. "Why don't you explain it to me?"

"Pappy—no!" Morgan breathed. "You're not supposed to—"

"Because I'm betting you don't really know anything," Pappy continued. At the very least, this might be their chance to find out exactly how much the Ueys knew.

"You're either remarkably ignorant or you're stalling,"

Chakarvarti said. "No matter. Either way, I'm happy to play along."

Pappy smiled humorlessly. Especially since Chakarvarti himself was playing the exact same stalling game while he freed the Dunsland from Pappy's rockslide.

His smile faded. Which meant he and Morgan had that same rapidly closing window to figure out how to immobilize the vehicle permanently.

But how?

Their best bet was obviously their single remaining cement bomb. But getting it past two groups of shieldbearers would be nearly impossible, especially now that the Ueys knew how dangerous the weapons were. In retrospect, he now realized he should probably have taken a bomb over the ridge and attacked with that instead of his oxy-tank rockslide.

On the other hand, given the problems he'd had scaling the brittle rock, there was a good chance he'd never have made it up the ridge with the bomb intact, and might possibly have ended up cemented to the lunar surface himself.

Unfortunately, even if he wanted to take that risk now, there was no way that trick would work a second time. Chakarvarti might have pulled back his flanking team, but they were certainly still on the other side of the ridge near the Dunsland where they could guard against another sneak attack.

"The Mimic is an alien device," Chakarvarti said. "One of your mining groups dug it up approximately seven months ago, and your leaders have been attempting to keep it all to themselves."

"Well, finders keepers, as the saying goes," Pappy said. If he could somehow figure out how to rig more monofil traps . . . but while there were already two more of those in place, hidden in more of the ground cracks along the Freeway, the Ueys now knew what to look for and it was doubtful they'd be taken in again so easily. Even if they didn't spot the traps before they were triggered, that kind of snare depended on the Dunsland tank rolling over the loops fast enough to entangle the monofil solidly around the exposed parts of the wheel and axle. If the Ueys simply kept everything to a crawl, then stopped the second the monofil appeared, they could extricate themselves with little trouble.

"Hardly," Chakarvarti said. "This isn't just some interesting oddity. The Mimic is a replicator: a device that can copy and manufacture virtually any nonliving object."

Pappy winced. So the rumors he'd heard were true. Damn. "Seriously?" he asked, putting some scoffing disbelief into his voice. "Big deal—I've got a printer in my office that can do that."

"I doubt it," Chakarvarti said. "The Mimic isn't some upscale 3-D printer with three or four materials it can draw on. It does a complete scan of what you want duplicated—a *complete* scan, mind you, down to the atomic level. It then takes whatever scrap or garbage you've loaded into its hopper, sifts through it all for the specific atoms it needs, and builds a duplicate of its sample, again from the molecules on up. Are you really going to pretend you hadn't heard about any of this?"

"No, but it sounds very cool," Pappy said. "And United Earth thinks it deserves this thing *why*?"

"Don't be a fool," Chakarvarti said, an edge of bitterness in his voice. "You have fifty thousand people. Earth has seven billion. Seven million of them die every year from hunger alone, and that doesn't even count the millions who are malnourished. The Mimic would be a godsend for these people."

"In what way?"

Chakarvarti spat something. "Are you stupid or just lacking in imagination? Put in a loaf of bread, add a neighborhood's worth of garbage into the hopper, and that neighborhood's children will no longer be hungry. Feed in the pieces of a truck, add in the rusted metal from a scrapyard, and that bread can be taken across the city. Put a hundred gallons of petrol in the Mimic with anything that contains carbon and hydrogen, and that bread and that truck can travel to the most inaccessible of villages."

"Sounds like a lot of work for one humble little Mimic to handle," Pappy said.

"It wouldn't be alone for long," Chakarvarti said, warming to his topic. "Reverse-engineering will give us ten of them. Then the Mimics themselves will create a hundred, then a thousand, then a million. Hunger wiped out. Poverty wiped out. Sickness wiped out—put in a vaccine, and every child in every country will be protected."

"Good thing food will be free," Pappy said. "Because everyone except the people who shovel garbage into the hoppers will be out of work."

"You think anyone will care about back-breaking labor when they finally have food to eat and clothes to wear?"

"No, actually, I don't," Pappy said, his stomach tightening. "Because it'll never happen. Not the rosy picture you're painting, anyway. If United Earth gets the Mimic, the leaders will keep the benefits for themselves."

"They wouldn't dare."

"Since when?" Pappy retorted. "Leaders dare whatever they damn well please. And since they're the ones with the guns and the armies, they usually get away with it."

"Not in this case."

"Yes, in this case, too," Pappy said. "Because for everyone who wants to lift the poor out of poverty, there will be two more who don't want their constituents thrown out of work."

"Those unemployed people won't care."

"Those in power will," Pappy said. "Because their sole job *is* to hold onto their power." It was hard to see from his vantage point, but it looked like the Ueys' rock-clearing bucket brigade was starting to slow down. If he didn't come up with something fast, it was going to be too late. "You think the politicians will risk losing the next election because all the voters have been thrown out of work? You think the manufacturers are going to give up the profits they make from selling widgets to people? You think the military types will put bananas in the Mimic when you can shove in a single tactical nuclear weapon and have a hundred of them by dinner time?"

"Not all leaders are like that," Chakarvarti insisted.

"Not all, no," Pappy agreed. "But the humanitarians will be the first to be mowed down by the more vicious types. You sound like one of the good guys, Colonel. If you win, you'd better watch your back."

"Ridiculous," Chakarvarti said. But to Pappy's ears he didn't sound entirely convinced.

He hoped so. Right now, turning Chakarvarti was about the only plan he had.

There was pressure on his sleeve. He looked down to see KC clutching his arm with one hand and making a slashing motion across his throat with the other. Frowning, Pappy muted the transmitter. "What is it?" he asked.

"I'll take it," KC said, a slight quaver in his voice.

"What?"

"The bomb," KC said. "You need to get it to the tank. I'll take it."

Pappy sighed. Drugs or blood loss—either way, the man was starting to slip from reality. "Thanks, but you're not up to a walk," he said. "Anyway, they'd kind of notice you carrying something that big."

"I'm not going to carry it," KC said. "You put it in my oxy carrier. As long as I'm facing them, they won't see what it is."

Pappy stared down at him. So much for drugged delusions.

And it could work. It could actually work. The bomb would fit into the oxy-tank carrier on KC's back, and it would be hidden as long as no one got a good look from the side. Once that discovery happened, he would be close enough to make a run for the Dunsland. If he was fast enough, and the Ueys were slow enough, he should be able to unload the bomb, get it under the tank, and detonate it where it could completely scramble the works.

There was only one, small, minor problem. "And you'd breathe what in the meantime?"

"*You* made it back on fumes," KC said. "If you can, I can."

Pappy grimaced. He hadn't realized KC had even been aware of his little sortie, let alone had noticed that he'd been without his own tank when he came back. "Okay, we'll try it," he said. "Only *I'll* take it, not you."

"Don't be ridiculous," KC said, some strength and determination returning to his voice. "You weren't invited. I was. I'm taking it."

"You'll never make it," Pappy insisted. "Even if you did, you'd never make it back. You want to be their prisoner?"

"No, but it beats bleeding to death."

"We'll get the MASH truck here."

"Not until we hammer the Dunsland." KC grunted with exertion as he got another grip on Pappy's arm and started to pull himself upright. "You want to give me a hand? Or are you going to make me do it myself?"

"Sergeant MacLeod?"

"Stay put," Pappy ordered KC as he turned his transmitter back on. "Yeah, I'm here, Colonel."

"I thought for a moment that you'd left us," Chakarvarti said. "Everything all right?"

"I was checking on my friend," Pappy said, scowling across the open space at the Ueys. Unfortunately, KC was right. Pappy hadn't been invited to drop in for tea. If he headed across alone, they would know something was up.

But if he was simply helping an injured soldier who couldn't navigate on his own . . .

The upside was that he might be able to paralyze the Dunsland for good. The downside was that he and KC would both end up prisoners. Or worse.

But they were out of other options. With two lines of shieldbearers standing guard, the only way to get the cement bomb close enough was for Pappy to carry it there.

"How is he doing?" Chakarvarti asked. "My offer to treat him still stands. I'll even send some unarmed men to assist him, if you'd like."

"I appreciate that." Pappy braced himself—

"Wait a second," Morgan spoke up suddenly. "I've got an idea. Stay put, and stall him. And I'll need that last bomb."

Pappy frowned. Surely she'd worked out the same logic he had. How in the world did she think she could slip it past the shieldbearers?

Maybe by throwing a couple of oxy tanks first to confuse them?

In fact, he realized suddenly, that might work. The bomb's outer shell didn't look anything like that of an oxy tank, but the Ueys wouldn't necessarily know that. If he and Morgan both sent oxys toward the tank, and then one of them threw the remaining bomb—

"You're obviously still not convinced," Chakarvarti said. "Very well. While you consider—and while your friend bleeds to death—let me put one other factor into the mix."

"You going to say *please*?" Pappy suggested, squatting down and picking up the cement bomb. Of course, now that the Ueys knew about the bombs, lobbing it across to Morgan carried its own set of risks. If the machine gunner was fast enough, he could blow it open and probably cover him, KC, *and* Morgan. Another juicy tidbit for the future history texts. "Come to think of it, did anyone at United Earth consider saying *please* in the first place?"

"I don't know," Chakarvarti said. "Not my department."

"I suppose not," Pappy said, eyeing the ground between him and Morgan. Theoretically, until the detonator was armed, the bomb should be able to handle a bounce. Theoretically. "So why exactly do you think this Mimic thing—*if* it exists, and I'm personally not convinced it is—why you think it's in Hadley instead of one of the other domes?"

"We don't," Chakarvarti said. "If it isn't, we'll pack up and leave you in peace."

"And head to the next colony?"

"I have my orders, Sergeant, as do you," the colonel said. "But let's talk about that. Your orders, I assume, are to protect Hadley Dome?"

"And all of Luna."

"But mostly Hadley Dome?"

"Mostly," Pappy agreed.

"All right. So what then are you planning to do when the aliens who created the Mimic come looking for it?"

Pappy frowned, throwing a look at Morgan. But her attention seemed to be alternating between her rangefinder scope and her hand computer. "Who says they're even around anymore?"

"Who says they aren't?" Chakarvarti countered. "And if they are—and if they decide they want it back—are you and Luna really prepared to fend them off?"

Out of the corner of his eye he saw Morgan duck down in her foxhole and come back up with her coil of monofil. One final look through her scope and she began counting off loops of the cord. "You think you can protect it better?"

"Of course we can," Chakarvarti scoffed. "We have the militaries of two hundred and four countries to draw on."

"What about those seven billion hungry citizens?" Pappy asked. Morgan had reached whatever count she was going for and had taken her knife to the proper loop. "You get an alien war going and a lot of them are going to die."

"*You* get a war going and *all* of you will die," Chakarvarti retorted.

Morgan had ducked down out of sight again. "Maybe it won't come to war," Pappy said. "Maybe the aliens will ask for it nicely. They might even say *please*."

"And if they don't?" Chakarvarti persisted. He was starting to run out of patience, Pappy noted uneasily. That probably meant the Dunsland was nearly cleared and ready to roll. "What if they just come tearing in and plow up the landscape until they find it? Are you willing to take that risk?"

"Like you said," Pappy told him. "Not my department."

"Pappy?" Morgan murmured in his ear. "*Now*."

Clenching his teeth, hoping to God Morgan knew what she was doing, Pappy lifted the cement bomb to his chest and gave it a shot-putter shove toward her.

The Uey machine gunner was ready. Unfortunately for him, his training still wasn't quite acclimated to the lower gravity and lack of air resistance. His shots slashed through the space above the bomb, digging up more lunar dust a few meters past his intended target. Before he could adjust his aim Morgan snatched the cylinder out of its arc and once again dropped down out of sight.

"You refuse to cooperate," Chakarvarti said. "So be it. The record will show that the United Earth forces did everything in our power to avoid unnecessary bloodshed."

"Hardly," Pappy said. The Ueys who'd been around the Dunsland's rear were moving away now, clearly getting ready for it to pull out. But if continuing the conversation could buy Morgan a few more seconds... "You could have continued negotiations instead of bringing soldiers here to shoot us down and destroy our homes. And you still can, because there's still one factor you haven't added in."

"Which would be?"

And then, out of the corner of his eye, he saw the cement bomb shoot out of Morgan's foxhole, arcing toward the Ueys. So she'd used the catapult after all.

Only the bomb was going too high.

Pappy cursed, following the cylinder with his eyes. If Morgan had intended to overshoot the shieldbearers, she'd certainly succeeded. Even as the first trio leaped upward in response it was abundantly clear that the bomb would sail well over their heads.

The problem was that it would also sail well over the Dunsland and splatter its contents over the distant landscape.

He'd asked Morgan earlier if the catapults could be set for high angles. She'd told him they couldn't. Maybe she thought she'd figured out a way to do that anyway.

But if that had been her plan, she'd failed. Pappy's years in the SAS had given him an eye for judging a shell's trajectory, and this one was heading into the sky at no more than forty-five degrees.

Could Morgan be trying somehow to cut off the tank's retreat? After all, if the goal was to keep the Mimic in Hadley, then letting Chakarvarti get hold of it wouldn't gain him anything if he couldn't escape with it.

But Pappy knew the terrain back there reasonably well, and there was no spot he could think of where a splash or a lump of vacuum cement would do anything but pave over the rocky ground. Did Morgan know something he didn't?

The three shieldbearers were nearly at the top of their group jump, and as Pappy had already anticipated they would end up far too low to intercept the bomb. On the ground behind them, the second row of shieldbearers now went into action, this group throwing their shields up into the sky toward the soaring missile.

But the shields hadn't been designed for throwing, and the Ueys certainly hadn't had any practice with the technique. Two of the shields immediately started tumbling, not so much of a problem without air resistance to slow them down, while the third stayed more or less upright. But the first two didn't have enough momentum to intercept the bomb, while the third reached the necessary height but ended up a couple of meters to the side. As the shields and the shieldbearers floated back toward the ground the bomb reached its zenith—

And directly above the Dunsland it jerked to an abrupt halt.

Pappy blinked in surprise as the bomb seemed to hover for an instant in empty space. What the *hell*—?

And then, as it began to fall straight down, he caught just the slightest glint of sunlight reflecting off part of a line behind the cylinder.

Morgan had used her monofil to tether the bomb to something in her foxhole. Now, having reached the end of its leash—and having evaded all Uey attempts to block it—it was dropping straight down toward the Dunsland.

The Ueys instantly spotted the unexpected threat. But it was too late for them to do anything to stop it. Some of the soldiers, who'd been moving away from the tank in anticipation of once again getting on the road, turned back to try to intercept the bomb. But their momentum was starting out in the wrong direction, and they still were unaccustomed to the footing and the rules for low-gee movement. None of them made it more than a couple of steps back before suddenly stopping and again reversing direction. Chakarvarti, no doubt recognizing the threat and the inevitability of its success, had presumably ordered them back rather than have his soldiers immobilized along with his vehicle. The bomb continued its leisurely fall . . .

It hit the ground right beside the Dunsland's left rear wheel, right where Pappy's earlier rockslide had left a mound of broken rock, and exploded into a cloud of white foam. The cloud collapsed to the ground, leaving the Dunsland, the rock, and the lunar surface locked solidly together.

Pappy took a deep breath and looked at Morgan. She gave him a tight smile through her faceplate and lifted her hand in a thumbs-up. Pappy nodded, smiling and gesturing back, then turned back to the Ueys. "Colonel Chakarvarti?" he called.

"I'm here, Sergeant," Chakarvarti said. His voice was tight with controlled anger, but Pappy could hear a hint of grudging respect beneath it. "Nicely done."

"Thank you," Pappy said. "You and your men were able to stay clear of the burst, I hope?"

"We did," Chakarvarti said. "And we still have weapons."

"I thought we'd agreed that we didn't want to start the bloodshed today," Pappy reminded him. "I mean, apart from your shooting my man."

"I have a mission."

"Which you can no longer complete," Pappy said. "You can run over us, you can kill everyone in Hadley, but you can't bring the Mimic back to Tranquility. Not until you get your Dunsland free, and I'm really doubting you can." He considered. "*If* the Mimic is even here. Which I don't concede."

"There are four other tank units I could call."

"There are four other units and *one* other tank," Morgan put in. "The other three Dunslands weren't up to the terrain and climate."

"Your commanders really should have thought things through a little more thoroughly before rushing into this thing," Pappy added. "So here's how it's going to go."

He jerked a thumb toward the two Ueys still cemented to the ridge. "Your two men will probably run out of oxy before we can get them free. We can give them each a fresh tank, good for four hours. We can also call Hadley and have them send out some hammers and chisels to get them loose. But we're not going to do any of that until all of you—and I mean *all* of you, including the ones guarding the other side of Waffle Ridge—are back inside your vehicle."

"I need to deploy at least a pair of sentries."

"No, you don't," Pappy said. "Consider yourselves on parole, with the Dunsland a mobile POW camp of your own making. Well, with a bit of our help, I suppose."

"Very well," Chakarvarti said stiffly. "I assume you'll want us to block the viewports, too?"

"No need—we can do that ourselves from here," Pappy said. "And remember: we've got a really impressive array of sensors, and we know *exactly* how many men you have. We don't move until they're all inside the tank. Get cute, and your two men here will suffocate."

"There will be no tricks," Chakarvarti said darkly. "And once they're free?"

"That'll be up to Hadley," Pappy said. "They may decide to send you to some neutral point where your people can pick you up. Or they may decide we'll keep all of you as our guests for a bit while the politicians and diplomats talk."

"I see," Chakarvarti said. "I will just say one more thing, Sergeant MacLeod. Beware the thought that this is over. It is not. In fact, it has barely begun."

"I agree," Pappy said, peering through his scope. The Ueys were walking along the side of the Dunsland now, heading for the rear hatch and their forced seclusion. On the sail, the machine gunners had secured their weapons to the cages and were climbing down. "In that case, let me offer you a final word as well. You say you want the

Mimic. But I'm guessing that some of United Earth's most powerful would be just as happy to see it destroyed. If it can be destroyed in a war with Luna, so much the better, because that way they won't have to take any of the blame."

"That would be a terrible mistake," Chakarvarti said. "The people of United Earth desperately need the Mimic."

"I'm not arguing," Pappy said. "Here's my point. Those aliens you mentioned, the ones who might want to come back and retrieve their magic replicator? If they do, we're going to be in serious trouble if all we can show them is a pile of scrap. You might make sure your leaders—*all* of them—know that simply destroying the Mimic isn't an option."

"An interesting warning," Chakarvarti said thoughtfully. "Yes, I'll be sure to pass it on to my superiors." He paused. "All of my men are now inside. You may begin your rescue operation."

"Thank you," Pappy said. "Once we've confirmed that, we'll get some people out here and get to work."

"Thank you, Sergeant MacLeod," Chakarvarti said, with just a hint of dark humor. "It has been a most interesting encounter. I look forward to our next."

Pappy swallowed hard. "As will I," he said, trying to sound like he meant it.

He keyed off his transmitter and plugged in the comm cable back to the dome. "Eagle Four to Hadley," he called. "Uey tank's been neutralized; repeat, Uey tank's been neutralized. Get that MASH truck rolling."

"On its way, Eagle Four," the controller said, and there was no mistaking the relief in his voice.

"And get some materials techs out here with vac cement solvent," Pappy continued. "If you can free up a mining crew with a deep-radar, that would also be handy."

"I'll put in the request," the controller promised. "Let us know if you need anything else."

Pappy keyed off. "I wondered about the hammer-and-chisel bit," Morgan commented. "I couldn't believe you'd actually forgotten we have solvents for that sort of thing."

"If the Ueys knew there was a solvent, they'd have fallen all over themselves trying to figure out what it was," Pappy pointed out. "Better to keep them guessing."

"And we *don't* know how many men Chakarvarti has."

"True. Again, he doesn't know that."

Morgan huffed out a sigh. "I hope you know what you're doing," she said. "Bluffs and half-truths can only take you so far."

"I know," Pappy said, wincing as images of Birmingham once again flickered across his memory. "But that's strategy. Not my department. Nice work with the bomb, by the way. I think a field promotion to corporal is in order."

"I'm honored," Morgan said dryly. "Here it comes."

Pappy looked behind him. Rolling up the Freeway was the massive vehicle that Hadley had converted into a MASH truck. "Great," he said, reaching down and getting a grip under KC's armpits. "KC? You still with us?"

"Where else would I go?" KC murmured back. "Getting pretty sleepy in here. I'm getting tired of bleeding, too."

"We're about to take care of that," Pappy assured him. "Morgan? Can you hold the fort alone until the reinforcements get here?"

"Sure," Morgan assured him. "Anyway, I've still got a viewport or two on the Uey tank to take care of. After that, I was thinking I'd see about getting one of those rifles away from our neighbors."

"Yeah, I'd watch that," Pappy warned, glancing over at the ridge as he pulled KC upright and eased him onto his stomach over the edge of the foxhole. "They may not be *completely* helpless. And one rifle isn't going to do any good."

"You haven't been listening," Morgan said darkly. "All we *need* is one."

Pappy stared back at her. Thirteen lunar colonies. Fifty thousand people. One rifle.

And the Mimic.

"Damn," he muttered. "Right. This is going to change things, isn't it? This is *really* going to change things."

"Pappy?" KC said.

"What?"

"Not your department."

"Yeah." Pappy took a deep breath. "Come on. Let's get you patched up."

UNDER THE HILL

⊕

by Michael Z. Williamson

Engineer Andre Crawford skipped down the corridor, using the best gait for fast travel on the Moon. He always felt like a kid back in South Chicago when he did. It was fast, though, in the low G.

He reached Control, the pressure doors closed for security, not due to atmosphere worries. The scanner recognized both him and his ID and opened the staggered doors in turn.

Luna Central Operations sounded as if it should be an exotic place. It was even jokingly referred to as "Main Mission," which someone had dredged out of the depths of old sci-fi and had to explain. More often, it was dubbed the "Ops Module" or just "Control."

It wasn't nearly as roomy as a TV show would have it, though. The space was about as tight as a warship or TOC. People had room to walk, barely, and consoles with minimal spare space. Polarized screens and noise-canceling shrouds made it work, and expensive gear was cheaper than making more space.

He knew why he had been called. The UN landing at Hadley was only a precursor to the one that just landed here.

The good news was the element trying for Hadley Dome had been stopped.

Luna Village might not be so lucky. The UN force was throwing more of its troops and assets at the main habitat, probably hoping for both visibility and intimidation. Three ships had landed just over the ridge, giving them limited concealment and cover. Satellite imagery caught a bare glimpse of the craft, one of them with an ArctiTrak debarking, before the satellite feed had gone dead. It wasn't clear yet if the controls had been compromised or the satellite destroyed.

ArctiTraks worked well on the lunar surface. From that landing site they could reach the main lock in an hour.

As he stepped inside, he noticed Control was almost silent, which meant crew were furiously busy. Also, he realized all the uniforms were Lunar Operations only, no Kosmolock, Boeing, or TRW contractors.

Across the round facility, he spotted Colonel Zeiss next to Steve Coffman, the senior commo tech, and usually roving, not sitting a console as he was now. Zeiss was the only military person present. The entire staff present were very select, and many were on their alternate shifts.

Andre made his way over and nodded a greeting. Zeiss made a half salute, half wave. Commo Tech Coffman just glanced and flicked his eyes.

Andre took in the display. It showed bandwidths, frequencies, strength and quality, as well as interference.

The Lunar Village primary commo was still active, but

there was very strong local jamming, presumably from the UN landers or the command craft in orbit.

Coffman said, "I can probably burn a signal through if we have to. But who would we call?"

At least Lunar Village had resources. Whatever the Moon had as far as materials and power, this was the place for it. It was also very secure. The habitat was only partially domed, being built into a tunnel through the crater rim with structure protruding out each side.

Still, the encroaching force had professionally built weapons which, while not ideal for the Moon, were purpose designed.

On the Loonie side, there were several hastily constructed booby traps and a bunch of improvised materials from the warehouse, under the command of Andre Crawford. Crawford apparently had the mission because he was both one of the senior engineers, and a veteran of the US Army.

He'd supervised construction of the traps the two days previous, as soon as it was known there were UN ships inbound. Now he'd have to put them to use.

"You realize I never saw combat, only did support, right?" he said to Zeiss.

Colonel Zeiss, Bundeswehr (Retired) said, "You understand military ops, military engineering, and our equipment. That makes you the right man."

He inhaled and tensed. "Fair enough, and I agree. I just want you to understand I was never actually faced with killing anyone. And no matter how peaceful we try to be, that's a possibility here, when things get stressed and ugly."

Zeiss nodded. "You know that. That's why you're in charge of it."

"Roger."

Andre sighed. Even on the Moon, human beings could find a reason and a way to go to war.

He'd need some good support. He thought for a moment and spoke.

"I want Malakhar, Morton, Rojas and Godin."

Zeiss said, "They're all here. They're yours."

"Thanks. Patch me through, please, Mr. Coffman?"

Coffman nodded and said, "Sure thing." He pinged their phones and had all four on a split screen he swiveled to Andre.

"Hey, guys, it's on. Meet me at the Ops Room off the main lock."

They all agreed, looking nervous or sober or both, and he gestured for Coffman to kill the channel.

He turned and asked, "Colonel, can you clear the regular personnel out of there fast?"

Zeiss replied, "We already did. We said it was a pending solar storm, everyone to move inside and forego regular duties. They'll shortly realize that wasn't true, but I hope a lot of them will enjoy the downtime. It's not as if everyone couldn't use some."

"True that. What orders do you have? For me?"

"Hold them as long as you can. Minimize casualties. Deny knowledge of anything. Refer them to us, and we will not be responding. Shrug and sound without clue. Stall for every second you can before acting, and between. You'll have to wear them down by attrition, though daylight may help. Their timing is based on the find, not on the environment. Use the minimum force necessary, but if you have to, do whatever you need to stop them entering."

Taking all that in, he replied, "I don't want to provoke them into escalating."

Zeiss said, "Exactly. Be as measured as possible. That's why I chose you."

"Thanks." *I guess*, he thought. "I better move fast."

He turned and left. The doors closed behind him, followed by a supplemental air curtain. The Moon was buttoning up.

On the track outside, there was a Quad waiting for him.

He climbed on, flipped the power, and rode the designated path toward the main lock.

He reflected that the complete dearth of anything lethal, even a few handguns the police could have used, was possibly a planned move on the part of the Ueys. Or, it may have just been media-inspired paranoia over explosive decompression, even though it would take a lot more than a pistol, or even a rifle, to puncture the outside hull, and holes in the regolith of the inner habitat were pointless, even if possible. Meteorites whacked the structure regularly, often not even scratching the metal. Only twice had they made a pinhole.

The police had stun batons, which were rarely needed, granted, but would be singularly ineffective against actual gunfire. Nor would they do anything through a vacuum suit.

There were a handful of antiarmor rockets, intended for blowing protruding rock faces down. Inside, though, those were suicidally dangerous.

Fighting here came down to either poking holes in people, hitting them hard, or, if they were in vacuum, damaging their breathing equipment or containment. That additional factor was something the Loonies worried about constantly, and the Ueys might not have thought about.

Under the Hill, spaces maintained pressure protocol but the main passage did not. The air curtains were kept open, but could be dropped automatically, from any control station, or individually if needed. The Quad Track paralleled the walkway, which was empty due to Zeiss's stand-down order. Unusually empty. Normally there were dozens of people moving through it with carts and dollies, walking to jobs, rolling Quads. He had the only Quad and he counted eight people during the trip, three of them Security. That was definitely going to arouse suspicions and couldn't be maintained long.

It took only a couple of minutes to reach the main lock. It was uncommon to see the large screen noting LOCK SECTION CLOSED. Even more so to see it devoid of anyone working even if it was. He parked the Quad, leapt off, and stepped into the Lock Operations Room, which everyone knew as the Hut.

Possibly on Earth a gate control might still romantically be thought of as a hut. Here it was just a hole bored in the regolith, with power conduits and lights, a bare-sheet titanium floor with some imported static mats, and desks and chairs. As with everywhere up here, one brought their own fliptop computer, plugged in, and used software and access codes to build a work center. The conduits ran to the main trunk, out to the airlocks, up to the surface antennas, and all had standard plug connectors spaced along them. There was a wire fence separating the Hut from the Support Cage that held tools, suits, parts, and incoming supplies that would get sorted and dispensed. Farther back the passage was the main Supply Cage that took all the palletized resources.

Really, the number of people who knew about the device made the pretense of secrecy silly. It was almost certain that everyone in Echelon 1 knew the rough details. The labor, support, outside contractors and family members might not, but all those with pull almost certainly did. He'd picked his four-member crew because they definitely knew, but that was secondary to their usefulness. They were in because they were ace engineers even by Loonie standards, very trustworthy, and calm under hazard.

Ravi Malakhar had done the materials sampling of the device's case, or tried to. The case was impervious. There was speculation it wasn't quite matter as humans understood it. Scans reflected off or got absorbed, and there wasn't any consistency as to which. He was very good with observation and data. The more of that they had regarding the Ueys, the easier it would be. He was a slender Indian and looked older in the face than he was, but was quite fit.

Stu Morton had figured out some of the small amount of coding they understood so far. The controls on the thing were very organic, taking hand motions and translating them into instructions. He could code equipment remotely, or secure it against intrusion. It was assumed the Ueys would try to hack into commo. He'd coordinate counters. If only his Liverpool accent didn't make him sound like a Beatles movie.

Laura Rojas was a crack fabricator, and had been here eight years. There wasn't a detail of the lunarscape she didn't know, nor any of their equipment. She'd helped create, on the fly, some of the tooling that had failed to penetrate the device. That was more success than anyone else had. He'd watched her gain a little mass due to the low G, but she was fit, just tiny, barely 160 centimeters.

Roderick Godin was in because he'd been the mission engineer when the "gadget" had been found. He'd been cool enough to secure the item in place, clear the area, call for observation and photos, approach slowly and then wait for further instruction. "Rod from God," as several women nicknamed him, was also really good in a crater or crevice, and understood structures. Andre had a special project for him.

Andre would rather none of them were involved in the defense, given the information they had. For them to get killed, or worse, captured, could screw the whole deal. However, there was no one who could be relied upon to defend against an armed force without having the knowledge, which still needed to officially be held close. It made a certain amount of sense.

So here they were.

He shook hands quickly. He mumbled and nodded because his brain was still thinking.

Then he remembered to act as well as think.

"Sorry, let's move. We've got to secure resources before the Ueys arrive. Lock down, lock up, clear out power and oxy, unsafe the traps, get back here and hunker down."

He didn't bother with a vacuum suit yet. There was no time.

There were a handful of others at their disposal, who only knew there was a dispute, not the cause. He wasn't going to involve them yet. He knew Ravi and Rod had observers who could support them.

Not that it mattered. It wouldn't take long for news of the UN landing to get out, and of the dock being secured. There were plenty of science and industrial projects outside that required access to vehicles. Those were all on hold. That hold, even justified as "solar activity," wouldn't last more than a few hours.

As far as weapons, they had nothing ready made. They had explosives in expedient production, and various chemicals, but the goal was to avoid violence as long and as much as possible, for both PR and out of humanitarian gestures. Melee implements were plentiful—titanium geologist's hammers with the rock chisel end sharpened to an edge, chisels ground down and mounted on tool handles as pikes, pry bars. Those would readily crack a faceplate or split any hose connection. Though he wasn't sanguine about using them. The incoming troops probably had better and more recent hand-to-hand training than he or his people.

They had an effectively limitless oxygen source, as far as the engagement went. The intruders had only what they could bring on their ship and vehicles. Keeping them from acquiring resupply locally was first on the list. If they ran out of oxy, or eventually water, the fight ended. They might also have issues with power. Certainly the power plants on the ships would have plenty, but changing that energy to usable form for vehicles and suits took time and equipment. A man charging his suit batteries and filling up on breathing mix wasn't combat effective.

The plan was to delay, stall, hinder, then if need be damage or injure, and if all else failed, kill, but only after the Ueys had made the first aggressive move.

The devices and events constructed over the last three days, since the UN launch, with either secrecy or careful cover stories and work orders ready to go. They were still hidden, and nothing appeared out of line. However, to maintain the pretense of normalcy, the lock itself had been left operational until now.

Crawford and his men and woman were almost in a panic as they rolled into the Outer Bay. He felt very exposed this far from the main habitable area without a pressure suit even within reach.

The Outer Bay had a light sheet floor over the regolith, framework pressure doors, and parking slots for four ready vehicles to recharge, reload, refit and get back out. There were racks for batteries, tanks and bottles. It made it quick and efficient to supply and resupply outside functions without entering deeper into the maintenance and support area of Middle Bay. During a busy project, the four rollys would be nonstop ferries of people and sundries.

He pointed around the bay and ordered.

"Okay, load the oxy on that goat trailer, then pull power lines on the rollys. We'll take those in."

Rojas said, "Those aren't all gonna fit."

"Right. We'll make more trips, and try to dismount charging ports as well. If we have time, we'll take the batteries. If we can't do that, we'll try to disable the vehicles some other way."

"If you say so." She didn't sound convinced.

"Yeah. We'll do what we can. Let's move, okay?"

The bottles were easy enough, it was just tedious to move so many. The ready racks held enough for an entire shift of three work crews to be outside, right about a hundred tanks.

"Stack them neatly. We can dump to unload, but the neater, the better for loading," he said.

Ravi had been just tossing them. He grumbled, but started aligning them for a geometric pile. And thank God for .16 G.

Those all fit, with room to take all four power cables from the other rollys.

"Hurry," Crawford urged. Once everything was piled, he jumped on the saddle, powered up and rolled in to the Middle Bay, then past Lock 3A and 3B to Inner Bay and Maintenance off to the side. That was big enough to pull pressurized maintenance on a single rolly, and for two others to pass each other in turn. There was just room to back the trailer carefully inside the main hab, Lock 4. The haulers used for palletized cargo were specialized for that lock and used in trains, not singly.

Barely. He scraped one side and almost jammed a wheel before he got it backed in.

"Just toss the stuff off and we'll go back for more."

Really, more labor would be useful. On the other hand, it would only take one sympathizer to wreck the whole thing.

He scraped back out, the vehicle thumping and rising,

then back down in the low G, as one of the trailer wheels caught on the hatch frame.

For the second trip, two of the large recharge tanks fit on the trailer, along with charging ports. There was still power in the battery banks, but the Ueys would have no way to charge or draw from them without bringing or making a Charging Interface Unit. The batteries could be dismounted and used as is, but that would take time the Ueys probably couldn't spare.

His phone beeped. He pressed the button on his collar and heard Coffman. "They're rolling into view."

"Crap, guys, we go now."

He bounded across the garage in two leaps and slapped the button to close Lock 1. Then he turned to the remaining recharge tank, pulled the hammer off his belt, and cracked the safety disk. The tank began a slow hiss as it vented into the enclosed space.

"At least we're not losing that air," he said. "Kick it."

Rojas shrugged and took the wheel, and rolled back through to Inner Bay. Morton followed, disabling the lock control on this side, then doing a bypass on the inner control. He couldn't smash it completely; it housed all the circuitry here. There was a manual override for emergencies. No one had foreseen needing to cut lock controls and run them remotely. It was cheaper, faster and safer to build one box for each hatch and simply run a control line in. That was going to bite them in the ass now. They couldn't cut it without surrendering control to the Ueys. The Ueys could cut it and take that control, and probably would.

The maintenance section in the Middle Bay was empty.

That meant lots of room for Ueys to get in, but nothing for them to hide behind. When it came to booby traps, this entrance was as good as could be hoped for.

They needed to get on those booby traps.

"Rod, you know that divot right about the middle of the entryway floor? Reinforced with lattice?"

Godin said, "Yes."

"Can you open that section and mine that lattice?"

The man nodded, wrinkled his brow and said, "I need an hour."

"Faster if you can. We might not have more than that. They may come straight in."

"Can I have Rojas with me? And Ravi, can you get the charges? I'll need at least ten. One hundred grams each."

Malakhar said, "I'll get them now. Do I need authorization?"

Crawford said, "You have it." He pointed at his screen. He'd already pinged Control and gotten approval.

The three skipped off.

Then he said, "Stu, can you prep those transducers we talked about? I want them up high out of reach."

Morton said, "On it, boss," and skipped away.

The transducers could generate enough sound pressure to be heard in five percent atmospheric pressure. They were armored against impact, and Rojas had fabbed a second cover for them that should stop bullets. Properly placed in one of the locks, they would hopefully be very effective stun and distraction devices.

All that set, Andre took a few moments to peel out of his coverall, skin into a leotard, and pull his friction suit on. He had his helmet and bottle right there in case he needed them.

Back to the fliptop he had as a control console, he looked at the screens and written report. Nothing was coming through on audio yet.

"Can you hear me, boss?" Godin came through his headset.

"I have you."

"I'm wired into the channel here. Didn't want to use radio."

"Good." And that decision-making ability was why he'd grabbed these people.

Godin said, "Ravi is prepping the charges for me. Laura is helping me open the floor panels. Worst case, we pull out and there's a big hole in the floor they have to work around. What are they doing?"

The video feed showed three ArctiTraks lumbering evenly around the ridge cut.

Crawford gauged them and said, "Approaching by vehicle. At that speed, you still have ten minutes before arrival. I'd say they'll need ten to debark and arm for entry. Which also assumes they're in a hurry. They're certainly visible and can't expect to surprise us."

"Roger. I'll update as we go. I'm pulling the wire. Give me a channel squelch and a word 'go' if we have to run."

Crawford nodded to himself. "Sounds good. Signal is quelch and go."

Right then, Coffman came on. "Andre, we have two friends of Ravi's who are going EVA for observations."

"Yeah, he mentioned them. What do you have on this element out there?"

On screen, Coffman shrugged. "The same camera you do, sir. SELSAT has nothing. We don't know if it's dead or jammed."

That was bad. "All three? Shouldn't two be over the horizon at present?"

"Yup, nada. The colonel doesn't want to put a skimmer up because that would be obvious and possibly provocative. We're waiting for them to come to us."

"Got it. Whatever you do see, keep me informed. I may not notice everything."

"I'm listening in. What you've been reporting so far is good."

"Glad to hear it." But as much as he liked being in charge, this was a bit outside his comfort zone.

The element was large. He looked over the imagery and tried to think. Three ArctiTraks, possibly sixty Ueys. Ground staff . . . space crew, if they were double trained, and probably were . . .

Ravi came back through the door.

He said, "Hey, boss, I'm in their way. What do you need?"

Crawford replied, "Hang here until we have more info."

"That I can do. Want me to look?"

"Please."

Turning his head back to the screens, Andre tried to estimate against known landmarks.

He said, "Estimate a hundred men? Figure three Traks with twenty each plus support?"

Malakhar agreed. "That seems a fair appraisal. Anything on sat?"

"Coffman says they're down."

Malakhar scowled, his lean face looking odd with the expression. "That's not good. I may be able to get a powered drone up, or I have a man outside who can slingshot a camera overhead and try to retrieve it later. Both have advantages."

Crawford said, "Yeah, I do want to know. On the other hand, I don't want to waste anything too soon, or give away our knowledge."

Rojas came in right then and said, "Boss, they have to know we know. I wouldn't worry about that part." She sounded out of breath.

"True," he agreed. "Which leaves finding out now, or waiting. It's not as if it's going to change the troop numbers."

The talk was necessary, but agitating. Andre prompted again, "Okay, get me whatever you have."

Malakhar said, "I've got an observer going up Peak Five from the outside. We painted his suit tan. It'll flake off, but should drop his profile a lot. He has a laser signal he can beam to the tertiary receiver. Coffman's the only one with access."

"Well done, thanks."

"No problem. I've got another guy behind the outcropping who's going to launch the camera, then duck inside. We get one shot, so tell me when you want to do it."

Andre chewed his lip and thought.

"Don't let them get close enough to catch him. But when they're a few hundred meters out, I say do it."

Malakhar said, "I count three vehicles, but it's likely there's two more out behind the ridge."

He nodded. "Right. Do it when you see fit."

"Roger."

"And we need to get that emergency hatch moved into position and sealed."

Morton said, "I'll do that now. Laura, help?"

"Yup," she said, and bounded back to her feet.

Godin leaned his head into the Hut and said, "I'll help. I'm done in Outer Bay."

"Good."

The emergency lock mounted into position anywhere a precut slot existed. Those were in the rock every twenty meters, and in the habitrails every fifteen. The idea was a leak could be isolated to the smallest volume possible, and then repaired or worked around.

But an emergency lock was just that. It wouldn't handle many sudden significant pressure shifts but it might handle one. It bought time in an emergency. This wasn't the emergency it was built for, but it would still work.

Out in the main passage, Morton and Rojas mounted the lock base, set the sides, and cranked the tension up. Godin latched the mounts. Andre watched through the door, while turning back to his screens every few seconds. Once they had all four sides in the precut slots, Morton pulled, twisted and slapped the button that extruded sealing goop all the way around. It was effectively airtight; leakage should be in grams per minute or less. It wasn't proof against an overpressure slam either way. They'd need to avoid that.

Andre was back at the screens as the three returned. There was a video feed from up high. That man on the ridge had good imagery, though his field of view was limited.

Malakhar took a look at the scan and said, "Yup, two more. Now, that's three plus two that we can see. We're assuming a lander-type Albatross C. That doesn't mean they didn't strip down and squeeze another vehicle in, or that they didn't land another craft farther out. I don't see a reason they would, but it's not impossible."

"Got it," Crawford said with a nod.

An overhead image at an oblique, ballistic angle showed the exact positions of the Uey craft and vehicles. They were well clear of any feasible weapon from here, out of view of the dome or the tunnels, but close enough to make their own support and recovery easy.

Malakhar stared at his screen and replied, "Yes, Albatross C, single, can carry five ArctiTraks and most of their gear would be inside those, or wedged between. We're looking at everything they are likely to have. They may be able to lift if they abandon everything here, or if they get a fuel drop from an orbiter."

"Good."

Ravi continued, "Okay, my man outside is now inside. The man up on the peak can hold for four hours on his oxy supply if you need him to."

"If he's comfy, it can't hurt to do so."

Malakhar pointed. "He even sent a pic."

The image showed a suited figure draped in a hollow, one leg hanging over a formerly sharp edge he'd hammered flat. From any angle, in that color, he'd be tough to see, and no one should be looking. He was flashing a peace sign.

Crawford had to grin.

"Yeah, as long as he can last. More intel always helps."

He stood, stretched and looked at the other three.

"So let's summarize: We have three airlocks, one of them twin. We installed an emergency unit as a fifth. Four sections, five hatches. We can secure controls from in here, but that could be bypassed eventually. We need to stop them from entering or causing infrastructure damage that would lead to personnel evacuation. We want to minimize casualties, and avoid first use of force if at all possible. We've improvised several nonlethal weapons and the three of you can hopefully fab gear as needed against incursions. It's dawn here, and as the sun clears the peaks, it will get hot fast. That means they'll need to force entry or build shelter. Ultimately, we win if they surrender or run out of oxy and retreat. They win if they achieve entry and control the entrance."

Morton said, "Of course we never needed lethal or projectile weapons here, and they'd be dangerous in a habitat. And whether that was intentional or circumstantial, they're going to exploit it."

Crawford nodded and scowled. "Yeah. I said all along that pistols wouldn't breach the sheathing, nor most light rifles, and that they'd be useful in case of a rebellion or even a criminal threat. Everyone ignored me. Then Gresham freaked out last year and stabbed five people before he got dogpiled."

Rojas said, "I'm not sure firearms would have changed that outcome."

Andre shrugged. He'd seen knife fights on the South Side. "Probably not, but if it happens once, it can happen again. We can discuss it another time. I just wish we had them now."

The four sat down to wait. That was the main thing in war: boredom. All parties would maneuver, sit around, maneuver some more, change positions. Eventually someone would attack or, more likely, trip over the enemy. Then the fight started.

"Make sure we keep the coffee full," he ordered. "Food regularly. We can talk, or move around, or plan. I don't want anyone playing cards or gaming. We need to notice motion on the screens and messages. No outgoing messages. Everyone's phone is off, right? And the suit comms are for official use only."

"Yup."

"Yes."

"Got it."

"Ravi, please confirm."

The man had been fiddling with his fliptop to get the screen at a good angle.

"Yes, I understand. Sorry."

He was usually taciturn and didn't communicate much. He had to be reminded that for this, verbal confirmation was a must for record.

From his raised position, Colonel Zeiss looked around Central Operations, then at the external view on the large screen. Often, that carried news or mission footage. Now it just showed the majestic scenery. It was almost high enough resolution to fool the human eye into seeing it as "real." Almost.

Even though the moon ran on Zulu time, lunar sunrise was relevant to several functions. It was also very pretty. The main screen showed a polarized view of a bare glow peeking through a notch in the rim wall. That tendril that might just be a prominence added to the grandeur.

Zeiss felt reasonably calm under the present circumstances. He had some of the best people on the job, and it was unlikely the UN wanted violence. The wrap-up at Hadley Dome indicated that.

On the other hand, he also had some of the most stubborn and cantankerous people, and they were getting aggravating.

Zeiss had only a moment to appreciate the canned view, as approval requests and advisories started chattering in.

The hope was to stall any EXTAC—EXTernal ACtivity—until the dispute was resolved. Otherwise, a lockdown phrased in that way would guarantee rumors as to why. Those would be bad if true, potentially worse if wild speculation. Nor was it possible to bottle this many people up, even with hard vacuum outside.

Zeiss asked, "What's the word on the Uey landing?"

Coffman said, "No movement yet, from any available source. We still have nothing from SELSAT. Definitely compromised."

"Who else knows that?"

Coffman replied, "Just my section. No one has any urgent commo queued."

Solar activity did sometimes interfere for minutes at a time. But that was minutes. He needed hours.

Okay, so he felt a little stressed. "I wish they'd get on with it."

Coffman agreed, "Yes, sir. Meantime, I've automated 'in queue' notifications to all senders, and a 'possible interference' advisory. Which is true. We have interference."

That was clever, and just beyond Zeiss's grasp of English. He was very fluent, but his German mind-set didn't let him play words with the foreign language like that.

"Just not a natural cause. Yes," he noted.

Coffman warned, "But, sir, within a few minutes, there are going to be angry queries, and I don't know what to say."

"Yes. I'll see what I can devise."

He turned to his private console and wired connection. "Crawford, update when you can."

Andre heard Zeiss's order and replied, "I will, sir. We've finished prepping infrastructure. Now we're waiting for commencement."

"I understand, Zeiss out."

He and his people waited, with every screen on every device split to show command input and the outside cameras.

Crawford asked, "What's their roll time from there, about ten minutes?"

Godin said, "Ten minutes for us. They should take about twenty to be cautious, plus whatever threat protocols they want to use."

He calculated. "So, figure eight as a bare minimum if they go balls out, and we're already five into that. Nominal thirty. Possibly an hour."

Godin agreed. "That seems reasonable."

"Okay. I could definitely use a sandwich."

Rojas put in with a grin, "The cooler has egg, chicken, cheese, mustard and peppers. Make your own damned sandwich, boss."

He grinned. "Don't mind if I do. Anyone else?"

Morton said, "Yeah, sure thing."

"Go for it. Make your own damned sandwich," Andre tossed back.

He would like some roast beef, but that was very scarce up here, and usually from a tank. Tank-raised meat did not taste like real meat, no matter who claimed so. They weren't likely to get any from Earth this month, either. Chicken, turkey, tuna and salmon were their primary meat proteins, and lots of egg. The cheese also wasn't great, being made from powdered milk fat solids.

In the list of minor repercussions, the McDonald's down the passage wasn't going to have any burgers for as long as this lasted, only chicken.

The mustard was okay. They made their own vinegar and grew their own mustard seed, among other spices. The bread was real, though with rice as well as wheat it was a bit crumbly.

Still, he had a fresh sandwich and coffee.

The coffee was okay. They grew that under lights, and it didn't have anything like the complexity of Earth coffee, because they didn't have the soil. It was hot and well made, though.

Malakhar said, "Here they come. Three ArctiTraks, probably with ten each, twenty if they stuff. But I have no idea how much volume they're using for equipment."

"Right." He shoved the rest of the sandwich in his mouth, chewed, swallowed, guzzled the last quarter cup of coffee and turned to his console.

For now, he had plenty of imagery. He assumed that would stop eventually. But he could clearly see the vehicles rolling around the cut in the ridge. They were in line, about five hundred meters separated.

They stopped well back from Lock 1, and dispersed a few meters apart. Hatches dropped, and suited troops debarked, in tan pressure suits with rifles and small buttpacks under their oxy bottles.

He said, "Remember, these are all space-qual troops, so they're elite. Don't underestimate any of them."

The troops moved quickly, rolling out what appeared to be a genny cart, and an oxy bottle supply. They were ready for an extended stay.

In a few moments, three of the troops almost casually detached from the group and started moving zigzag toward the lock. Two more followed a few seconds behind.

Rodin said, "Looks like a recon team first. Smart. They're armed with G56 rifles and pry bars. I don't see any other weapons or relevant tools."

Andre said, "Well, we can't do anything until they do something."

For now, the outer lock wasn't secured. There were advantages to having the troops inside where pressure and vacuum could be adjusted. He'd hoped for a larger element, but this would do.

Lock 1 was designed as an outer pressure curtain against leaks, and slid like a hangar door. It was powered, but also had a rack and pinion for manual opening. The three-man element opened it manually and slowly, cautious in their entry. They cranked it about a meter, just enough for easy entrance. They certainly expected explosives or similar. They stood clear as it slid, then lurked back while making careful scans with a drone ball, handheld sensors and a sweep with an old-fashioned stick.

That's it. Come on in.

Even inside a suit, that gesture from the leader was a shrug. The three stepped forward and in, holding an arc against potential attackers. They were aiming at the walls and looking silly, but he had to admit it was a valid stance to assume a threat from any direction. They even scanned overhead.

Good enough. This stage was a combination of delaying and disorienting. Here was the first obstacle.

He clicked the safety, then pressed the trigger button. Lock 2's latch clicked, twisted, there was a hiss . . .

. . . then Lock 2 slammed against its stops as ten atmospheres of pressure found an escape.

The blast of air was mostly oxygen, which they could refresh from Lunar regolith. Nitrogen was too valuable, and needed for the hydroponics farm. All that mattered was the pressure front, which roared, hissed and sighed into the open lock and out into vacuum. The gust blew the first troop straight through the hatch, his feet catching on the rim and causing him to flail and tumble. He slammed into the two Ueys outside, and they all sprawled across the powdery road.

The other two were a moment behind, buffeted and battered against the lip as the pressure inexorably forced them through as it escaped. One cartwheeled dramatically before bouncing on his helmet and sprawling in a long slide, like the ultimate base-steal in baseball.

Andre wasn't sure if they were injured from being

blown across the moonscape. One may have strained a thigh as he bounced. All three were well outside, though.

There was a seconds-long pause, before others rushed to their aid, with screening troops in front and responders behind. Very quickly, they all got back behind the cover of their vehicles.

Andre could close the hatch and do this again, but then the Ueys might find another route, blow some seals, or otherwise cease engaging. The goal was to keep them here as long as possible.

The open lock invited them to try again, this time to close the hatch as soon as they entered and proceed to secure Lock 2, which was just big enough for a vehicle to move in, then into the Maintenance Bay. That had nothing of relevance. The batteries and oxygen were in here now. The tools in Maintenance weren't anything their ship didn't have. And the Ueys had to be wondering why Lock 2 was still open, inviting, taunting them.

That Middle Bay would mean the Ueys could only admit a small contingent, and would have to secure it to proceed, then the next. Then, the fifth hatch hastily erected inside allowed more bottlenecking, and the entire habitat was able to use pressure doors and curtains as additional setbacks.

The delay was palpable and irritating, no doubt by intention. That was to be expected. Nothing here needed to be accomplished in seconds or even minutes. Hours, however, would run out even the oxygen supply on those support vehicles. It wouldn't be terribly long before the invaders did something.

"Is the second stage ready?" he asked. He knew it was.

"Got my finger on the button," Godin said.

"Good. Stand by."

With two locks wide open and daring them, a larger contingent approached, skipping from cover to cover— boulders, a lip of melted regolith, the lock frame itself. This time, it was four armed in front, and two guys with gear, presumably technical specialists.

Everyone knew the Loonies had no weapons. Still, having been once caught, this element moved up slowly, with impressively even spacing, given that they had no experience in low G.

They darted into the Outer Bay, slid against the wall for the Middle Bay, then skipped one at a time through Lock 2.

Once inside, one of the techs slapped the hatch release, and nothing happened.

He turned to look, slapped it again, then hopped over to the lock to close it manually.

Once there, he realized that he lacked leverage, and waved for another to assist.

It was then that the monitor found their commo frequency.

"—take two of us. You brace me, I'll push."

"Got it."

It wasn't encrypted, but then, they hadn't had much time.

Nothing else useful was said, so Andre sat patiently while they closed and dogged Lock 2.

The one said, "I think the O_2 controls are bollixed, too. We have to get inside the next one and try to pressurize from there."

"They can't blow us out again, can they?"

"No, we're in vacuum and closed. But, if they try to overpressure us, you'll need to be ready to inflate your suit to counter it, or you'll be squashed from pressure."

Very good, dammit. It sounded like their technical expert actually knew physics.

Ah, well, squashing them wasn't the plan. Yet.

The intruders moved forward, and one of them shot a load of gunk at the monitor camera, which didn't matter since that camera was no longer in use and just a decoy. The camera Andre was watching was miniaturized and hidden.

The Ueys' pace was cautious, but brisk as they moved down the walls of the Outer Bay, then against the frame of Lock 2.

Using hand signals only, they gestured, then shuffled into position and stacked.

"Ready?" Crawford asked again.

Godin grinned and said, "I am."

Right then, the Ueys swarmed across the threshold, crossing through each other, rifles out and sweeping.

The moment all of them were within the frame, he snapped, "Now!"

Godin tapped the key, and the second trap was sprung.

Three strobes flashed at three different rates, at ten thousand lumens each. The flashes from two were short enough duration not to trigger faceplate polarizing. The other was just long enough. Between them, the troops should be disoriented with dazzling flash and dark fields of vision.

As the light show faded, another burst of oxygen

cleared out three tubes full of bouncy balls. In fact, they were roughly shaped lumps of super silicone gasket goop, formed and let set.

With that pressure behind them, and in low G, they impacted like fists, then bounced away. Some careened around like billiard balls in a 3-D table and came back for a second thump. The dazzle, darkness and thumping had all six on the ground, struggling or unconscious.

They were all clear of the frame, and Crawford punched for the hatch to close, locking them in.

The door swung, then slowed and stopped.

Crap. Yeah, the troops were inside, but a chunk of silicone was not. It was in the door track.

Okay, the lock would have to stay eighty percent closed. It was just barely wide enough someone might squeeze back out. If they tried, he was going to let them. He had Lock 1 dogged now. That would take time to breach.

And time was what the Loonies needed. Every minute here was a minute the Ueys weren't inside, and were using oxygen. Their supply was much more limited.

"Okay, do I leave the lock evacuated and force those troops to use their oxygen? Or pressurize it against another attempt at a breach?"

Morton said, "We should have had someone ready to swarm them." He didn't sound accusatory, rather, embarrassed. None of them had thought of it.

Andre replied, "Yeah, but no way to predict how effective that was going to be, and we can't spare people for hand-to-hand against professional troops."

Godin suggested, "Leave it for now. We'll watch outside for movement, and they're consuming oxygen in there."

"Right."

The stunned troops recovered and rose slowly. Once up they looked around. One of them cautiously blocked the open lock hatch with his weapon, then turned around to see what the Middle Bay looked like.

They chattered with helmets in contact, no radio. Smart.

Then there was a transmission. "Command, we were attacked. We appear to have been pummeled with elastic projectiles causing minor injury only, and we were stunned. Sergeant Plexer has a damaged tank valve and will need extraction."

"We are unable to enter the outer lock. It has been sealed and barricaded from inside."

"What is your time frame for entry, over?"

"Unknown, over."

"Crap. Lunar faction, if you are monitoring this frequency, we are in need of assistance. One of our party has a damaged oxygen supply and his helmet contains only a very short duration. Will you accept temporary truce and let him exit?"

That was a tough one. Certainly, prisoners were useful, and treating them well would avoid escalating the situation, might help defuse it. But, admitting to having hacked their commo already . . . on the other hand, it wasn't encrypted.

"Andre, they sent that in the clear."

"Yeah. Let's hold on a moment, though."

The NCO in charge called again. "Lunar faction, are you monitoring this frequency?"

Crawford said, "Let's give him one more."

Almost a full minute went by, before the call came again.

"Lunar faction, please respond."

He activated then keyed the mic and said, "UN element, this is Lock Control. We have your frequency. Please confirm, over."

"I hear you, Lunar. Over."

"What do you need?"

"This incident has damaged the oxygen supply for one of my troops. Will you permit him to exit?"

Andre waited several seconds, then said, "I think it would be better if we brought him in here. It's faster, and we've got plenty of oxy in the habitat."

"Are you proposing to detain him as a prisoner of war?"

Less of a delay on that. Diplomacy. "I'm not aware of any war. But if you are asking do we intend to keep him from re-engaging, then the answer is yes. And will he be treated humanely? Of course. We may eventually want to discuss damages and protocol violations, but that's for Control to decide. I'm just the gatekeeper."

"Fair enough. How do we proceed?"

He waited several more seconds. On the one hand, they might think he was either just a flunky or indecisive. On the other, it was all stall. A minute here, a minute there. Eventually it might add up to hours.

"You will place your weapons in the next airlock for us to secure. You may then admit your troop and he will be allowed to remain, unharmed, until resolution."

The Uey sounded really suspicious as he asked, "Why do you need the weapons?"

"We don't intend to allow you to keep them. At this point you constitute a threat. You are asking for additional terms to that detention. You can argue, but your man has what, another minute or so in his suit?"

"We have your word on his safety?" That did sound like a genuine question.

"We have used the minimum force possible so far and intend to continue to do so. You have my word."

"And may we have your name?"

Why not? "You first."

"Lieutenant Kasanga of the African Federation, detached to Operation Clarity."

"I am engineer Andre Crawford." And now he had the operation name, which sounded like one of the randomly generated ones that didn't tell anything.

Kasanga said, "We will comply."

He cut communication. "Morton, Rojas, go get them." He switched on to Central. "Mr. Coffman, I could use a medic."

"Doctor Nik is inbound your way."

"Thanks."

He worked the controls and opened Lock 3A. The Ueys piled their weapons up, though he assumed they retained a hidden pistol or knife somewhere. The video showed them taking a good look for whatever intel they could get. The plenum between 3A and 3B was just a connector without much of anything. It just allowed locking through from habitat to an unpressurized bay.

It took long seconds to balance pressure and open the inner hatch—Lock 3B. Morton skipped in, grabbed the rifles, brought them back and started clearing the actions.

Rojas manually slammed 3B. Andre started the evacuation process and stood ready to cycle again.

Kasanga called, "Engineer Crawford, please hurry. His blood oxygen meter is reaching hypoxia."

"About five seconds . . . opening hatch."

The troop staggered in, and one other came with him for support. Reasonable. And why he'd disarmed them.

He punched for pressure, hit the override and had the hatch motor work against the differential until it cracked seal. There was a whuff and a gust and there was breathing air from Bay 3.

The second Uey twisted the helmet latch of the first, who gasped and started breathing hard.

The door finished its swing, and Morton stepped through to greet them.

"Welcome to the Moon. Precede me that way and through the open door to your right."

Crawford watched on camera, and saw the shadows down the passage as they approached, then them enter the other side of the fence in the equipment cage.

Morton said, "Please sit over there and do not make any sudden moves."

The escort realized all four rifles were now in the hands of Loonies. He nodded and assisted his buddy over.

"He should lie down for now."

Crawford agreed, "Yes, do so. Also, you will need to remove your harness. I see tools and equipment we could find troublesome."

The man didn't argue. He helped his buddy lie back, then unsnapped his harness including his oxy bottle.

Doctor Nik stepped in, glanced for approval, which Crawford gave with a nod, and let himself into the cage.

He checked the man's suit monitor and said, "He

should be fine. Bring him some water. Take it easy, sir. You'll need a few minutes to recover."

The second man said, "May I report in to assure them we are well?"

Andre said, "Yes. I've already assumed you're going to try to pass intel. As soon as you do, I cut the signal." He handed over a wired mic.

The man scowled, took the offered mic, and said, "Clarity, this is Sergeant Vinson. Aigule and I are both well and unharmed. They have our weapons. I count five of them. The third lock is—"

"I cut you off after 'weapons.'"

The man shrugged. "Of course I was going to try."

"And of course you were going to lose. Please consider yourselves our guests, rather than prisoners. Either way, escape means entering hard vacuum without even a helmet. I recommend against it. If you succeed, you suffocate instantly. If you fail, you will probably have been injured. There's no benefit to either of you."

There was a message from Coffman. "Paul will be at the Hut shortly. We'll transfer these two in."

"Roger." He checked the corridor monitors. "I see him."

Security Officer Paul arrived with two others. The Ueys were bound with cable ties, hooded with pillowcases, and looked very wary as that happened. Then they were marched out in front of the security officer with one of their rifles.

Andre said, "They'll each be put in a separate compartment. That should minimize risk."

Morton asked, "And if we capture enough to run out of compartments?"

He smiled. "We declare victory conditions."

Having transferred the two troops in, the Ueys in the Middle Bay sat to conserve oxygen. One of them tried to pry the elastic goop out of the track, and the hatch closed more. He stuck a tool in the latch side to prevent it being closed by the Loonies and apparently decided not to keep messing with it without support. The element outside waited.

There were obviously lengthy discussions ongoing with the leadership, possibly all the way back to Earth.

Shortly, the outside element trotted to one of the vehicles and pulled out a roll of material and some struts. Then they started assembling it.

Rojas noted, "Mylar sun shield."

Malakhar said, "For note, the shadow is nowhere underneath it this time of day. Quite distant. We can knock it down with no risk of injury."

Andre smirked. "Heck, a properly placed gas bottle will blow it across the landscape."

Rojas added, "Especially if we can find a way to cut it with debris then blow it to shreds."

The element outside were almost certainly trying to open Lock 1 intact. It existed for a reason, and even if they succeeded in entry, they'd need it, too. It was probably also sturdier than their gear could easily override. Blowing a hole in it would be easy. Actually opening it to admit entry was a different matter.

It was obvious they were using tools, moving around, probing, trying to determine some way to force an almost featureless aluminum panel on a grooved track.

Crawford asked, "What do your observers have, Ravi?"

Malakhar said, "There are two small detachments patrolling slowly through the crags, and they will probably find the personnel hatches. I told Coffman, who says Zeiss is aware."

"Good. But most of them are right here?"

"Yes."

"I'd question their logic, but really, this is the best place to get a force in. The narrow passages are bottlenecks and could lead to a lot of casualties. Here they can get more force in, and maneuver."

During all this, the troops in Middle Bay were still sitting there patiently, not using more resources than they had to.

"Does this matter?" Rojas asked. She looked tired.

"How do you mean?" Andre asked.

"Even if we win, do we win? What do we win?"

Andre had to think about that. He stretched back in his chair.

"I don't know," he said. "On the one hand, if the Ueys do keep it secret, there's no benefit but no loss. On the other hand, I can't imagine it staying secret. Too many scientists would want it to be public, and too many people would benefit."

Morton said, "I rather think there'd be a lot of fighting over it, with serious physical assaults to secure it for one group or another. Probably national, but possibly corporate."

"Very possible," Andre agreed.

Godin said, "If it gets out, there's guaranteed violence. If it stays secure, guaranteed violence, but you know, we have plenty of violence without it. I don't see it having that much of an effect on things overall, as far as that goes."

Andre said, "Logistically it matters. Military engineers are a force multiplier for an army. We let them move faster, be secure, pin the enemy in place. That takes money—logistics. If I could have as many mines and traps as I wanted produced on-site by shoveling crap—even literally crap—into one end, it would definitely make it easier."

Godin said, "And that would apply equally to everyone who had one, right? Even poorer, less equipped armies."

"It would. There'd be no superpowers anymore."

"Not really a bad thing, then?"

Andre thought. "I don't know. I mean, at present the superpowers are basically the US and China with Brazil, India and Japan moving up fast. I certainly don't fear the Japanese with it. The Indians I'm not sure about. Sorry, Ravi."

Malakhar looked up from his screens and shrugged. "I agree, given our internal issues and some of our fringe groups that the government is not able to control."

"But say some of the more rabid nations, like some of the Arab countries of thirty years ago, get it, or some of the Stans. And then there's any number of groups who could become national powers if they had it, and as long as they have enough people, this means they will have enough material. The entire power dynamic of Earth is about to change."

Rojas said, "So they're not going to let us keep it, no matter what."

"I don't know," he admitted. "There are military, diplomatic, cultural and economic factors and I'm nowhere near an expert."

Godin said, "If someone thinks they can make a buck off it, they're not going to destroy it."

Morton cocked his head and raised his brows.

"There are groups opposed enough to capitalism that bombing it will be their first response. They'd rather have nothing than let anyone profit."

"Yup," Andre agreed. "All we can do is hold off for now and see what's next. For now, everyone should take a bathroom break in turn and get more food. And we need some water bottles."

"I'll go," Morton said, standing.

It was an hour later when Lieutenant Kasanga came over the radio.

"Lunar Element, Engineer Crawford, we are low on oxygen."

Theoretically, those were six-hour tanks with good filters. But they'd been exerting since arrival, and their trip from the ship was probably an hour. So two and a half hours? Yeah. No one had thought to use fresh bottles for a short incursion into an airlock.

Andre opened the mic. "Are you asking to surrender?"

After a long pause, the response was, "Yes."

"One at a time into the lock. Gear first, then the individual in a stripped suit."

He cycled them in one by one, and they were escorted off, hooded, to further detention.

He examined one of the gas bottles left behind. It

probably held twenty minutes of oxy. So they hadn't been desperate, but were certainly thinking ahead to avoid being so.

How big a reserve did they have in those vehicles? Replenishment tank or individual bottles? On the Moon, spare bottles were the rule. Lose one, you went on. Lose an entire replenishment supply...

He said, "We need to find a way to attack their support vehicles."

Godin said, "I've got a skimmer. We can shovel it full of dust at the pit out east."

"Is it out of view now?"

Godin explained, "As in, it's out at the hole where we found the thing. Remember they were doing geo surveys and mining outlines. They still are."

Crawford asked, "Okay. Who's piloting?"

"Seville."

He understood, he thought. "Aha. She hops to the pit, loads up with dust, flies over and opens the bay."

Godin said, "It'll be really messy to load it into the craft. There will be sealing issues and then we'll have to clean it all out afterward."

He understood. "Right. Still, it'll be a lot worse on their vehicle than the skimmer."

Godin said, "Yes. Want me to get her going?"

"Have her load up and stand by. We want to stage our response. Every time they think they're making headway, we knock them back down."

Godin turned to his console. "Got it. I'll code a message through."

Right then, the radio came through in clear.

"Lunar Element, this is Colonel Arris, UN Forces. I request response."

Crawford waited ten seconds, then keyed and spoke. "Go ahead, Colonel."

"May I ask who I am speaking with?"

"Sure, why not? As I told your lieutenant, I'm Andre Crawford, systems engineer."

There was dead air for about fifteen seconds, then Arris said, "Ah, here you are. You served with the US Army."

Crawford agreed, "I did. What about it?"

Arris said, "I want to discuss our positions, and hope to resolve this peacefully."

Crawford counted five. "I can talk. I can't make any decisions. That has to go through Control."

"I understand. I am unable to get a response from your Central Operations."

Five more seconds. "Okay."

Wait . . . Command wasn't answering Arris. But, Command hadn't told him not to talk to the Ueys. So the Ueys might think this was unsanctioned. That was interesting and potentially useful.

He typed a quick query to Command.

Zeiss responded, *Correct. As I said, we decided to ignore them, force them to deal with you alone for now. He tried to contact us on the official freq about 30 seconds ago. I was just sending that note. If it gets complicated you're authorized to ask us for advice, ask us to step in, or ignore him. Basically, keep him talking and unaware of anything else.*

He typed back, *Roger, but we might want to split his attention shortly. Distraction. I'll see what I can arrange.*

And as long as they were talking, the clock was running.

Arris said, "Ultimately, we have the upper hand."

He paused again. It was all delay. "You believe so?"

The colonel said, "We do. We have weapons and position."

Crawford waited his standard five seconds and said, "We have weapons now. And your troops are our prisoners."

He could almost hear Arris smirk. "We have a lot more than six weapons."

Crawford had to smile. "We have oxygen recycling and food. Do you propose a siege? We'll win."

"Until we bring more forces from Earth."

Leaning back to feel casual so he'd sound casual, he replied, "That takes time. Something we have a lot of."

"Something you have a finite amount of. Eventually our positions reverse."

He really did sound casual as he said, "Eventually."

Arris said, "We need to talk about the device."

"What device?" He'd rehearsed sounding as casually ignorant as possible.

"The device that is the reason we're here."

Noncommittally, he said, "I'm listening."

"You understand what it is, yes?"

"No. I don't know of any 'device.'" Actually, he knew a lot, but the longer they talked, the better, as long as his people kept an eye out for maneuvers.

Malakhar smiled and winced, and looked impressed at the flat-out lie. Andre had to stifle his own giggle.

"It didn't occur to you to ask why an armed force was landing with demands to enter, and orders for same?"

He replied, "One of the things I learned in the Army was not to ask questions about things I didn't want to need answers to. That's also good policy here, with all the military, technical and research secrets floating around."

Arris said, "Interesting. But you were told not to admit us." He didn't sound convinced.

"That is correct."

Arris said, "And have gone to lengthy measures to delay us."

Crawford leaned back in his chair and replied, "Those were my instructions."

"You understand my orders place me superior to your command authority."

That ploy. "Well, I'm sure they do from your point of view, but I don't recognize it."

"You don't recognize UN authority?" Arris sounded surprised.

"Not from outside, without a bona fide emergency. Central Operations is fully functional, and there's no reason for external control. They told me to hold out any incursion. I wasn't given a reason, but seeing as they're functional and not under any kind of duress, I'm assuming their orders are legit. Talk to them."

Arris sounded irritated as he replied, "As I said, they are not responding."

"Well, I'll send them a query. Right now, in fact. Stand by."

He did nothing for a measured thirty seconds. Really, this was eating up minutes.

He keyed and spoke, "Okay, that's done. You should hear from them as soon as they have comm time. But you understand I can't speak for them and have no control over their decisions."

Arris said, "I—"

Crawford cut him off and said, "So tell me about this device."

Arris replied, "It's a fabricator. Raw material goes in, it processes out as product."

"So, a printer?" He tried for just a hint of scoff.

"No, this is far more sophisticated. Much like a science fiction replicator."

That was a good rough approximation. Someone with firsthand knowledge had probably leaked.

He replied, "I see. Or rather, I don't. Why invade over that?"

Arris sounded surprised at the question. "The risks of it. Any weapon one wants, instantly."

Crawford replied, "Or food. Medicine. Shelter. Apparently, though, you and your bosses went immediately to the bad potential."

Morton whispered, "Andre, they're charging Lock One now."

"Case in point," he said. "You have no desire for a peaceful outcome." He slapped the channel closed.

"Let's do Round Two," he said. "They're actually going to try to blow their way in." He punched an alarm to Control.

"Explosion possibly imminent. Stand by for decompression protocols, and probably seismic as well."

Coffman replied, "Understood."

Was he justified in using lethal force yet? They hadn't so far, but this could be considered an imminent threat, except of course, the Ueys would argue with the known status of the locks that it wasn't.

"Go with the dust," he ordered. Though eventually someone was going to become a casualty.

Far back alongside the ridge, six emplaced fougasse detonated, their initiation felt as a rumble through the regolith. In vacuum, the tons of dust they launched prescribed near perfect parabola, arcing up and back down to land in a huge, coordinated pile on and in front of Lock 1, utterly burying several Ueys.

"Run the vid, count them," he ordered. "And go with shot two."

Outside and right of the entrance was a boulder that had been moved when the track was cleared. Several others had been stacked around it, then, over time, arranged into a loose sculpture. It had been there for a decade and no one questioned it.

Last week a large bladder had been erected among the rocks, and shoveled full of dust. A centrifugal pump spooled up, throwing the dust in its scroll out across the moonscape, followed by the dust above it, as it trickled in, like a massive hourglass. The blower would jam soon enough, or abrasion would cause failure. Until then, though, they were using electricity but wasting no oxygen.

That blew a huge stream of dust across the way, blocking pretty much any frequency of sensor, and almost certainly clogging equipment.

"Hopefully, that will take them a while to dig out," he said in satisfaction. Clicking open the general channel, he asked, "Colonel, are you still there?"

"Well done, Mr. Crawford."

"Thank you, sir, though I think we can do better. Would you like to give us another chance?"

"You can hold the mock derision. I am impressed. On another level, not at all. We know how this ends."

"Not my department, Colonel, as we've discussed."

He cut the channel. Let Arris stew for a while.

The video feed from the observer was fascinating. The dust had settled instantly in vacuum, and the pile was impressive. It wouldn't be hard to dig through in this G, but it would take time.

However, Arris knew there were no serious weapons in play, and simply had a hundred troops descend on the pile and dig like dogs, tossing the dust into a wider dispersion. It didn't take long for them to turn it from a mound to dig through into a pile they could merely wade through.

The sunlight, though, had to be sweltering and draining their suit power, and the dust clung to everything from static, made worse by solar ionization. The troops were constantly wiping their visors with gloves, then someone brought towels. It didn't help. That dust was flour, worse than Arabian Desert sand. It was probably contaminating a lot of their gear, too. Potentially even some weapons, though only a handful of troops were armed for this detail. Most of their gear was still in the vehicles.

Twenty minutes later, the pile was a broad pan rather than a sloping mound.

"That was an impressive and quick workaround," he muttered. "I think we have to consider the outer hatch permanently compromised."

Rojas said, "They're not in yet."

A flash, crack and rumble indicated the Ueys had

blown the latches on Lock 1. Approaching again, they started cranking the manual. That not working, someone brought up a Johnson bar and started prying. In moments it was big enough for passage.

Andre said, "Well, bring them on. They've lost some O_2. They've lost lots of time. They probably are fine for food but water in those suits can't last long."

Rojas said, "I'm trying to calculate their power use for cooling, based on that suit model and probable power pack. It looks like they'll need a recharge every couple of hours."

"Yep, some of them are already rotating back to the trucks."

"The question is how many spares they have."

Godin said, "Well, they're rolling up a fourth vehicle."

Crawford looked at the scene. "Interesting. I expect they're tapped out now."

Godin had data on his screen. "Given the size of the lander, I don't see how they could have more, unless they ripped out safety equipment or power or air margin to make room. I don't think they had any expectation of having to do more than secure the corridors."

"I agree. What's here has to be it."

Godin said, "But it looks like the outside troops did a complete change of power, and possibly refilled their water. I think they have eighty to eighty-six effectives, assuming four crew and command in each vehicle, minus the six we have."

Crawford wiggled his fingers as he counted, and said, "If we can detain another twenty or so, I think they'll stop. Of course, that's temporary, not permanent."

Godin said, "We can dust that support truck in about thirty minutes."

"Good. We can't really pick a time, either. Once she's committed, it's all or nothing."

Godin said, "They're stacking."

"Yeah, I see."

They were professional. They formed up as if they expected an armed reception, then spilled in through the open hatch.

They shuffled around and forward, feet in good contact with the ground, weapons and eyes panning all sides, above and below.

"I guess we can drop that support now," Rojas said.

"Yes," Andre agreed.

Several of the troops were right atop the classic pitfall they'd hurriedly excavated under the deck. The bolts for the plates had been removed, and pull pins inserted in their place. The hole underneath had been filled with a binary cement that would set quickly once the seal was broken. It hadn't been used on the first round both to save it for the second round, and because there'd only been three soldiers. There were at least twenty now.

"Do it," he said.

She tapped her controls, the deck plating opened up under several of them and they went down in a tangle. The others formed a circle facing in and another facing out, protecting their mates and looking for a threat.

The Uey radio chatter was encoded now, and the Loonie systems hadn't cracked it yet. There was lots of traffic, though.

He couldn't see well from the monitors available, but at a guess, six of them were in the hole.

Some of those above reached down and tried to pull their friends out. One of them got his hand stuck and started kicking in agitation. He wasn't going anywhere, either.

"I wish we had popcorn," Godin said.

Crawford grinned. "It is amusing. We know it's not lethal, and it's just going to stick worse for a bit. They're definitely tied up."

He isolated still images and counted.

"Looks like seven in the hole and twelve more on top trying to help them, plus four sentries."

The troops' approach was still professional. The perimeter guards turned to watching the bay. One of them walked around, pointing his weapon, and one by one the cameras went dead. Shot.

One sensor remained functional. There was a device mounted behind the lock control that looked in, ostensibly to check the outside of incoming vehicles. It was a thermal imager. That worked, and Andre even had a frequency shifter to put it into something easier to parse.

The Ueys worked feverishly, pulling, trying to cut, prying with tools, lowering cords. More and more stuff, more limbs of those in the hole, and occasional rescuers got bound in. The volatiles were almost evaporated by this point, so it wasn't going to get worse. It wasn't going to get better, either.

Two troops came in unspooling something.

Godin said, "Support conduit. Oxygen line and a power

cable. They're trying to establish a beachhead with outside support. Just like we do in a crater study."

"Right. I wonder if they brought a solar array or are just working off onboard power?"

Morton said, "If they did, it lengthens their engagement time, but not significantly. I'm estimating they started with twelve hours of duration, assuming they brought full capability. They've used four."

Just to split Arris's attention, Crawford called him.

"It's like this, Colonel: you can get in there and we can't really stop you. You can eventually find a way to cut your men free. In the meantime, you'll be running oxygen to them and your rescue element, exposed to anything we would choose to do, and hindering your own advance. My suggestion is to let us release them, since we have the solvent right here. Then, of course, we keep them until we resolve this."

Arris sounded frustrated but very formal as he said, "That is not within my operational limits at this time."

"Fair enough. Well, good luck." He closed the channel.

It was fascinating to watch. The outer sentries never wavered, even though nothing was coming from either direction. The troops in the hole realized struggles only made it worse, and remained still, though suit motion suggested they were still breathing at an accelerated rate.

Shortly, a repair bot of some kind trundled in on silicone tracks. Its operator followed along, and brought it right to the perfect edge of the hole.

He fastened it down with anchors, and it deployed arms that extended out holding tools for the men below to use. The machine then put out a boom that ran across the gap, so they could use it for leverage.

Another small device ran out along that beam and lowered itself down.

The robot wasn't sufficient. It lacked both traction and reach. Shortly, four more troops came in, with a toolbox and portable power pack.

To no one in particular Andre said, "This should be interesting. Patience."

The Uey techs brought in some spare oxy bottles. They spent long minutes trying to figure out how to change bottles in the hole, then gave up. Crawford watched in fascination as one built a manifold from spare fittings, then ran hoses to each suit via the Onboard Supply Valve.

Well, good. They'd be able to breathe as long as someone kept bringing them bottles. The workers above had a terminal from the conduit they could use for recharging themselves and the bottles for the victims.

They worked furiously, taking a sample, pulling, twisting, spraying solvent, using a radiant heater, waiting for an analysis of the sample, yanking with sheer brute force. It was all to no avail.

The one with his hand stuck came up suddenly, his right forearm and hand bare. They must have cut the fabric to free him. As his skin got puffy and blotchy, one of the rescuers rolled a taut mesh glove up his arm, then taped it in place with a contact tape. That should let him evacuate, at least.

Godin almost giggled as he swiped a switch and a pack hidden in the roof bracing popped open.

SPLASH. A loogie dropped from a hidden tube. More

cement spattered across the freed guy and three others. It didn't accomplish much immediately, but then two made the mistake of touching each other. They became instant conjoined twins. One other skipped back and tumbled. He remained supine on the deck.

The original casualty tried instinctively to wipe himself off and immobilized his arms.

"When did you do that?" Andre asked.

Godin said, "After I was done with the hole. I climbed up with some excess balloons."

"Well done. It's highly entertaining. I just hope we don't come to regret it."

Godin shrugged. "Yeah, they have to be getting pissed about now. Still, ten immobilized."

But at this point, the Ueys had an entire element moving in and out of the Outer Bay, power conduits, O_2 lines, etc. They were also getting lots of imagery of the second hatch.

The ground rocked, the walls boomed, dust erupted from every surface, and gear tumbled.

"Blasting charge," he said.

"Cutting charge," Malakhar corrected. "They were able to get a cutting charge in place. Vacuum made it safe. It's not as if an airlock is a vault."

"Right."

The video playback showed very little effect on the Ueys, and that was good discipline, he had to admit. Or else they hadn't been told to expect it. No, they had twitched, but not much. They just kept working, and only tensed momentarily. In the high vacuum, all they'd suffered was a little debris and dust. Inside, though . . .

Yes, Lock 2 was dismounted enough it wasn't going to close or seal. There was a huge distortion along the frame. It had already been open, too. This was just sabotage to ensure access.

Two locks down, four to go, because Lock 3 was a double. The Ueys thought there were only three, so any surprises would have to wait. After that, the inner defense would take over, and that could get ugly. It involved the weapons acquired so far, more goo, overpressure and melee weapons. That meant there'd be actual casualties.

For now, though, they were in the Outer and Middle Bays of the port.

The inner locks were smaller and easier to crack, though. Especially the emergency lock.

"We knew they couldn't be kept out forever," Rojas said. "They've been minimal so far. A larger charge could have done additional damage to the structure, or they could have just bombed us."

Godin nodded. "Yeah, but they're trying to minimize collateral casualties. Once they reach us, don't expect them to show any kind of restraint if we resist."

"We're not speculating because we don't know," Crawford said with some force.

"Sorry." Godin looked embarrassed.

As a reminder, he said, "Speculate on known factors. They've been very restrained, so have we. We hope that continues."

Morton said, "They are pissed, though."

He had to smile again. "Yeah, but they've freed two, plus the three who got stuck up top. Another element of eight came in. They're in the Middle Bay, trying to drill

Lock Three-A, and the rockwall next to it." He pointed at the imagery they had, as the Middle Bay's cameras went dead.

Godin agreed, "I see."

"I'm glad for that double personnel lock, though. I guess they were right that the personnel section should have double sealing from the work section. Has it ever been used?"

Godin said, "I remember testing it, but we always leave B open, don't we?"

"Yup," Andre said. "Until now."

He switched to the backup, a tiny little self-contained device that had a fisheye lens and low resolution. It sent an image every sixty seconds, scrambled. It was low enough power the Ueys might not notice it.

Godin continued, "I'm guessing once they punch through, they'll either try to equalize the pressure, or shove a charge through from the inside."

Studying the image, Andre said, "I think you're correct. They have what could be a charge sealed into one, and are pumping pressure into the other. Specifically, they're pumping oxygen in. Want to bet that'll be followed with something reactive?"

Malakhar said, "It'll stratify."

Crawford said, "Twin charge. The first agitates, the second ignites. Thermobaric charge and massive over-pressure."

Malakhar squinted and nodded. "Plausible. I can't say how effective it will be without seeing more of their equipment."

"We'll just have to monitor."

Rojas asked, "How are they doing on unsticking those guys?"

Godin pointed at his screen and said, "They hauled out the one they had, managed to slice between the other two by UV cutting the bond. They're slowly getting another loose."

And damn did the man look uncomfortable as they peeled the adhesive. He was bent forward in a very awkward position, almost but not quite leaning against a support someone else had stretched into place for him. As Crawford watched he reached it, and his relaxation was visibly obvious.

He said, "The longer they're tied up here, though, the shorter they are on oxy, and the longer they're not actually inside."

He was repeating that, but it was to reassure himself they might pull this off. It was all a waiting game.

Rojas asked, "Do you think there's going to be some sort of deal?"

He shrugged. "Dunno. We'll delay them until we're told otherwise."

"Yah."

Godin asked, "Can we get a another emergency lock in place?"

He shook his head. "Not in time, and not in a relevant location."

"Can we barricade?"

He'd already thought about that. "We can drive some equipment in, but it won't stop them wiggling through."

"No, but it does stop them bringing heavier stuff

through, and means they have to acquire oxygen from us, or run yet another supply route."

"True. Well, I guess I can spare the two of you for five minutes."

"Got it."

"Stack a couple of the rolly loaders about a meter from Lock Four. They'll be able to crack the seal, but not open it."

"Okay. Laura, let's move."

The two jogged away.

While that happened, he was going to try to distract Arris some more.

He keyed the radio mic. "Colonel, I see you making progress."

"Indeed we are, Mr. Crawford. Once we disable the fourth lock it's all over."

"Oh, I wouldn't say that, sir. The entire base is compartmentalized. We know where you are, after all."

Arris almost sighed. "Andre, the rule during the Middle Ages was that once the bastion walls of a castle were breached, the defenders surrendered. Any additional resistance only prolonged the inevitable and needlessly increased casualties."

He was actually aware of that. "Well, since this isn't the Middle Ages, and as far as I know, no one has taken casualties yet, I think we can change the tradition."

"Possibly. Your resistance shows ill intent for the device."

"How do you figure? By not turning whatever it might be over to a hostile force, we're the bad guys?"

Arris replied, "You are, in effect, hiding stolen property from the police."

"Sorry, what stolen property? I'm assuming this thing you're talking about is alien in nature. Or are you claiming this is something you created, transported here and carelessly lost hold of, and now you want it back? And how do you figure you're the cops? You're an invading army." He didn't want to risk further discussion of the artifact, so he switched to, "By the way, I see you finally figured out which mix we used for the glue."

And that meant no one in his section had leaked any intel to them. It wasn't that proprietary. The manufacturers listed solvents in the documentation. The mix was slightly esoteric, but a quick doc search would have found it. Presumably they had to ask Earth, with circumlocutions to avoid blurting out info for anyone with a radio receiver in the scatter path of the tight beam.

Arris said, "It wasn't that hard."

"No, but it took you a while. We're monitoring how much oxy you're using, and comparing that to the capacity of your . . . transport." He actually wasn't sure how many ships they'd brought. But he could estimate the mass of equipment so far. They really were serious.

He also needed to avoid trying to be clever. That's how slips happened.

Arris said, almost casually, "There are always more ships."

That was a really, really good opening. He pinged a warning, entered a code, and another fougasse detonated. This one was obliquely aimed toward the Lock 1 entrance, and blew a hurricane of dust and gravel against the troops working there. Several were buried in the settling pile. On the monitors, a huge stream arced, bounced, rattled and settled quickly in the Outer Bay, with some reaching as far as Lock 2. At that angle it didn't enter, but the floor and the hole were a mess.

"True," he said. "And as we've learned here the hard way, there's always more dust."

Every troop there had to have a static-charged sheen of dust obscuring their vision, and refreshing itself with each footstep. It all added up. Eventually they'd quit.

He hoped.

The exposed cement was neutralized now, crusted over with debris. All the Ueys had dust adhering to their mask lenses, and certainly some was clogging joints and connectors. Those would have to be cleaned before further oxy transfer.

The oxy lines run from outside were still intact, but the manifold end they'd been using to supply their crew inside was now buried. An element was frantically digging dirt away around that, using a couple of shovels, some available pieces of board, and gloved hands.

That also showed a lack of forethought. Loonie vehicles, like vehicles for Earth wilderness, all carried shovels, picks and winches. They didn't bother with axes here. They had long prybars instead.

Godin and Rojas arrived back, panting.

Rod said, "We put two rollys right in front of it, wheels touching. They'll have to crawl under. So we ran a pipe section under there. It's going to mean they have to weave through one at a time. If need be, we can crack them or sack them or shoot them as they do, with good odds."

"Excellent. But I really hope we don't have to, because

I assume these guys do know how to fight, and that means people die."

"We also set a sensor pack. It's on your feed."

He gave a thumbs-up, held up a hand, turned back and keyed the mic to outside.

"So I'll offer a deal," he said. "You stop drilling through the current lock, I'll pressurize the outer one so your troops can breathe. There are patches to seal the hole you made. I'll leave a vac gap between us."

Arris replied, "Do you really think I'm going to surrender?"

"Surrender? Not at all. You can leave any time you wish. Then if you want to call off the truce and resume, you can. But the only condition under which I can offer a temporary cease-fire, and breathing air, is if I can be assured the hostilities stop in the interim."

There was a short delay that felt as if it contained a frantic consult.

Arris sounded as if he'd been given orders. "When you relinquish the artifact, all this ends and there's no harm to anyone."

"If the artifact exists, I have no information or control or ability to negotiate for it. You need to talk to Control. But if it is real, and you're going to this much effort over it, I can't see you leaving people around to talk about it."

Arris replied, "Why not? Once it's secure, it doesn't matter."

"Am I supposed to assume our scientists here haven't already analyzed this thing and how it works? If you apparently know what the process is, so do they, and if they've had hands on, they may even know how to duplicate it. In any case, this is about you, me, our personnel, and breathing air. Would you like some?"

"We'll be fine."

The channel went dead.

"Blast," he muttered.

"Sir?" Rojas asked.

"I was hoping they were actually low enough to take that deal. It would slow them a bit."

She said, "They seem pretty sure of themselves."

"They may be. And that may be because they have more than we think they do, or they've miscalculated their resources, or are just putting up a false front. Which is also relevant for us."

"Act cool?"

"The important thing," he advised, "is to not admit that we're running out of options. If they realize we're out of tricks, they'll come straight in."

Malakhar said, "They wouldn't if they thought they'd die in the process. We do have a bit more explosive."

"I understand the logic. Control doesn't want to do it." Nor, truthfully, did he. A peaceful solution was much to be preferred.

It was near an hour later that the colonel called back.

"Mr. Crawford, I would consider a temporary truce if the offer is still open."

Sure. "Maybe."

"I have six troops whose respiration gear was damaged by the dust. I would like to transfer them inside."

He left a usual pause, then replied, "Certainly. Should I deduce you don't have that many spare parts handy?"

Arris almost sounded condescending. "You may deduce as you wish. Do we have a deal?"

"Send them to Lock Three. Send your crew there out. I'll let them in."

"You understand I may have to use additional force to re-enter that space," Arris advised.

"You do what you gotta do. We'll do the same."

He realized he'd admitted they still had video. Well, almost.

"Colonel, since you saw fit to take out our cameras, I'm going to trust that six and only six troops will enter."

"That is what I said."

He opened Lock 3A, and six troops stepped through. He closed it fast. If it wasn't for the extra lock beyond it, he'd have declined. You could fit a hundred troops inside the Inner Bay. Once he had it closed, he opened 3B.

In they came, visible on the next camera. Six of them. No weapons, no gear at all. Just suits with two-minute emergency bottles protruding from the necks. They unmasked. Five men, one woman, looking very sweaty, disheveled and exhausted.

At Lock 4, there was a lot of shuffling while they figured out to crawl between the wheels of the rollys, up over the pipe between them, back down and between the other side's wheels, and out. Then they realized there was yet another lock. Their expressions suggested they were not sanguine about their side's chances. Good.

He nodded and signaled.

Morton and Godin met them and directed them into pressure.

And now he knew where their penetrations were.

While the transfer took place, Godin had bounced an IR illuminator through. The image was very fuzzy, being reconstructed from shadows and reflections, but the computer was able to clarify most of it. Godin pointed at two spots, and Andre asked, "Yes?"

"That is probably a rock-melting drill, that other is an abrasive bit through the metal bulkhead."

A tiny rolling drone added a minute amount of enhancement. Its aperture was small and its range short, and when 3A closed again, it died. The Ueys must have scramble protocols in place.

Counting, he said, "So, that gives us twelve of their hundred or so as prisoners."

Godin said, "And we know how to stop the incursion."

"What's your plan?"

"Now *we* fill that space with O_2. Specifically, right over where they're drilling. When they cut through, the flash runs back into their space."

Andre liked the concept, but ... "It might kill them."

"This is a war."

He thought furiously. "Yeah. It's not a weapon per se, and it's defensive in nature, and we might talk our way around it, and goddammit, we have to do something. You're right. Okay, fab it."

It wasn't an unpredictable outcome, was it? But the Ueys drilled and ground. The power cables he'd seen on the scan were heavy and armored. They were running power from the crawler outside.

Was it possible to interfere with that?

He asked.

Morton said, "Well, there are three options. I can

trundle down there in a rolly, and try to jam a shearing blade into the conduit. They will probably shoot at us. I doubt we'd die inside the vehicle, but good chance of being captured if we were close when they stopped us. I don't see how they couldn't stop us, as obvious as that would be. We could toss some rocks and hope to damage the cable, but that armor is designed to protect against rockfalls, and we've only got one-sixth gee in our favor. Rifles might work, but it would depend on range. It would take solid shots to break armor, insulation and conductor."

Godin said, "It's a titanium braid inside a fiberglass extrusion, with more fiberglass and double insulation. I don't think a small-caliber round is going to reliably penetrate. Likely get bound in the mesh. Also, that means LOS."

Andre said, "Yeah. Indirect fire is preferred. We need some sort of rocket or solvent."

Godin mumbled, "Solvent . . . or incendiary."

Rojas said, "Both. Red fuming nitric acid in a butyl balloon, and a binary of that with pure octane. But we don't have much of the latter."

That got Andre's attention. "Can it be ready in time?"

She looked serious and cheerful. "I can damned sure try."

That left one thing. "How do we deliver?"

"Torsion catapult," she said. "We'll have to drag it out of the old emergency escape hatch. Assuming that's not guarded."

Godin said, "It might be reasonable to take weapons out that way for self-defense."

Andre conceded, "Fair enough, but if that's necessary,

you're coming right back in, not trying to fight through them."

"Yes," Godin agreed.

Andre turned back to Rojas. "By the way, how long to make the catapult?"

She grinned. "It's done. One of the school classes did it as a project and were throwing rocks."

"Ah. Historical lesson?"

"That, and also physics. They did the math on projectiles and came up with both a table and an algorithm."

"Well, that would have been useful earlier . . . though possibly not. It would already be taken out. Go to it."

"On my way," she agreed. "Rod, Stu, you're with me." She started skipping.

Momentarily she came on the suit freq.

"I'm wired in for now," she said. "I've got scramble on radio, but going to assume they can crack that. So listen for me to talk around things if I have to."

"Good," Andre agreed.

"We're going out the E-hatch, there's a flat area out there we can launch from that gives us a nice beaten zone diagonally along the conduit. I'm going to throw as much as we have until we get it or the spotter says we're getting rushed. I'll be leaving the 'pult outside."

"That sounds correct and is approved," he said for record.

She said, "Rod couldn't find any octane in the chem storage here. I have three of the RFNA and one hydrogen-and-fluorine binary with RFNA to help boost it."

"One. Well, make them count."

"That's the plan. We're exiting now. Any lasts?"

"Good luck," he said.

The old emergency lock had been built during construction, as a personnel hatch. It was barely big enough for a suited man. Then it became an emergency exit in case of damage to Lock 1, after some rockfalls. All that having been fixed, it was officially abandoned and not on the blueprints. They'd have to force it open, then because the Ueys would certainly find it, barricade it afterward, possibly with a rockfall. He recalled the Egyptian pyramids and their complicated shafts.

He turned to the images from that observer on the ridge, and saw faint movement of them getting into position. The natural depression outside the hatch had been carved, beaten and filled with concrete debris into a rough level. It was okay for moon bikes or trailers with balloon tires. It didn't work for a catapult on polymer casters. The three of them dragged and pulled their catapult.

Beyond them, he saw Ueys trudging back and forth, for tools and probably for rest breaks, to their vehicle park. It was amazing how close everyone was, without being within sight, and of course, there was no hearing.

Laura Rojas was surprised how fast the catapult was ready. The kids had done a good job of making it sectional. She and the men hauled the arm out, then the base and uprights. They got it pointed in the right direction, then tapped and pushed and thumped it into better alignment until she was satisfied. She had her tablet, a level, a protractor and some string. In a couple of minutes she had what should be the right torsion tension, based on the known test. The device had T&E screws she adjusted slightly. That should be it. Thumbs-up.

The two men cranked the arm down, she set a heavy balloon in the bucket, then adjusted the thing some more with a couple of kicks and a nudge. It had shifted during cranking. And goddamn, it was hot out here. She could feel the suit cooling unit running at max, and power was only going to last an hour, tops.

Godin hopped up in the low G, found a foothold on the ledge, and put his tablet just barely over a rock lip so he could record.

She stepped back and made sure the lanyard and pull release were straight. She took up slack and snapped her wrist down.

The arm swung, slapped into the detent, and rocked the whole assembly forward. The balloon sloshed and wobbled as it arced up, then seemed to just drop straight down. An optical illusion caused by parallax and distance. But there it was.

Godin hopped down, drifted to the ground, and skipped over.

In review, the balloon splashed down about a meter past the cable, throwing dust and splatters.

"Crap."

She gave a thumbs-up acknowledgment, not an okay sign of "We're good." She rolled her forefingers "again" and went for another balloon from the box. It was interesting how hand signs and even ISL had come into use here. Lots of sites didn't allow radio commo because it interfered with instruments. So they already had a pidgin when needed.

It was a good bet that some of the fluid from the shot

had splashed on the cable and was eating into it. It wasn't a good bet there was enough, though. And no bet on adjusting the throw. A minimal variation in mass would affect the next shot more than any change of position.

Morton hopped down from his perch, and held up his tablet. He ran the vid.

One of the Ueys apparently saw the impact and ran roughly toward it, then stopped. Probably his helmet camera was forwarding the imagery to their command.

In a few moments, four of them had gathered, seemed to realize that was dangerous, pulled back, and tried to back-azimuth from the streaks left from the impact. The liquid had already started boiling off.

Again she signed, "Understood. Again." It was all they could do.

They reset the catapult and she checked angle and inclination.

Morton went back up while she made fine adjustments. The unit had moved four centimeters, which didn't seem like a lot, but would be at that end. The only way to do that much lateral was a kick. Then switch the tablet back to Nav and fine adjust. No one ever went outside without a tablet as backup commo, navigation, data recording. These units were built tough and accurate. You could die without them.

That reminded her how goddamned hot it was, and how she was panting even with this little exertion. Hopefully that meant the Ueys were struggling, too.

Morton came down and held up his tablet. She watched.

Already, the Ueys had a team of six organized, who

started outward, keeping within clear sight of each other, but eyeballing for the Loonies. Then, one had some sort of sensor. Probably thermal or other spectra. That wouldn't do them any good, hopefully. The catapult had no signature.

Sonar didn't work in vacuum and it seemed unlikely they had any kind of radar setup with them. They'd expected direct fire and would be looking for thermal flashes. This was cold. They'd have to eyeball it.

They gazed all over, with no particular focal point, so they hadn't estimated the trajectory yet.

She shrugged and signed, "Watch between shots." That last sign was normally used to mean explosive shots or "blasts," but its meaning was clear.

She stepped back and pulled the release. The second bomb arced up, contents slopping about. It flew tumbling, slowed, then started down out of sight.

Morton pointed and signed for Godin to move up and take over vid, while he hopped down to show the ongoing report to Laura.

Troops had shot at the balloon.

They stopped almost at once and stared at one individual, who was gesticulating wildly and apparently chewing them out for the folly.

The balloon splashed down a meter short, but almost in a perfect line with the first one.

That was better. There was definitely a splash pattern across the cable now. It wasn't as good as an impact, but there were shimmers and vapor off the casing.

Thumbs-up, okay, more, clenched hand for "correct."

Godin came down fast with his tablet.

It showed troops turning around and started bounding in the general direction of the team.

He touched helmets. "Shoot now, make it count," he said.

She nodded and went for a balloon.

The Ueys would need a couple of minutes to get here, and up through the rock. They'd probably want to leapfrog to avoid exposure. Really, there was time for a shot.

Part of her kept feeling exposed, that someone might pop up any second.

So far, no one had done any shooting. They'd still be able to run or dodge and knew this terrain, and worst case, capture left them on the Moon in an atmosphere-controlled environment.

No one had done any shooting yet.

No one except Laura Rojas and her team with acid and hypergolic liquid.

Godin and Morton levered the arm back, she placed the balloon. This one sloshed a lot. She checked position, then checked it again, forcing herself to be methodical.

From his lookout, Morton kept a thumb up. Safe so far.

She shuffled back and behind. She found her lanyard, checked alignment, then tugged.

The bag broke.

She hopped away and avoided being splashed.

As the fluid fumed across the arm, the catapult flung the residue in a long, pretty spray around the axis. The remaining dregs flew, probably far too far.

One round, totally wasted, and a good marker for the Ueys.

Behind the catapult, the rock fumed momentarily.

Laura fumed in a different context.

Godin signed, "What do next?"

She replied, "Shoot more, hurry, load," and gestured to indicate the splashes that were damaging the catapult.

They levered fast, she loaded the HF container very quickly and very delicately. If it burst . . .

And fire.

No, she wanted to shoot. "Fire" was what would happen at the other end.

She pulled the lanyard.

The container arced spaceward, peaked, then started back down.

She was already scrambling up to watch, and for reassurance on the approaching troops.

In mid-trajetory, the HF ignited. The acid spill had done enough damage to pierce the balloons.

The flash started as a jet, where the two components met. It spread rapidly in a bright ring, turning into a glare all over.

"Dammit," she muttered.

That first jet of fire had shifted the trajectory slightly. The fireball was already lit and probably at full effect . . .

. . . As it crashed directly onto the cable, about a half meter right of the existing damage from the acid spills.

The fire was a glorious, roiling ball, as heated corrosives and oxidizers consumed each other and the cable housing, then the insulation.

It suddenly burned white.

Rod touched helmets and gloated, "Their O_2 line just failed."

The glare was blinding for a few moments, as pure oxygen supplemented the nitric acid. Even the metal cabling burned.

The automatic pressure switches cut the oxygen flow, but by then, a meter of conduit was slagged.

Then there were sputtering electrical sparks from a dead short, followed by a decreasing glow from the starving fire.

She slapped their shoulders and signed, "Back inside. Quickly."

Morton pointed at the catapult.

"Leave. Run."

There were already dust puffs from bullet impacts erupting from the rocks around them. Luckily, motion, low G, and bad angle made the Ueys' aim pointless.

Rojas was panting as she staggered back in.

Andre whooped. "Hell yes, it worked! And they don't seem to have a spare conduit. Probably a mass-transport issue. They're busy trying to shear as close and clean as they can to splice it. Meanwhile, they lost the oxygen in the pipe, and a bit more before the pressure safety kicked in."

Still panting, Rojas asked, "How long can they do this?"

Morton said, "I don't have any info on a support ship inbound, but I don't know how many landed. They could ferry stuff by Trak, but that's going to take time."

Andre took a bite of the stale sandwich on his console.

For that matter . . .

He pinged the channel. "Colonel, how are your troops doing on food, water and relief facilities?"

"We ate before this started. A few hours' hunger is a minor inconvenience, and there are rations in our transport. Water we have, and as for the waste water... well, it mostly evaporated straight out when they drained it in your tunnel." The man sounded almost amused.

"Fair enough. I just wondered because I have a really good sandwich here."

"Mr Crawford, would you like—"

"More guests? Certainly."

"—would you like to retreat inside your habitat now? I have been authorized for weapon release."

Cold adrenaline ripples ran through him.

"Meaning?"

"Meaning with three missiles, or emplaced charges, I can simply blow the doors off, and leave your main passage, per my blueprints, open to space. I have clearance to shoot any adult in the open as a hostile threat, now that you've used incendiaries and caustics. The latter which qualify as chemical weapons."

What the hell?

"Huh? You're inside pressure suits."

"They release toxic gases, which would be lethal if we were not wearing protective gear. Per the letter of the law, that constitutes chemical weapons."

That was... "Ridiculous. You're in vacuum. You're separated by vacuum, and a suit you can't remove."

Arris sounded smug. "I assure you our legal staff have made the determination, and are prepared to defend it at the World Court in the Hague."

Shit.

"I guess it depends on how many people you're willing

to kill in the name of peace. Including your troops, who are dispersed within the habitat. A fact we've already logged for release, including with the Red Cross."

Arris said, "That's your side of the story."

Andre said, "Of course. You can write whatever story you want. At the end of the day, you'll have murdered even the innocent people in here, who have no way to evacuate or choose sides about a device you claim exists and they've never heard of. And your own troops. I guess that's a decision you'll have to live with."

Arris was unwavering. "I have orders, and weapons."

Andre tried really hard to sound condescending rather than pleading.

"For that matter, you have a bunch of troops who are short of oxy and power, and I doubt you can last long with what's aboard your vehicles."

"There are other elements inbound."

"Did they tell you that? Because my seismic gear doesn't show it." He was lying, because the seismometers were not on his screen. He swiped furiously and brought them up.

Local tremors only, within shape and amplitude he saw all the time. Which didn't mean there wasn't a soft vehicle out there, but anything putting ground pressure on rubble should be pressing that into the surface and generating fractional effects.

Arris's tone suggested a shrug. "That is as it may be. I have control of the first two locks, I am going to destroy the third one now."

Think. Think.

"Colonel, have you considered what a trained engineer

and crew could have done in the last twenty-four hours with more corrosives, more flammables, explosives, pressure vessels and electrical power? You got that one taste so far. Want to try for the seven-course banquet?"

Arris sounded very relaxed. "War is not without casualties. We've both been lucky so far."

Andre realized he was talking too much again. "Logistically we have the upper hand here."

"Then this should be to your advantage."

It was time to log off before he said something he'd regret. "Fine. You've been warned. I'm going to enjoy ice cream now."

He closed the connection.

He sighed deeply.

"Well, let's see if he's bluffing, threatening, or going balls out."

Andre noted ironically he was bluffing about the ice cream. Nor did he want any. A beer wouldn't be out of line, though. Except he needed his wits. More coffee. He poured another cup, watching it splash lazily in the low gravity. That was always fascinating. The cups were shaped to roll splashes back in, and looked oversized, until you tried to pour.

Malakhar said, "They're still drilling, according to sensors."

"Good . . . on the sensors working, I mean. Any guess on cut through?"

"The door could be any time. Acoustics suggest there's only a centimeter left. It wasn't armored, just thick enough to support itself."

"Yeah, it wasn't a hard one."

He looked at the screen, which displayed Malakhar's feed. The image was animated from acoustic and sonic inputs and representative only. Personnel locations were fuzzy approximations.

Right then, the drill did break through, and a rush of pure oxy enveloped the mechanism. Somewhere in the motor, a tiny electrostatic spark flared, and what must be a nimbus of flame engulfed it.

Both drills stopped, and troops scrambled to aid the operators who'd just taken a flash burn.

About a minute later, the rock drill started back up.

Malakhar said, "Figures. It was a good flash, but without an atmosphere in there, it's not significant, likely just scorched a suit and faceplate."

Morton said, "I'm worried about that rock drill."

"Oh, why?"

"The rock cut is near the lock controls."

Andre checked his feed. "I've got it switched to central."

Morton said, "Yes . . . but the outer ones stop here physically. That one's not airwalled from the network. Nor are you."

"Shit."

Morton said, "Yeah, if they have a good tech, and get into that, they can do a lot of havoc."

Andre said slowly, "We . . . I should have caught that when we were setting up. Alright, someone go disconnect the box and see about plugging that hole at the same time?"

Morton said, "I will. How do you want it isolated?"

"Just unplug the control line from the terminal inside

Lock Four. Don't damage it. We may need it later. Then get into Inner Bay and see if you can hinder them more. They still only have pinholes."

"Got it."

Morton closed his faceplate and bounded off.

Andre asked, "Ravi, can you keep an eye on my feed and give me any notice of entry?"

Malakhar said, "Probably. I don't think they'll have a pre-built hack, and we've got excellent compartmentalized security. But anything on your system could be compromised, and they might manage to open Lock Four."

"You have spare system cable?"

"In the storeroom, yes."

"Okay." He grabbed a pair of sidecutters from the toolbox, and put them around the cable next to the terminal. "You shout, I cut."

"Got it."

Morton was back in a hurry, panting.

"I was able to disconnect it," he said between gasps. "No one can operate it now. I pulled the wires and the commo cable."

"Good."

Morton continued, still breathing hard, "They're working on that hole in the door. Explosives, I think. Stuff squeezing through the hole."

Andre said, "That makes sense. They'll try to crack it and break it loose, which will also damage the seals and render it unusable. But we can get some sensors in there. Ravi?"

"Yes, this box," the man replied. He held up a tray with

several varieties of drones. It looked as if some would roll, others bounce or fly, and give several views. As long as they lasted, they'd provide useful intel.

Morton said, "Okay, I'll take those now."

Malakhar handed him the box and said, "Just slide it in smoothly on the floor. The modules know what to do. Let them go."

Morton grinned. "Got it."

He turned and bounded back, and Andre closed the door behind him.

Godin said, "We should button up now. If they blow one and decide to use a rocket for a one-two, we're boned."

"Yeah."

Crawford kept a close eye on the monitors while donning his helmet, clicking the seal and checking oxygen flow. He had four hours in the bottle, and they had several spares on a cart they could drag with them in a hurry.

Several feeds popped up on Malakhar's monitors as the drones went active. Morton could be seen closing 3B, from multiple angles. Godin's screen showed others.

BANG!

The floor shook as Lock 3A was breached. Some of the feeds went dead.

Andre looked at Malakhar, realized his expression was hard to read through the plate, and started to ask as the man replied, "Three A is dismounted."

"So they're in the connector between Middle and Inner."

Another explosion rattled everything.

"That was 3B," Godin said needlessly. "They didn't

waste any time. Probably slapped a charge and got behind the wall in Middle."

Andre felt a cold chill.

"Crap. Is Morton alive?"

Godin said, "I can't see, but probably not. Pressure trauma from decompression to vacuum, and from the blast. Probably stunned, down, and not sealed. I'm sorry."

"Hopefully they have him prisoner. If they reached him fast . . ."

Malakhar was trying to look positive and not succeeding. "Maybe."

Rojas sighed. Godin cursed and punched the wall.

Andre shook his head. "Can't worry now."

Malakhar said, "We no longer have control of our own locks. They can hardwire Lock Four from their side. All we have is the emergency curtain."

Andre pulled the cable that connected his system to Lock Control, since it was no longer needed.

"Right, but they can't get into the rest of the network yet," he said. "Any way around their hack?"

Malakhar shook his head. "Not fast. I guess we figure out how to hack in ourselves. I'll get working on that."

He scanned and dragged images.

Morton was dead. That was a tough one. Was this all worth it? If resistance didn't change the outcome and did leave some dead and others subject to legal penalty?

Malakhar said, "I think I have it. Laura, can you go cut Line L-4-O-X?" He pointed to his screen.

She squinted. "Down the main passage? Yes. With what?"

"An axe. Cutters. Whatever it takes. Sever and separate."

"Will do."

The Indian worked feverishly, using two styli to tap keys until he could widen the touchscreen enough for gloved fingers. Then they fairly flew across the surface.

"Okay, I'm disengaging everything from inside. We'll be the only control point, but we can't risk them accessing other files."

"Right," Andre agreed.

Rojas came back at a skip.

"Got it," she said.

Malakhar cocked his head. "Just in time. They were plugging into the terminal. That won't do them any good, but now they have to breach the emergency lock."

Andre said, "Good."

"We still have camera lines there, though."

"Can we—"

Malakhar said, "Morton cut them with wire cutters."

"On this side?"

"Both. This side as he went in, there once he was . . . inside."

Blast. "Okay. We know they're past the vehicles, though, just not efficiently. They're having to hand-carry oxy and use batteries only until they finish that splice. How is that coming?"

Malakhar said, "My observer reports they'll be done soon. Also that he's running short on cooling power, even with a field battery with him."

Had it been that long? "Noted. He can leave whenever he has to, and should come back if he can."

Malakhar nodded. "He was told. He says he'll hold out to the end."

Andre raised his eyebrows. "Good man. What else can we do to slow them, then?"

Godin cleared his throat and said, "I do have the skimmer and that dustbin. She's loitering and can arrive in five."

"Right. Well, if you can get it into the rear of that support vehicle, that would do wonders."

"I'll tell her."

Andre cautioned, "I don't know that they can't shoot it down."

The man nodded soberly. "Yeah, she knows. It's Seville. She'll fly fast, low and through the Fangs," he said, referencing two tall peaks of the crater rim. "They shouldn't see her."

"Good. Go."

Godin listened to his headset, and reported, "In fact, this says she's two minutes out."

"I hope that's soon enough."

"She says there's a rock inside the load. One big one, enough to damage the vehicle."

Andre said, "Or anyone it hits. But we're past that point now."

"'Fraid so. You'll see it right in that saddle, any moment."

The skimmer came over the ridge unseen by the Ueys. It was several seconds before they reacted. Likely, it had to be sensed, interpreted, IDed as a Loonie craft, and then reported.

They didn't appear to have any antiaircraft assets. It was further confirmation that they hadn't expected any outside resistance, only busting a lock and holding everyone at gunpoint.

Several of them stared up at the craft, others took cover behind rocks, assuming a bombing run. Anywhere out of line of sight would be safe, with no atmosphere for overpressure.

Seville angled in, likely using autopilot with a preprogrammed trajectory.

Too late, the Ueys figured out the intended target and ran for the ArctiTrak's hatch. They probably assumed a bomb or mass-impact weapon. In the low G, two of them bounced up above the ground. With better self-control, one managed to slap the close button as the bay doors opened on the skimmer above.

The dust dropped out like a brick, one solid mass with no atmosphere. It dropped slowly and got a little fuzzy as internal friction started it separating. It was powdered pumice, not as dense as water, and in this G, negligible in impact.

The rock inside the dust, however, was big enough to wreak some havoc. Not much, perhaps. It would bounce inside, break something, and maybe it would matter.

The ramp had barely closed to knee height when the pile sloshed into the back of the vehicle, filling it.

"Well done!" Andre shouted.

The vehicle rocked, indicating the boulder had in fact entered and rattled around. Something in there was damaged. Something critical?

Possibly crew.

The hatch jammed with a pile of dust. That was a huge load, spilling out, around and over. The vehicle was buried forward to the front wheels.

Rojas almost gloated. "They'll have to shovel that out,

and it's going to be everywhere inside—under, behind and in equipment. Any gas connections will need to be wiped clean. And as soon as they turn on any inside environment, it's going to blow into a cloud. It may not have stopped them, but it's certainly hindered them."

Andre said, "I expect all their support equipment, and main commo, is in there. The individual vehicles have short-range transmitters, and of course they can relay through a remote to their lander. But that one probably can burn to Earth directly. That may no longer be possible. They pulled their power tools out of there. They won't be doing that now. We probably slowed them significantly."

"Hopefully. It looks like we're wearing them down."

He said, "We are. I hope it's fast enough to matter."

The Ueys went to dig the dust out, scooping and pulling. As before, it static-clung to their face shields and suits. They had to take frequent breaks.

Andre said, "I wish we had another load right now, for them, or one of their personnel vehicles."

Godin pointed. "Yeah. See the guy heading to the truck?"

"I expect he's getting an oxy bottle. I wonder how many spares they have, and how many they can reach."

Godin said, "We can try another, but there's risk of them shooting one down, or trying to rush us and wreck things. That's not slow."

Andre agreed. "Yes, that's good for now. We stage our responses."

The troops dug, heedless of the solar influx beating

down on them with its long shadows. They managed to clear enough to lower the ramp partially, though it stopped well above plane. More spilled from inside, and they kept throwing that.

Eventually they worked inside, but it was only a partial fix. They'd have shade, they might reach spare bottles, but any equipment back there was still endangered.

Godin said, "Oh, here's the pic the pilot got as she passed overhead."

Andre turned around to take a look.

The image was difficult to discern due to sharp shadows. The area in shadow was near black, with just the barest hint of illumination from inside.

Rojas said, "I've got this." She gestured and Godin stood up.

She sat down and got to work.

First she cloned the image and left the raw. That second one, she blew up to examine.

"That looks like one of their boots there. That angle suggests it's being worn."

Andre looked at it. He'd not have caught it, but he had to agree with her. That was good. "I concur."

She kept itemizing. "Three oxy bottles there, and I'm guessing from the spacing they're in a rack, probably connected to a manifold. In fact, what's the scale here?" She glanced down, wrinkled her brow and said, "Probably an old Dash Eight. When were these vehicles made?"

Godin said, "Eight years ago. That makes sense."

"Okay, so that gives them at least two full charges per person."

"Is that another bottle there?" Andre pointed.

"On the floor. Empty or discarded."

She reduced the image, shifted, chopped off everything in sunlight and brought up the brightness on the rest.

"God, that looks like crap," she said. Even chopping off the area in direct light left saturation from the reflected rays. That and the internal illumination created a lot of irregular outlines. "I'm going to say that ghost is the tech whose boot we saw in sunlight."

Andre followed the outline and said, "He's bent over a bench."

"Yeah, likely prepping components for something."

"What about back there?" he pointed.

Rojas said, "That is just barely another person. I think that's the arm. That might be the helmet shadow on the forward airwall."

Godin asked, "Is there a driver as well?"

Andre said, "Typically, the driver is part of the element, and especially here with them having limited support."

He looked over the array of images and considered.

"Okay. Two crew. They apparently weren't injured. No one evacced them or looked overly concerned. That's definitely long-range commo gear. Figure they have enough oxygen for sixteen hours nominal, which means under ten the way they're exerting."

Rojas said, "They could detach someone back for more supplies. Is it wrong of me to hope they were injured?"

She was icy calm, but there was hot anger under that.

Andre tried to sound neutral. "No, though it won't really help."

"It would certainly be fair, though."

Then his brain caught up with the comment about going back for more supplies.

"They could, but I suspect they figured to resupply off us as soon as they secured entry. There's still nothing to suggest a large logistics footprint."

Malakhar commented, "That means in another six hours or less they have to either be back at their craft, or cry uncle here. They need at least a half hour, call it an hour with safety. Five hours."

Andre said, "Hopefully before that. I can't risk cycling them in that fast. And we need to watch out for a sympathy ploy."

Rojas was wide-eyed. "You think they'd violate Geneva like that?"

"We aren't at war. They're police as they see it. Don't count on them abiding by anything. Especially after claiming residual vapors in vacuum constitute a chemical weapon."

"Good point." She was looking pissed, but still acted calm. She trembled slightly, though.

He said, "But, in the four hours they've had, they've done some damage. I don't think we can hold them another six. Or even four."

Godin noted, "They're now using the lock and passage as their sun shade. But outside is brutal if they're going back and forth."

Rojas looked at the outside of the image, full screen. "We damaged their solar package. That means they've got onboard power for everything, and the conversion cell aboard each vehicle."

Godin said, "That will still last well over the remaining time they need."

"I have another aerial picture and report," Malakhar said. "Their numbers are down. I think they detached some for the Old Lock."

Andre felt another adrenaline burn and said, "Crap. The only defensive measure possible there is a rockfall." He looked around. "I guess that's up to me, since I've done them."

Godin said, "I've done one here. Want me to do it?"

His tone suggested he'd enjoy it.

"Yes. You need to pop the lock, shoot the protrusions outside, drop the debris. Keep the backblast outside, and remember arming distance."

"I'll let you know if it's clear," Rojas said.

Good point. "Yeah, no reason to open it if they're right there."

Malakhar added, "And I've got imagery from the skimmer, and our man on the mountain. There actually was an element heading for the Old Lock, but it looks like they couldn't get over the ridge even in low G, and are now heading back."

"Good." That was less of a concern, then.

Looking at the view, Godin said, "Well, they picked the low saddle, which isn't the easiest route, just least altitude."

"Right," Malakhar agreed.

Andre asked, "Are there enough in that element to account for the balance of their force?"

"No!" Rojas replied. "But I do see several on a dolly crawler. It looks like they're heading back to their ship."

"Interesting."

"Two with probable suit damage, including the one who got stuck. One other who may be an exertion or heat casualty, or has a suit malfunction. There's one driver and one other I think is escort."

"So, five out of commission for now, and the twelve we have detained."

Malakhar said, "A notable amount of the element. Given their support numbers, and the count on those moving around, we've probably cut their effectives by a quarter."

"And run out half their time," Andre said. "They have to be exhausted."

"It's working, boss," Malakhar said. "Also, my observer is going down for oxy and power. He'll be back in a half hour."

"I'd ask for quicker, but I know how much of a struggle even that is. I'm glad of the support."

The man leaned back and mused, "I wonder how much support we actually have among the other Loonies."

Andre said, "Probably a very mixed bag."

Rudy Zeiss did not like the American trait of doing as one pleased. Or possibly it was a civilian scientist habit. The military people he served with understood patience, chain of command, and inquiry. Some of the workers here . . .

The disturbance outside resolved as Doctor Cheung Lee, who despite his Chinese name, was born and raised in San Diego. He was apparently a brilliant scientist, but he had no ability to comprehend resource limits, time constraints, or other people's feelings.

Lee pushed right past the Entry Controller, who shrugged at Zeiss and looked sheepish. It wasn't his fault. His task was to log people in and out and account for them, not be an actual guard.

As Lee strode right through the middle of the consoles, he started demanding loudly.

"Colonel Zeiss, I need to talk to you."

Zeiss sighed and made an attempt at being good natured. That was hard, seeing as he'd just lost a man.

"I presume the nature of your issue precludes an appointment, Doctor?"

Lee replied, "It does. I demand to know what is going on."

As he approached, Lee almost ran into Zeiss, apparently not having a good internal grasp of inertia on the Moon even after three months.

"Doctor, I don't take demands. That's why I have a commission." Zeiss gestured faintly at the badge on his chest. "However, I am happy to answer clearly phrased questions within the limits of my authority and your need to know."

Lee paused and breathed. "Then what is going on, sir?"

Zeiss looked around the entire complex and replied, "This is the control room. We're currently monitoring several EXTACs, planning a schedule for June, working on arranging lift and drop for personnel and supplies, and dealing with a solar storm."

Lee had the sense to shrug off the deflection. "You know what I mean, sir. The apparently alien device we've not been informed about."

Zeiss replied, "I'm not sure what you're referencing,

but if there's an alien device, you seem to have been informed by someone. As I noted, not all activity falls within your . . . purview or need to know. Nor mine, for that matter."

Lee stood up almost to Zeiss's height and said, "Sir, I recognize your military reticence and will not be toyed with. The UN wants the rightful property of humanity, and it certainly can't be trusted to a conspiracy of anti-communitarians and military officers here."

Zeiss kept his eyes clearly on Lee, only peripherally watching the two security guards moving up behind him. Coffman had called them.

He said, "That's a rather serious charge about my staff, without any grounding in reality."

The guards very smoothly each took one of Lee's arms.

The sergeant, Tyler, on his third tour here, said, "Sir, you must leave Central Operations at once."

Lee didn't struggle, but said, "Then this shall be taken up with higher authority."

Coffman said, "Good luck with that. We have no outside communication at this point."

Lee gave him a cold stare and said, "It is illegal to restrict my communication."

Coffman grinned. "Actually, no. It can be restricted on the colonel's orders, your section's orders, my say-so, or that of anyone who is Echelon One and has a security concern logged. But what I said was, 'we have no outside communication.' I am unable to get any signal outside of moonside LOS."

Lee started to say, "Well, if you—"

Zeiss cut him off with, "Doctor, while I respect your

expertise, I must place you under observation. You may work in your lab or lodging. You may not approach other groups or any communication equipment. I hope this will all be resolved shortly and you will be happy with the outcome."

Lee sounded very scholarly when he said, "That latter will not happen, sir."

As he left, without trouble, Zeiss muttered, "I am glad security remains loyal for now."

Coffman must have heard him, as he replied, "As long as the orders are in writing, and within their limits."

"That's the best we can ask for."

Coffman said, "He'll blab. Or try to."

Zeiss said, "If he sounds crazy enough, they'll be busy. It's not as if they can get out without our help anyway. I've hard-locked inside the surface interface. They'd have to break out, as much as the Ueys have to break in."

Operations Officer Gallatin came over, and spoke very quietly.

"I hate to ask, sir, but at what point do we give it to them?"

Zeiss said, "We don't. Physicist Cutsinger is trying to figure out how to hide it or destroy it. Hide if we can, destroy if we must. But no government can be trusted with that."

She said, "You better destroy it, then, sir. They won't stop looking, and they'll shake people down until they get it."

"For now, we have it as a bargaining chip, because they don't want to destroy it."

"I'm not sure," she said. "They might assume it's

immune to explosive decompression. The value of a bargaining chip is directly proportional to the value of just killing and taking it. Are we going to be martyrs?"

Even the dispute was causing panic. Either it had to be destroyed, or it had to be so widely shared that no one had an upper hand. The irony was that universality solved more problems than it created, but sole possession would only lead to negative outcomes, either in repression or fights for possession.

He wanted to be reassuring, and said, "No, if it comes to that, we let them have it if we can't dispose of it. But I don't want to live in that future."

Coffman was close enough to overhear even whispers, but was utterly trustworthy. He put in, softly, "The intel will leak out eventually, if it hasn't already."

Zeiss agreed. "Eventually. In the meantime, it's the ultimate tool of repression, and I don't trust the Ueys to keep it. Some asshole will abscond while 'studying' it and it all comes crashing down. We have to keep it here as long as possible, or destroy it."

Coffman said, "Seeing as the lab can't touch the shell with any known force, I'm not even sure a nuke will hurt it. They're able to crack the controls, but not damage it. It's like it was made to withstand attack. Or two-year-olds."

"Either is possible," Zeiss smiled. "I certainly wish more of our gear was resistant to scientists or two-year-olds."

Coffman sat up, held a finger in the air, and said, "Sir, the UN officer is calling directly for you."

That was expected. "Ignore."

The commo tech nodded and tapped, then said, "Yeah, but maybe they have an offer?"

Zeiss shook his head. "No. They can back off and make an offer. There's no fair deal with a knife at your throat. And there are reasons I can't talk to them."

"Understood, sir, but plausible deniability only goes so far."

"Yes, but it exists until proven otherwise," he replied.

Coffman said, very quietly, "One of our people had to leak the info."

Zeiss said, "Yes, and that disturbs me, but I can't address it at this time. Do we have anything else on observation?"

Coffman shook his head. "Still nothing."

"You have the feed from Technician Malakhar's observer, yes?"

"I do, and from the cameras. I'm wondering if we can launch a sounding rocket?"

Zeiss considered. "Maybe. They can't have much in the way of overhead cover. The worst case is they shoot it down. But we'll have to let a mapping crew know what we're doing, given the all-hands notice on radiation. Let's wait for now."

"Yes, sir."

Andre sighed and rubbed his eyes. They were gritty.

"Well, we're whittling them down. But we don't have much left to keep them out with. And if they think this won't work, they just might crack the roof."

Godin asked, "Really? For the . . . device?" He was Canadian. Canadians tended to be very civilized about such things.

Andre said, "If they either want to assure they have sole control, or simply prevent its existence, yeah."

Rojas put in, "For that matter, why aren't we uploading the blueprints to makerspace?"

He said, "That's still under discussion in Control. There are political ramifications to doing so. Also, they haven't completely reverse engineered it yet."

Godin shrugged. "Okay. So load it as we go."

"Yeah. Remember what I said about any terrorist org wanting it? Any separatist or rebel group? Organized crime? Disorganized crime? For every bit of good it does, it also does bad."

Godin shrugged again. "Once someone finds out, it's all moot."

"Right, but while it's here, there's some delay on that."

The young man said, "Delay . . . just like we're doing to them stealing it. In the end, it will get out anyway, over our dead bodies or theirs."

"Wars never make sense, son." Never had, never would.

The radio pinged again. It was Arris.

"Engineer Crawford, since I'm unable to reach your leadership, I am contacting you again."

"What do you need, Colonel?" he replied.

"I want to persuade you to do the right thing regarding the device."

"Regarding a device I know nothing about other than its claimed existence? Okay." While talking, he gestured to Malakhar and Godin to look for an incoming attack.

"It does exist, and it's not safe here, without proper oversight."

Andre keyed the mic, let it go, waited a timed thirty seconds, then said, "Stand by one moment, please."

He really wanted Control to handle this. He felt far over his depth. He called Coffman.

Colonel Zeiss heard Coffman call. "Sir, flagged message from Crawford. He says the Ueys want to bargain."

"Tell him to stall and cut them off. I have confidence in him, and the less I'm involved, the tougher the Uey position."

"Understood. What are his limits if they do try to bargain?"

"Did he ask that?"

Coffman said, "No, sir, but I'd like to tell him."

"They can surrender. That's the bargain."

"Understood."

Zeiss still had a base and operations to run. With the sun up, heavier power loads were sustainable, and industrial research and local production of resources came online. Then, there were science projects that required sunlight, or mixed shadow and sunlight, many of which took place at remote sites.

He had EXTACs that were actually critical, even with an invasion, and he was trying to find some way to clear people to sites that wouldn't be in LOS and could continue, with the fabricated advisory that there were radiation issues.

It wasn't uncommon to move personnel out through secondary locks that were either closer, less crowded, or more private, depending on the function involved. SolGen had their own remote station, and often used an overhead hatch to launch their commuters. Unless they needed an entire plant assembly, they didn't use the main lock.

Much of the lunar operation was inside. The selenology,

solar science, and vacuum physics processes and research, though, had regular trips in Rollys. It wasn't going to be easy to stall them for hours or days.

He knew it was tough on Crawford, but the longer Zeiss stayed uninvolved, the better the position when he had to. He had no intention of betraying his people, but he could start a lengthy investigation that might string things out in court, and lead to publicity the UN wouldn't want.

He also still wanted to know who the leak was. He would find a way to rotate them home, assuming this concluded favorably.

"Mr. Coffman, get Astronomer Victor and ask him to help delay EXTAC. He knows the issue, and he can create a far better story than we can."

"Got it."

Andre got the reply. It was unrealistic, but at least it was a simple order. They could surrender or go to hell. Fair enough.

He keyed the mic and spoke.

"Colonel Arris, you're saying this is some sort of material fabricator. I'm familiar with the concept, of course. We have printer mills here that can produce almost any part from a blueprint. This would be more than that, then."

Arris replied, "Exactly. A material fabricator that takes raw material, possibly even unprocessed material, and delivers a broad range of product."

At once, Andre replied, "At what energy cost?"

The pause was at Arris's end. When he finally replied he said, "We don't have that information. Not until we get hands on."

Andre waited again, then returned, "If such a thing really exists, and if it is powerable with anything smaller than a five-gig pebble bed, every terror group in the world will be producing bombs. Every gang making guns and ammo. It won't feed anyone. People want to kill each other and you know it. Northern Ireland. The Middle East. Balkans."

Arris said, "Exactly. Which is why it has to be under UN control."

No delay again this time. Andre said, "You know that's crap. When has the UN ever kept a secret from one of the member nations? The primary Security Council did fairly well with nuclear weapons, but once non-power nations got that knowledge, it was pretty well global in short order. Anything we might find here is safer here where none of them can touch it. We have a four-hundred-thousand-kilometer vac gap."

"So are you admitting to knowing about this device?"

Crap. Stop talking. "No, sir, I'm just analyzing a problem you have described. It's what engineers do."

Malakhar was gesturing, and Andre took a look. There were UN troops moving into a formation behind Lock 4. The sensors didn't give detail, but that was probably a couple of squads.

"I think they're going to try a cutting charge," Malakhar said.

Andre looked back to the radio as Arris replied, "If you have it you will leak the information. Your leadership has little control over outside data management, with all the contractors and scientists here. The proof of that is that I know about this device that you claim not to."

Andre let Arris stew while he looked at the movement on the screen.

"Laura, Rod, we need to overpressure that as much as we can, so when they open they're slowed. It will also mean they have to reconfigure their suit pressure."

He pinged Control. "I need anyone who you can trust with a lethal weapon right now."

Coffman replied, "We have your feed. Colonel Zeiss is already heading that way with Captain Touro and four security."

Andre breathed relief and said, "Make sure they hurry."

He turned quickly back to the radio and spoke to Arris. "Right, so to prevent us leaking it, you want to take it closer to the people who can exploit and abuse it. Have you considered the logic of that? I think we're done on this exchange, sir."

He clicked the mic off again.

Turning to Malakhar he said, "Okay, so they're down to about eighty, and we've accounted for forty in the outer tunnel and support around the vehicles, is that correct?"

Malakhar said, "Yes, that's correct. Inside there appear to be two clusters. One is right near Lock Four; the other is farther back. They seem to be rotating for oxygen. It looks as if everyone that went outside got food when they did. They also left a huge pile of trash to clean up later. Jackasses."

"We still think they're low on oxy?"

Rojas said, "Given the bottle exchange rate, and the capacity of the ArctiTraks, I figure they have to be. I don't think they can last three more hours at a strain, two if they're smart. If they conclude they can't secure resources here within an hour, their only logical move is to ask for terms."

"Assuming their leadership is logical," Andre said. "Just because we see it, and even if Arris sees it, doesn't mean Earth will. In which case he'll be honor bound to carry through to the end."

Godin added, "And when people get desperate bad things happen."

Right then, Malakhar sat up and shouted, "Here they come! They're backing up fast, I think it's a—"

There came the muffled thump and tremor of an explosion. This one was smaller and more controlled than the last.

It was a swarm attack.

The pressure monitors on the emergency lock indicated an instant drop. The cameras showed Lock 3B dismounting, and blowing roughly back into place from the overpressure. Smoke and debris rushed through the gaps and filled the occupied section.

One of the troops levered the lock door open, and another stuffed a ladder through to block it. The ladder jammed into the rolly parked across the hatch. They suddenly realized their rush wasn't going to work.

After a moment's pause, one dropped to his knees and led the way with others following, between the wheels, up over the pipes, and down and in. Their progress was slow with the encumbrance of weapons and gear, but they proceeded steadily. One of them pointed at a camera and it went dead. The remote crawler camera still had a limited view. The other camera was behind them . . . and it went dead.

Things were moving fast now.

Andre half-shouted, "Okay, ready on those transducers and start pumping up pressure in the emergency lock. It should have a fifty percent design overload, and I guess we're going to test that."

He added, "Let's hit the audio."

He had the transducer controls and dialed it up. First was a loud boom, powerful enough they heard it through here, muffled by the bulkheads. Then he dialed it down to low subsonic.

"I'm just going to sweep it as much as I can. Ultra, sub, and back."

He was betting on disorientation, combined with suit fatigue and the double impact of their blast and his pressure wave.

Godin said, "I'm not sure about damage, but several of them are on the ground, squirming."

"Good." He kept sweeping the frequency.

They definitely didn't like that. Combined with fatigue and heat, it had to be rough.

But the Ueys held the entire section. There was one more hatch between them and inside, an emergency lock with no other support that wasn't going to have any real effect except possibly psychological, though it would channel them.

The transducers could hit 170 dB, which even with the protection of a suit and headphones should be painful. Most of these guys were helmetless. That meant they'd closed Lock 2 so they could use Loonie air, even though transferring in and out was restricted when they had pressure. Also, since the transducers were cone type, each momentary noise should hit like a punch. Andre felt inspired, so he chose an excerpt from the *1812 Overture* for score. Each cannon blast suddenly spiked to 170, while the noise generally ran about 130. And man, those subsonics were awful. He could feel them here.

Malakhar said, "They're slowly crawling out, and they're helmeted and dropping pressure. Really, they should have stayed in vacuum, but that tells us how low they are on oxygen."

"We'll take it. If all it did was get them sealed up, it's still a gain. But we're out of options now. They're against the emergency lock."

Rojas said, "Yes, but it's been six hours. They're running short."

To reinforce that, Arris called.

"Mr. Crawford, I have at least five troops down. I would like to ask again for your hospitality."

Andre thought, *Good*, but . . . as far as the Ueys were concerned, this was the final lock. There was no way to open that without breaching containment, officially. He couldn't let them know about the emergency lock yet.

So he said, "That's going to be a problem. You know where you are."

"That's the response I expected, sir. I will make do out here for the little time it takes. By the way, as a courtesy, your man Morton is here, and in our medical vehicle. He has suffered some vacuum trauma, but is alive. I will treat him honorably, but I have no space for additional casualties. Please consider that."

Rojas and Godin whooped. Even Malakhar pumped his fist.

Alive! Thank god.

"Thank you for the information, Colonel. I appreciate your courtesy and honor. I wish I could offer more help."

"You are welcome. Shall we proceed?"

He tried again.

"Colonel, take the deal. This isn't worth dying for."

Arris didn't sound nearly as confident as he replied, "I do not have authorization to do so."

He was almost pleading as he said, "Sir, I am not at all out of defensive measures. But at this point, I'm out of nonlethal defensive measures. You are advised that further incursion will result in grave risk to human life."

Arris recited, "I must again order you to stand down."

He cut him off. "Sorry, that has to go through my command, not between us."

It was a dance they had to dance, and it was really, really irritating. But Morton was alive!

Arris responded, "I understand. Thank you for considering the request."

"No problem. You're welcome to sit there and breathe oxygen, however, since you have control of the facility for now."

Arris said, "We may do that."

Oh, really?

Andre turned and ordered, "There are no more elements that surrender. They could have been breathing air there, or they have a vehicle they can reach in minutes without hindrance. That was in fact an attempt to either see our defense, or gain access by someone with knowledge or skills. They bought this, they have to pay for it now. Laura, repressurize the emergency section."

"Already doing it," she said. "Back up to previous."

"What pressure are you reading in there?"

She said, "Nine atmospheres as you requested, and it seems to be holding."

Good. "No sign of leakage?"

"No. What were these tested at?"

He said, "The requirement is momentary overpressure of six, sustained three. I think they were tested at nine and six, in a lab setting with solid mountings. Twelve is pushing to max theoretical. But if you're not finding any strain, see if you can pump it up."

Looking at monitors she raised her eyebrows and said, "I'm not sure the pumps can do that, but trying."

Zeiss and his support skipped in right then, in vac suits with rock armor. There was one woman he recognized. She was Hawaiian or similar and bulky enough for a fight. The rest were all men he remembered as being veterans.

He closed the freq, and said, "I'm glad you're here, Colonel. What are your orders?"

Zeiss said, "You are still in charge, Engineer Crawford. I'm here with backup. What are *your* instructions?"

He summarized fast. "They're going to try to blow the Lock. We still have that emergency hatch. We've overpressured and overoxygenated to hinder movement momentarily, and we used transducers to try to stun them. If they enter the main passage, we expect them to be hindered and slowed, and we'll need to shoot while trying to block them in."

Zeiss said, "Understood. I'd hoped to avoid violence, and you've managed very well so far."

"Thank you, sir. And I need you down the hall

wherever you can best shoot from." It felt odd to be giving orders to the Guy in Charge.

"We'll do that now," Zeiss agreed.

While that element skipped off, he took another look at the information they had. Then he started scrawling figures on screen. Was that . . . possibly, yes. If . . .

He leaned back, checked the time and the video feed, and glanced through his numbers.

"This is complicated," he said. "But I think we can cause more overpressure, without undue risk to the emergency lock. Rod, can you check my figures?" He turned his fliptop so Godin could see.

Godin had more experience with this sort of thing, and Andre wanted his opinion for safety.

Reading through, the man replied, "If I follow this, you want to use a deflagration to cause overpressure, focused inside the primary lock, relying on the constriction of the hatch to minimize shock against the e-lock."

Andre gave a thumbs-up. "Correct."

"Did you account for the choke and funnel effect of the shot?"

Yes. "I think so. As best I could."

Godin said, "I think so, too. I believe there's a small risk of popping the seals, but it should still retain structural integrity."

Andre asked, "Fair risk?"

"Yes, do it."

Andre said, "Thanks. Laura, three tanks of acetylene are getting pumped in."

"Won't it stratify?" she asked.

"Not quickly with the blowers going, in this gee."

"Three?"

Andre said, "It's more than enough, and more than we should spare."

She stood up and grabbed her tool belt. "Got it. I'll need a thread adapter."

"Hurry. They will probably cut through in a few minutes."

"They are stubborn," Malakhar agreed.

More waiting, as the Ueys kept their preps going, with only secondary intel available on exactly what those preps were.

Shortly, Laura reported, "It's done. I managed to get a ratio of about eighteen to one. I'm not sure how you plan to ignite, though."

"A low-order charge will agitate and provide flame front. It won't be efficient, but it will generate overpressure. But it has to be on their side. That means the bottleneck of their opening restricts the pressure wave enough not to damage our lock. We hope." He looked at Godin for reassurance, who thumbed back.

Malakhar said, "They appear to be closing the hatch behind them. They must figure we plan something, and will open back up after breaching. That explains the numbers."

"It also means they expect a fight. Are our people behind cover?"

"Yes, there's a forklift as well as the pillars. It'll stop rifle fire."

"Then we hope that's enough."

There was a rumbling crack as a charge breached the airlock containment.

"Smackdown!" Godin shouted.

Drone sonar and imagery showed the Ueys getting bowled off their feet as the pressure equalized between sections. Adding in the explosive gas, it was a bit over six atmospheres even after balance.

The volume and low charge meant no one had died, but damn, did they look shaken.

All of them were still moving, but they'd obviously been hit hard and wouldn't be doing much for a while. Two of them rolled to their knees and stood.

Meanwhile, Uey troops pumped the pressure down on their side and opened the hatch. The camera just showed them diving through, reasonably well controlled in the low G, and offering support positions to each other.

Another element rushed in to check the downed troops, and didn't seem overly panicked.

Then two more came through, leading others forward to the open lock.

The body language of the troops just sagged. After all this, there was another lock, one they didn't have on their plans. Which suggested there might just be another behind it, and another.

They huddled and conferred. They really weren't sure what to do here.

Rojas muttered, "I hope they don't realize a basic charge will blow that thing right off its seals."

Andre said, "I don't think that's going to occur to them at this point. They're short on oxy, short on personnel, and haven't achieved objective."

Still, there was movement and conference. Their technical element came in and painted the camera, but

Andre assumed they were examining the hatch itself. Certainly it was an emergency unit. It wouldn't be too hard to dismount. But doing so might leave them in an open crossfire with Loonies in reinforced positions. Or they might be facing yet another hatch. Or they might be confronted with heavy equipment. They had nothing to go with from here.

At least, that's what he hoped they were thinking.

"Come on," he said quietly through clenched teeth.

It was fifteen minutes before the radio channel opened. "Mr. Crawford?"

He grabbed the mic, made himself wait, breathed slowly, counted time, then replied, "Yes, Colonel?"

"You have blocked us again. I would like to propose a resolution."

Was that what it hinted at? He felt prickly and exposed.

He waited, slowly, watching the seconds tick by.

"There's only one set of terms I can accept as a resolution, sir. I believe you understand that."

Arris said, "It appears I don't have the backup I was supposed to have."

"Is that a 'yes'?"

"Mr. Crawford, I reluctantly accept your offer of recovery."

WIN!

He took a long, deep breath to steady his nerves. He didn't want to stutter and giggle.

"That's fine. I require your surrender and parole in order to proceed. And on behalf of all UN forces accompanying you, whether under your command, attached, contract or otherwise in the element we are taking."

After a short pause. Arris replied, "That was amazingly thorough."

"I've dealt with bureaucrats and our contract lawyers. Do I have your word?"

Arris agreed. "You do. I am ordering everyone accompanying me to abide by those terms, and I will vouch for them."

"Very good, sir," he said as politely and professionally blandly as possible. "You will need to assist with transfer operations."

Arris said, "Certainly. Please tell me what you need."

"I need you to reengage any working lock in a very specific fashion. Is your technical specialist ready for instructions?"

A few seconds later, a different voice said, "This is Captain Gul. I am ready for instructions regarding the outer lock."

Andre motioned to Laura, who nodded and switched in.

"Captain, this is Fabricator Rojas. You will be reengaging the lock controls through a commo line that will be isolated at this end. If my signals show any power loss or other indications of trouble, we'll have to evacuate. Is that clear?"

"It is."

"Please open the box and find the LCP23 on the left side . . ."

After that, he had them clear the non-destroyed cameras as best they could. It was enough that he could see all the hatches from both sides. They wouldn't be trying any rushes.

Andre told Arris, "The procedure is you put all the weapons into the innermost lock. We secure those. Then your people come through four at a time. We'll do this as fast as we can, but there will be a cycle time as we have them desuit and relocate inside."

"I understand," the colonel replied. "I will send through my most junior, and those shortest of oxygen first, along with your Mr. Morton. I shall be last."

Whew. "I will continue to furnish atmosphere inside the lock. Understand that at the first sign of trouble, I will evacuate it. This does not mean I don't trust you. It means I can't trust anyone. Something twitches, I punch the button. So for our sake and yours, please instruct your element to keep their helmets in place or immediately accessible."

"I understand and will comply."

He was still prickly nervous. "Very well, sir. You can disarm now."

Saying it didn't cause much relief, but seeing all the rifles piled did help. The troops doing so unloaded and cleared them all in the process.

Rojas and Godin checked the weapons as they retrieved them, piled them all into a trailer on a quad, and drove them down the passage to where one of the security officers could take them to be secured. Andre wasn't sure where that was and figured that was safer.

That done, he called Arris and said, "You may proceed."

Each cycle took a full minute to lock, clear and open, and the security officers made the Ueys desuit, then patted them down, before escorting them into the habitat. They must be getting placed into empty cubes and trusted locations where they couldn't reach any equipment, and what about the sympathizers up here? This might not be over yet.

There was Morton, and Andre said, "Ravi, you're in charge for a moment."

He skipped out into the passage.

Morton looked shaken, and was obviously having trouble breathing. That might be with him for a while or for life. But he was alive. Two of the Ueys were assisting him, and Doctor Nik was arriving on a Quad, with two medics and a gurney.

"Stu, glad you made it, and thanks."

Morton smiled weakly. "We did it."

"You did. Now lie down and do as the good doctor tells you."

He shook hands, and Morton's grip was still firm. He'd be fine.

As the number of Ueys waiting dropped, Andre did relax a bit. Having what were effectively human shields scattered inside was useful, as was a few dozen weapons and some extra equipment. He wasn't sure yet what the crew aboard the ships would do. Could they even launch out? Likely not.

Watching on vid, he had to give the Ueys their due. They were all fit, all wrung out, all near complete collapse. They'd given it everything they had. Stout, worthwhile people. They'd do well here. Though he didn't think any applications would be accepted unless this resolved favorably.

Was that even possible? Probably the only solutions were to destroy the device so no one had it, or crack it and share the schematics publicly. Hopefully the good would outweigh the bad. Though he expected some terrorist nukes to be among the first round of creation.

It took an hour to move them all in and separate them. He was given a partial update from Control. The Ueys were literally scattered with no means of communication. Quite a few were in lockup, others in secondary habitats with no vac gear. That should keep them from mischief, and he'd offer whatever he came up with, but it wasn't his problem after this.

Arris was the last, after all his troops. That was the proper thing to do.

The colonel was not at all what Crawford expected. Despite the soft voice, he was huge. He had to work out daily to be that chiseled, and that wasn't a standard-sized suit.

But he sounded so gentlemanly and mild. His hulking exterior didn't hide the sheepishness and disappointment in his demeanor, either.

"Mr Crawford, I congratulate you on a very stubborn and successful defense."

"Thank you, sir. I appreciate your professionalism and graciousness in minimizing casualties. If only the politicians could be as courteous."

Arris carefully turned off his helmet power and placed it on the deck.

"Are you recording?" he asked.

"I am."

"Can I ask you to pause it for a moment, for a personal comment?"

That was a bit dodgy, but it could be useful.

He hard disconnected the mic.

He said, "If you face this way, the cameras won't see your lips move."

Arris turned and seemed to relax quite a bit. "Thank you. I am clear here?"

"You are."

The man said, "For all our sakes, I hope to persuade you to just destroy the device entirely. As you noted, it offers provocations to groups we'd have to fight, and could lead to endless internecine warfare between nations and separatist groups who have just in the last few years been persuaded to reduce their aggressions."

"This is unofficial?"

"This is me as an individual who will be charged with wading in to clean up messes caused by people with far less moral compass than you. Please consider it, and you can open your channels again now."

"Yes, sir. And welcome to the Moon."

"Thank you. It is possible I will ask to remain."

MOONDOG

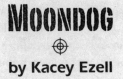

by Kacey Ezell

Back home, she'd been a ballroom dancer in her free
time. Mostly Latin dances, with a smattering of smooth
routines here and there over the years. She wasn't a
superstar, but she'd been to a few competitions, brought
home a few trophies. Mostly it was just a good, fun way to
stay flexible and in shape. That, coupled with the more
intense athletic training that was always part of the job,
allowed Leiko Soloway to feel like she was a fairly graceful
individual. Like she was in control of her body and its
movement.

But that was back home, before the divorce that had
sent her into a freefall of wild decisions and ended up with
her accepting a five-year contract to work security here,
in Rinehart Dome.

On the moon.

"It's easier if you don't try to walk."

Leiko looked up to find the speaker, a young, blond
male fellow passenger in his mid-twenties, smiling at her

with an understanding expression in his blue eyes. "The reduced gravity throws your rhythm off. Try hopping, like those old videos of the first moon landings? It's easier to keep your balance that way."

"Thanks," Leiko murmured, and looked back down again at the smallish overnight bag that held her possessions. She'd dropped it in favor of grabbing the exit ramp wall in order to keep from falling on her face under the feet of the other passengers disembarking from the moon shuttle.

"Let me get that for you—" The young man bent to grab the strap of her bag, but Leiko was faster, her hand shot out in a block that rapped against his forearm hard enough to bruise. The young man hissed and bounced backwards, cradling his arm to his chest.

"Ah—I'm sorry," Leiko said, "It's just . . ."

"No, it's okay," the young man said, his wide grin returning. "I forgot, you Earthers are paranoid about theft when you first arrive. I should have known better. You don't have to worry, though. People don't just take your stuff up here."

"People aren't people up here?" she asked as she gathered her courage and bent to pick up the bag. She straightened slowly and looped the strap over her head and shoulders.

"Ha!" he said. "Yes, we're still people. But it's not acceptable to take what isn't yours. We're a small community, when it comes down to it. Everyone knows everyone, and DomeSec would find out sooner or later. There's only so many places to hide. I'm Ryder, by the way."

"Leiko," she said, taking his outstretched hand and shaking it. "Thanks for the help."

"You're welcome. First trip to the moon?"

She nodded.

"You're doing better than most. Ready to give it another try?"

"Sure." She shifted her bag around so that it sat against her lower back and resolutely let go of the wall.

"Atta girl. Remember, hop, don't walk." He demonstrated, bending his knees and pushing off in a split-legged jump that took him a few feet further down the corridor.

"Right." Leiko flexed her own knees and tried to mimic his movements. Once again, years of following choreographers paid off as she executed a neat, graceful little hop to land beside him.

"I did it," she said, smiling up at him. Perhaps it was silly, but she felt as flushed with victory as a toddler who finally manages to let go of the furniture and walk to their parent.

"Good work!" Ryder said, "I knew you could! Now that we've got that out of the way, want to head to baggage claim? I imagine you've got more stuff if this is your first trip up here."

"Nope," she said, her smile fading. She patted her bag. "This is it. All my worldly goods . . . for the most part. I travel light."

"Wow, okay," he said. "So then you're probably headed to check in somewhere . . . ?"

"My job. They said to come by the station when I arrived. I guess they have housing lined up for me here."

"Oh! That's cool. Where do you work, then?"

"Rinehart Dome Security."

Ryder's blue eyes widened and his eyebrows climbed high enough to hide behind his oh-so-casually tousled wisps of blond hair. "DomeSec? Really?"

"Yep," she said, giving him a half smile. "What's wrong, I don't look like the type?" She knew that she didn't. Her long dark hair, relatively petite build and almond shaped eyes didn't exactly give off a "security professional" vibe. It was one of her big assets.

"Well . . ." he shrugged his shoulders and smiled again. "Not really. Most of the DomeSec guys are pretty big dudes. I didn't think they hired women. Working with the dogs is a pretty physical job."

"They hired me," she said with her own shrug. "Want to show me where it is?"

"Sure thing! It's just this way . . ."

As they bounced through the arrival terminal and out onto the Dome's main thoroughfare, Ryder regaled her with his life story.

"I wasn't born up here," he said. "Though I've lived on the moon most of my life. My parents were two of the original colonists that laid the foundation for Rinehart. Mom's a structural engineer and Dad's a hydrologist. They took a three year sabbatical on Earth to have me and my brother, and then moved back up here as soon as we boys were old enough. I grew up here."

"Really?" Leiko asked, fascinated despite herself. "How did that affect you, growing up in reduced gravity?"

"Mostly it made my mom a fanatic about our workouts," he said with a laugh. "And she'd send us down to our grandparents' for a few months out of every year. So we could develop properly."

"That must have been expensive."

"Part of the contract," he said with a grin. "Mom's pretty highly sought-after, so she could name her terms. She designed Rinehart Dome, you know. Named it after her best friend Jill. She was a nature photographer and artist back on Earth. That's the reason Rinehart has its signature landscaping. Mom did it as a tribute to her friend."

"That's pretty cool," Leiko said, taking a moment to look around. Unlike the stark moonscape she'd imagined, the interior of the dome teemed with color and life. Someone must have added nutrients to the lunar soil, because plants spread out in every direction: grasses, wildflowers, ground running vines. Tall stands of bamboo stretched up higher than Leiko had ever seen at home. Fruit trees that looked old enough that they almost had to have been transplants interlaced their branches in a gorgeous arch over the top of the elevated pedestrian walkway where they stood. Leiko looked down and to the left, where large wheeled vehicles rolled by on big, balloon-like tires. Most of them had cargo beds filled with rock, or cannisters and crates of cargo. Unlike the rumbling engines of vehicles back home, these behemoths were quiet, save for the crunching of gravel under their wheels.

"Electric?" she guessed. Ryder nodded.

"They're unloading the shuttle you came in on. Rinehart has the third largest shuttleport on Luna, so we get the supply shipments for several of the nearby domes. They're headed to the distribution center, where the stuff will be collated into smaller shipments and then sent out via rover."

"Sounds efficient."

"I try," he said. "That's my job. I'm a loggie for the company."

"I see. So are you headed to the distribution center, too?"

"Nope. Last day of vacation," he grinned down at her and pointed at an intersection up ahead, marked by flowering vines. "We take a right up here. I always take an extra day to reacclimate when I get back from my grandparents' house. I highly recommend it."

"Yeah, well, I don't think I'll be visiting Earth anytime soon," she said, surprising herself with how bitter she sounded. "There's not much left for me there. Thus, I'm here."

"Fair enough." Ryder seemed disinclined to question her further, and she felt a surge of gratitude for the polite, gregarious young man. He continued chattering on about his family and his job as they took the right turn and headed up the block for another half kilometer or so. Eventually, the ground started to slope upward, and Ryder came to a stop at the top of a small hill.

"Here we are," he said, gesturing expansively at the unassuming structure before them. It was a concrete building the same color as the gravel underfoot, which meant that it was probably made of Lunar materials. The squat block building had no windows, and only a single metal door in the front. It also boasted a chain link fence extending out either side and circling back to enclose a generous perimeter. The lush ground cover stopped at the line of the fence, and only grey lunar gravel remained on the other side.

"Inviting," Leiko said. Ryder laughed and clapped her lightly on the shoulder.

"I think it's all part of the image," he said. "Good luck! It was really nice to meet you, Leiko."

"Thanks, you too," she said, turning toward him and holding out her hand. He took it and shook it warmly.

"If you ever need to get ahold of me, you can just call the distribution center. The landline number is listed in the directory, and I'm channel 8 on the LMR."

"Land Mobile Radio? They work up here?"

"Lunar Mobile Radio," he corrected, grinning. "Just a modification or two to deal with the different atmospheric conditions . . . that is to say, none at all! But yeah, they work. Call me anytime, and do let me know if you need anything to get settled in, okay?"

"Okay, thanks, Ryder, I will." She found to her surprise that she meant it. Despite her usual anti-social nature, she seemed to have made a friend already.

The moon was a weird place.

The door to DomeSec was locked.

After waving goodbye to Ryder, Leiko walked up to the metal door and examined it, lips pursed. No handle, no obvious buzzer or doorbell . . . how exactly was she supposed to make her presence known? She had just raised her fist to pound on the thing when she heard a short chime and a tinny voice filtered down from a speaker somewhere above.

"May I help you?"

"Uh, Hi. I'm Leiko Soloway? I've just arrived. New hire?" She hated the way her voice rose up as if she were asking questions rather than stating undeniable facts, so she gave herself a mental kick and resolved to eliminate that behavior.

"Just a second."

There was a deep *thunk*, and then the door swung outward as a burly, olive-skinned man in a dark blue uniform pushed it that way.

"Come on in." The man's voice was deeper when not being filtered through the speaker, and she tried to flash him a confident smile as he held the obviously heavy door open and squeezed to the side to let her pass behind him into the spartan room beyond.

"Thanks," Leiko said, looking around. The floor and walls were the same bare concrete as the exterior of the building, with the occasional drain set into the floor itself. A short hallway stretched straight ahead, with two doors on either side as it went. A fifth, double door faced them at the far end. The entrance door clanged shut behind her, and she fought to turn her instinctive jump into a turning move that hid her startlement.

"Welcome to Rinehart," the big man said. He held out a hand that was easily the size of her face. "I'm Hollis."

"Soloway," she said, taking his hand in as firm a grip as she could manage. He quirked the corner of his mouth in a smile as they shook.

"Yeah, you said. First time on the moon?" He turned and gestured for her to follow as he led the way through the first door on the right of the hallway, and into a tiny concrete-walled office.

"Yep."

"Well, we're glad you're here. I'm the deputy chief of DomeSec here on Rinehart, been here about five years. The Chief's out right now, but he told me you were inbound sometime today. How was your trip?" He pulled a utilitarian chair out from under a corner desk and sat, gesturing for her to take a seat on the tiny, slightly dilapidated love seat that squatted against the near wall. She shook her head slightly and leaned her shoulder on the door frame instead.

"Uneventful."

"Good deal. We've got you set up with quarters not too far away. You probably passed it on your way if you came from the terminal. You walked?"

"Bounced," she said, echoing his half-smile. He chuckled.

"Yeah. Bounced. For sure. Do you want to go there now? Get settled in? Get some rest?"

"Not really," she said. Hollis's dark eyebrows rose up toward the dome of his bald head. "I feel like I've been lazing around for the last several days."

"Ah," Hollis nodded. "Yeah, it feels like that sometimes. You're a little restless, gotta work that out before you can sleep?"

"Something like that."

"Welll . . ." he stretched it out, looking closely at her. She fought not to straighten up and stand to attention under his assessing gaze. "Do you want to meet your partner?"

A tiny thrill of excitement spiraled through her, but she pushed it down. This was a test. First impressions were always a test.

"Sure, if it's convenient."

"Good a time as any," Hollis said. "Your file said you're an experienced working dog handler. What do you know about our moondogs?"

"You breed, raise, and train them here, so they grow up adapted to lunar gravity and conditions," Leiko said. "The breeding program is still touch and go, with about one litter in four actually resulting in live pups. But if they survive to be born and complete the training, the moondogs tend to be hardy, tough animals, suited to their role in mine safety and security work."

"Done your homework, I see." A note of approval threaded through Hollis's voice. "Lower gravity tends to make them taller, but more delicately built. We compensate by keeping them weighted the whole time they're growing up. There's been some papers on it."

"Like I said, the trip was uneventful. Plenty of time to read up."

"Well, so far you're dead on. Did your reading material talk about the suits at all?"

"Just a little bit, mostly focusing on the weighted aspect. I gather that the neuro implants that allow the dogs' brains to interface with their vac-suits' chemical receptors are still proprietary tech?"

"Very much so," Hollis said. "We don't even have the full specs, though our vet happened to be on the developmental team for the implant. But she's as good as her word on the non-disclosure agreements, so we don't get anything out of her. What you need to know is this: each dog is fitted for their own customized suit. The helmet plugs into the dogs' implants. They get the implants before their first birthday and grow up using the suits, so it's very natural to them. Thanks to the implant, the dog actually *smells* in a vacuum. That is, the chemical receptors in the suit communicate the appropriate scent profile to the olfactory receptors in their brains, and they react accordingly."

"Neat," Leiko said.

"I thought so. We'll get you working in a suit asap. Most handlers have to do a bit of catching up, since unlike their partners, they didn't grow up wearing a vac suit."

"Makes sense."

"But for today, It's probably enough if you just meet Ryu. He's . . . a lot."

"Dominant?"

Hollis met her eyes and nodded, his expression serious. "He's a bit of a problem dog. For some reason, he's convinced he's in charge, and he's a big guy. To be honest, I'd pair you up with any other dog if we had anyone else. But if we had anyone else, we'd probably have to put Ryu down. He's just too hard to work."

"Maybe he hasn't met the right handler yet," Leiko said, carefully keeping her emotions out of her voice.

"I'm hoping you're right. And for his sake . . . and yours . . . I hope you're the handler he needs. Honestly, we probably should have put him down already. Still want to meet him?"

"Sure. A brief introduction. I'll need to get his file from you and go through it in detail later."

"You got it," Hollis said as he pushed back up to his feet.

They headed back out into the hallway and turned

toward the double doors. As soon as Hollis pushed the right one open, a cacophony of barks rose up, echoing off the concrete walls.

"Enough!" Hollis said, his voice sharp and pitched to carry. "Y'all know better than that!"

Sure enough, the dogs fell silent, and Leiko stepped out into the kennel area.

It was about what she'd expected: a perpendicular hallway with a line of wire-fronted kennels facing the doors they'd come through. Each kennel had a large window set high in the wall to provide light, although Leiko could see light fixtures over her head as well. The kennels themselves had no frills to speak of; each consisted of a simple concrete floor with a drain set in it, three concrete walls, and the chain link fourth wall with a door.

"This is Mida," Hollis said, pointing at the dog in the nearest kennel, who looked up at them with an expectant expression. "She's the youngest of the group. Next to her is Sly, then Jugger. And Ryu is on the end."

Leiko bounce-walked down the line of kennels, ignoring all of the dogs. She imagined she could feel their curious looks as she passed them. She made her way to the end and stopped right in front of Ryu's door.

He was huge. She could see that even without looking directly at him. She took her time and examined his kennel, letting Ryu get a look at her before she paid any attention to him. He lay against the back wall of the kennel, well clear of the puddle of sunlight that poured in through his window. Not far away, a metal water bowl sat upside-down on the floor, and a thin sheen of water ran from it to the drain. She wondered why no one had gone in to clean it up.

As if in answer to her thoughts, a deep warning growl rumbled forth from the back of the kennel.

"Knock it off," she said, her own voice low and calm. "I'm not even looking at you. You're convinced it's all about you, aren't you?"

The growl intensified.

"Oh, shut up. You're not scaring anyone here, you spoiled pup. Hollis, do you have a squeegee?"

"Against the wall on your right," Hollis said from his vantage point near the double doors.

"Thanks," Leiko said. "Billy Badass here has kicked over his water dish and made a mess of his kennel. I'm gonna clean it up for him."

"Sure you want to do that?" Hollis asked.

"Yup," Leiko said, still in that calm, unconcerned tone. "Unlock his kennel for me, will ya?"

She glanced at Hollis out of the corner of her eye and caught his shrug, but he pushed a button on the end of a row of them near the door, and Leiko heard a quiet *click*.

So did Ryu.

He bounced up to his feet, moving like lightning in the lunar gravity, and started barking and growling loudly enough that Leiko felt the pressure change on her eardrums. The other dogs picked up his cry, and for just a second, she thought she just might drown in the cacophony.

"KNOCK IT OFF!" she shouted, and all the dogs fell silent.

All but Ryu, who quit barking, but continued growling and snarling at her, his lips pulled back to showcase teeth as long as her little finger. Leiko still refused to acknowledge this, and turned to grab the squeegee before turning the metal handle of Ryu's kennel door and letting herself in.

For a moment, she wondered if he might attack her. She held the squeegee loosely in front of herself, just in case she had to use it to hold Ryu's bite off of her throat long enough for Hollis to come rescue her. But the big dog didn't move, just stood at the back of the kennel and growled.

"I'm not here for you," she said softly. "I'm just here to clean up your mess, Billy Badass. Bet it sucks that you've got a wet kennel now, doesn't it? Maybe you shouldn't knock your shit over, hmm? Maybe you should act like the grown-ass dog you are instead of trying to pass for a spoiled puppy who insists on getting his way? How's that for an idea?"

As she talked, she started to use the squeegee in long, sweeping strokes to pull the water toward the floor drain. She moved slowly and methodically, watching the way Ryu circled away from her so as to be on the opposite side of the kennel from wherever she stood. When she got to the water bowl, she bent down to pick it up.

Silence was her only warning. Ryu had kept his steady growl going the entire time she worked, so when he suddenly stopped, she knew something was up. She lifted her head just enough to catch a flash of brindle black and brown before she felt the full impact of a charging moondog. Instinct alone had her reaching out and clamping one hand tightly around his muzzle, holding his mouth shut as she wrapped her other arm around his body and twisted, using his momentum to take them both to the floor. Somehow, she managed to roll so that Ryu's body was pinned under her slightly greater weight. She felt him try to yelp, then to snarl and snap, but she'd been a dog handler her entire adult life. When she grabbed a dog by the muzzle, the dog's mouth stayed closed.

"This is not how you're gonna act with me, Billy Badass," she said softly, almost purring into Ryu's pointed ear. "You don't scare me. You are not in charge of me. I've seen a hundred dogs like you, and I'll see a hundred more when you're gone. You try to hurt me, and I promise, I won't be the one getting hurt."

He squirmed under her, his back feet scrabbling against her thighs as he fought to regain control. Slowly, carefully, she got her feet under herself and pushed up to her knees and elbows, still holding Ryu to the floor. For the first time, she looked in his eyes.

"But if you trust me, if you work with me, I'm gonna take care of you," she said, pumping sincerity into every word. She took the hand she'd wrapped around him and slid it out from under him as she rose up. Slowly, softly, she started to stroke behind his ear. "You don't have to be scared anymore, Ryu. I'm here, I'm in charge. I'll take care of things. You just have to trust me and do what I ask. Got it?"

Dogs understood tone, not words. She knew that. She'd been taught it all her life, and had taught that principle to her students in turn. But right then, it really did seem as if Ryu understood her, because he stopped moving, stopped growling, and just stared back at her in challenge.

"You want proof?" she asked. "Trust you to earn your trust? Fair enough, Billy Badass. Fair enough."

Outside, she could hear Hollis stifle an expression of disbelief as she slowly let go of Ryu's muzzle. Her other hand slid down to his chest, holding him lightly on his back in a submissive posture. Ryu looked at her, considering, but she tilted her head slightly to the side and raised her eyebrows as if to ask if he really wanted to do something he'd regret.

Instead, he twisted his body and got back to his feet. Leiko let go of him and straightened up, but she remained sitting on her knees, even though Ryu's head was now even with hers. He took a half step backward, still watching her. When she didn't move, he walked back toward her and put his nose up under her chin, snuffling as he pulled her scent in through his wet nostrils.

"Holy shit," Hollis breathed, his eyes narrowing. "I've never seen anything like that. How in the hell did you tame psycho dog so fast?"

"Oh, he's not tame," Leiko said. "He's just playing nice for the moment. He's still gonna push me for a while yet, but I think we've got the start of an understanding here, don't we, Ryu?" She reached out and stroked the deliciously soft fur between his ears, and the tip of Ryu's tail began to swing just the tiniest bit.

"Still. I thought he was gonna try and kill you! He cut up his previous handler but good. The guy quit, went back to Earth."

"You didn't think I'd want to know about that?" Leiko asked, her voice deliberately mild.

"It's all in the file," Hollis said, a bit of a defensive tone leaking into his words. "I didn't think you'd go in to the kennel right away!"

"Even after you unlocked it for me?"

Hollis looked uncomfortable enough that Leiko let out a low chuckle. She felt Ryu's skin shiver in response under her fingertips.

"It's okay, man," she said. "I get it. I'm proving myself to you as much as I am to this guy here."

"I guess," Hollis said. "But after that? Shit. I don't think you gotta prove anything to anyone. I've never seen Ryu take to someone so quickly!"

"I trusted him," Leiko said. "You'd be amazed at how much of a difference that makes." She patted Ryu on his head and then pushed gently on his chest.

"Go lie down again," she told the dog. "I've gotta go, but I'll be back in a little while. I'll get you more water, as long as you don't knock it over again." Ryu looked at her, and Leiko could swear she saw a spark of mischief in the dog's eyes, but he obediently backed away enough that she could get to her feet. She surprised herself by laughing again.

"Oh yeah," she said. "You're gonna be a handful, all right!"

Over the next few weeks, Leiko and Ryu got to know one another. The moondogs' daily training regimen included extensive work in their weighted training suits, both inside and outside the dome. Every time Leiko approached his kennel with the heavy suit draped in her arms, Ryu would leap to his feet, his body quivering in excitement. Leiko would work them until they were both falling-down exhausted, but every morning, Ryu's enthusiasm returned.

"Something new today, Billy," Leiko said as she stepped into the kennel one morning about three weeks after she'd arrived. In her arms, she carried her own vac suit, and a lighter, stripped down version of Ryu's.

"You're graduating him to the operational suit, huh?" Hollis asked from behind her. Leiko turned and jerked her chin at him in a hello, and he nodded back at her. "Sure he's ready? No one's taken him off weights yet."

"That's why he's so big," she said. "He is what you guys made him."

"He's a psychopath," Hollis said. "I don't know how he hasn't killed you yet."

"I haven't let him. Besides, we trust each other, don't we, Billy?"

"Crazy fucking dog. Crazy fucking handler."

"That's how we like it," she said as she unlocked Ryu's kennel. Truth was, she didn't much care what Hollis and the other handlers thought. They were well-trained and mostly a disciplined lot, but every one of them, including the Chief, had been willing to give up on Ryu and have him destroyed. No wonder he hadn't trusted any of them, and had acted so aggressively. She'd have done the same in such a hostile environment.

"But I'm here now, aren't I?" she murmured for the dog's ears alone as she unlocked the newly upgraded kennel lock with her fob and stepped inside. "I'm here and I've got you. No one's gonna hurt you, Billy Badass, because we're gonna work together and show them all what you can do. So let's get you in this suit and go see what's what."

"Where're you taking him?" Hollis called from the door.

"Lock Three." Leiko held the suit legs open while Ryu stepped obediently in. She grunted softly and pulled up hard, making sure the vac suit sat snugly around his legs and belly before continuing the dressing process. "There's a shipment going out from the distribution center, and we're gonna scan it. My friend Ryder said they're including some demo equipment. Should give Billy here a bit of a workout."

"Interesting," he said, softly. "That's an elegant solution. And it beats being tied to the damn vidlink like me. I'd even go out with you to watch Psycho there if it would get me out of this conference call back to Earth. Damn thing's supposed to take all freaking day."

"Yeah, thanks. I figured we might as well get what practice we can."

"Sure," Hollis said, snorting softly. "But keep the tether short, Leiko. I still think that psycho's too crazy to be allowed near too many people. More and more I think he's just a waste of training and a waste of a dog. He really shoulda been put down." He looked at her with sober, concerned eyes.

"With respect, Deputy Chief, I disagree," Leiko murmured, just as she became aware of the low, rolling growl coming from Ryu's chest. She turned and thumped the dog just between his front legs.

"Knock it off," she growled, lowering her chin and staring into his eyes. "Behave yourself."

The growling stopped, but the stiff defiance in his body language remained. Leiko thought about correcting him, but couldn't face the hypocrisy of it. She agreed with Ryu, Hollis was a dick.

"Come on," Leiko said then, speaking to herself as much as to the dog. "We've got work to do. Let's get these suits on."

Less than half a standard hour later, Leiko led Ryu out through the grey gravel training yard and onto the thoroughfare. She wore her own armored vac suit with the visor retracted so that she could speak and hear normally. Ryu's helmet included a smoked visor that shaded his eyes, and made him look even more formidable than usual. Leiko keyed the button to turn on Ryu's hot mic and heard the rhythmic panting of his normal breath. She set her own radio to vox, so she could speak and Ryu would hear her commands inside his helmet.

"Ryu. Hold." she said, and Ryu, who had been idly sniffing around, froze. His attention sharpened, intense and unwavering as he stared at her and waited.

"Gape."

Ryu obediently yawned widely inside his helmet. Leiko checked to make sure that the flexible chin piece expanded as advertised without compromising the suit-to-helmet seal. Below that, the suit's hydraulically actuated "prosthetic jaw" opened up, revealing the shark-like rows of serrated tungsten steel teeth.

"Snap."

Ryu let out a growl and snapped his mouth shut. The steel teeth slammed together hard enough to make a ringing sound. From her research, Leiko knew that the pressure of the suit's bite was enough to snap a fully grown male human's femur. Which was a pretty neat trick, all things considered.

Leiko did one more check of the seals on both her suit and Ryu's, and then the two of them set off in an easy, hopping lope toward Lock 3. They moved well together. She'd become more accustomed to working in lunar gravity, and Ryu stayed glued to her side, his tether curving slackly between them.

"Feels good to get out and move, doesn't it?" she murmured, looking down. His near ear twitched in response to her voice. "I can tell you like the non-weighted suit. You feel strong, don't you? Like you could go forever? Yeah, Billy Badass. Me too, buddy. Me too."

Neither one of them had broken a sweat by the time they arrived at Lock 3. Leiko slowed to a more pedestrian pace and looked around for the distribution vehicle she'd been told to find.

"Leiko? Ah, I mean, Officer Soloway?"

Leiko turned, moving her whole body rather than just her head, and gave Ryder a solemn, professional head nod. Beside her, Ryu stiffened, but did not growl.

"Ryder," she said. "Let me introduce you to my partner, Security K-9 Ryu. Just look at him, please. Don't hold out a hand or approach him in any way."

"Is he dangerous?" Ryder asked. "I've never seen one this close before. That suit is something else!"

"He can be," Leiko said, with a small smile for her friend. "But he's a professional, and he'll listen to me. We appreciate you letting us take this opportunity for training."

"No problem," Ryder said. "I'm happy to help. I just

can't believe how *big* he is! This is really cool. So, you want me to show you to the convoy?"

"Please," Leiko said. "And please ask your people to basically ignore us. Ryu won't bother them as long as they don't bother us."

"Of course. It's just right over here. We are just a touch behind schedule, so I'll just introduce you to the convoy supervisor—"

Boom.

A wall of brilliant, searing light rose up out of the third vehicle in the line and raced toward them as the ground turned sideways. The light picked them up and hurtled them through the manufactured atmosphere, only to slam them down on the soft, lush ground cover just inside the dome's airlock itself. Pure instinct made Leiko toggle her visor down with her tongue switch as she flew through the air, so her face would be protected from the debris that would follow. Torn, twisted metal and pulverized moon rock rained down on them as soon as they hit the ground. The force of the impact drove the air from Leiko's stunned lungs, and she lay still while her body remembered how to breathe.

Next to her, Ryu whimpered. Leiko blinked inside her helmet and gasped. Finally, after what felt like ages, her diaphragm relaxed and she pulled in a great whooshing breath of air.

It tasted like burnt metal and stone.

"Ryu," she said, her voice ragged. "Ryu, I'm here, buddy. Are you hurt?"

Her visor was covered with dirt, but she didn't want to retract it just yet, in case there was a secondary explosion

or something. She swiped at it with a gloved hand, and
that helped a little. She heard Ryu whimpering again, and
felt something press against her side as she rolled over and
fought her way up onto her hands and knees. Another
swipe at her visor didn't yield better results, so she took a
deep breath and toggled it open, then looked out on a
scene of devastation.

Gray lunar dust hung thickly in the air, coating her
mouth and nose with every breath. Her ears rang with a
high, insistent buzzy sound. It almost sounded like one of
her helmet's speakers were blown, but she could hear
Ryu's whines coming through just fine. She shook her
head to clear it and immediately regretted that decision
as a sudden, throbbing pain in her skull resulted.

"Ryu," she groaned again. The whining intensified, and
the body pressing next to her pressed harder. She looked
down to see the dog leaning on her, his suit covered in a
layer of dust, his own visor completely obscured. She sat
heavily down and pulled off her vac gloves, using her bare
hands to wipe his helmet clear.

"I'm all right," she said. "You're all right. I'm right here.
What the hell happened? An explosion? Oh bloody hells,
Ryder!"

She pushed herself up to her feet, despite her
wobbliness and the pain in her skull. Ryu leaned into her,
nearly knocking her over. She reached down and wrapped
his tether around her hand, using that anchor to steady
herself as she squinted into the dust.

"Ryder?" Leiko called out, coughing. "Ryder?!"

Ryu snuffled, and let out a short bark that nearly
brought Leiko to her knees. She clenched her fist around

his tether, and felt him step forward, favoring his right side.

"Ryu?" she whispered. The dust swirled around her and the Moon threatened to tilt sideways again, but Leiko swallowed hard and forced herself to stay upright. *Come on, girl,* she told herself. *Get your shit together! The dog is trying to tell you something. Figure it out!*

Ryu pulled again with another whine, and Leiko felt herself stumble forward. She managed to catch herself before she spilled onto her face, but Ryu wouldn't let up with either the whining or the pulling, and she had no choice but to hop along as he pulled her toward the heat where the explosion had been. Her balance had been knocked askew by the blast, but she managed to stay upright until Ryu came to a dead stop and stood, quivering in intensity as he stared at a pile of rubble. He let out a short, perfunctory bark.

He's alerting! Ryder!

Leiko fell to her knees, adding two more sharp pains that ricocheted up into her battered body. But she ignored them and began to pull chunks of debris off of the pile with her bare hands. Ryu, too, came and began to dig, his wide, dinner-plate paws causing showers of little stones to go bouncing and rolling away. Eventually, they heard a metal clang, and Leiko traced her fingers along the edge of what had possibly once been a cowling on the convoy vehicle. She took the best grip she could with her bare hands and heaved, lifting with her legs and her back as it inched upward bit by torturous bit. Ryu continued digging at her side, until between the two of them they created a space large enough for him to get his head and front body into.

"Get him out," Leiko grunted, knowing that it wasn't a command that Ryu knew, hoping that he'd understand what she meant anyway. She heard a lot of snuffling and whining, and then Ryu began to back out, haunches first, pulling a dirty, bleeding Ryder with him. Ryu had found Ryder's arm and grabbed it with the helmet's jaw. Somehow, he had managed enough control not to crush Ryder's bones. At least, she hoped that was the case.

Somewhere in the dust, Leiko heard voices.

"Help!" she screamed. "I've got a survivor here! He's hurt! Someone please!"

Someone she didn't know and could barely see stepped forward and grabbed Ryder's free arm as it flopped out of the hole in the debris. Ryu growled softly, but let go and backed up when Leiko gave him the "drop it" command.

"We've got him, ma'am," a voice she didn't recognize said. "You can let that go."

"How many are missing?" she asked.

"We . . . we don't know."

"Get Ryder to the medic. Ryu and I will help you find who's left." She let the former cowling drop with a clang and scrubbed her hands over her face, then bent down and pressed her face to Ryu's helmet.

"Good boy, Ryu," she said. "Now let's find the others."

"It wasn't an accident."

Leiko looked up from the hospital bed where she'd awakened. She and Ryu had searched the rubble, finding eleven more survivors buried under the debris and dust from the disaster. That was the last thing she remembered. Best she could tell, she'd passed out after helping to pull that last survivor free. As far as she knew, those eleven, plus Ryder, Ryu and she herself, were the only survivors of over fifty people at Lock 3 that day.

"Come on, Leiko, I know you're awake," Ryder said from the bed next to her. He reached out and pushed aside the curtain that separated them. "Sit your bed up and talk to me. You've got to talk some sense into the guys at DomeSec. There's no way this was an accident!"

"Why not?" she asked softly. Her ears still rang, though it was getting better. Loud noises tended to cause the ringing to flare up in volume and intensity. "You said yourself that the cab that blew had all the mining demo equipment in it."

"Yes," Ryder said, snorting softly. "But it didn't have the primers, or any of the other components! We don't transport them together because we're not idiots. Someone *rigged* that cab to explode, and we just got very, very lucky."

"Ryder, there's over thirty people dead. I don't think we can call that lucky."

"We can if the alternative is a couple thousand—like the entire population of Rinehart Dome!"

Leiko pressed a button on her control pad and the head of the bed angled upward to a sitting position. "What?"

"Remember what I said right before the blast?" Ryder asked, his bright eyes ringed by lurid bruises. White bandages covered the top of his head and ran down under his chin, and his whole face looked puffy and sore. But none of that seemed to matter to him, so intensely was he looking at her. "That we were running a bit behind schedule?"

"Yeah, so?"

"So, I've done the math. If we had been running on

time, that cab would have blown just as it was passing through the airlock. A blast of that size would have compromised both the inner and outer gates! It would have compromised the entire dome."

"What?" she asked again. "But . . . who would do that? And why, Ryder? There's no motive for that!"

"There's one," he said grimly. "But you might not have heard about it. I only heard myself this morning. The Ueys are here. They've already had skirmishes with a couple of the other domes."

"Skirmishes?"

Ryder nodded. "They demanded entry to Hadley Dome and Lunar Village. And fought when they were denied. They want something they think we have, but they don't know where it is."

"What do they want?"

"I don't know. They haven't come here yet, but with our spaceport, I bet we're not far down the list. And what better way to get inside than to stage an 'accident' and swoop in to 'help'?"

"But that would require them to have a man on the inside," she said.

"Exactly." He nodded slowly. "Someone's playing saboteur."

"You know this sounds like a bad conspiracy theory, right?" She tried to raise her right eyebrow, and winced when the movement made her head start to pound.

"But you believe me." It wasn't a question. Leiko let out a sigh, and then nodded slowly, carefully.

"I believe it wasn't a total accident," she said. "I'll look into it when I get returned to duty."

She'd expected that to mollify him. With his easygoing personality, Ryder wasn't generally one to push. But this time, he shook his head in the negative.

"That's not going to work," he said softly, glancing around before leaning closer to her. "We don't have enough time. If I'm right, we've got to find the saboteur ASAP, otherwise you know they'll try again, and more people will get hurt."

"Can we call them anything else?" she asked, groaning softly as she shifted in her bed. "Perp, or Unsub? I just . . . let's not get overly dramatic until we have to, all right?"

"Fine. Unsub, then. As long as you tell me what it means."

"Unknown subject. Why'd you pick that one if you didn't know what it meant?"

"I like learning new words. Anyway, my point is this: We don't have time to wait for you to be returned to duty. We've got to find the unsub *now.*"

"Okay," she said slowly, scrubbing her hands over her eyes. "Let me think about this. If what you're saying is right, then this individual has access to the components needed to detonate a cab's worth of explosives. And the knowledge to make it happen. That list has to be pretty small, right?"

"Knowledge . . . no." Ryder made a waffling motion with his hand. "A lot of the mining crews have demo experience. Access, though—we keep primers and components locked down pretty tight. And I just did our accountability audit. We're not missing anything. Haven't been since I took over the directorship three years ago."

She looked at him sidelong.

"It's not you, is it?" she asked, mostly joking.

"What? Shit, no!" Ryder said, swearing for the first time in their acquaintance. "How could you think I—?"

"Relax," she said, letting the corners of her mouth lift in a tiny smile. "I don't. I'm just giving you a hard time. Besides, if you'd had residue from working the explosives on you, Ryu would have alerted—" Leiko sat bolt upright, ignoring the piercing, blinding pain that stabbed behind her eyes.

"Where is Ryu?" she asked.

"Your dog?" Ryder shrugged. "I think they took him to the vet. I overheard the nurses talking earlier. He apparently wasn't happy when you went down. He wouldn't let any of the medics approach. Luckily, the first of the other DomeSec guys was on scene by that point and he tranqued him."

Her eyes narrowed.

"Which DomeSec guy?"

"Hollis. The deputy chief."

She should have been surprised. With his all-day conference call, Hollis wouldn't have been in a position to hear the calls on the LMR system. The fact that he was the first guy on scene was weird. She supposed someone could have told him about the emergency, but still, *any* of the other guys should have shown up first.

But she wasn't surprised. Which meant that he'd already piqued her gut's interest. And the fact that *he'd* been the one to take custody of Ryu? Well . . .

"We gotta go," she said, pushing her blankets down to her waist and pulling the IV tube out of the saline lock they'd put in the back of her hand. She swung her legs to the floor and pushed up to her feet, disregarding the way it made her head pound.

"What? Why? What happened?" Ryder asked, blinking rapidly as he fought to catch up.

"You're right. Something is off, and Ryu's the only trained explosive detection dog DomeSec has right now. Hollis hates him, and he shouldn't have been able to get to Lock Three at all, let alone be first on scene."

"Besides you."

"Besides me. So yeah, something is off. Plus, think about this: Hollis has access to explosives components as well. They're part of our mine rescue kits."

"That doesn't make him a saboteur!" Ryder protested. Still, he was out of bed and pulling a T-shirt on over his head. Leiko looked down at her own hospital gown and cursed before she saw the skintight underlayer of her vac suit lying neatly folded on the chair beside her bed. She snatched it up and began pulling it on.

"No, but if he is, and he was near the cab, Ryu will be able to tell, which is why Hollis tranqued him. Think about it. He's a trained moondog handler. Hell, he trained Ryu. Why would he need to tranq him? We have commands and procedures for when a dog's handler is incapacitated. If Hollis is the unsub, then he wants Ryu out of the picture because Ryu is a potential vulnerability! If only we had a ride! We need to get to the vet's ASAP!"

Ryder stared at her, and then grabbed an LMR from his bedside table.

"Trans, Director. Need a cab at the hospital entrance. Now. Perfect. Thanks. Director out."

Leiko paused in the act of buckling her duty belt over the suit and raised her eyebrows. "That was fast."

"When you need something, call a loggie," Ryder said with a ghost of a grin. "Now come on, they'll be here in about thirty seconds."

Rinehart's resident veterinarian, Dr. Taketou, had her own office and clinic. It was conveniently located near the animal husbandry compound, where the moondogs and other lunar variants of Earth animals were bred and tested. Unfortunately for Leiko, this put it across the entirety of the dome from the hospital. And while Rinehart wasn't anywhere near as large as an Earth city, the roads and streets were unusually congested with vehicles.

"It's the 'accident,'" Ryder explained as their driver took yet another detour to avoid gridlocked traffic. "It's thrown all the timetables off and everything is chaos. If your guy really did do this, I'm going to punch him in the face for that alone."

"Warranted," Leiko said, pushing against the seat to avoid sliding into him and aggravating their existing bruising.

Eventually, they arrived at their destination. Dr. Taketou's front office windows were dark, with no sign of movement within. Leiko stepped up to the door and waved her security credentials over the lock. It clicked. She pushed the door open and crept over the threshold.

Inside the darkened reception area, all was still. Leiko turned back over her shoulder and waved to Ryder to follow her. She laid one finger on her lips to caution him

to silence and moved on silent feet to a door emblazoned
with the name CANDACE TAKETOU, DVM.

At first, the office itself looked just as deserted. But just
as Leiko was getting ready to move on, a low, broken
moan drifted out from behind the doctor's heavy wooden
desk. She crept forward just enough to see Dr. Taketou
lying on the floor, her white lab coat askew, a trickle of
blood flowing from her nose to a puddle beneath her
cheek on the carpet. Behind Leiko, Ryder let out a soft
gasp.

"Radio for help and stay with her," Leiko said lowly.
She turned around and grabbed the LMR from Ryder's
slack fingers, then held it up in his eyeline. "Do it, Ryder.
I'll find Hollis."

Her friend nodded, his wide eyes locked on the
sprawled figure of the veterinarian. But he keyed the
LMR's mic and called for immediate medical assistance.
Then he knelt and began to take Dr. Taketou's pulse.

Leiko spun and bounded out into the hallway, then
back toward the double doors that led to the lab/surgery
area. As she approached, she heard a soft, despairing
whine.

She hit the doors full force, throwing them wide with
the impact of her body. She had just a moment to register
the scene: Hollis standing at the operating table, his back
to her, loading a syringe from a small glass vial, Ryu lying
on his side, his brindle tail and feet twitching as he fought
to overcome the fading effects of the tranquilizer that
Hollis had used earlier.

Though mass and power weren't her strength, Leiko
put everything she had into that charge, and she impacted

Hollis from his right side, reaching up to knock the syringe out of his hand as they fell to the ground.

"Get. The. Fuck. Away. From. My. Dog!" Leiko ground the words out between her teeth as she fought to get control of the larger, heavier officer. Despite his initial surprise, Hollis recovered well, grabbing the collar of her suit and using his larger mass to roll and force her down to the floor beneath his weight.

"Soloway," he said, giving her an ugly smile. He moved his forearm up to press against her neck. "Why am I not surprised? Ever since you've arrived, you've been a pain in my ass. You and this damn psycho here. Do you have any idea how excited I was to learn that you were going to be at Lock Three today? Finally, I thought. Finally my problems will solve themselves. Just in time for me to get a fat payout from the Ueys and make my way off this godforsaken rock! Five years of my life, wasted."

"Why didn't you just leave? Why blow up a convoy? Fuck, man, we *talked* about this!" Leiko asked, grunting as his forearm ground down over her throat. From the corner of her eye, she could see Ryu slowly lift his head. *Keep talking, asshole.*

"And do what? Live in poverty back planetside? No thanks. I'm going home, but I'm going home in *style*. I've been killing myself training these stupid dogs . . . thank God for the Mime or whatever it is the Ueys are looking for. I get wind that they're looking for it, I make a call, drop some hints. Guy asks if I can help them out a little bit, and *cha-ching!* There's my chance! St. Tropez, here I come!"

"So you murdered almost fifty people for vacation

tickets?" she gasped. His pressure on her windpipe increased.

"No, you stupid bitch. The convoy was supposed to be in the airlock when it blew! No one would have been hurt if they'd gone on time. But you had to hold the whole thing up flirting with the director. Those dead people are on *your* head. Not mine!" He reared up, pressing down hard enough that she saw stars. At the edge of her hearing, she started to hear a rushing, roaring sound. The need to breathe was a physical pressure, making her mouth gape, her eyes bulge. Blackness closed in from the edges of her vision. The roaring got louder and louder . . .

A missile of fur and teeth hit Hollis from the side, knocking him off of her. The roaring sound of her own blood faded, replaced by Ryu's snarling and growling as he bowled Hollis over onto his back. Unlike his handler, Ryu was well versed in grappling with someone bigger and larger than himself and completely comfortable in lunar gravity. Leiko blinked away the last of the stars and found herself watching with a peculiar detachment as her partner used his great length to reach up and clamp his jaws around Hollis's throat.

"Soloway," Hollis called out, panic soaking his voice. "Call him off!"

"Do it yourself," she whispered, her voice failing her after being strangled. "Oh wait, you can't, can you? Ryu doesn't trust you enough to follow your commands. Huh. I wonder why."

She pushed herself up to a seated position and fumbled at her duty belt for the restraints she kept there. With a steady, grinding stream of growls, Ryu held Hollis perfectly

still while she cuffed him at hand and foot. She'd just
clicked the last binder shut over Hollis's ankle by the time
the doors burst open again and the medical team spilled
in, followed closely by her boss, the Chief of Rinehart
Dome Security.

"Soloway! Hollis! What the hell?" the Chief asked.
Hollis opened his mouth to talk, but Ryu gave a warning
growl and the former deputy chief remained silent.

"He's a Uey plant, sir," Leiko whispered. "He's the one
who caused the demo cab to blow up this afternoon. He
assaulted the doc and strangled me. And if you test the
contents of that syringe, you'll see that he was attempting
to murder K-9 Ryu."

"What? Impossible!" the Chief said. On the floor,
Hollis's breathing accelerated.

"Ryu, release," Leiko said, projecting as much as she
was able. Her partner obediently opened his mouth and
backed away from Hollis, though the low, warning growl
never ceased. "It's true, Chief. Check his message logs and
interview the doc. Hell, check the security footage here.
It sounds crazy, but it all checks out. I'll bet the Ueys just
sent a message offering 'assistance' after the explosion
today, didn't they?"

The Chief blinked, startled. "How did you know that?"

Leiko gave a tiny smile and pushed up to her feet. "Gut
feeling. Check the logs, chief. Interview the doc. I've got
to go take care of my dog."

"So the Chief told them to fuck off?" Leiko asked, her
voice still a ragged whisper. Despite the lingering pain in
her throat, she smiled as she threaded her fingers through

the velvety soft fur between Ryu's ears. The dog thumped his tail once on the hospital bed mattress in response. He laid his head down on Leiko's chest, moving gently enough that he didn't disturb her healing contusions.

"Pretty much," Ryder said, with a small smile of his own. "He told them that we could do very well without any more of their assistance. They, of course, protested that they knew nothing of Hollis's claims, but they'd almost have to say that, wouldn't they?"

"Diplomatic bullshit." Leiko nodded. "So what happens next?"

"Well," Ryder said. "Talks are continuing. I think they'll keep trying to negotiate a way into our dome to look for this thing that they want. None of us know what the hell it is, and if it had come through Rinehart, the distribution center would know about it. Honestly, if they'd just asked, we probably would have let them in to look at whatever they want. But now it's trickier for them, and they know it."

"Think it will come to an open war?"

"Maybe," Ryder said, his voice sobering, his grin disappearing. "It has at other domes. And if it does, I don't know how long we can hold against them. Rinehart's not really a fortified location, not for military purposes."

"No," Leiko said, stroking Ryu's ears. "But it is our home."

"It is. So if the Ueys want to fight, I guess we'll fight. But not today. Today, my good friend Ryu is going to make sure you stay in your bed and rest as you should."

Ryu thumped his tail again, and Leiko snorted a laugh.

"We need you, Leiko. You and Ryu. So rest up, because this might be just the beginning."

THE MIMIC
⊕
by Travis S. Taylor

"... and in other news the Secretary General of the United Nations of Earth Council encouraged the nations of the planet to pass the System Revenues Act, describing it as a small price to pay for the infrastructure Earth governments are supplying to the Lunar, Belt, and Mars businesses and citizens. She stated plainly that, quote, *'it is expedient that new provisions and regulations should be established for improving the revenue of this planet's governments and it is just and necessary that a revenue should be raised for defraying the expenses of defending, protecting, and securing the same so that our extraplanetary citizens' needs are provided for.'*

"In response to Secretary General Carlize's speech Mayor Hamilton of the far side Lunar Colony Aldrinville posted a vlog stating that his citizens would not be taxed without due representation and direct infrastructure funding for his constituents..."

⊕ ⊕ ⊕

"Hey, Jimmy, turn that to the match, will ya? Nobody here wants to hear the Earthers justifying raising our taxes again," a lady sitting near the muffin counter looking over her touchpad said gruffly.

"Hear, hear." David raised his coffee cup and nodded in agreement along with most of the patrons of the coffee shop. David would rather see the soccer match between Luna 11 and Swigert Dome than listen to Earthers excitedly raising taxes on Loonies they'd never met and whom they'd never asked. The teenage barista behind the counter just shrugged and changed the screen.

David Sandeep had been on the Moon for at least two decades now—a citizen of Aldrinville. If he were still on Earth, he would be considered an old man, but as far as lunar geriatrics were concerned, seventy-seven years old was just on the other side of midlife. The lower gravity seemed to take much less toll on your body parts, and it didn't cause wrinkling near as bad as Earth gravity did. He had hoped to live out a long, peaceful life at Luna City in the Luna Village Dome but the rent there had continued to go up and up and finally about five years ago had reached a point that was higher than he had planned on and hadn't fit in his retirement budget. Hence, Aldrinville it was.

Aldrinville was the fifth "official" colony that had been built on the Moon and it had more or less grown out of necessity as a home for the radio astronomers, physicists, and engineers that made pilgrimage to the lunar-crater turned-giant-radio-telescope some kids had built as a reality television project about a decade back. The original colony was nothing more than an inflatable hotel and some buried habitat canisters, but over time the nearby volcanic dome of the Compton-Belkovich region just around the limb on the far side and a bit to the north had been excavated and turned into a habitat dome.

David had always had an interest in the Search for Extra-Terrestrial Intelligence, or SETI as it was often referred to, because of his expertise in language interpretation. He had been a multilinguistic translator for various companies over the years and he had a keen interest in ancient languages. So he had moved to the farthest and most isolated colony on the Moon not only because of the low rent, but because of the people there. Aldrinville was, indeed, the most out of the way, isolated, and least thought about of the present-day thirteen lunar colonies. It was on the far side of the Moon like the more recent colonies Luna 11 and Luna 12. It wasn't a mining effort like Luna 11 and Luna 12, so it was both out of sight and out of mind for the people from Earth not interested in the big radio telescope. That's not to say that there was no mining that took place at Aldrinville, especially in the dome excavation efforts, but the main industry and purpose of Aldrinville was the dish.

Before leaving Earth David had hopes of retiring and sitting in coffee shops chatting about life, taxes in New Delhi, politics, and so on. But after a heart murmur had given him a scare during his daily walk along the banks of the Yamuna River it was time for seriously rethinking his life. The doctors wanted him to have some sort of robot heart surgery—every single one of them except for one: a friend of his brother's who was a geriatrics research physician for the Indian Space Research Organization, ISRO. After having a short glass of wine—that had turned into a tall one—with him at one of his brother's many social gatherings, David was bitten by the "Moonbug."

The research physician had convinced David that, provided he could survive the trip to the Moon, once he got there his heart murmur would no longer be an issue due to the lower gravity and less stress on the body. David hadn't cared for heart surgery, so he decided that if he were going to die it would be on a rocket lunar bound.

That had been almost twenty years ago. At first David had hoped to retire in Luna City spending his time on the Moon sitting in coffee shops chatting about life, taxes on waste product disposal and air scrubbing, lunar colonial politics, and so on all the while he watched the Earth below going on about its Earthly business. After the population and business boom in the Luna Village Dome his plans had been shifted, once again, to sitting in coffee shops of Aldrinville—there were two—and chatting about how one might go about detecting and interpreting some alien signal if one was ever received by the giant crater-sized radio telescope. Such a retirement, David had incorrectly thought, would be uneventful, relaxing, fun, and most importantly free of stress as far as he or his heart were concerned. He might miss seeing the Earth below, but the view of the stars from the far side was unbelievable. He might even consider his coffee shop exolinguistics as a "second career" someday. A second career that was pretty much apropos of nothing and of little interest to most, which was exactly how he wanted it.

He did somewhat miss the walks along the toxic-foam-covered banks of the Yamuna, and watching birds fly about, but he didn't miss the sweltering summers or the threat of dying from heart failure or a stroke. The temperature in the Aldrinville domes was always a perfect twenty-two degrees Celsius and there were the occasional cargo and passenger spaceships flying over to the port near the North Dome that were way more interesting to watch than any birds. For all intents and purposes his retirement was good.

Then, his "retirement" had come to an abrupt halt—an unexpected very sudden abrupt halt. And his second career had suddenly become immediately apropos and highly stressing. David had been sitting in the usual coffee shop discussing the finer points of ancient glyphs and modern computer algorithms with one of the "usuals," Carla Pruitt, a post-doc mathematician from Tycho State, when a team of miners had come in from the west volcanic dome excavation project. David had seen them in the shop before and sort of knew them—mostly he knew their faces. They usually had talked about finding riches like diamonds or obsidian or in one case thorium and uranium ores on their various excursions across the volcanic expanse, but not this time. This time it was something else, something that had them spooked.

"Hey, fellas." David nodded over his coffee cup. "Find anything new today?"

"You wouldn't believe it if we told ya," one of them replied. David recognized the man as one of the newer shift workers who had just come in from Luna 8 down near the South Pole Dome.

"Shut up, Thomas! We ain't s'posed to be talking about that," his older companion and most likely his crew chief scolded him. David knew the man. He'd been in and out of the coffee shop for about as long as David had, and he always went to the counter when they called the name "Jerry." The workers from the construction and excavation crews always stood out in their light gray coveralls that had retroreflective orange stripes between the ankles and knees on both legs and from wrist to elbow on both arms.

"Seriously, Jerry? Who would believe us anyway?" the new recruit scoffed at his boss in return. "I'll talk about whatever the Hell I want to talk about."

"We signed nondisclosures, idiot, and there are a lot of ears and eyes in here," Jerry continued. "You want to keep your job and keep gettin' paid you'll shut your trap."

And that was the end of it as far as David knew. The foreman Jerry had shut his man up and that was that. David respected nondisclosure agreements and getting paid. In his former life as a translator he often had signed nondisclosures and had heard and said things he could never repeat without heavy financial, and sometimes criminal, penalties. On the other hand, it did leave David very curious as to what was going on, but it also sounded like added stress that had little to do with a relaxing retirement plan of drinking coffee, looking at the stars, and chatting up new, attractive even, post-docs. David finished his conversation and his cup of coffee and returned to his quarters. There was an encrypted video email waiting for him.

"Hello, Dr. Sandeep. I am Aldrinville Dome Mayor Alton Hamilton. Approximately seventy-two hours ago a mining and construction crew on the west excavation project discovered..."

✦ ✦ ✦

"As you may or may not know, Dr. Sandeep . . ." The LoonieCart II driver, Ken, according to the name on his coveralls, was talking like a tour guide nodding and waving his arms about. The bright orange retroreflective stripes on his yellow hard hat and gray sleeves fluoresced as they drove past the LED work lights placed along the excavation road every twenty or so meters.

"The volcanic dome on the west side of the caldera of what must have been, according to lunar geologists, a volcano a billion years ago has to be at least over a kilometer across and made this natural giant cavern we call West Aldrinville now. All the natural domes around the caldera you already know as North Aldrinville and East Aldrinville. There have been no attempts as of yet to excavate anything on the south side."

David just nodded knowingly as he white-knuckled the "oh-shit handle" over the passenger-side bubble door as the gray lunar tunnel walls zipped by only a couple meters to his right. The gravel made a continuous crunching noise that was the perfect base tone for the oscillating high pitch whine of the electric wheel motors and the *thump-thumpi*ng sound coming from his heart beating out of his chest. The driver must have been down that particular path so many times that driving it was second nature to him. At what David was certain was top speed for the LoonieCart II they approached what looked like a sheer lunar volcanic obsidian wall in front of them when suddenly, and unannounced, the driver pulled the rear brake handle and put power to the front right wheel. Gray dust sprayed about as the buggy slid into almost a perfect ninety-degree turn.

"Some of it was filled in over the eons and some not,"

Ken continued his tour-guiding, barely looking at the road. David continued to hang on so tightly that he thought he'd lose feeling in his fingers. "But as you can see from all the work we've done here as the excavation and repurposing of the natural volcanic dome has continued over the years, more and more of the structure we are exposing—well, it just doesn't look natural, does it? Almost as if it had been previously excavated and maybe even structurally shored up in places—see over there?" He pointed at the very high ceiling of the cavern they were entering. "We didn't do that."

"Uh-huh." David only nodded, not about to loosen his grip on the handle. "Really, if we didn't do it . . ."

"Yeah, that long lunar obsidian beam. That thing's got to be thirty meters long, several meters thick on each side and must weigh millions of kilograms! It is one big, long beam that looks to have been cut, poured, or who in the Hell knows how it was built, but no geologist has been able to explain it away by a natural process."

"Fascinating," David muttered through his gritted teeth.

"Yeah, and then there's this . . ."

Ken whipped the buggy around a spoils pile to the left of the path, almost bringing it up on two wheels, and then slid to a halt. The buggy rocked forward and back several times as the springy suspension damped the momentum of the abrupt stop. Lunar regolith and dust glittered like fireflies all about them in the light as it settled slowly in the low gravity. The driver was looking at David and then back in the direction of the headlights and then back at David with a big smile on his face.

It took a second for David's eyes to adjust to the lighting. When they did, he could see a giant megalithic archway that David thought was most certainly made of the same lunar volcanic obsidian-type material that was so black it was almost blue. The arch was at least ten meters wide and twice that tall. David's jaw dropped. There were strange, ancient glyph markings all around the entrance, and as his eyes continued to adjust to the scale of the opening he could see a tunnel leading inward and downward at what looked to be a shallow angle of about ten degrees.

"What the bloody Hell?"

"My sentiments exactly, Doc."

"Why'd we stop? Do we walk from here?"

"Ha-ha! Walk? Nope, we're a good half a kilometer out. I just wanted you to be able to take all this in before we venture down to 'the belly of the beast,' as they say."

"Wait, a half a kilometer? The dome is only about a kilometer across." David was confused. "Come on, Ken, it can't be that big. We have to be at the west edge of the dome by now already."

"We're not going farther out, Doc. We're going downward at this point. The tunnel here sort of corkscrews down a bit and then turns back south in sort of a dogleg. You'll see. Hang on, though, 'cause it is a little bit bumpy from here."

The ride down the tunnel was anything but "a little bumpy." The excavation machines had left huge tracks pressed into the regolith and there were rocks from cave-ins eons old that had been crushed up by tunnel borers and left as detritus strewn about. The walls of the tunnel appeared in most places to have been cut out of the Moon with precision, but in others there seemed to be natural caverns that opened up around them that whoever had built the place had made use of. It was along these more natural spaces where the cave-ins and stray materials were scattered. After about seven complete loops on the corkscrew they turned out of the descent like exiting a parking garage right onto a turnpike within a passageway that made the Chunnel on Earth look like a toy train's tunnel. Finally, the tunnel stopped at what appeared to be a solid wall ahead of them a good fifty meters.

There were floodlights spraying fluorescent white against the gray floor and black walls. Several vehicles moved around, one zipped past them heading the direction they'd just come from—and there must have been thirty or more people scurrying about. One of them David recognized as Jerry from the coffee shop a few days before.

David was doing his best to take all of it in, but the fact that they were looking at artificial structures inside the Moon that had to be ancient and certainly weren't man-made was beginning to register in his mind. He was looking at something actually built by people that didn't come from Earth or people that lived on Earth long before the present civilization had.

"Alright, Doc, this is it." Ken uncharacteristically slowed the buggy down and parked it cautiously before bouncing out. "Follow me."

"One helluva door, Mr. Mayor." David looked up from his computer pad to shake the politician's hand as he approached. David had pretty much been in front of that door for two weeks doing his best to decipher the glyphs on the wall with hopes of gaining entrance into whatever was on the other side of it. So far, he had made only a little progress. Very. Little. Progress.

"Dr. Sandeep, I hope you have figured something out and we can open this sucker up soon? Not sure how much longer we can keep this thing quiet and the press will become a nightmare. And then the damned Ueys will probably try to tax us with a finder's fee before they try to confiscate whatever is in there."

"Short of blasting it"—David scratched at the back of his head and made a sour face—"not really, no progress as of yet. Well, if you don't count that I think they don't have an alphabet."

"Don't listen to him, Mr. Mayor. Since David got down here we've uncovered a basis for their language." Carla Pruitt, the mathematician and friend of David's who'd also been brought in on the project, offered her hand to the politician.

"You mean you have discovered their alphabet?" the mayor asked as he turned back to David.

"No alphabet," David grunted and started to explain before being interrupted.

"I wouldn't say 'alphabet,' sir," Carla said. David had worked with the lady for a couple weeks now and realized that she spoke up whether it was politely her turn to or not. He actually liked that about her. Had he been twenty or thirty years younger he might just have been an intriguing older man to her, but as it currently stood, well, he knew he was the *old* man of the group. But one never knew what others might think of as old, especially in a frontier like the far side of the Moon.

"Whoever these people were, their language was more character or symbol based, I believe. More like ancient Egyptian, Mandarin, or Japanese perhaps. Not sure yet." David pointed at a couple of characters on the wall about a meter to the right of the giant door. "These symbols here, at first I thought it was a symbol for our solar system. See how there is a central point with multiple concentric rings about it? The fact that they are circles rather than ellipses like planetary orbits threw me. But Sarah, over there, one of the physicists, pointed out how it looks like a molecule with multiple atoms bonded together. See these overlapping rings here and how there are two planetoids only in the intersecting ring? This is some polymer or other thing that apparently all chemists and physicists know about."

"Covalent bond," Carla added.

"Yeah, that." David nodded. "Been a while since high school chemistry."

"Why is that on the wall by the door?" the mayor asked. "Is it a textbook or something?"

"Damn good question." David shrugged. "Sarah, over there, again, she's a physicist, well, she thinks this is telling us what's in this room. Like, there's an x-ray symbol on the door at a hospital x-ray room or a toxic chemical symbol on a storage cabinet in a lab. At least that's what she says. I've never personally been in a lab with toxic chemicals."

"So, she thinks this is a polymer or whatever room?" The mayor looked as confused as the rest of the team had been.

"I don't think so. I think it is more like a chemistry room or a place where molecules were made or reacted or something. I've asked her what molecule this is and she says it isn't anything she's ever heard of before. If we could just find the open switch we could go in there and look."

"Hmmm. Keep trying."

"Right."

"What I want to know is who told them we found something down there!" Mayor Alton Hamilton wasn't quite shouting at the young female face on his monitor but it was as close as a politician could get to shouting and get away with it. "Damn it!"

"I don't know, Mr. Mayor. Perhaps it was one of the workers."

"Find out who it was and clamp this down!" Alton pointed out the window of his office at the West Dome. "All we need is the Earthers trying to make claims on whatever it is we find in there. Whether it's worthless or priceless we need that dome to expand the city into. If the damned Earthers try to make claims we might be in court forever over ownership and their pockets are waaay deeper than Aldrinville's are. Then on top of that the bastards will tax us for it somehow!"

"Understood, Mr. Mayor. Who should we put on this to track it down?" the young lady asked.

"I have a thought. Get Benny and Nathaniel in here ASAP." Alton paused and thought.

"Nathaniel I understand, sir. But, you sure you can trust Benjamin?"

"I can trust Benny to be out for Benny. As long as I know that going in, well, I won't get any hopes dashed," the mayor explained. "Where are you right now, Tami?"

"I'm at North Dome. There's some kind of skirmish over here about the Earthers taxing any outbound shipment and some of the locals are protesting and picketing the port authority."

"Goddamnit, this is getting out of hand. The damned Earthers are treating us like secondhand citizens. History repeats itself."

"Yes sir, it does."

"We have to get into that room before they decide to come up here. Put somebody else on that uprising and get over here. I need my top cop."

"Yes sir."

"Benny, come in and have a seat." Alton eyed his old campaign manager slash enforcer slash whatever the hell needed to be done guy as he entered. Benny used to be his right-hand, under-the-table guy, but that had been many years and millions of dollars since. "You know Nathaniel."

"Nate, how the hell are you?" Benjamin Atkins took the man's hand in a strong handshake. Seeing the two men brought back memories of them marching from hab to hab in Aldrinville convincing residents that they needed to be a full-fledged colony with an elected leader and council. Alton had heard rumors that Benny had strong-armed or paid some of the would-be citizens into agreeing but he could never prove it. He hadn't tried to find evidence that hard either. Some things were just better left undiscovered.

"Fellas, I'm not sure if you've met but this is Captain Tamika Jones, sheriff of Aldrinville." Alton nodded to Tami.

"Never met but seen her on the vids." Nathaniel Ray smiled. "Nice to meet ya."

"Likewise sir. And I have to say I really like your company's blond ale," Tami added.

"Yes, one of our big sellers," Nathaniel shook her hand.

"Alright, so, let's get down to it." Alton sat back in his maroon leather executive chair and placed his hands on the oak desk in front of him. The chair only briefly squeaked as he wriggled himself into a comfortable position. He reveled for a brief moment as to how much it cost to get that thing on the far side of the Moon. "What do you know about the West Dome excavation?"

"Only what I've seen on the news, Al. What's all this about?" Nathaniel looked sincere. Benny had remained quiet and that suggested to Alton that he knew something. Benny always had his eyes and ears open for what was really going on and where the next quick fortune would be made. That reason alone was why Alton kept him on call, always.

"Benny?"

"I know that one of the construction companies I'm a shareholder of and on the board for was suddenly given a hold-work order and their guys are sitting idle and not getting paid." Benny crossed his legs and made himself more comfortable. "I also know that there is something going on there that you, Mr. Mayor, don't want the Earthers to know about."

"And why is that, Benny?" Alton raised an eyebrow.

"I did a little checking. I noted all the work crews that were stopped had Earthers in them. The few crews that are still working, well . . ."

"I see."

"What's going on here, Alton?" Nathaniel was clearly in the dark. That meant he hadn't been talking to anybody, which in turn meant he could likely still be trusted. But Benny had connections that might be useful in the near future if things with the Ueys went south.

"Fellas, a few weeks ago while excavating the West Dome, we found something," he started. "Something very old and not built by us."

"Holy shit . . ." Nathaniel whispered. "Not us, then who?"

"Exactly, Nate," Alton continued, "There is some kind of ancient habitat or construction down there. And there's a room that has this big-ass door we haven't been able to get open yet. But I'll bet you a dozen donuts that there is something big just waiting for us. *US!* I mean for Loonies not Earthers. We found it. It belongs to us. It could be something worth trillions or something worthless that Earthers will still pay billions to see. As long as we maintain ownership."

"Now I see why I am here, Al." Benny smiled. "You need me to run a smoke screen and to find out what the Earthers already know."

"You got it." Alton looked over at Tami. "Keep your hands clean, Benny. And don't put me or Tami in any precarious predicaments like back in Luna Eight."

"Al, that was no predicament. That was, um, necessary."

"Well, we need to keep the Earthers' grubby paws off whatever we find here," Alton said.

"So, you're speaking out of both sides of your mouth," Benny said, expressionless. "Do what is necessary or not?"

Alton decided the best response was silence and a nod.

⊕ ⊕ ⊕

"Sarah, why is it, you think, that there is no freakin' doorknob on this thing?" David Sandeep had been studying the glyphs and symbols of the ancient, maybe alien, language for more than a month and was getting quite frustrated at the fact that all he seemed to be able to do was stare at the giant basalt-and-obsidian door and wish it would open. The mayor had been pressuring them to make progress and it was clear to David that for whatever reason there was time pressure to their work.

"Perhaps they didn't use doorknobs." Dr. Sarah Rollin shrugged. "Maybe doorknobs are a human thing. Or maybe they evolved beyond them. I mean, your quarters door has no knob per se."

"Well, it has a wireless key connected to my biomarker, which is kind of a knob," David argued.

"But David, you're making my point for me." Sarah smiled. She was a bit older than Carla the mathematician and could at least be his granddaughter. At almost six feet tall with short bobbed black hair and three blue teardrop tattoos at the corner of her right eye, David saw her as quite fetching. She was still very young, but fetching. "Yes, you have a metaphorical, or more precisely a virtual, doorknob, but no physical doorknob."

"I get that, but why can't we figure out what the virtual doorknob is? There's no instructions or information here anywhere about it." David was still perplexed.

"Wait, what'd I miss?" Carla said as she and Jerry entered from the shadows behind the floodlights, each carrying two cups of coffee.

"David wants to know why there are no instructions on how to open this door here anywhere," Sarah recapped.

"Shit, man, are there instructions on the door to your apartment, or the men's room, or Hell, any door you've ever seen? I mean, we've been using doors for thousands of years probably. Hell, who even invented the door or doorknob?" Jerry handed David a cup with his name on it. David nodded graciously and took a long pull from it. The aroma of the steamy black coffee stimulated him only enough to want more. So he took another longer sip, this time burning his tongue.

"Careful, man, it's still very hot," Jerry said as a throw away joke.

"Uh, thanks." David grinned. "Okay, no door user's manual. Alright, then. We have to find the keyhole, the knob, or whatever ancient alien analog there is."

"Well, I say, I just go get the big rig down here and ram the sucker." Jerry shrugged. "How thick do we think this thing is? A foot, two, more?"

"It would be a shame to destroy the door, and what if we triggered some sort of collapse or cave-in?" Carla looked over David's shoulder at the tablet displaying the glyphs around the door. "I just don't think we're ever going to solve this thing. Look, I mean, even the picture of the molecule here is incomplete."

"Incomplete? What d'ya mean?" David truly was out of his element and high school chemistry had been a very very long time ago. "My uh, chemistry is a little rusty."

"This isn't high school chemistry," Carla continued. "I am a mathematician, so you're thinking why do I know it? Well, my master's thesis was on numerical analysis of the complex molecular dynamics in long chain polymer synthesis methods. That just means that the way we synthesize polymers like plastics, and some modern nanocomposite metamaterials, is in a lot of cases magic. Well, I worked out some detailed computer models using various numerical methods that allowed me to predict the most likely outcome of a particular synthesis method and what type of polymer chain mess it would make."

"All I got was blah blah mess blah chains blah." Jerry waved his hands about.

"Not really my gig, Carla, but I know what polymer synthesis and such is," Sarah replied. "So what does that have to do with the pictures here not being complete?"

"Well, look at this covalent bonded molecule here by the door." She pointed at the glyphs that were originally mistaken as planetary orbits. "This is the bond between two atoms, or maybe more but it is hard to say because, where are the rest of the atoms? Just to the right here there are multiple blobs of different sizes about each other that might be confused as constellations against the sky beyond these orbital things. But if I take a marker and connect them all, guess what?"

Carla took a red felt-tip dry-erase pen from the duty white board and started marking on the grayish-black wall, connecting the dots in a particular way. The red barely showed with enough color against the lunar obsidian to discern where she had marked but it was enough.

"Holy shit!" Sarah nodded, understanding what she was looking at. "It's a long-chain polymer. But why these other dots?"

"That's just it, Sarah. No polymers are really just two-dimensional long chains. They are almost always twisted up around each other like a pile of spaghetti. What if these dots here are the ends that we are looking down on? But, where are the others? Where is the spaghetti?"

"Damn." Jerry smiled back at all of them. "You keep talking about spaghetti and we're gonna have to break for lunch."

"I'm with Jerry here," David said. He was confused and had no idea what Carla and Sarah were going on about. "So what? They didn't draw all the molecules in perfect order on a block wall damned near as hard as diamonds."

"That is just it, David." Sarah turned to him following Carla's agreeing nods. "Everything else on this wall looks precisely drawn. Look at any ancient glyph or character. Slight changes in them might change the meaning of the character. We looked at these things with extremely high resolution and the edges of each character and line are pristine, precise, and exact."

"So, then . . ." David still wasn't there yet.

"So, whoever made these made them precise and most likely they are very accurately depicting something. Something complicated. Maybe even something we don't understand," Carla said.

"Oh, I see, but . . ." David wasn't really sure he saw. "Then what exactly is missing and where is it?"

"I don't know." Carla shrugged. "But I'm telling you, we're not seeing the whole intent of these glyphs."

"Not seeing? Or not understanding?" Jerry asked.

"Does it matter?" David dismissed Jerry's questions as if they meant the same things.

"Well, I don't understand it exactly, but I know when we are mining in the darkest tunnels we can illuminate the walls with an ultraviolet lamp and we'll find certain gemstones. They uh, glow sometimes," Jerry explained. "So, we have lamps put on the head of the drilling rigs that we can change the colors of."

"Fluorescence, phosphorescence, refraction, sure, that makes sense to me," Sarah said. "You think this thing might glow in the dark?"

"Infrared!" Carla snapped her fingers. "Do we have any infrared cameras or goggles anywhere?"

"Of course!" Sarah slapped her palm to her forehead. "IR spectroscopy! That's how we look at polymers to find the types of hydroxyl groups, double bonds, and various other parts of the molecules."

"I've got an IR mask with a digital output in the mini excavator." Jerry turned from them. "I'll be right back."

"So, David, you have done it?" The mayor looked excited, nervous, and tired all at the same time. David had seen some of the news boards in what little time he'd had to himself. The tax issues between the Earther companies and the Loonie ones were getting worse. Three mayors including Mayor Hamilton, and two governors of the thirteen lunar colonies had signed an accord proclaiming that those five colonies would not accept nor allow Earth company ships charging taxes on any export cargo to land at their ports whether they were bringing needed goods or not. It must have been weighing heavy on his shoulders.

"Well, it wasn't really me, Mr. Mayor." David cleared his throat sheepishly. "Carla was the one who realized that there was something missing about the wall."

"That so, Dr. Pruitt?" Mayor Hamilton gave the post-doc mathematician a politician's smile.

"Well, I realized that we were missing something and then Sarah figured out that we needed to look at the wall in the infrared spectrum," Carla replied. "But we weren't expecting what we found."

"And that would be what exactly?" Hamilton asked.

"Well, we realized that the people, the...eh, the whatevers that built this place, saw deeply into the infrared spectrum and so our human eyes just simply aren't seeing all the artwork on the walls."

"Or the doorknob," Jerry butted in. David almost laughed as Jerry added, "Um, we found the doorknob, Mr. Mayor."

David could see it on the mayor's face that he wasn't completely getting the gist of what they were telling him. Thinking about it, none of them truly did either until they put the infrared work goggles on. It was one thing to think about seeing through a completely different rainbow spectrum and a totally other thing to actually see it, experience it, and perceive what is meant by things in that range of lower energy level light.

"Here sir, put these on." Sarah handed the mayor a pair of goggles that looked just like the ones that they all had propped up on their foreheads. "See this button here? Hold it down once you get the goggles fit over your eyes and the spectrum will shift to the infrared."

David watched as Mayor Hamilton slid the goggles down and from his body language could tell that the mayor was just as flabbergasted as they had been the first time. Hell, David was pretty sure he reacted that way every single time he turned the goggles on. So, he slid his goggles down, pressed the button, and once again was put in awe as the room seemed to light up with icons and two-dimensional drawings of three-dimensional objects. By the door was an outlined circle glowing in the false orange color of the IR goggles. Within the circular placard were two handprints that looked like human hands but had much longer, much skinnier fingers with almost no palm area. One hand pointed upward while the other pointed downward.

"It's an elevator door," Mayor Hamilton stated as he reached out and depressed the downward pointing hand. It lit up and then a shimmer in the doorway appeared. "Holy Hell!"

"You think that's crazy, Mr. Mayor? Slip your goggles up and look at the door," Jerry told him.

David did the same just to see the look on the mayor's face.

"There's no opening?"

"Oh, it is there, sir. But somehow or other only the visible light bounces off it and the infrared goes right on through. It's a perfect way to camouflage a doorway that you wouldn't want people who see in the visible to find," David explained. "That suggests that they knew about humans and our eyesight range."

"Is it safe to go in?" Hamilton asked.

"Oh yes. We found some very interesting things," Sarah said nonchalantly. That surprised David because he didn't feel there was anything nonchalant about the entire ordeal. "Mostly, it looks like the place was abandoned or vacated a long time ago."

"Vacated?" The mayor seemed disappointed. "Abandoned?"

"Well, there is a piece of, um, equipment I guess you'd say that was either too big to move, or so cheap they didn't care to leave it behind," David added.

"And what is it?"

"No idea. We just found it yesterday."

"Show me."

"Tami, I think it's time we start a bit of subterfuge with the Earthers. Somehow by now, and Benny will figure out what they know through his channels, Earthers must have got wind of us finding an alien gadget up here," Alton said. He and Nate sat across a tall barroom table from Tamika. Nate owned a pub in almost every colony and each of them had a special room in the back only ever used for "business talks."

"Good idea, Alton." Nate sipped at one of his local brews and looked to be in deep thought. "I could start some rumors through the pub circuit. We'd just need to know what rumors to start."

"And I could have an update briefing sent to all the colony security services," Tami agreed. "I think we start by implying that we've moved whatever it is we leak that was found."

"Where did we move it to?" Alton thought out loud. "It would have to be a complicit colony."

"Shawna at Luna Thirteen?" Nate suggested. "She's always been on the Free Luna side of things."

"Too much and too small as of now. The place needs to be big enough and far enough away that if the Ueys go there we'll have time to react here." Alton tapped at his personal data engine tattoo and the three-dimensional projector kicked on. He spun some icons about until a map of the Moon with dots for the colonies appeared before them. "Let's see just where should we send this thing."

"Luna City is plenty big enough," Tami suggested. "Politically, though, I think they're still on the fence because of all the Earther tourist money."

"I don't know, Tami, what I'm hearing through the grapevine is that the business owners are getting tired of the cargo import to export ration being too far out of whack. And now with this new tariff," Nate looked over to Alton and shrugged. "You see this beer? It is damned near perfect. The color is a beautiful gold, fragrance is strong but not pungent, and the taste is just on the edge of ale to bitter. It should be making me millions in sales back to Earth, but the import fees on some of the ingredients plus the export fees on getting it back to Earth makes it profit on the margins. Depending on port fees, some quarters gain, some lose. Guess where I make it?"

"Luna City?" Tami asked.

"Luna City," Nate confirmed. "I've had several discussions with the Town Council about it and the governor is starting to listen. It's just the damned hotel cartels make so much damned money and are keeping the lobby up."

"Luna City isn't right yet." Alton held up a hand. "Not there."

"My younger brother runs a diamond mine down at Luna Eight," Tami said. "You have good relations with the mayor there."

"Luna Eight, the miners buy a lot of the pilsners down there." Nate held up his schooner. "I funded a lot of the mayor's campaign."

"Luna Eight." Alton held up his glass. The three tapped schooners gently and drank on it. "So who's gonna slip up and leak the info to Benny? He's terrible at poker. He has to think it's the truth."

"What are they gonna do with it, Benny?" the assistant to the Undersecretary of State for Lunar Commerce asked quietly over the beer mug before taking a long swig and in response making a screwed-up face from the taste. Benny almost laughed. Luna Pale Ales took some getting used to.

"The Loonies like their ales very pale and very hoppy. Makes the ones coming from India back in the day pale in comparison." Benny laughed at his own pun and noted how his brother-in-law had failed to catch it. "They have to be that way, though. The super hoppiness and high alcohol content keeps the beer good for very long periods of time. We either constantly produce it or make a big batch and store it. Some think it's cheaper to do the latter. I just know that I've made a serious amount of loot selling LPAs back to you Earthers."

"The artifact, Benny?"

"Oh, yeah, well, I dunno. What are they gonna do with it? Hell, James, I'm not even sure they know exactly what it does yet. Alton really wouldn't even like the fact that I'm telling you about it right now."

"Well, the Loonies can't keep it for themselves you know." James-Phillipe Sergeant took a second taste of the pungent lunar beverage. "Do they not serve wine here?"

"Certainly, but mostly only the tourists and nonlocals drink that stuff in here. You want to stand out? I'll order you a nice chardonnay from California."

"I see. Skip it." The assistant to the undersecretary forced himself to sip at the mug.

"I'm not sure how the Earth governments are going to keep the lunar governments from keeping it to themselves." Benny smiled. "Finders keepers and all that."

"No way that will go over with the UNE. The tension over the taxes on the import cargo is bad enough. If Mayor Hamilton tries to keep this for himself there will be Hell to pay," James-Phillipe replied.

"Now just hold on, James, what kinda Hell are we talkin' about?" Benny never liked the idea of physical actions if there was a way to steer a situation toward making money. "There's bound to be a way we can all make hay here."

"Between you and me and this godawful liquid, the secretary general has had enough of the colonies and he has the backing of the driving interests of the Security Council." James leaned back and sat the mug down as if he couldn't take it any longer or as though it were a chess piece and he was declaring checkmate—or submitting.

"Does that include the United States?"

"It most certainly does."

"Well, that changes things, don't it?" Benny rubbed at his chin briefly in thought but wasn't sure what his best play would be. He knew that Mayor Hamilton wasn't going to give up the "thing," especially if the Earthers wanted it so badly. There was a play, but he just couldn't put his finger on it yet. The big issue was where he wanted to be standing if the UNE backed by the Big Three of the Security Council showed up looking for a fight.

"Benjamin, my friend." James-Phillipe opened his hands wide, cocked his head sideways slightly, gesturing with a come-here motion of his fingertips. It was clear that James wanted Benny to trust him. "We've known each other some time now, brother-in-law. You and my sister do not need to get caught up in the things that are to come. Have you considered an exit strategy from this place? My sister would like to see grass and sky again someday. Can you tell me the exact location of this thing, Benjamin?"

"You ask a question I'm not sure I know the answer to." Benny put on his best poker face, picked up his mug and chugged the rest of the lunar pale ale down. He also thought about moving back to Earth. He wasn't sure that was physiologically possible any longer. He'd been on the Moon for a decade or more and at that point without serious fitness efforts it would be difficult to go back to a six-times-larger gravity field. His wife on the other hand had treated every day they'd lived there like a visit, she had worked out and prepared for a return home religiously. Benny was torn by the situation. He had maintained political loyalty to Alton for years. But James was family. It wouldn't hurt to tell him what he knew for now. "James-Phillipe, all I know is that the mayor had it moved down to Luna Eight to keep it away from the port squabble going on here at Aldrinville."

⊕ ⊕ ⊕

"I'm telling you, Alton, the Earthers are planning something. My guys in the cargo union are telling me that they've been given extra leave hours with directions that they had to use them within the next four weeks. There is more going on here than we know." Alton Hamilton listened to his friend Nathaniel Ray go on and on about the impending doom, but Nate had always been like that. He mostly based his fortune-telling on the waxing and waning of his alcohol sales. In the end, he was actually a pretty good prognosticator.

"Nate, just what kind of *something* could the Earthers be planning?" Alton shrugged. "It takes two days for any transport to get from the Earth to the Moon and we'd know they were coming. Besides, we don't have any army up here anyway."

"That's my point, Al," Nathaniel replied. "We are a soft target."

"Well, shit, I never thought of it like that."

"One good incursion force and they could be down there and grab that thing before we could do jack about it." Nate always oversold his concerns, but this time Alton thought his friend might be right. "If only that damned alien elevator had a security code on it."

"Could you put one on it?" Nate asked.

"I don't know. Why not?"

Nate only shrugged.

"We need a security plan, militia, police, something . . ." Alton stopped mid-sentence and tapped a button on his desk monitor. "Tamika, get in here to my office as soon as you can."

⊕ ⊕ ⊕

"It's something the mayor wants," the construction team foreman was telling Jerry as David approached the "elevator." But the construction work had it blocked off a good ten meters. Metal walls were going up with lunar concrete being mixed and poured into monolithic upright forms.

"What is going on, Jerry?" David asked.

"Security barrier is being constructed and we'll all be given access codes and biometric identity badges," Jerry explained. "Apparently, the mayor ordered it. So, I guess we get a couple days off."

"Huh, reckon why he decided on that?"

Carla and Sarah had decided not to take the few days off while the construction crew was building the security barrier and door system for the mayor. Instead, they'd decided to go for a drive. As it had turned out, it was a long drive—a very long drive.

"Let's stop here and put out another geophone," Sarah radioed to Carla. She was white-knuckling the open top buggy as they spun along the edge of a small crater west of Aldrinville. The basaltic-looking rocks mixed in with the lunar soil was a unique visual mix of shiny black and silver flashes in the sunlight. As the buggy came to a rolling stop some of the regolith dust hung in the air in a slowly developing arc. The sunlight glittered through it and split into rainbows at various angles.

"That's pretty," Carla marveled at the diffracted light as she worked her fingers. "Some drive."

"Well, we needed to do it," Sarah agreed with a nod

of her suit helmet. "I'll place this one. You set the coordinates for it in the computer."

"I got it." Carla reached over to the back stowage and slid the tablet out of its cubby. With the tactile fingertips of her suit's gloves she started working through the menu of the software to log in their current lunar coordinates as the location for geophone number seventeen. "I wouldn't have thought we'd have to come out this far."

"Tell me if you get the signal," Sarah told her. "Yeah, what are we, a hundred and fifty kilometers now?"

"Hey, Luna, how far are we from Aldrinville West Dome?" Carla asked.

"You are currently two hundred and thirty-one point three kilometers from Aldrinville West Dome," the tablet responded.

"Seriously?"

"Yes, I am always serious, Carla," the tablet added.

"I got it, Sarah. It just popped up." Carla tapped at a few pull-down menus and then sat the tablet back in the cubby. "This has to be enough of them."

"Can you see the thumper?" Sarah asked.

"Oh, I don't know. I already put the computer back. We've been out a good while. Wanna head back?"

"Sure. I suspect David will flip when he realizes what we've discovered." Sarah climbed into the passenger seat and strapped in. "Some brilliant insight of yours there."

"I don't know about brilliant, but somebody had to ask the question." Carla stepped on the accelerator slowly and turned the buggy pointed eastward.

"What question is that?"

"Where exactly the alien stuff *is*?" she answered. "We've just taken for granted that it's right under the elevator door."

"Yeah, I always had," Sarah agreed.

"Well, now we can measure it exactly."

David scratched his head with his left hand as he extended the computer tablet with his right. His right arm was just about getting too short for him to continue reading the screen without help, especially in the dim visible lighting of the Artifact Room. A couple months prior his only worries were if there'd be somebody at the coffee shop to shoot the shit with while he wasted away his retirement.

Had they not found the dang alien printer whatsit and had he not been an expert at linguistics maybe, just maybe he might have made it through the first interplanetary war unscathed. In fact, David was pretty sure that he might not have ever even been involved had he not just happened to be in the right place at the right time, or perhaps it was the wrong place at the right time, or even perhaps the right place at the wrong time. It made his head ache trying to figure it out, but whichever the case it was, he felt as if he were pretty much screwed.

David had spent more than three months now studying the *artifact, object, thing,*whatever. He was never happy with what to call it. He wasn't much of an engineer, but he had tinkered with cars and motorcycles and an occasional busted blender earlier in his life, so he wasn't mechanically inept, either. Besides, he had scientists, engineers, technicians, and even excavation crews to fall back on even though most of them were lunar mining or construction oriented; in some fashion or other they were all learned. As it had turned out, once they had uncovered the full set of marks David truly was the most suited for deciphering the instructions, if that's what they were, that were written all over the device.

The Object was tall; it was at least four meters high. It was about a meter and a half on one of its horizontal dimensions and a good seven meters in the other dimension. In visible light it looked dull and almost like an odd-shaped mechanical device constructed of smooth bluish-black obsidian-like materials. But with the infrared goggles on it was vibrant and had all sorts of writings, drawings, depression- or membrane-type controls, and other mechanisms that would be completely missed by the naked human eye.

David had overheard one of the engineers saying something like, "It appears to be able to print out things in large pieces, maybe even a full two meters cubed."

Which was really freaking big. But appearances could be deceiving also. As far as he was aware nobody had yet to get the thing to print anything.

It wasn't like the desk 3-D printer that he had in his apartment to print out small devices and tools that a person might need for everyday life on the Moon. In fact, if David had needed anything larger than a spatula printed out he'd have to either traipse off to the marketplace to buy it or have one printed and shipped to him from a local shop that had larger print capabilities. The Object on the other hand, well, if they ever figured it out, looked to be large enough to print out things the size of a motor for a

LoonieCart or maybe even a full-sized environment suit in one printing.

David sat in front of the main display of the Object with his IR goggles on. The false color images filled his field of view with strange alien-looking writing and characters. Looking at the images before him gave him the elation that he—and Carla, Sarah, and Jerry if you were going to get nitpicky—were deciphering a completely new language that mankind had never seen before. He tapped at one of the glyphs before him on the device's input screen or monitor or, well, it wasn't a monitor per se, like an old school computer or device that you might find in a modern day human dwelling or office, and it didn't have a direct-to-mind link like some of the other more modern technologies. But it was the data interface for the Object and "monitor" was as good a word for it as any. Maybe "interface" would suffice but it seemed too little or common a word to describe it as far as David was concerned.

There was something else. It had a set of glyphs on the side and the glyphs seemed to morph as you needed them to, and the key was knowing which glyphs you wanted to morph. You didn't actually touch it, it just knew that you were thinking about that particular set of glyphs. How it did that was beyond David. He just accepted it as technology that the engineers and scientists understood, or would understand, once he figured out the instruction manual. No, it was more like they would understand it once he'd figured out which language the instruction manual was written in, then he learned said language, and then he read the manual and explained it to everyone else.

One of the physicists from Luna 8 had said something about quantum entanglement and the human brain functioning like a quantum computer and it got the entire team buzzing about the idea. David wasn't so sure how any of that was actually helpful in translating the instructions which in turn would enable using the Object for its original intended purpose or at least some purpose useful to the Loonies reverse engineering it.

In fact, if it weren't for Carla and Sarah, the mathematician and the physicist, helping decipher the glyphs, David would be completely lost on the nuances of atomic and molecular physics and chemistry and quantum information mathematics that were involved in the alien glyph language. The weird symbols used for those sciences were pretty much an alien language to David as well.

And were it not for the mayor pressuring him and warning that the Ueys were coming and gonna take it away any day now, David would much rather just sit back, relax, and take his time on the project. He had always worked much better without pressure. But he'd seen the news. He and the rest of the Loonies working there knew that if the Moon was going to keep any autonomy in their lives then a stand was going to be made soon. And the Object might turn out to be a key component of that autonomy.

"Hey, Luna, what time is it?"

"It is seven fifty-five, David."

He looked up as he heard the buzz of the elevator door and Carla walked through the translucent opening that always appeared in the IR goggle view. He nodded to her and paused from looking at his work briefly. She was carrying something in her hand that looked like a two-meter-long metal pipe with holes and gadgets connected to it. The one end of the thing was very pointy. She was also fidgeting with her security badge, trying to get it back in her hip pocket.

"Good morning,"

"Good morning, David." Carla smiled her very youthful grin at him and scanned the room. The purple streak through her shoulder-length ponytail just reminded David how young she was and how old he was. Rhetorically she asked, "Hasn't Sarah gotten in yet?"

"Um, we're the first ones here. What you got there?"

"Oh, this is just a surprise. If it works then I'll tell you about it." Carla raised an eyebrow and sounded a bit cagy to David, but what did he know.

"Okay, then." He shrugged but still watched her with interest as she placed the pipe upright into the floor and folded three legs down at one-hundred-twenty-degree increments about the pipe. Each of the legs had an L bracket that met flush with the floor. Carla depressed some pushpins and they held in place, allowing the thing to stand upright by itself. She stepped away to the tool bin and returned with a hammer drill and six long masonry screws.

"Uh, Carla, you need a hand?"

"No, thank you," she said. Carla finished placing the rock screws in and tossed the drill motor to the side. She then pressed a button on top of the pipe. "Oh, yeah, fire in the hole!"

The pointy end of the device glowed red hot and then there was a very loud *BANG!* David nearly ruined his pants.

"What the HELL was that?"

"Wow, that was louder than it was outside." Carla shook her head and fingered at her ears. David noticed she had earplugs in them. She went back to work sliding the outer pipe up over what was apparently an inner pipe that had just been hammered into the floor and then she tossed it aside. The metal on rock *clankity-clank* was nowhere near as loud as the explosive had been. She tapped a few buttons on the device and a light started moving up and down the shaft of it. A very low bass tone sound started to oscillate in the room. "Well, that won't be too annoying, I hope."

The elevator door buzzed again and Sarah and Jerry stepped through laughing about something. David was still trying to stop his ears from ringing and couldn't make out what they were saying. He noticed that Carla was removing the earplugs from her ears when she looked back at him.

"Oh, David, I'm sorry. I should have warned you. Are you okay?" Carla asked.

"Yeah, but do you mind telling me what is going on?"

"So you see, Mr. Mayor, you are not at all where you think you are." Carla pulled up a projected map of the Moon and zoomed into the West Dome area a bit. "Sarah and I placed geophones—they detect seismic vibrations—along this path here where the red dots are on the map. We basically took the old gravel road path the kids used back when to go between Luna City and Aldrinville."

"When did you do that?" Mayor Hamilton asked.

"When we were shut down to have the security doors

installed," Sarah said, waving a hand over her shoulder as if to point to the elevator door behind her. "We hated wasting all that time so we put it to good use."

"I see. Go on."

"Well, then we placed this thumper here into the rock floor and turned it on," Carla continued. "The geophones, after a lot of computer processing, managed to detect the thumping and we used the delays from all seventeen of them to triangulate the position of the thumper."

"Just like triangulating on a radio source, I get it," Mayor Hamilton said.

"Well, guess where we are?" Carla asked him. "No don't, 'cause you won't get it right. We are right here about three hundred kilometers west and a bit north of the West Dome and about two hundred meters beneath the surface of this crater here."

"Wha—?" The mayor was dumbfounded.

"That's exactly how I responded, Mr. Mayor." David laughed. "But we've checked and double-checked with different techniques now and it's true."

"But how?"

"Well, first of all, we have to realize that the elevator isn't an elevator," Sarah explained. "It's a transport of some sort."

"It might even be a teleporter like in science fiction movies but we don't know anything about it yet," Carla continued. "For now, just knowing how to use it is good enough. We still have to figure out how the Object here works before moving on to the next crazy thing."

"I agree with that." Mayor Hamilton still looked bewildered.

"There's more," David added. "Well, a couple of things."

"More than this?"

"The transport has more locations."

"There's only the up and down button on the door?" Mayor Hamilton said, perplexed.

"Well, kinda," Carla said. "There is an up hand and a down hand. And they are both the same hand."

"Yeah, I've seen them. Used them."

"Ah, so, do this," Carla held her right hand upright out in front of her. "This is the up hand and if I hold it upside down it's the down hand, right?"

"Sure."

"Well, first hold your hand upright then slowly turn it clockwise to the downward pointing position. There are all these points between upright and downward that are locations too. The hands aren't buttons. They are starting and stopping points on a dial." Carla smiled as she continued to move her hand slowly through the positions along the imaginary hand dial.

"Oh my God." Then after a brief pause he continued. "Have any of you tried this?"

"Not yet. We wanted to tell you first," David answered.

"It could be dangerous, might not be. Who knows?" Sarah added.

"This team is my A-team," Mayor Hamilton said. "I don't want anything happening to you. I'll get some others to work on the elevator thing. We need to stay focused here on how to make this thing do whatever it does."

"Well, realizing how the door works gives a bit more insight on how the aliens built their instrument controls.

Before we were thinking buttons. Now we need to think of three-dimensional spinners and dials," Carla explained.

"I see. Good." The Mayor nodded in agreement. "What else?"

"Well, as you'll note, Jerry isn't here today." David motioned around the Object room. "We sent him out to the location above us to survey for a spot where we might build ourselves a back door."

"A back door? Yes, that is a very good idea. But it must be a secret back door and only we know about it. Tell him to do it but with a minimal crew. And I want to have your team moved into here with all the supplies and creature comforts of home. This is your new home for now. The room is big enough we can set up private quarters. I'll have that started."

"Wait, what?" David, Sarah, and Carla said mostly in unison.

"Listen, I know it is inconvenient for you. And you can come and go as you need to, but I'd prefer you stayed here for safety." The mayor seemed to know something they didn't. "I don't trust the Ueys. And I think they have gotten wind of our project here."

"Oh my God! It's terrible." Jerry was almost in tears as much as he was fuming with anger. The big projector in the center common area they had created showed the Luna 8 dome collapsed on the southernmost side with plumes of dust floating about randomly from escaping air currents. There were four UNE transport ships sitting just outside the dome with dozens of Earther troops moving about. The team couldn't believe what they were seeing.

"... as it stands the casualty rate is estimated to be in the forties to fifties with at least nine confirmed deaths so far. It is unclear what the point of the attack is and a spokesperson for the United Nations of Earth has yet to comment. The coalition of Lunar mayors and governors are meeting in a nondisclosed and confidential meeting this morning to determine how to respond..."

"What were they trying to accomplish?" Carla asked. "I mean, why attack a mining colony like Luna Eight?"

"They were looking for something," David said sternly. He had been expecting something to happen before too long. The mayor had been warning them something was coming, but up until this point it hadn't been real. "Something that might be very valuable. Not sure why Luna Eight, though."

"You mean they were looking for the Object?" Sarah asked.

"That's exactly what I mean."

"I bet the mayor somehow led them to thinking it was down there to see what they would do," Jerry added. David could see from the look on his face that he was ready to start punching the next Uey he saw. "And boy did they do something."

"I bet they don't have two dozen firearms down there. They were all just sitting ducks." David leaned back on the old couch that had been brought in for them and sighed. "We'd better figure this thing out before they figure out where it really is."

"The first thing I want it to do is to print out me an alien ray gun!" Jerry said angrily. "Then we'll show those bastards."

"Where we gonna get the blueprint for an alien ray gun?" Carla asked.

David stared at the images before him and there were several that would seem to change from one shape to another and then back to where it started. He was beginning to think that the first images you saw when interacting with the Object might be a ready prompt like on an old school computer.

"Don't ask me," Carla shrugged. "It just knows what you're thinking. I think. The really interesting part is it seems to interact with all of us at once. How do we keep too many chefs from spoiling the soup once we do figure this thing out?"

"This is that brain-is-a-quantum-computer thing again, right?" Jerry, the construction crew foreman, had seemed to acclimate to the physicist's language quicker than David had. His orange-striped coveralls looked monochrome in the IR goggles. "So, what if I change my mind in the middle of a print?"

"No, uh, I don't think it works like that, Jer," Sarah responded. "Think of it more like you sent a file to the printer and you are waiting for it to print. I guess you could hit the cancel button somehow."

"More than that." David looked a bit annoyed at their conversation. "I think there must be a very complex drawing package or blueprint package down to the atoms or molecules input into this thing somehow before a print can be done."

"That would make a lot of sense, David." Carla sat down next to him, putting on her goggles. "Our systems all require detailed three-dimensional models and print material descriptions. But how do we think in those details without saving and editing along the way?"

"First things first. Let's just get the thing to print something even if it is just a blob of goop," David suggested. "Then we fine-tune."

"Well, the printers have printer material spools. Where do we put the print materials into this thing?" Sarah walked around and around the Object waving her arms about. David guessed she'd done that a million times. "Where is the print button on this thing?"

"I'm thinking here, just thinking, mind you." Jerry sat down and pulled up an image on his tablet of an apple. "Man, I wish we could have apples here on the Moon anytime we wanted them. D'ya think we could just print an apple?"

"That'd be nice, Jerry." David started to laugh but then the alien device lit up even more than it had been across the infrared spectrum. There were spots in the middle that saturated the goggles so brightly that he had to shut his eyes.

"What did you do, David?" Carla and Sarah both exclaimed while jumping backward, putting distance between them and the Object.

"I didn't do anything!"

"Hey, look!" Jerry pointed at the flat tray on the right side of the device. "Something is printing!"

"It looks like a page or a solid sheet." David reached down as the lights on the printer subsided and the printing noises stopped completely. "Well, Jerry, I'll be damned."

"What?"

David held up a piece of material that felt almost like paper or maybe it was very thin plastic or sheet metal, but in the middle of it was a drawing of an apple in orange infrared false colors.

"Hang on a minute," Sarah said while lifting her goggles. "You all should look at it in the visible spectrum. Jerry, what type of apple were you thinking of?"

"Pink Ladies. I used to love them with peanut butter as a kid. Haven't had one since I moved to Aldrinville." Jerry almost licked his lips as he described the fruit.

"Well, here ya go! One Pink Lady apple." David smiled. He handed the printout to him. "I doubt it will be as tasty as you had hoped."

"A picture of an apple? What good does that do us? I was thinking of this picture here." Jerry held up his tablet and the image was almost identical to the printout from the Object.

"Wait, Jerry, that's it!" Sarah clapped her hands triumphantly and looked as if she were going to bounce off the floor in the light lunar gravity. "You were looking at a two-dimensional image and thinking of that image, not an actual apple."

"But why Jerry's thoughts?" Carla shrugged. "We've all been imagining things, I'm sure. I mean, I'd kill for a cup of coffee with a triple-shot espresso about now."

"I don't know, but maybe it just likes him." David turned to Jerry and handed him a tablet pen. "Jerry, hold this in your hand and look at it and think about it and focus on it and wish for it just like you did the apple."

"Uh, okay, David." Jerry took the pen.

⊕ ⊕ ⊕

"Too many people know where it is already," Tami agreed with the mayor. "All the crews that were down there excavating the dome. Some of them will talk to their friends and family on Earth."

"Yeah, but all they know is there's a big crazy room under the surface." Mayor Hamilton leaned back into the seat of the LoonieCart II as they zoomed down the old gravel Aldrinville-to-Luna City pass. The gray regolith was building up on the front bumper section on the cart thick enough to write your name in. He suspected his suit looked similar. "Only the research teams and us know about the Object. I certainly didn't think that the Earthers would do a hostile takeover of Luna Eight when they thought it was down there either."

"The Earthers want whatever it is that we've got, Mr. Mayor. How'd the other mayors feel about our gambit?" Tami kept the accelerator all the way to the floor. "I mean, they couldn't have been happy about it."

"They were mostly pissed at the UNE for authorizing the damage of a multibillion-dollar habitat dome. And now the citizens there are forced to live in shelters and under siege." Alton looked up and pointed at an outcropping at the rim of a crater about a kilometer off the roadway. "There it is over there."

"What are we going to do about it? The attack, I mean?" Tami slowed down and edged the buggy off the main road. There were clear construction vehicle tracks to follow. "We'll need to sweep these tracks."

"Good idea," the mayor agreed. "As far as the attack goes, first the Coalition of Lunar Mayors and Governors is suing the shit out of the UNE. We filed the injunction this morning."

"Good luck with that."

"Yeah, and, I want you and your sheriff counterpart from Luna Eight to file criminal charges against the commander of the attack squad. Find out who it is and I want him made Luna public enemy number one! I want him charged with murder, destruction of property, terrorism, Hell, jaywalking even. Charge him with everything you can imagine."

"That's a good idea. Always great to have a bad guy for the public to point at." Tami eased the buggy around the edge of the crater and down the switchback that had been put together in order to carry equipment to the bottom. "Wouldn't hurt to find out who gave the order from Earth. We could charge them with conspiracy to commit mass murder."

"Do it. Whatever it takes." Alton unbuckled himself and looked up toward the rim of the crater. The Moon was big. Nobody came out this road any longer since the highway had been put in. As long as they swept the tracks from the old road nobody would ever find this place. "I can't think of a better secret hidey-hole. Pull the cart into the alcove so no orbital flights can see it."

"There isn't one expected today, but good practice," Tami agreed.

"Who knows if the damned Earthers have tossed out some tiny spysats we haven't detected yet. We don't want this place being revealed at all costs."

The two of them stood at the edge of the two-car garage-sized opening looking out at the crater. From out there looking in, the entrance would appear no more interesting than a million other shadows or caves in craters on the far side of the Moon. They were over three hundred kilometers from the nearest city or dwelling of any sort and the far side of nowhere was as good a description as any as to where they were. Where they were exactly, was about two hundred meters above the alien room that housed the Object. They turned and walked down the path the earth-borer had made and in the low gravity, the two-hundred-meter walk downhill was pretty easy.

"They had to blast the outer wall to get through to the room. Whatever the aliens did to the basaltic rock made it superstrong," Alton explained. "Jerry, the construction foreman, he said he's never seen anything like it. But in the end they managed."

"No security on the airlock?"

"No need. We had a ready chamber built to accommodate larger numbers in case we have to stage troops out here too. But nobody can get through the security doors to the Object without access." Alton cycled the airlock outer door and then the inner door light went green and slid open. "In we go."

"Are we putting in other rooms like this at the other locations?"

"We'll get to that. Right now, we need to worry about protecting our main asset here." He worked his way out of the spacesuit and kicked it into an alcove that had been cut out of the rock wall. "We'll go back the easy way. I wanted to make the trip out and to leave a cart out here. We really need to bring several out here. And start caching suits and weapons and food and air."

"I'll get on that."

"That doesn't seem right though," Sarah said.

"I'm not so sure I understand. What do you mean?" David wasn't sure exactly what the physicist had on her mind and was more distracted than startled by the new backdoor light turning green and opening. The mayor and the Aldrinville sheriff entered unannounced and un-expectedly.

"Mr. Mayor." Jerry jumped up from the couch to greet the two. "I see you found the back door."

"Yes, great job there, Jerry." The mayor shook his hand. "You know Sheriff Jones?"

"Yes, sir."

"Tami, this is Dr. David Sandeep, Dr. Carla Pruitt, and Dr. Sarah Rollin. These four have been the A-team in deciphering the alien technology and language," the mayor said proudly. "I hope we are getting closer, team?"

"Every second, Mr. Mayor," Jerry said excitedly.

"Any word from Luna Eight, sir?" Carla asked. "I have some friends down there and I haven't heard from them at all."

"The Ueys have cut off all the comms through open channels. They've claimed there was a terrorist plot to steal goods and services from the UNE and some other nonsense."

"The only info we're getting is scuttlebutt through underground channels, but worse than that, our people on Earth tell us that more ships are being loaded with troops and equipment and being readied for launch,"

Sheriff Jones added. "If you ask me, I'd say the Ueys are planning to come show us Loonies who's boss."

"Tami, no need to spread scary rumors," the mayor scolded. "Changing the subject, tell me some progress."

"Okay, sir, we have made the thing print—we can all get blobs of goop," Sarah told him. "And for some reason Jerry has been able to think a couple items to it and it printed a shell of them but not a one-to-one likeness. More of a rough mold as such."

"Why Jerry?"

"That is the million-dollar question," David answered. "He seems to be connected to the thing somehow and we don't know why. My theory is he happened to touch just the right buttons in the right order before anyone else did and it connected to him. We'll figure it out."

"Well, it seems to me like just letting a person think of the three-dimensional object, while that's interesting and efficient, it could be inaccurate as hell." The mayor turned to David and only sort of glanced at Jerry. "I mean no offense, but I couldn't think of exactly how to build a hammer much less a complicated piece of equipment. So, unless the aliens had better minds than we do, there's got to be more, right?"

"Yeah, I agree and we've talked about this before." David was excited that Jerry was able to get things to print even if they were just hollow shells of what he was looking at.

"It takes months to get a blueprint, a three-dimensional design drawing right, I'm guessing. Exactly right, I mean," Jerry agreed with them. "Just look around the excavation site here." He waved his arms about, pointing at the room, the giant door, and upward to the roadways leading down to the alien construction.

"What about it?" The mayor shrugged.

"We took weeks to get survey maps drawn up from the ground-penetrating radar and the geology maps. Then we had to use the lunar positioning trackers to guide the excavators. Engineering a thing has to be at least that complex. Hell, I've only ever printed out toothbrushes and buttons and little doohickeys that I needed around the apartment. And I got full-up blueprint downloads for all of those from the web. We needed a special tool to remove the field coil on one of the mini-excavator wheel drives when we were digging the East Dome and it took the LoonieCart company engineers two weeks to get it right. I couldn't have imagined or thought of all the parts of my toothbrush at once, much less a really complicated thing. No way."

"You built the backdoor shaft pretty quickly," Tami noted.

"That was straightforward," Jerry said. "Drill down, set up support girders, drop in a readymade airlock, build a door. Still took five guys and a week."

"I see," Tami said.

"You're right, Jerry." Sarah nodded. "You have to know where every screw goes, all the tolerances for the holes. You have to know the distance between all the parts, the materials each of the parts are made of. There's a lot of inputs there, more than just thinking of the picture, I don't think a human can do that. Right?"

"Well, maybe whoever built this wasn't human and maybe they were smarter than us." Jerry smiled and shook his head. "Might be we humans ain't evolved enough to use this thing."

"That is an unacceptable answer, David," the mayor said. "I can't accept that we can't figure this thing out."

"That could be, but I think even these aliens were smart enough to realize that thinking of something on the fly isn't the way realistic things are designed." David couldn't accept that the builders of the device were that super or godlike. "They had to have physical limitations if they were organic beings, didn't they? The handprints on the elevator buttons look like living creature hands, not like robot hands."

"We need to give this thing a blueprint of something and see what it does," Jerry stated.

"Okay. I see what you're getting at." David thought. "So tell me something, then. How do we do that? How would we input something that complex into that thing?"

Sarah walked around the Object for a few moments and let out a flabbergasted sigh. "I've got no clue what to do. I was hoping the glyphs would tell us how."

Jerry stood up from his camping chair and started walking about the tall alien device as well. The two of them ran their fingers over cracks, icons, and any other places that looked different from the smooth obsidian-like material it was constructed from.

David watched them with interest, half-expecting Carla, the sheriff, and the mayor to join them. But they didn't. Carla's mind was focused on patterns in the glyphs that she and David had recently found. Carla thought the patterns were mathematical, but David was hoping for them to be a language primer.

"Well, on this side, there's an output that nothing ever seems to come out of." Jerry pointed.

"Hey, you're right! Every time we've thought of something it always comes out of the other side." Sarah walked back to the other side where the printed material had always emerged.

"Yeah, I've noticed that. It kind of reminds me of an Easy-Bake Oven." David laughed. "A very big, grayish, obsidian-looking, alien Easy-Bake Oven."

"An easy what?" Sarah looked at him. "I'm not sure what that is."

"I know what that is," Sheriff Jones said. "I used to have one, like, forty years ago."

"You've never had an Easy-Bake Oven." David looked at Sarah with a smile. "I thought all little girls played with those things."

"First, sexist. And second, how old are you, David?" Sarah asked.

"Meant nothing by it." David laughed.

"Hey, and it doesn't matter, because they still make Easy-Bake Ovens. They even have them on the Moon," Jerry added. "David, I think you're right."

"Yeah, my great-granddaughter has one back on Earth. I have videos of her cooking with it." David felt lonely briefly, thinking about how he'd never go back to Earth again. But that was the trade he'd made for living twice as long. He looked up at the mayor, who was watching intently but remaining quiet for the time being.

"Okay, now I'm curious," Carla looked up from her tablet screen. "Never heard of it."

"Well, David, don't leave us hanging. What is an Easy-

Bake Oven?" Sarah put her hands on her hips and tapped her foot on the solid rock floor. "I guess I never cooked as a child. I was always building bicycles and playing with computers and playing video games."

"There's something wrong with a generation that never had an Easy-Bake Oven." He laughed.

"We're waiting! Are you going to tell me and Carla what it is or not?"

Jerry just looked back and forth between the women and David, but he didn't say anything. David could see a grin forming at the corners of his mouth.

"Alright, alright." He said, waving his hands. "Hey, Luna, show me some full images of an Easy-Bake Oven." A three-dimensional display popped up from his smart tablet before them, showing the child's toy cooking device. "You see, Sarah, you mix up the ingredients in this pan here and you slide it into this side of the oven. It's like a conveyor and as the pan goes to the inside, the heating element inside cooks the cake and then you reach in with your handle and take the cake out from the other side. It goes in one side, it comes out the other. It goes in one side as mixed-up ingredients comes out the other side as a cake."

"They're pretty good, too," Jerry added. "I think they quit making it for a few years, but you know how it is with retro toys these days."

"Oh, I get it. It is just an oven, but why'd they call it Easy-Bake?" Carla asked.

"Well, it's all put together easily so kids can do it. It's just a sample packet with water that you mixed together."

"I see. That looks like fun, but I never really was a big cake fan," Sarah said. "Too many carbs."

"Who doesn't like cake?" The mayor finally broke his silence.

"Not the point, I think." David laughed and shook his head.

"There really is something wrong with you. You know that?" But she was smiling when she said it.

David looked at the three-dimensional image of the Easy-Bake Oven projected out of his tablet and then back at Sarah and then something struck him. He had an idea that he couldn't let go. He looked back at the Easy-Bake Oven, three-dimensional picture, and then back at the diagrams. There were three icons beside each other on the face of the Object's "monitor."

"Hmm? Three icons, three-dimensional thing." He thought.

"Say that again," Sarah said.

"Look, there are three buttons here, right? Well, we know that we are wanting to print in three dimensions. Right?" David pointed at the glowing and morphing icons on the upper right of the "monitor."

"Damn." Sarah smacked her head with her palm. "Of course, that's probably X, Y, Z, or R, theta, and phi, or any other three-dimensional coordinate system in the alien language!"

"Well, I guess other than the funky handprints and the infrared stuff everywhere, we don't *really* know that aliens built this thing. I mean . . ." David said half-jokingly.

"Seriously. Can you really believe that humanity made this thing? Some advanced ancient human race that saw in the IR and had long goofy fingers?" Sarah cocked her head sideways at him. "We still don't even know exactly what it does."

"I just told you what it does. It's an Easy-Bake Oven." David paused for effect. "An alien Easy-Bake Oven. We should try making a cake."

"Ha!" Carla sniggered. Jerry guffawed. Sarah wasn't quite as amused.

"How does it know what to bake, though?" Jerry asked. "I mean, you mix chocolate cake mix in the pan, you get chocolate cake."

"Somehow we have to tell it what to bake." Carla touched her tablet stylus to her right temple in thought.

"Wait, I have an idea. Let's put some materials on this side and let's think of a three-dimensional model and then let's see what happens."

"Okay, but it can't be that simple."

"Well, let's start with simple and go from there."

"Where do we input a three-dimensional model?" Jerry asked.

"Don't know. Let's put some stuff through it and see what happens." Sarah was on board with the plan now. "We need some basic building materials."

"Carbon, metals, paper, plastics, are all right here." David walked across the alien room and found the human-designed and -built trash can and poured the ingredients out onto the side of the Object that nothing had ever printed out of. When he did, several of the icons on the front of the device morphed into different symbols.

"You don't think this thing just looked at the trash and figured out what materials we just put there, do you?"

Sarah looked very excited. She studied the objects closely and then it was clear she had a plan.

"I want to try something." She scooped all of the materials off of the input side back into the trash can, and then she looked for something specific. There was an aluminum can from a soft drink dispenser there, so she took the can out. "This is only aluminum, mostly. There may be some impurities in it."

"Holy shit! That's it, Sarah!" Carla clapped her hands together and then excitedly pointed at one of the IR icons. "Look, I think you just discovered the symbol for aluminum."

"Oh wait, there are two symbols." David looked closer and he could see that two symbols had indeed appeared and by each symbol there was a bar that seemed to be like a percentage bar graph. The one to the left was almost completely full and the one to the right was almost completely empty.

"I think we've just discovered what the symbol for aluminum is, Sarah. And this other symbol is probably tin or carbon or some other impurity." David looked back at her. They now had a way to decipher the glyphs.

"Are there two of the same thing in there?" Jerry asked.

"Well, here's a plastic spoon from yesterday and you can take mine from my lunch if you want to." Carla started digging through her backpack. "Here."

"What are you doing, Jerry?"

"A hunch." Jerry took both spoons and examined them. "They look pretty much the same. Close enough."

He broke one of the plastic spoons into multiple pieces and then set the broken pieces on the device. Jerry stood in front of the Object's "monitor" holding the spoon in his hand and focusing on it. A beam of infrared energy reached out from the Object and scanned the spoon in his hand. Had they not been wearing their goggles they would have never seen it. The tray holding the broken spoon pieces slid into the inner workings of the Object and the infrared goggles saturated again, the flash blinding them all briefly.

"The spoon is mostly one thing, with some of three other things," David said.

"Plastics have all sorts of stuff in them. Carbon, oxygen, hydrogen, nitrogen, could be sulfur or chlorine," Sarah stated. "We'll need to get known sources to calibrate the symbols."

"Eureka!" Jerry shouted, somewhat startling David. "A brand-new spoon."

"Very nice!" Mayor Hamilton clapped his hands.

"Look at this icon, here. Now there are two of them." Sarah pointed at the "monitor."

"I want to try something now." David took a plastic bottle out of the trash pile and placed it on the Object input tray. "Think of the spoon again, Jerry."

"Okay."

A moment later two spoons slid out of the output side.

"There are three of the icons this time. I think this is the object counter." David pointed where Sarah had before.

"Do some more!" Jerry said. "Try it without plastic this time."

"Okay." David scrounged through the trash and pulled out some pieces of a paper box and he grabbed the aluminum can. He sat them on the input tray. Carla got up and placed her Styrofoam coffee cup on the tray as well.

"Ready, Jerry."

The counter ticked away. After a couple minutes there were eight spoons made from materials that weren't plastic. There were several of the element icons lighting up showing empty bar graphs beside them.

"It didn't just copy the spoons because it didn't have all the right stuff," Carla surmised.

"Can I try something?" Sheriff Jones asked.

"Sure, what do you have in mind?" David looked up at her and watched as she unholstered her handgun.

"Here, take this round as the blueprint." She slid a bullet from the magazine and handed it to Jerry. She then slid two more out and sat them on a nearby worktable. "You have some pliers anywhere?"

"Oh, yeah, I see what you're doing." Jerry turned to a wall cabinet. "Tools in here."

He pulled out a hammer, some needle-nose pliers, and a pair of vise grips and handed them to the sheriff.

"Alright, if we pop the lead out, and then just pour out the powder"—Tami managed to unload the rounds onto a paper plate—"this should be enough ingredients to fix them back."

"Hold on. Let's make it a little harder." David reached in and plucked out one of the lead bullet tips and then took the aluminum fork from the previous run. "Let's see what it does with this."

"Alright, Jerry, do your thing." The mayor clapped him on the shoulder.

"Um, okay." Jerry took the plate of the broken bullets and the fork and sat them on the input side. He then held the good round in his hand and focused on it. The beam of infrared light hit the bullet and the system flashed. The materials icons on the monitor showed multiple material symbols with multiple percentage graphs and then on the other side appeared two perfect-looking bullets.

"Wow! Let me see those." The sheriff picked them up and examined them very closely. "I expected there to be one with a lead bullet and one with aluminum, but this looks more like some amalgam of the aluminum and lead in both. Hold on a sec."

Tami took the rounds and chambered them into the pistol and then walked to a far corner of the room. *Bang! Bang!* David was expecting her to fire the weapon, he guessed, but he was also startled by how loud it was.

"Cycled through fine. No stovepipes. Good rounds." Tami nodded approvingly.

"The A-team!" The mayor sounded elated and was almost bouncing up and down. "You've done it! You just got this thing to copy bullets! Now *that* is going to be handy in the days and weeks to come."

"No, it didn't copy them, Mr. Mayor. Since they weren't exact duplicates the device did its best," David said. "Our object, thing, artifact isn't a copier. It's a mimic!!"

Mama's Express

⊕

by Travis S. Taylor

It didn't really matter to Paul that there were people at Luna 11 that hadn't had a drink of fresh water in almost three months or that any of them had actually reverted to diets of protein shakes if they were lucky. Many of the Luna 11ers were down to a few hundred kilocalories per day, which meant they were flat-out starving to death. All of those stories were hard for Paul Jennings, captain of the cargo hauler *Mama's Express*, to really believe or at least connect to. At least until the United Earthers had allowed one ship through the blockade for humanitarian reasons— for political optics and soundbites was more to the truth.

One ship was allowed through the Ueys' formidable blockade orbiting the Moon—the *Mama's Express*. One ship out of hundreds that up until a year prior carried trade and commerce goods back and forth between the Moon and Earth. The economic symbiotic relationship between the two had ground to a screeching halt once the war had broken out. Paul had once been the captain of a very lucrative ship, but the UE forces didn't have quite the logistics requirements of thirteen lunar colonies.

"*Mama's Express*, we have you locked in on lidar. Just switch on the ALS and we'll bring you in," the Luna 11 port authority voice said. Paul switched on the automated landing system, then leaned back, and relaxed.

"It's in your hands, Luna Eleven," Paul replied. He sat back and waited for the hauler to come to rest on the hangar platform and then for the airlock tube to attach. Once the pressure equalization lights chimed on Paul sighed and then stood up. "Time to go to work."

Mama's Express was a typical privateer hauler about thirty meters long and ten meters on each side. Haulers of the type were reminiscent of the river barges from Earth— no frills and designed to hold maximum cargo for minimum mass and volume. Paul had started as a freelancer making the cargo runs from Earth to the Moon and back. Up until the Earthers started acting all foolish about possession rights on the lunar colonies it had been a fairly lucrative endeavor. But for the past nine months or so, the only business had been logistics to the blockade, which was no way to make a living. And this humanitarian run wasn't making him more than breaking even. To top it off, the damned Ueys wouldn't let him bring an offloading crew.

"*Mama's Express*, you are free to disembark," a voice from the other side of the cargo door shouted. It was followed by three loud metal *clang-clang-clang*s against the bulkhead. Paul depressed the cargo lift door control and the tail section began to swing open making a loading ramp. As the door fell slowly against the floor Paul noticed three scarecrows standing by with rifles pointed in his general direction. The men's faces were all sunken inward and dehydrated and looked like a scene from a horror movie. Paul did his best not to stare.

"Uh, hi," he said cautiously. "Capt'n Paul Jennings. I'm the only crew aboard. Cargo hold, as you can see, is full of stuff. Where would y'all like it?"

"Captain Jennings, we'll unload this. In the meantime you have to come with us. Your presence is requested in the pub." One of the scarecrows motioned with the rifle.

"Uh, okay. Is that thing loaded?" he asked. "If it is, why don't you point it in a different direction."

"Yes, it is loaded. It would be difficult to hold the Ueys at bay with unloaded weapons, would it not?"

"Man, I don't know. I'm just a hauler captain. Heard you folks down here were starving so I brought food and medicine and stuff. From what I see, you could use a bit of it yourself." Paul continued along in front of the scarecrow and was uneasy about having that rifle in his back the whole way to "the pub," wherever that was.

The pub actually turned out to be just that, a bar. It was one of the Loonie brew pubs that seemed to be in all of the colonies. The scarecrows he passed along the way were hard to look at. Paul had never really seen a starving human being before, but once he did he realized it was the most wrong and disturbing thing he'd ever seen. The fact that one group of humans would do this to another group of humans he'd thought was a primitive thing of the past. Whatever the Ueys were after on the Moon couldn't justify *this*.

"In here." The scarecrow with the rifle nudged him through the outer pub area into a dark room in the back. "Sit."

Paul sat. Three minutes later another scarecrow appeared and placed a tall schooner filled with a golden hazy and very hoppy-smelling beer beside him with a small bowl of nuts. Paul looked at the nearly thousand calories sat beside him and started to offer it back.

"Don't. They wouldn't take it anyway." A well-fed individual that Paul recognized offered him his hand. "Nathaniel Ray. You are?"

"Captain Paul Jennings." Paul shook the well-known Loonie beer tycoon's hand and sat down.

"Call me Nate," the man said as he sat across the coffee table from Paul in a red leather wingback chair. "It's all a show, Paul."

"A show? What is?"

"The scarecrows. The siege." Nate waved his hands about. "The visible tier of people here are all volunteers. They are being kept alive and healthy but on a near-to-nothing diet. The goal is political warfare. We want the Earthers to see what their government is capable of. I won't tell you how just yet, but we've got plenty of food here."

"Aren't you afraid I'd tell this to somebody out there?" Paul wasn't sure if these Loonies were too trusting, naïve, or if he was being set up somehow. He sipped the beer. It was very hoppy. "Why tell me?"

"We need an ally from the other side of the blockade. You managed to get yourself chosen to make this humanitarian run. So, honestly, you are the first person we've been able to make the proposition to."

"What proposition?" He sipped the beer again. "Not bad stuff."

"I know, right? Took me months to get that one right. Then all this had to happen. It's just sitting there in the barrels downstairs and I can't move it. Costing me a fortune." Nate grimaced. "But that's not why you're here. Although, you might could move some of this back with you if you'd like. I would cut you in for a good piece."

"Ha-ha-ha. The Ueys might let me back through the blockade with it, but then I'd have to explain why y'all are starving down here if you have all this beer and nuts laying about," Paul said. "So, what the Hell is really going on? You had to know that."

"Just making sure you did, Paul." Nate leaned back in his chair. "And you are right. We can't move the beer right now. But someday."

"Then what?" Paul shrugged. "What is your proposition?"

"Imagine that you had a machine that could pump out any object, device, machine—whatever that your culture, your society, your army might need," Nate said over his steepled fingers resting against his chin.

"Sounds great, but there's a catch. There's always a catch."

"Very true. The catch is that you have to have the ingredients the devices are made from as raw materials in order to build them. While the Moon has an abundance of things like carbon, titanium, even metals lying about the habitats and cities, there are some things that just are missing. Things we need." Nate sighed. "We can make guns all day long, but we can't make enough gunpowder to reload the bullets."

"Well, how about that?" Paul realized what this was all

about finally. The Loonies didn't have any ammunition to fight back with and if the Ueys figured that out they'd be sunk. "The Ueys would never let me through the blockade with gunpowder."

"No, they wouldn't. But we don't need gunpowder."

"Wait, you just said you needed gunpowder."

"I said we can't make enough gunpowder to make enough ammunition. We have all the carbon, nitrogen, sulfur, magnesium, and other things. What we are missing is potassium nitrate. Well, we can make the nitrate, we need the potassium." Nate sighed and leaned back. "Apparently, there just isn't a stable ready source of potassium here on the Moon."

"Potassium?"

"And here in a few minutes we're gonna video you and the doctors analyzing all these scarecrows out there and guess what? They're all gonna be suffering from hypokalemia as one of the side effects of the starvation." Nate smiled. "You know what hypokalemia is, Paul?"

"Let me guess, potassium deficiency?"

"Ding-ding! Give the man a prize."

"So, we need you to make another humanitarian run with potassium-rich foods, vitamins and supplements, cream of tartar, sports drinks, and even hide some potassium metal in there if you can manage it," Nate explained. "The doctors will give you a list."

"That might could be done. I know a guy that does runs out to the Belt that might could hook me up with some larger chunks of potassium. Might could hide it in the structure somewhere." Paul pondered the idea of helping the Loonies out. "But there's still a big question."

"What's in it for you?"

"Bingo. Give the man a prize." Paul finished off the beer. "What's in it for me other than a trip to prison if the Ueys figure out what is happening?"

"We'll never let you be a willing accomplice," Nate assured him. "As far as you know you are purely doing a humanitarian run. And, if things work out, setting yourself up for a very lucrative future."

"Lucrative? How so?"

"Paul, if we suddenly could repel the Ueys we'd be a free market. Even more than we've been for the last thirty years." Nate leaned in toward him with a raised eyebrow. "And, Paul, I'm always looking for distribution lines I can trust. This would put you in on the ground floor of what might be billions, maybe trillions in future revenue."

"You had me at billions." Paul smiled and rose from the chair. "Let's go look at these scarecrows and see if we can't get them some sports drinks or something. Thanks for the beer."

"If you're not going to eat the nuts, we'll recycle them." Nate frowned. "Lot of potassium in them, you know."

"Didn't know."

"It's just medical supplies and foodstuffs! You hold me up much longer and I'll have a cargo hold full of rotten bananas and avocados and antibiotics that are going to be useless!" Paul shouted almost nose to nose with the young lieutenant commander holding him at gunpoint. "Check your logs. This is the *Mama's Express* on a Red Cross humanitarian mission to Luna Eleven and it has been approved by the UNE! This is my second run. Haven't you people seen the news vids?"

"What the Hell is going on here, Lieutenant Commander Haines?" A man with three full blips on his collar stepped through the UNE carrier's cargo hold doors, through the airlock and onto the *Express*.

"This man has a cargo for the sieged colony and there are three ships in convoy with him. His manifest is nonmilitary humanitarian goods, but I was only given notice of one ship, not three. Sir, I wasn't aware we were letting more ships through the blockade."

"I already explained that! We had the opportunity to get much-needed foodstuffs to the starving and dying human beings on the Moon below! If we don't get this food there now it will be bad before we can distribute it. The bananas are already turning black!" Paul continued to oversell the predicament with hopes that the captain of the blockade would just not want to deal with him. "I have no weapons of any sort on board and we're approved by the Red Cross and the UNE!"

"Captain Jennings, is it?" the blockade captain asked calmly.

"Yes."

"Captain, this is just a bad day for you. We have things going on and nobody is supposed to be getting through the blockade today." But the captain paused and was clearly perplexed by the situation. Paul was causing him trouble he didn't want. "You're only going to Luna Eleven with this, right?"

"Yes sir, humanitarian goods only. I mean, have you seen the scarecrows down there? It's terrible." Paul waved his arms about at the cargo. "I'm just hoping some of this stuff can get to them and keep some of them alive. I've never seen children so frail looking!"

"Captain, if I let you through with this cargo, I won't be able to let you back for an unforeseen time to come. We're about to clamp completely down on the Moon and nobody will be going in or out. Not even humanitarian missions."

"I see." Paul hesitated slightly. *Fortune favors the bold*, he thought. "Sir, I'll gladly sit down there for weeks if that's what it takes to get this stuff to them."

"You might end up one of them, Captain Jennings. Do you understand what you are asking for here?"

"Yes, I do."

"I see." The captain looked at the lieutenant commander briefly then nodded approvingly. "It's a noble thing. Good luck, then. Don't try to return or we'll be ordered to open fire on you."

"Understood. And thanks, Captain . . . uh, sorry, I didn't get your name."

"Blalock. Captain Blalock," the man told him. "We'll see if you're thanking me in a few weeks when you start getting hungry too."

"The bananas and avocados are mostly going bad, Nate," Paul explained as he walked him about the cargo hold of the *Mama's Express*. "The potassium should still be there, just not edible."

"Didn't plan on eating it anyway," Nate laughed. "But three cargo haulers full of bananas is only a start, not sure if it's enough to run a war."

"Good thing I brought you more than just bananas and avocados, then." Paul grinned from ear to ear. "Look here. You see this bulkhead here? Does it seem out of place to you at all?"

"Not sure what you mean. It just looks like a bulkhead at the aft end of a cargo box." Nate pounded his hand against it and there was nothing unusual about the metallic clang sound it made. "Should it look out of place?"

"Well, if you measure the outer length of the ship this cargo hold should be a good five meters longer on the inside." Paul leaned against the bulkhead. "I asked around before making this run. I had a feeling it would be my second and last one through the blockade and I knew this might be our only shot at getting you what you need. On the other side of this wall is a container filled with petroleum jelly and inside of that petroleum jelly is a five-meter-by-five-meter-by-three-meter chunk of pure potassium metal. I had to hock everything I own and take out a loan against the *Express* to pay for it, but it's there. The other two ships have similar holds but they're filled with potassium metal ion batteries. Most of them are old and bad but there's a lot of potassium there. I had to autonav them down. Ueys wouldn't let me crew them. The guys I, uh, borrowed them from are gonna be pissed that they ain't getting them back anytime soon."

"Brilliant! Paul, just brilliant!" Nate clapped him on the shoulder and shook him happily. "We'll get to tearing all this down and moving it. So, looks like you're gonna be with us for a while now. Maybe in the time to come we can figure out a way to get your ships out of hock."

"Maybe, but unless they were destroyed or something so that the insurance would pay off the loans, I'm not sure how. Whatever we do, it'd better pay dividends in the long run," Paul said.

"I'll see to it that your finances will be taken care of. That is assuming we survive all this." Nate pointed out through the viewport of the hangar bay at the expanse of the Moon stretching out to the east. There were flatbeds pulling up with people in spacesuits holding rifles. One of the trucks had a cover over the back and was painted up like a Red Cross ambulance. "So, in the meantime, we need to figure out how to move cargo both across the surface and underground from colony to colony. Interested in another job?"

"Maybe *Mama's Express* can stay in business, just not as an interplanetary hauling company." Paul looked out the window at the ambulance and had an idea. "What needs to get where first?"

Lunar Fury

⊕

by Josh Hayes

⊕ ONE ⊕

Go to the Moon, they said. It'll be fun, they said. Yeah, sure.

I looked at the chaos unfolding around Swigert Dome. The news of the blockade had spread like a wildfire, and the residents were scrambling to find refuge against the battle everyone knew was coming. A battle that no one here could fight. Willing, sure. Most of these people wouldn't give it a second thought, but what were they supposed to do, throw rocks and paint at the Earthers?

Swigert's "Garden," as its residents called it, wasn't as much a garden as it was a large common area in the middle of the dome. It was used for everything from random storage, to entertainment, to just a quiet place to relax after a long day at work. Well, quiet under normal circumstances. Right now, it was filled with a lot of scared people, all wondering if they would live through this debacle.

And they weren't the only ones.

At one end, a man and a woman were hauling what looked like everything they owned in several duffels, dragging three children behind them as they hurried toward safety. A vac-suit sleeve stuck out from the side of one bag and I couldn't help but think how optimistic they'd been in taking the time to pack it. If the Earthers broke through the outer dome defenses, pressure suits wouldn't do a damn thing. But if it made them feel better...

I felt for them, I really did, but there wasn't anything I could do for them. Nothing but stand here and watch and make sure they didn't kill each other before the real fighting started. Several of them had already asked me if I knew anything about Earth allowing people to make the trip to Tranquility, but so far, I hadn't heard anything but "keep everyone calm and keep them inside."

Yeah, easier said than done.

"Hey, Thompson!" the voice yanked me back to the present as Shepard jogged toward me. The top of her Swigert Dome security uniform—navy blue, trimmed in silver—was unzipped, a red shirt underneath.

"What's up, Shep," I said, checking my watch. "I'm not due for relief for another hour."

She waved a dismissive hand through the air as she came to a stop, bending over and putting a hand on her knee. She spoke through long breaths. "Been... looking... all over. Reynolds is looking for you. Wants you down in Operations ASAP."

I frowned. "Operations? What for?"

"Hell if I know, I was just sent to deliver the message and take your place."

I pulled the radio off my vest and held it up. "Why didn't you just call me?"

"We tried. Looks like the Earthers stepped up their blockade and are jamming all the comms."

"Of course they are," I said.

Shepard straightened, her breathing starting to slow. "I can't believe it's really going to happen."

"What's that?"

"A war on Luna," Shepard said. "Even saying it doesn't sound real. Like a bad dream."

I couldn't disagree, but I didn't think "war" would be the best description of that particular scenario. "Lot of steps to go through before that happens."

Shepard's expression changed to one that might have been a relief. "You think so?"

"Not even the Earthers want war up here," I said, mostly believing it. "It's not like fighting a battle back on Earth. The circumstances are a lot more . . ." I trailed off, searching for the words. "Dire. Besides, as long as there's women and children up here—"

Shepard frowned. "What the hell is that supposed to mean?"

I raised my hands in mock surrender. "I didn't mean it like that. Just meant, that with families up here, they won't just start bombarding us. No one wants that kind of blood on their hands."

She looked around, taking in the scene I'd been staring at for the better part of three hours, and shook her head. "They're all scared as fuck."

"They're not the only ones," I said. "Listen, if the comms are down, don't get caught up in something. If people start causing a ruckus, let it happen and stay away from it. One of us against all of them are worse odds than us against Earth."

⊕ TWO ⊕

I found Trina in the operations bunker, an expansive chamber filled with rows of small computer terminals. Each row was arranged in concentric semicircles on descending levels. The main control station was a raised platform at the front of the room, where Trina Reynolds, Swigert's Head of Operations, stood orchestrating the madness, calling out orders with the cadence of a practiced conductor.

Sporadic radio transmissions buzzed through speakers in the corners of the room, the traffic clipped and unreadable. She held a headset to her ear, a finger pressed into the other, obviously trying to make out the transmission over the cacophony of the room.

"No, I didn't copy, Ryan, say again," Reynolds said. She looked up as I approached and waved me down. I stopped at the small stepladder leading up to the command station and put a boot on the bottom rung.

"What's up, Chief?"

She held up a finger, listening.

The screens behind her showed views from one of the dome's external feeds, giving her visuals of the entire outpost and a few from orbit. In the center screen, four Earth Fleet ships hung against the backdrop of stars. The image seemed almost peaceful, if it weren't for the fact that they were endangering every human on Luna with their ridiculous stunt.

"Look," Reynolds said. "Just deal with it. Thompson's here, I'll get back with you in a bit, okay? Right."

Reynolds set the headset aside and came over to the top of the ladder, shaking her head. "Just one time, *one time*, I'd like something to go right around here."

"Wouldn't be Luna otherwise," I said.

"Never would've imagined it getting this bad," Reynolds said. "And it's only going to get worse. They've already tried to attack Hadley once. Fortunately, some crazy son of a bitch managed to stop them with some paint and a tank of O_2, but that will only slow them down. They've really got a hard on for that damn Mimic."

The Mimic, I thought. There'd been countless rumors about the artifact they'd found, and I wasn't sure if I believed any of them. Some ancient alien God, some deep-space alien probe, some type of faster-than-light travel, all of it seemed ridiculous to me. Of course, I was the expert on exactly none of those subjects so no one was asking my opinion on what we should do with it, whatever it was. If it'd been me, I would have told everybody to stay the hell away from it. Don't know that I've ever seen anything good come of messing with stuff that people don't understand. But what do I know?

I let the silence hang for a moment, then raised an eyebrow. "You wanted to see me?"

Reynolds shook herself. "We got a call from Hadley Dome a few hours ago. They were supposed to be sending over what they called 'much-needed supplies.' Supplies that were"—she checked her watch—"supposed to have been here an hour ago."

"What kind of supplies?"

"They didn't say. *Wouldn't* say. Said they were worried about the comms being tapped and didn't want anyone to know exactly what was going on."

"Sounds reasonable."

"Maybe."

"So where do I come in?"

"I need you to find it."

I coughed. "Find it? You're not serious."

"As a heart attack. They said it would tip the scales of this conflict in our favor, and if there's even a small chance of us coming out on top, we have to take it. We know the most likely route they'd take, I've already had it loaded into this pad." She held out a small, palm-sized data pad.

I looked over the map. "It could be anywhere. You know that, right? I mean, it's not like you can just hop on the turnpike."

"It's not an ideal situation, no."

"Ideal? You're asking me to go on a walkabout in one of the most hazardous environments known to man during one of the most dangerous conflicts in history, to look for . . . we don't even know what."

"If you can't do it . . ."

I held up a hand. "I didn't say I couldn't do it, but I'm going to need some help."

"Boyd and Lang are already getting suited up."

I chuckled. "Figures. Do you have any idea how big this thing is? Kinda need to know that kind of information."

"They just said it was coming on a flatbed track, that's all I know."

"Except that it should've been here by now."

She nodded. "Except that."

"Are we expecting any problems?" I put a hand on the pistol holstered on my hip.

"I doubt it," Reynolds said. "Even if the Earthers figure out what's going on, I don't think they'd be able to deploy any units fast enough."

"But it *is* possible."

"The longer you stand here talking to me, the worse the odds get. Look, just go out there, find out what happened to the transport and bring it here. It'll be fine."

It didn't sound fine. In fact, it sounded like it was a gigantic clusterfuck and Reynolds was throwing me out right in the middle of it.

Fantastic.

⊕ THREE ⊕

The garage was about the length of a football field, with a low ceiling and two rows of round concrete pillars running down the center. It wasn't as big as the Garden, but as spaces on Luna went, it was damn right expansive. Swigert Dome owned several kinds of vehicles from squat eight-wheeled haulers to fast single-passenger cars, though the cars were more an ATV than anything you'd find back on Earth.

I found Boyd and Lang loading up three of the quads,

strapping on additional O$_2$ tanks to wide cargo platforms on the back end. Both were already suited up, save for their helmets. Each had a pistol holstered on a thigh rig, the grips manufactured so the weapons were usable even with their thick gloves.

Lang's long blond hair looked like she'd just gotten out of the shower. She was shorter than Boyd and me, at five-four, but could beat us both any day of the week in cardio. She nodded to me as I approached, pulling hard on a strap holding one of the tanks to the cargo rack.

"'Bout time you showed up," Boyd said, dusting his hands off. His black hair was cut short, and he had a thin, almost imperceptible line across the top of his upper lip. I wouldn't have been surprised if he spent more time getting ready than Lang did.

I tapped the radio clipped to my shoulder. "Radios are shit."

He laughed. "I've been saying that shit for weeks."

"What have you not complained about since you got here?" Lang asked.

Boyd waved her off and moved to load another tank onto his quad, strapping it down next to the first. "Yeah, well, when shit's broken, shit's broken. I already got you loaded up, boss."

"Thanks." He'd laid out my suit over the quad's center seat, the helmet resting on the headrest. I moved one of the suit's sleeves aside to see the quad's control panel, which flicked to life when I tapped it. "You guys know what we're doing?"

Lang shrugged. "Do we ever?"

"She's got a point, boss," Boyd said.

"We're going to find a transport, sent from Hadley to us. It's about an hour past due and the brass seems to think it's extremely important to our mission here."

Boyd laughed. "Sure it is."

I initiated the quad's start-up sequence and diagnostic protocols, then kicked off my boots and unclipped my gun belt. I slipped on the suit, leaving the helmet and gloves on the seat as I worked through the quad's system menu, pulling the data from the pad Reynolds had given me.

"Where we heading?" Lang asked, coming up behind me. She leaned over my shoulder, watching as the nav computer loaded the data. A small screen above the steering wheel displayed a grayscale map of Luna, landmarks shown in yellow, the route outlined in red. "Oh, great, not only do we not know what's going on, we don't know what's going on in the middle of nowhere."

There was a lot of open space on the Moon, unclaimed territory or unusable territory that nobody wanted. On any normal day that wouldn't have been a problem, but with the fleet of enemy ships running an illegal blockade and attacking our settlements, there wasn't any telling what could happen. Not only that, but anything to do with the Mimic was sure to get someone's attention, attention we didn't want or need. I just hoped I could find it quick. The sooner we got back the sooner it became someone else's problem.

"The batteries will give us about twelve hours," Boyd said. "And we've got enough O_2 to last about twice that."

I pulled on my gloves. "I'm hoping to be back well before that."

Boyd climbed onto his quad. "Yeah, well, you know what they say about best-laid plans."

"Yeah, I know."

We left Swigert ten minutes later, driving through hundreds of vehicle tracks that spread farther and farther apart as we drove deeper into the barren, gray wasteland that was Luna. Most of us just called it the Gray and no matter how many trips I've taken, the landscape never becomes any less intimidating. Something about the emptiness of it all.

The sound of my breathing echoed inside my helmet, but outside the almost haunting stillness was enough to drive a person crazy. It was like a dream, didn't feel right. It'd taken several months to become accustomed to it. In fact, that had been my hope when the Earthers had first arrived; that the terrain would be so disorienting, they wouldn't be able to handle it and they'd just decide to pack up and leave.

But that was too much to hope for. They were here until they got what they came for, or until we kicked them back to Earth. And the way things had been going, I didn't have high hopes for the latter.

Our trio of quads bounced around on the rocky terrain, kicking up trails of dust behind us. The shadow of Swigert Dome sprawled out in front of us, the massive structure stretching almost a half a mile in diameter. It wasn't beautiful, but then again, it hadn't been built for comfort or pleasure; it had been built for survival, like everything on Luna.

I'd had my doubts about coming here, to Luna, not going to lie about that. Worried that I would miss the creature comforts of Earth. Hell, the simplest thing, like walking out your front door without making sure you are completely sealed in a vac suit to enjoy the afternoon breeze, for the sun on my face, swimming in the ocean. The things you people back on the Big Blue still take for granted every day.

But after a few months, I didn't even miss them anymore. I'd even come to consider Luna home, more than Earth had ever been. Life on Luna really makes you appreciate what was truly important in life.

We continued on for another twenty minutes before coming to the mouth of the Shona Crater Pass. Engineers had carved out a ten-meter-wide pass on opposing sides of the crater, reducing the travel time between Swigert and Hadley by almost an hour. We sped through the entrance single file, the walls of the pass stretching up some thirty feet. After clearing the pass, we passed several large mounds of dirt and rock, removed during the excavation, and old earthmovers left abandoned.

Above us in the star-filled sky, humanity's birthplace was a blue crescent, and a beautiful backdrop to the ships sent to steal what was rightfully ours. And its residents were coming to kill us.

"What I wouldn't give for a nice railgun about right about now," Boyd said. He overexaggerated his movements, miming firing a rifle at one of the ships. "I could end this thing right now."

The ugly monstrosity looked like it had been pieced together from several random modules. Its long central chassis was an amalgamation of scaffold mechanical compartments, oxygen tanks and propellant canisters arranged around the fuselage.

"Or maybe you can make it worse," Lang said.

"How the hell could I make it any worse?"

"They could start hitting the domes with kinetic strikes."

"Ain't going to do that."

"Might," Lang said. "You don't know. Never thought they'd attack us either, but here we are. I have a bad feeling that this thing is going to get a lot worse before it's all said and done."

"It's our job to make sure that doesn't happen," I said with more conviction than I felt.

"When did you become such a hero?" Lang asked.

"I'm no hero," I said. "But sometimes things need doing, and when you're it, you're it."

⊕ FOUR ⊕

"Look," Boyd said, pointing over his steering wheel.

I followed his finger, looking over the gray, barren expanse. Craters and boulders threw long shadows across the desolate landscape, and tucked between two large columns of stone, I saw the transport. The engine hatch on the front of the flatbed's cab was propped open and two men in vac suits were standing next to it.

"You've got to be kidding," Lang said.

Movement on the ridge to the south caught my attention. A cloud of dust kicking rose up from behind the wall of a large crater, whatever was creating it hidden behind the ridge. I didn't need to see, I already knew.

"Shit," I said.

"What?" Lang asked.

This time it was my turn to point. "There."

They both followed my direction, and both cursed in unison. I scanned the terrain between the disabled multitrack and the dust cloud and estimated we had about ten minutes, maybe fifteen at the outside, before they reached us.

"Shit," I repeated, and gunned the throttle.

The two men turned as we approached, and even though I couldn't see their expressions past their mirrored face visors their body language was obviously apprehensive. They stepped away from us as our quads skidded to a stop.

"Don't worry, we're friendly. From Swigert," I said, my digitized voice projected on the suit-to-suit channel. I pointed to the large container strapped to the multitrack's flatbed. "You got something for us?"

The two looked at each other, seemingly trying to decide how much they should say.

"Listen, I get it, but we don't have a lot of time." I pointed toward the column of dust. "They're coming, and I guarantee you they're not going to be as friendly as us. What's wrong with your track?"

"Batteries are shot," the man on the right said. "Thought they had enough juice to make it, but I guess with the extra load it wasn't enough."

They spread apart so I could look. I'm not much of an engineer, but reading power levels on a battery is something a four-year-old could do on Luna. And all four battery modules were dead.

"What were they at when you left?" I asked.

"Just over half," the second man said.

Boyd stepped around them, craning his head to see. "What the hell you guys thinking taking a vehicle with half power? How did you drain all the battery power?"

"We were in kind of a rush," the first man said.

"Rushing is a good way to get dead out here," Lang said.

"It doesn't matter now," I said. We needed to get moving. I turned back to the quads. "Boyd, grab your batts. You two, start pulling the old batteries out. Come on, let's move."

"Wait, what are you talking about?" the first man asked.

"Batteries are batteries," I told him, already unlatching the housing on my quad. "And ours have full charges."

Boyd jogged back to his quad and followed my lead, removing the housing and disconnecting the batteries. "We're going to need all the batts from your quad, and mine, to run that thing, and even then—"

"It'll work," I said, cutting him off.

It took us five minutes to get the battery disconnected and transferred. Each cell weighed eighty pounds lunar and every time I set one down I was terrified I was going to smash a finger. The track driver and Boyd connected the new batteries in parallel, linking them together to provide the maximum power possible. A minute later, the track's engines hummed to life, and the driver was climbing into the cab.

"Looks like everything is powered up and ready to go," he said.

"All right, let's get moving," I said, pulling myself onto the flatbed. Boyd followed me up, and we braced ourselves against the waist-high case as the track started to move. It was eight feet long and four feet wide and didn't have any markings, save for the words PROPERTY OF HADLEY DOME stenciled across the front. Nothing to provide any clues as to its contents. Three four-inch nylon straps held it securely to the multitrack's flatbed. I had to fight the urge to pop the straps off and look inside, knowing that if it fell off, there wouldn't be any way in hell we'd be able to move it ourselves.

The pillar of gray-white dust was close now, maybe five hundred yards out. Close enough that I could see it was three distinct clouds; one seemed to be pulling away from the other two. So, a fast mover and a couple heavies. I wondered what the slower vehicles could be—another multitrack, a couple of the Earthers' tanks? Either way we'd be screwed.

I slapped the top of the cab. "Hey, come on! We need to be gone yesterday!"

The tracks whined briefly, and we lurched forward. It took another minute before we were rolling at speed, though it wasn't at all what I would call fast. Most transports on Luna weren't built for speed, they were built for versatility. For reasons that were painfully obvious right now, going fast was more than likely to get someone hurt or killed, and in a place that was deadly on its own, without any outside help, versatility and safety were favored.

Lang pulled up next to us. "This ain't going to cut it, boss."

"Yeah." I felt the urge to kick the cab and yell at the driver to pick it up but knew it wouldn't do any good. He was doing the best he could under the circumstances, just like we all were.

Boyd tapped my shoulder and pointed.

I followed his finger and gritted my teeth. "Shit."

Three hundred yards away, a quad sped out from behind a ridge, turning almost immediately to give chase.

"Well," Boyd said, "now what the hell do we do?"

⊕ FIVE ⊕

"We need to slow them down," I said.

"Yeah? And how do you suppose we do that?" Boyd asked.

"Lang, you need to convince him to go away."

Still rolling beside the transport, she looked up at me, then over her shoulder at the Earther. "What the hell do you expect me to do about that? You think if I ask him politely, he'll just turn around and go home?"

I tapped my pistol. "You've got thirty reasons for him to turn around right there on your thigh."

"And if he's got a gun too?"

"Make sure you shoot first."

Lang didn't respond right away, then without a word, angled her quad away from the multitrack, turning to charge the Earther.

The multitrack lurched, its right-side treads bouncing off a small crater. The sudden movement threw me back several steps, bumping into the case. I grabbed one of the straps holding the case to the flatbed and gritted my teeth, straining to keep from toppling over the side. I grunted as I pulled myself back upright and kicked the back of the cab. "Jesus Christ, pay attention."

"I tell you what," Boyd said, grabbing the other strap with both hands. "The way this is going, we'll be lucky to make it back even without those Earth bastards chasing us."

I didn't disagree.

I watched as Lang zigzagged through the field of boulders and small craters toward the lone Earther, wondering what he was thinking. I didn't see any weapons on the quad, and even if he had any, it wasn't like one quad was going to be able to stop us. I started to wonder if he was just a scout, keeping tabs on us until the main force could catch up.

As Lang closed on him, she started waving a hand at him, obviously trying to ward him off, but the Earther made no moves to change course. It might have been the first-ever game of Lunar Chicken.

"What the hell is she doing?" Boyd asked.

"Hell if I know." I toggled my radio. "Lang, what are you—"

At the last minute, Lang swerved to the left, drew her pistol and fired, sending a volley into the ground. Plumes of dust sprayed over the Earther as he drove through the powdered geysers before turning the wheel and veering away.

Boyd laughed. "Well, that's one way to do it."

The Earther made a wide turn, tires digging into the dirt, then accelerated back the way he'd come.

"Nice work, Lang," I said as the Earther cut between two large boulders and disappeared behind the ridge.

"That should make them think twice about getting too close," she responded over the radio.

I laughed and turned, scanning the landscape ahead. Swigert still wasn't in view, but we were closing on the Shona Pass. That was progress at least. "We get through Shona, we'll be home free."

"*If* we make it through," Boyd said.

"Well, that didn't last long," Lang said over the radio.

Boyd and I turned back around and watched as the two Earther quads came speeding out from behind the ridge again, followed by a six-wheeled rover. The armored transport had a rounded driver's compartment with a wide windshield that wrapped around the front, giving the operator a clear view of everything in front of them. The bulky, roughly cylindrical rear section was covered in armor plates, a mean-looking Kord 9P150 machine gun mounted on its spine. Two soldiers stood behind it, swaying back and forth with the motion of the rover.

"We're not going to make it," Boyd said.

I searched the back of the truck, looking for anything we could use to fend off the Earthers. The case was still strapped down, and we had our O_2 tanks. A few tools that we hadn't thrown out, and the pistols we each carried. Not that they'd do us any good at this range, and who knew if they'd do any good even if we were in range.

Maybe if I could manage a shot through a viewport, I might have a chance, but the chances of making that shot were slim to none, and that was considering I had a stable platform to shoot from. Riding on the back of this flatbed, bouncing around on the surface of the Moon at fifty miles an hour, trying to hit fast-moving vehicles weaving around boulders and craters, would make the shot damn-near impossible.

Mind racing, I turned back to the Pass, desperately trying to find a solution that didn't end up with us blasted all over Luna's surface. We had to take out that gun, but there wasn't any way we could get close without that gun finding us and turning us into so much slag. They'd see us coming a mile away.

Unless they didn't.

"Lang!" I shouted, beckoning her with both hands.

"What about calling for help?" Boyd asked.

I shook my head. "Even if there was help to send, they wouldn't get here in time."

"What are we going to do now?" Lang asked, pulling up beside the multitrack. "I'm not fucking charging that thing."

"Get closer." I stepped to the side of the flatbed where the small ladder hung down.

Boyd caught my arm as I stepped down. "Wait, what the hell are you going to do?"

I looked up at him, our eyes meeting through our visors. "We have to stop that rover."

"Okay?"

I waved Lang closer. "We're not going to make it back on defense. We're going to have to go on the offense."

"You're crazy."

"Yeah," I said, lowering myself down on the ladder. Lang had to steer around a cluster of rocks, then pulled close again, gunning the quad to match speed with the track.

Now, granted, this probably wasn't the most amazing idea I'd ever had, jumping off a moving vehicle onto another moving vehicle was pretty dumb under the best of circumstances, but it was the only move I had. My boot touched down on the quad's luggage rack. I focused on the rhythm of both vehicles, trying my best to gauge the best time to make the leap. Like there would ever be a good time.

I pushed off the ladder, brought my over foot over and crouched down on the back to the quad, grabbing the rack with both hands.

"Holy shit, boss," Lang said. "You're one crazy son of a bitch."

I let out a long breath as she angled away from the track. Well, no turning back now.

"All right, you're on now," Lang said. "Where the hell are we going?"

I pointed toward the Pass. "There. Find us a place to hide."

Lang hesitated and twisted to the side. "What the hell are you talking about?"

"Just do it. Hurry."

Lang gunned the quad; its tires dug into the soft gray powder, kicking up a wave of dust in our wake. We sped past the track, racing for the Pass.

"All right, genius," Lang shouted. "What's your plan?"

✠ SIX ✠

"This is nuts," Lang whispered, even though she didn't need to. Even if it hadn't been over the radio, the Earthers wouldn't've been able to hear anyway.

We were tucked down behind one of the larger mounds of discarded dirt and rock, just inside the entrance to Shona Crater, watching as the Earthers rolled past without giving their surroundings so much as a cursory glance. The soldiers behind the Kord 9P150 swayed with the rover's motion, each holding onto a waist-high rail that surrounded the space. Horrible situational awareness, but I wasn't complaining. The first hurdle of my plan was over, now came the hard part.

"Go!" I said, patting her shoulder once.

Judging by the wiggling of her helmet, I could tell Lang was shaking her head back and forth, but she gunned the quad regardless. The back end dipped slightly as we started off, the tires digging into the gray dirt, and thirty seconds later we were closing on the rover.

"Don't turn around," Lang said. "Don't turn around."

I drew my pistol and leaned forward. "Just keep her steady."

The soldier on the right shifted his weight, craning his body to see something ahead of the rover. The one on the left moved behind the Kord and pulled the charging handle back. They were getting ready to shoot.

"Hurry!" I shouted, leveling the pistol.

The sights danced in my vision. It was hell getting the gun on target, and even harder keeping it there. I gritted my teeth; my body tensed as I mentally prepared for the shot, trying to anticipate the motion of the quad under me and the rover ahead. I held my breath and squeezed the trigger.

The pistol bucked twice. Sparks shot off the rover's armor by the base of the gun mount, vanishing almost immediately.

"Shit," I growled, lining the sights back up. The unfocused image of the soldier behind the gun twisted, having obviously seen, or felt, the bullet impacts. I fired again and this time the rounds hit their mark, slamming into the soldier's back and side, knocking him into the Kord mount. His momentum carried him over the railing and over the side of the rover, his partner turning just in time to see him bounce off the ground.

The second Earther turned, obviously watching his comrade roll, then straightened as his gaze no doubt fell on our quad. I shifted aim and fired, the shots going wide as the Earther scrambled to get behind the Kord and bring it to bear. I fired until the magazine was empty; if we didn't succeed now, we wouldn't get a second chance. He managed to get the weapon halfway around before my bullets found him, sending him stumbling away from the Kord onto the roof of the rover's cab.

The pistol clicked empty, but I kept it leveled, waiting to see if the Earther got back up. The body bounced slightly on the armored roof, but otherwise remained still.

"Nice work, boss!" Lang said. She turned the wheel, angling us away.

"No," I said, reloading the magazine. "Keep going. Get right up on them."

I holstered the pistol, grabbed the roll bar above me and stood.

"What the hell are you doing?"

The quad bounced and rocked, knocking me into the bar. I gritted my teeth and tensed every muscle as we approached the rover.

"We still have work to do."

"Okay?"

"Closer! Get closer!"

Lang brought the quad right up next to the rover's back end. A short ladder, similar to the one on our multitrack, hung down between the back two sets of wheels. I shifted positions, ducking under the roll bar so I was standing on the very edge of the vehicle, and leaned over for the ladder, the surface of Luna a gray blur underneath me. My fingers wrapped around the rail, I held my breath and pushed off.

⊕ SEVEN ⊕

There was a half second of time, suspended between the quad and the rover, where I felt a terrifying sense of mortality. If I slipped or lost my grip, I'd fall and be crushed to death underneath the oversized wheels. I shook the thought out of my head and I pulled myself up the ladder, over the rail, onto the rover's roof.

I gave Lang a thumbs-up. "Get out of here!"

"Right! And where the hell am I supposed to go?" she asked, holding up both hands.

"Just stay back, those quads are coming back." I pointed as the two vehicles made wide turns, veering away from our multitrack back toward the rover. The driver must have called for help.

I stepped toward the machine gun and movement at the front of the rover caught my eye. The Earther soldier rolled over and pushed himself to his feet, a long knife in one hand. Without thinking I lunged forward and grabbed the gun mount, using it as leverage to propel a front kick into the man's chest. The sole of my boot connected and sent him rolling down the front of the rover. I felt the vehicle lurch as the tires ran him over and held tight to both the rail and the gun mount, keeping myself from being thrown clear.

The body appeared a second later, mangled and twisted, his suit torn in several places, venting streams of O_2. The Earther rolled to a stop and didn't move.

"Boss!" Lang shouted over the radio. "Eleven o'clock."

The first of the Earth quads was racing toward the rover; its operator had one hand on the wheel, the other leveling a pistol. I couldn't hear the shots, but I could see the weapon bucking as he fired. I froze, waiting for the inevitable impact, but nothing happened. He'd missed.

I shook myself, moving back to the Kord and twisting the barrel back forward. I pulled the charging handle to the rear then let it slam home. Leaning into the stock, I found the sight picture, found the Earther, and fired.

The weapon rocked violently as it fired, sending eight hundred rounds a minute down range. Plumes of gray dirt and rock shot into the air as the rounds slammed into the ground ahead of the quad. It went up on two wheels as it swerved hard to miss the attack.

"Come on," I said, shifting the fire to follow. The Kord 9P150 shook in my hands, firing in a steady staccato as rounds chewed through the lunar landscape chasing the quad.

The driver jerked the wheel again, turning away from the oncoming rounds, but it wasn't enough. A line of erupting powder and rock caught him, slamming into the rear and side of the quad, ripping through the chassis. His body spasmed as my fire found him. The quad swerved right, then left, losing control. The front bumper guard smacked into a knee-high rock, lifting the back end off the ground and sending the quad flipping end over end. Still strapped to the chair, the driver's lifeless body flopped around inside the roll-cage.

It landed nose-first and sent up a cloud of dirt and debris, coming to rest on its side, wheels still spinning.

"Holy shit," I whispered.

Sparks sprayed up from the rover's armored cab in front of me, pulling my attention away from the destroyed quad. The second Earther was still coming on, firing his own pistol, trying to take me out. I cursed, mentally kicking myself for losing focus, and scrambled to get the Kord on target.

I pressed the firing stud before I even had the weapon lined up. The first rounds hit to the right of the quad and twenty feet ahead. Another spray of sparks erupted off the side of the rover, shooting up in front of it and vanishing almost immediately.

"Come on! Come on!" I shouted. The sights were almost lined up—the gun clicked, going silent. Almost without thinking, I jerked the charging handle back, trying to clear the malfunction but nothing happened when I pulled the trigger. I flinched as sparks sprayed, frantically looking for why the gun had stopped firing. Then I saw it. The belt that had been feeding up from the ammo box mounted underneath the Kord was gone. I was out of ammo.

"You've got to be kidding me," I growled, ducking sideways, keeping the Kord between me and the oncoming quad. I drew my pistol, knowing it probably wasn't going to make any difference, and out of the corner of my eye Lang's quad came into view.

Her wordless warcry echoed over the radio as her quad cut across the landscape, closing on the Earther. I realized what she was planning on doing right before she did it, but didn't have enough time to warn her off. Even if I had, I doubted my words would've stopped her.

Lang's quad slammed into the side of the Earther's, the impact launching both vehicles into the air. Lang's rose above the other, flipping forward, debris from both vehicles filling the surrounding air. The Earther's landed first, its side digging a deep gouge out of the ground before rolling another ten feet, coming to rest upside down.

Lang's back end slammed down hard. The quad fell forward, landing on all four tires, bouncing several times before twisting and rolling to its side and skidding to a stop.

"Lang?" I shouted. "Lang, can you hear me?"

She didn't answer.

The rover jerked under me, quickly swerving right, then back left. I stumbled into the railing, grunting, straining to stay on my feet. They were trying to shake me off. I shoved the pistol back into its holster and pulled myself forward, ready to finish this.

⊕ EIGHT ⊕

The rover lurched again as I reached the forward rail. I held tight, shaking my head, silently cursing them. Carefully, I swung one leg over the rail, then the other. I dropped to the cab's roof and pulled myself forward until I could reach over the edge and grab the handle. Through the window, I could see the driver and passenger pointing, their helmets moving as if they were caught up in a heated debate.

I craned my neck forward and located the steps below the door. I held my breath, pulled the handle and threw open the door. Holding onto the frame with one hand, I slid over the edge and swung my feet down, hitting the step hard and drawing my pistol in the same movement.

I leveled it at the driver's helmet. "Stop."

The driver hesitated for a minute, obviously conflicted. The passenger's arm moved, and though I couldn't see what he was reaching for it was obvious, he was going for some kind of weapon.

"Don't!" I barked, "Not worth it. Put your hands on the dash."

Slowly, the passenger complied and I angled the gun back to the driver. "Now, stop this rover. Don't do anything stupid."

The driver nodded, the outline of his face visible through his darkened visor, then slowed to a stop.

"Turn it off," I said. After he'd gone through the rover's shutdown sequence, I stepped backward off the side step, then beckoned them to follow. "Guns stay in the cab."

I watched them disengage their five-point harnesses and slowly pull their pistols from the holsters on their thighs and toss them on the floorboard. The driver climbed out and I told him to get his hands up as the passenger slid across the bench seat.

"You don't have any idea what you're doing. Do you?" the driver asked.

"Move," I said, ignoring his question.

"Do your bosses have any idea the danger they're putting us in messing around with that thing?" the passenger asked. He followed the driver away from the rover, his hands up.

There'd been a time when knowing exactly what the Mimic was, and what it did, would've been extremely interesting. But right at that very moment, I couldn't have cared less. The only thing I knew for sure was that people like these men were willing to kill and steal for it. I wondered if the aliens that had built the damn thing had been as willing to destroy themselves over it as we were.

What if that's why they'd gone to so much trouble to hide it?

"Sit," I told the Earthers. I glanced at Lang's wrecked

quad, but there still wasn't any sign of her. I toggled my radio. "Lang, you there? Can you hear me?"

The only response I got was static.

"Boyd, you there?"

"Yeah, boss, I'm here."

"The rover's out of commission. You're clear."

"Roger that," Boyd said. "We'll come back and get you."

"No. Get the cargo to Swigert. That's priority number one. Once you get it off-loaded, grab a couple more guys and come back and get us. I've got two prisoners we're going to need escort."

There was silence for a moment, then Boyd said, "Okay, boss. Don't do anything stupid until I get back, all right?"

"Hey," I said, "it's me."

"Exactly."

I found some spare wire in a supply cabinet and made the driver tie up the passenger, then tied the driver's hands behind his back. With their ankles tied, sitting back to back, I finally took a breath. They weren't going anywhere, and with no signs of any reinforcements, it appeared as though our little adventure was drawing to a close. I disabled their suits' comm units and made sure they had plenty of O_2 left in their tanks.

I gave Lang's wreck another look, then nodded at my two captives. "You boys don't wander off now, ya hear?"

They didn't respond.

I reached the Earther's upside-down quad first, the driver hanging from the harness. Lang's quad was twenty feet away, on its side, and it was empty. I walked around the vehicle until I found some tracks that appeared to be someone crawling away and followed them to a boulder some fifteen feet away.

Lang was sitting with her back against the boulder on the far side, legs out in front of her. I knelt down and pushed up the mirrored visor of her helmet. "Lang?"

Her eyes flittered open, and a weak smile spread across her face. "Damn, you're ugly."

I let out a relieved breath. "Holy shit, you're okay."

She winced. "I guess. I'm pretty sure my leg's broken and I had to patch my suit. Lost a bit of O_2 in the process."

The gauge on her wrist showed her tank only had about twenty percent remaining. I took her hand and stood. "Come on, let's get you out of here. There's spare tanks on the rover."

She let out a pained gasp as I helped her to her feet. "Jesus, boss, easy."

"Sorry," I said, draping her arm over my shoulders. "We'll go slow."

The walk back to the rover took about ten minutes, and we had to stop several times to let her rest and check the seals on the patches. The two soldiers were in the process of scooting closer to the rover, but froze as we approached.

I put my free hand on my pistol. "I thought we'd discussed this."

The soldiers didn't answer, but I hadn't expected a response. Their shoulders slumped, and they leaned back against each other, resigning themselves to their fate. I found a replacement for Lang's O_2 tank, then sat down next to her and waited.

An hour later, Boyd arrived with six more security guys and the flatbed, now empty. We loaded the Earthers, securing them to the front of the bed with the same straps that had held the container they'd been after. It took four of us to lift Lang onto the bed and I took a seat next to her for the ride back. Boyd followed in the rover.

We pulled into Swigert's garage, met by more security and Reynolds. They helped haul the Earthers down and escorted them off for debriefing with Swigert's brass. A medical team loaded Lang onto a gurney and wheeled her off to the clinic.

I pulled off my gloves and helmet and ran a hand through my damp hair. Twenty feet away, the hard-plastic case sat facing away from me, the lip open. A handful of security officers stood around it, rubbing their hands together and grinning, making jokes and laughing.

I made my way to the front of the case, stepping up to it as the others backed away, giving me room. "Holy shit."

Inside were ten rows of identical matte-black rifles, stacked six deep, next to what looked like boxes of ammunition. Each box had the number "1,000" stenciled on the side in black lettering.

"Those would've been handy an hour ago," I said as Reynolds walked up.

"Nice, huh?" she asked, crossing her arms and grinning.

I picked up one of the rifles, feeling the weight, then pulled the stock into my shoulder and looked down the sights. It felt nice.

Boyd selected his own from the case. "All right, so we've got some guns, what are we supposed to do now?"

I pulled the trigger; there was an audible click. "Earth wants a fight. I say it's time we give them one."

THE BATTLE OF NORTH DOME

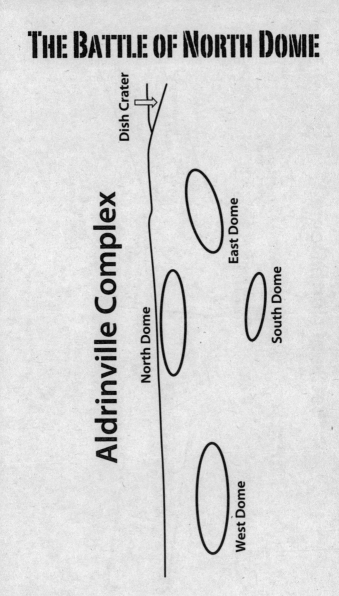

Battle of North Dome

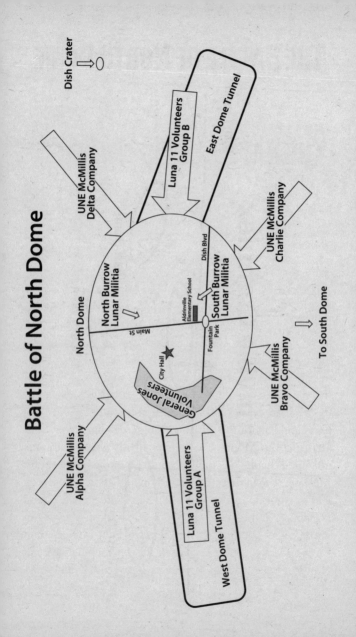

THE BATTLE OF NORTH DOME

✜

by Travis S. Taylor

"But why is this spot so important to them, Colonel?" Sergeant Reese Helms looked nervously across the vast gray landscape and the jagged edge of the meteor crater surrounding the research facility just outside of the North Dome of Aldrinville they had been dispatched to take and hold. The sergeant had been in scrapes on Earth before, but back home if you got shot up your blood didn't boil out and freeze at the same time. Fighting on the Moon, there was just something about it he didn't like.

No, there was everything about it he didn't like. Reese had signed on for the mission for the extra hazard pay and a trip to the Moon. He'd never in his wildest dreams imagined that he'd actually have to go into combat there. After all, who in their right minds would attack a research facility four hundred thousand kilometers away from anywhere, and to what end? But that had been over ten months ago—before the first skirmishes at Luna 8, then Luna City, the battle of Rinehart Dome, the Surrender at Hadley Dome, and most recently at Swigert Dome.

"Sergeant Helms," Colonel Marissa Suarez growled. She showed her full smile, like an alpha lion staring down his pride to show them who the boss was and to quit bothering them with stupid questions. "Who knows what this is all about? I don't. The whys and the what-fors—well, Sergeant, that ain't none of our business. Our business is to carry out the orders of the people who were elected and who are our bosses. Their orders were to take this facility at all costs and to the last soldier if that is what it took. It is our job to do just that."

"Uh, yes sir." Helms didn't like the answer. He didn't like anything about the predicament but there was absolutely nothing he could do to change the situation. His best move would be to follow the colonel's plan and hope he'd come out alive on the back side of it all.

"Helms!" Master Gunnery Sergeant Kelly Vors shouted over the comm net. "Get your butt over here and leave the colonel alone. Your squad is spread out so thin you could fly a shuttle between sentries and they'd never know it."

"On my way, Gunny!" Helms turned to Suarez and took in her larger-than-life appearance once more. She was legendary for her work in the Northern African skirmishes and had the scars and tattoos to back up the reputation. "Uh, thank you, Colonel. I needed to deliver this to you."

"What is it, Sergeant?" Suarez took the small data stick from him and studied it only briefly. She was too busy watching the radar showing the orbital insertion path of the incoming ship to worry about anything else.

"I don't know, ma'am. Alls I know is that General

McMillis told me to get it to you ASAP, ma'am. So that's what I did. Now, uh, ma'am, I need to get back to my squad."

"Very well, Helms." Suarez took the stick and inserted it into her wrist slot on her left hand. "And Sergeant Helms . . ."

"Ma'am?"

"Stay frosty and keep your eyes peeled. I'm counting on you."

"Yes, ma'am."

Suarez tapped at the data panel on her forearm until the information in the stick popped up on her visor. At first it just looked like maps and troop movements until the deck of cards started overlaying on the map. And right at the top within three hundred kilometers of her current location was the Ace of Spades, Mayor Alton Hamilton. About a hundred kilometers to the northeast was the King of Spades, Nathaniel Ray. The Queen of Spades, General Tamika Jones, was somewhere south of the West Dome about fifty kilometers. A few of the lesser cards showed up in almost every direction within a couple hundred kilometers of General McMillis's Major Attack Battalion. There were enough UNE forces right here concentrated with over four companies of more than one hundred soldiers each. If the data on this memory stick was right, the general could capture the Loonie Revolutionaries in one fell swoop and end this war before it got even further out of hand—if the data was real.

"Marissa, its Mac." Her officer's net buzzed in her ear.

"Yes, General? I thought I'd be hearing from you." Suarez tapped her forearm, pulling up a video window in her visor to see the general's face appear there. "Where'd we get this memory stick?"

"Apparently, we got this from a contact in the US State Department. I think we have a sympathizer in Aldrinville. According to intel reports this is real-time data. These are the hidey-hole whereabouts of the Loonies' top military leaders."

"If it's true, I say we go for the Ace of Spades to our west."

"I think that would take too long, Marissa. But we have Aldrinville surrounded and could take it. I think that would draw out all the top cards. I mean, this is their home." McMillis transmitted a map to Suarez's visor showing her an attack plan. "We pull in Alpha and Delta Companies up to the North Dome. Simultaneously you take Bravo and Charlie in eastward from your present position and break in through the southeast wall and we sack the city. Then the top cards will come running with their paintball guns and glue pots a-blazing. But we're ready for that nonsense now. This won't be like Hadley or Luna City. We'll decimate them like at Cernan Dome."

"Right sir, solid plan. We could take the city and then root them out from there. If they try to run over the surface, the blockade can swoop down and hammer them." Suarez liked the plan. She was getting tired of being on the Moon anyway. The UNE forces should have swept across the colonies months prior and put the Loonies in their places. "What's our timeline?"

"No time like the present, Colonel Suarez. The Loonie volunteers are so spread out it will take them hours to days to respond to us taking Aldrinville. We start with the

North Dome and we'll use that as our forward operating base. March your troops now. I want to make a push into the dome by morning. That enough time for you?" McMillis asked rhetorically.

"More than enough, General. We're moving out now!"

"Good hunting, Marissa."

"You too, sir."

"Are we sure they're on the move?"

"Yes, General Jones." The young volunteer stood at attention waiting for further orders. Tami rose from her chair and saluted the young woman then handed her a memory stick.

"Carry on. Send in First Sergeant Meeks and get this to Nathaniel as soon as possible. He's expecting it."

"Yes, ma'am."

Tami stood at the window in her makeshift quarters and stared out at the edge of what would hopefully be the next big dome excavation project for Aldrinville. No work had yet to be done on the southernmost natural volcanic dome structures but since Hamilton's A-team had figured out about the alien transport system a second, third, and then a fourth alien habitat had been found. The South Dome would one day be just as big as any other of Aldrinville's projects, especially since there were three major alien habitat rooms with more artifacts to be studied a few hundred meters below the interior caldera.

Tami watched as her army of volunteers made busy like ants on a mound moving about on a warm day on Earth. She just hoped that her ants would be able to hold out against the larger army of ants that were on their way.

"You sent for me, General?" First Sergeant Shawn Meeks entered her quarters at attention.

"Take it easy, Shawn."

"Yes, ma'am." Meeks allowed for a slight bend in his knees. Tami laughed out loud.

"That ain't easy," she scolded him. "Sit down."

"Yes, ma'am."

"And enough with the 'ma'am' stuff." She sat down behind her desk and sighed. "How many volunteers we got? Seventy? Eighty?"

"Current count is eighty-seven very raw volunteers. General McMillis is marching into the North Dome as we speak with over two hundred Earth-trained mercs." Meeks waited for that to sink in on Tami. She understood what he was telling her. "It could be very bad, Tami."

"Well, what I'm hoping is two things," she said, ticking off on her fingers. "One, our level of preparation will be a surprise to them. And two, Hamilton has something else up his sleeve that I hope scares the piss out of them."

"For a mayor of a small Moon town he's a damned good strategist." Meeks smiled even if somewhat somberly.

"We're lucky to have him." Tami reached into her metal desk and pulled out a small bottle and two glasses. She made two quick pours and handed Meeks one of them. "Free Luna."

"Free Luna." They tapped the glasses and swigged down the drinks.

"We gonna be ready to move out in the next hour?"

"Yes, ma'am."

"Well then, I guess it's time to go to war." Tami wasn't sure she could do it. She was going to have to send these eighty-seven kids into a meat grinder to face four companies of Earth troops. "You're probably the only actual veteran I've got, Shawn. Any last-minute words of wisdom?"

"There's no wisdom that I know of. Just keep your head down and don't get your ass shot off," Meeks said grimly. "I guess just do your job. That's the main thing. As long as our main focus is to get the job done, we'll make it through."

"Do your job. Sounds about right." Tami thought about what that job was. She had to draw the Ueys as deep into North Dome as she could so that Hamilton's and Ray's troops could flank and surround them. They were outnumbered and outgunned, but the advantage was that the Earthers would be thinking it was going to take them hours to get a company of troops across the fifty or so kilometers to North Dome. It was going to take about ten minutes at most. And all of her troops would be carrying the new *Mama's Express* rifles, not paintball guns. And this was the Loonies' home. She hoped all that would add up to something. But they'd still be outnumbered four to one, until Nate and Alton showed up. They just had to hold long enough for the plan to work.

"David, are you sure this is finished?" Mayor Hamilton asked, looking at the rocket-nozzle-shaped container the Mimic had just printed out. There were five others on the floor that looked identical and five rocket body tubes and nose cones. The nozzles were about a half meter tall and across on the top but only about five centimeters across at the bottom. The boxes had a cardboard and rubberized-like material filling them and intimately bonded to the metal walls, sealing the top. The multiple pieces were threaded and clearly could be connected together to build a much larger device. The hope was that they wouldn't be too complex to be put together on the fly without expert help.

"They're done, Mr. Mayor. All you have to do is light the fuse by pressing this button here," David explained. "They'll work."

"How did you know how to build these?" the mayor asked.

"I just looked it up on the internet. Then Sarah and Jerry and I played around with it a bit until we got it to work right. Carla designed the trigger circuit," David explained. "Sarah calculated the orbital mechanics and gave you the coordinates, right?"

"Yes. I'll place them myself," Hamilton acknowledged. "And they don't have to be guided or anything, right?"

"They're dumb rockets, Mr. Mayor. They'll fly straight assuming we designed them correctly. The test rockets we flew in the tunnels worked fine," David reassured him.

"They have to work, They have to."

"They will. I hope."

"Me too."

"Well, good luck, Mr. Mayor." David held out a hand and stood up. Hamilton took it and shook it solidly while nodding and looking him in the eyes.

"David, if it weren't for you figuring out how to work this thing, the Earthers would own us by now. You know that, right?"

"Took all of us, Mr. Mayor."

"Well, it's my turn now." He turned and gave a couple

of orders to others in the Mimic room. Several volunteers rushed in to pick up the launch boxes. "Let's move out through the back door. We'll take three vehicles with the lights on and I want the thirty troops with me spread out, making our group look as big as we can. We'll sling up as much of a dust trail as we can, too."

Hamilton slung a rifle on his back and made his way through the back door and toward the airlock. From there it was up the two-hundred-meter shaft to the garage and then westward across the old road toward Aldrinville and McMillis's battalion of Earther mercs. He hoped that the Ueys' eyes in the sky thought that his small band of troops heading to Aldrinville were all they'd managed to muster. What the Ueys didn't know was that there were over three hundred rifle-toting volunteers in the dogleg tunnel waiting to pour into the West Dome and then across the tunnel to the North Dome on his command. And if Tami and Nate were ready, they might just have a full-up defense force ready to surprise the Hell out of the Ueys.

The biggest concern was still the blockade. As long as the Moon was cut off from resupplies of certain materials, the UNE could eventually starve the colonies out. The damn Ueys could even do strategic strikes from low lunar orbit as they needed to keep the Loonies distressed. Alton knew that they could take back the domes they'd lost, but they couldn't hold them forever as long as that blockade was there.

At last count there were almost seventy space vehicles in multiple inclinations at about a hundred kilometers' altitude. You couldn't look up without seeing a damned UNE spaceship above. Alton thought of a comment that

Jerry had made that led him down this path. Jerry had looked up and said, "You know, Mr. Mayor, you couldn't throw a rock without hitting a damned Uey blockade ship."

"Too bad I can't throw a rock that far," Alton recalled saying to him.

"The southern wall is breached, ma'am. We can infil at your order," Master Gunny Sergeant Kelly Vors reported to Suarez over the command net channel. "Bravo Company is in place and ready. Charlie is a few minutes behind and they aren't quite through the wall on the southeast yet."

"Tell them to hurry it up, Kelly. I want us inside in ten minutes!" Suarez ordered.

"Yes, ma'am."

Looking at the HUD on her visor she could see that Alpha and Delta were on the north side of the Dome and were already moving inside it. She had yet to hear if there was any fighting going on and there had not been any casualty reports either. Marissa was guessing that the Loonies were going to stay hidden until the very last minute and then pull some engineering trap with glue, or concrete, or pitfalls, or pressure bombs like they had been doing up to this point in the conflicts. All she could really do for now was wait until Charlie's engineers cut through the dome and then the four-wave final attack on the Loonies could commence.

"Lieutenant Thomas, pull your squad and walk with me," Marissa called to the leader of a six-man forward recon unit.

"Ma'am."

"Thomas, take your squad on ahead of Bravo. I want you to push as deep towards the city center as you can. If you see unfriendlies, engage, but don't get yourself in a bind. What I want is for you to blaze us a trail to the center of the Loonie forces."

"Got it, ma'am."

"Go."

"Colonel, Charlie is through the dome wall. We can ingress on both sides now," Vors reported.

"Do it."

"Ueys are pouring in from all four corners of North Dome and are plodding through Main Street and Dish Boulevard like they own the city. For the most part all the civilians have been evacuated down to the tunnels and the alien rooms," First Sergeant Meeks told Tamika. "There are enough of them in place now, ma'am. No better time."

"Main Street of North Dome here is about a kilometer from the West Dome tunnel. We need to pull them away from there so Hamilton's men can egress and engage. Right here at the southern end of Dish Boulevard is where we hit. Let's move now fast and quietly. As soon as we set up in the shops along Jansky Drive and Bright Road running north and south we hit 'em."

This was going to be an old-school, hold-the-line type of fight. As far as she could tell, if they set up defensive lines along the two main streets and along the alleyways perpendicular, they could hold that little bit of town off from a frontal attack for a while. The Ueys had significantly larger numbers and would then try to flank them and they would be successful. That's when it would be an all-out hand-to-hand retreating fight to the West Dome tunnel.

"Meeks, send the order. Attack."

"Yes, ma'am."

Private First Class Kevin Mallet of the South Burrow Squad of the North Dome militia volunteers didn't like having to leave his visor on all the time. It made it hard to aim. But he also liked breathing and with the dome walls being breached by the damned Ueys he wasn't sure if the air was good enough. Main Street was so far from the outer dome wall that he wasn't sure it mattered, but one thing about living on the Moon was that you always had your suit on and ready in a time of crisis. PFC Mallet figured war counted as a time of crisis. He knew that General McMillis's battalion was coming for them and he knew that the North Dome militia was only a few squads deep and certainly wouldn't be able to hold the Ueys back. They were hopelessly outnumbered, but had been ordered directly from General Hamilton to hold the city.

"Mallet, get your ass down!" Corporal Martha Xhi shouted at him just as several rounds poked holes in the wall above his head. "What the Hell are you doing? Shoot back!"

"I count six of them there on Dish Boulevard just the other side of the coffee shop." Kevin let loose with several rounds from the nine-millimeter rifle. "Where the Hell is Ames?"

"There! On their left, about forty meters," Xhi replied. "Give him some cover fire!"

"Take that, you bastards! For Luna Eight!" Kevin

continued to fire in bursts and then he ducked back down behind the cover of the concrete barricade at the end of the alleyway. The mayor had the barricades placed there years ago and they were there to close off that end of the Main Street and Dish Boulevard crossing from traffic. The area was a pedestrians-only crossing with a big fountain in the middle of the street. On any normal day in Aldrinville you'd see the fountain covered with the college kids there to work on the radio telescope and the occasional family picnicking around the fountain. But this was no typical day. The shops were all closed. There were no families about. And the barricades and the fountain had been repurposed for fortification in a firefight.

"Xhi, this is Ames."

"Go, Staff Sergeant."

"We've got a forward recon team down here and they're laid in pretty good," Sergeant Ames started. "I need you and the rest of the squad to start pushing in to the south. I'm going to try and get close enough see if these new grenades work."

"Got it." Corporal Xhi looked to her left and Kevin could tell she was about to tell him to do something he didn't really want to do.

He looked down the line and counted PFCs James and Ruez on the other side of the street fountain. He was on her right and farther down from there was Lieutenant Gray's squad, but they looked to be pinned down by the forward recon team. It was going to be up to them to break things loose. Kevin managed to raise up and fire off three bursts of automatic fire before the barricade lit up in front of him with return fire.

"Holy shit!"

"Stay down, Kevin!" Martha bear-crawled behind the concrete street barricade until she was damned near crawling up his back. "Kevin, you see that doorway to the Ice-Cream Shoppe there? You and me are gonna make a run for it, then we're gonna cover James and Ruez to follow us. Got it?"

"Right now?" PFC Mallet asked. "You fucking kidding me? They're hammering the shit out of us!"

"If we stay here, we're pinned down, Kevin. Being pinned down is never a good thing. We've got to move. Now!" She pushed Kevin hard from behind and it was enough to force him to bear crawl forward and then rise to his feet.

"Shit! Shit! Shit!" Kevin repeated to himself as he bounced across the four-lane street in the lunar gravity in about three bounces and lost his balance on the last one, causing him to plunge face-first in a screeching crash into the glass door of the Ice-Cream Shoppe. The door must've been bulletproof glass or polycarbonate because he bounced to a stop more worse for wear than the door.

"Move it, Kevin!" Xhi was right behind him, almost stepping on his back as she burst through the doorway before him. Kevin bear-crawled up to his hands and feet and followed her. Several rounds splattered against the asphalt and the lunar concrete. The big glass window with the big red letters shattered and glass flew. "Back door!"

Xhi stood up and grabbed him by the shoulder, pulling him over the counter and through the kitchen area in the back. She landed into the back emergency exit door with her boot kicking it open. Kevin had enough of his wits about him to cover behind them with a sweep of his rifle. Quickly they cornered around the back and slipped to the next alleyway where they could see Jones and Ruez.

"How they Hell are we gonna get them across the street?" Mallet asked the corporal. "They're pinned down like the lieutenant's squad."

"No, we're going to hug this wall in a stack and take turns laying down fire. As the staff sergeant works his way down they'll just have to make a run for it like we did," Xhi explained. "Hopefully, between us, the staff sergeant, and Gray's squad, this little recon force will be distracted enough for us to close in on them. Jones. Ruez. Get ready to bounce.

"Okay, Staff Sergeant, now's as good a time as any," Xhi announced over the comm net. Then she looked back over her shoulder at Mallet. "Don't shoot me in the ass, Kevin.

"Right. Let's go!" Suddenly, the world seemed to move in slow motion for PFC Kevin Mallet. Corporal Xhi dropped to a knee in front of him, firing full auto ahead of them. Kevin leaned out and fired a round or two over her head and then hugged back against the wall as a round caught Martha in the chest, penetrating through her suit and out the back, spraying blood on Kevin's visor.

"Shit, I'm hit!" Corporal Xhi shouted flailing, backward into Kevin. He managed to grab the handle on the back of her suit and slide her up against the wall.

"Hang on, Martha!" Kevin yanked the instapatch from his thigh pocket and broke it in half to release the hardening agents. Then he slapped it against her chest. The bluish gel mixed with the red oozing from the hole in her suit until the flow stopped. He reached around behind her and felt for the exit wound but her suit self-seal layer had already filled it full of organic sealant.

"Missed my heart or I'd be dead already," she said with blood squirting out of the corners of her mouth. "But I'm out, Kevin. You've got to get the staff sergeant cover or he's done too. Jones and Ruez will follow you if you go."

"Damnit." Kevin wasn't sure what to do. He had known Martha since grade school. He didn't want to leave her there to die. "Martha, no."

"Kevin, it's bigger than you and me! Now go! That's an order, Private!"

"Right." Kevin tapped a transmit disk with a red cross on it and stuck it to Martha's shoulder molle strap. "Hang in there, an evac should be here soon. Jones, Ruez, we've gotta go!"

Kevin picked up Martha's ammo bandolier and tossed it over his shoulder. It stuck to the molle webbing and Velcro there as it had been designed to. He leaned out around the corner but was quickly pushed back by a hail of gunfire.

"Shit! This is a bad idea." He looked at what he was carrying and decided there was no real way out down the street. The street was a gauntlet run headfirst into a shitstorm and he didn't like his odds. And that gave him an idea. He looked up at the multicolored family-oriented businesses lining this side of the street. The buildings were mostly town-house types one connected to the other and were only one story tall. There were only a few that stuck up above the roof line with a second story. He reached in his belt and pulled out one of the new grenades and pulled the pin. "Here goes nothing."

He tossed the grenade to the top of the Ice-Cream Shoppe behind him and waited. The grenade exploded, sending debris flying in an arc across the street all the way to the other side of the fountain. A large piece of shrapnel flittered down and made a nice splash into the central fountain pool.

Most of the roof of the little mom-and pop-business caved in and that was just what Kevin was hoping for. He slipped around the backside of the alleyway where he and Xhi had just come from and reentered the shop. There was a hole in the roof that he could see the top of the dome through. He took a leap up onto the ice-cream counter and then another and was on a trajectory up and through the hole in the roof and came to a landing at the edge of the building's rooftop, almost falling over. Fortunately, one of the two-story buildings was between him and the Uey recon force so they had no idea what was going on.

"This will work," he said to himself as he started bouncing at top pace from rooftop to rooftop until he was only a few buildings from the Ueys. He could see that the staff sergeant was pinned down and looked to have been hit in the leg. Kevin slid to a stop prone on the edge of the last two-story building and steadied his rifle. He had perfect sniper view of the enemy recon team and with a light squeeze on his trigger he watched the red dot from the sight become a red mist where one of their heads had been. He shifted and caught a second one of them in the chest. And then the remaining of them trained their weapons at him.

"Oh shit!" Kevin backpedaled for cover. Then like a

flash the staff sergeant was on his feet and in the midst of the Ueys. He was firing and swinging the butt of his weapon like a madman. Jones and Ruez rushed the coffee shop that was making up most of the Ueys' cover and in seconds the enemy recon team had been neutralized.

Kevin looked to the west where the lieutenant's squad was and they were moving toward the staff sergeant's position. He checked his blue force tracker for the red-cross ambulance status and saw that there was a search team moving in on Xhi's location at that very moment. Then something caught his eye farther north up Main Street.

"Uh, Lieutenant Gray, this is PFC Mallet," Kevin called on the comm net.

"Go ahead, Mallet. And that was quick thinking taking the high ground," the lieutenant replied.

"Uh, well, sir, we've got movement about four blocks uptown headed this way."

"What kind of movement, Private?"

"Um, well, it looks like the entire damned Uey Army is marching this way!"

"What do you mean we lost the entire recon team? To who?" Colonel Suarez couldn't believe what she was hearing. "The damned Loonies couldn't have taken out a well-trained force recon squad with paintball guns."

"Colonel, they were loaded for bear. Full-auto rifles and grenades as far as we can tell," Master Gunnery Sergeant Kelly Vors responded back on the tactical net. "Our forward three squads are ready to move in but I'd recommend more."

"How many troops strong are they, you think? And where the Hell did they get guns and grenades?"

"I'm guessing they are less than twenty or thirty at best," Vors said. "No idea about the weapons, ma'am, but I'd suggest we assume they all are armed somehow. Should probably pass that intel up."

"General Mac is gonna want to know that. You're right. Hang on." She switched up a channel. "General McMillis, it's Suarez."

"Go, Colonel."

"We've seen armed resistance on the southwest end of North Dome. Rifles and grenades, sir," Suarez told him.

"Well, that's new, and maybe unexpected," McMillis replied. "How many Loonies you think there are?"

"We're estimating a few tens, sir."

"Not enough to be afraid of, Colonel Suarez. Keep pushing in and take the dome. We'll meet in the middle farther north. Mac out."

"Yes, sir." She switched back to the tactical net. "Vors. Keep pressing. I'm right behind you."

"Yes, ma'am."

"That is a full company at least marching straight for us!" Lieutenant Chris "Christy" Gray was pointing directions so rapidly his arms were waving about like a bird's wings. He thought he'd take off the ground if he kept it up much longer. "Staff Sergeant Ames, get the rest of the South Burrow Militia two blocks south of the fountain and I want you to lay out every type of IED, claymore, and kitchen explosive you can in the next ten minutes.

"Sergeant Moralles, keep the rest of the East Burrow Militia moving as fast as you can and get set up here and here by the elementary school. Use the building for cover and set the killing field up nearest the buses. If they start to overrun you hit the emergency exits and get outside the dome. Blow the buses and the school on your way out." Chris looked up to the top of the two-story mauve-colored clothing store where PFC Mallet was still perched. "Status, Private?"

"They're moving again, sir. I'd say we've got less than seven minutes until they are in range." Mallet sounded very nervous.

"Alright, get me ten good shots up on these buildings right here and there. As soon as your sights say they have targets in range start sniping. Get as many clean targets as you can then retreat. The rest of you are falling back now."

Chris nodded to the staff sergeants and waved them on. He took two bounding steps and put a foot against the wall of a single-story shop and grabbed the edge of the roof with one hand hauling him up. He got a run-and-go and bounded parkour fashion, grabbing the edge of the second-story roof next to Mallet. A couple quick pulls and a kick off the wall and he was rolling to his feet. Carefully, he found a spot a meter or so to the right of the young private. Hell, Chris wasn't much older than Mallet, but he'd been part of the militia longer. Up until about ten months prior that just meant he was part of fire brigades and emergency response.

"They're getting really close, sir," Kevin told him. "Should probably take cover. Jesus, it sure is a lot of them."

"We just need to slow them down, and draw them in. We don't have to get all of them." Chris thought for a moment about something useful to say, but didn't really have much. It was his first real combat too. "Kevin, what d'ya say we don't stay here too long and we live to fight another day, huh?"

"My sentiments exactly, sir." Kevin adjusted his sights and then turned back to the lieutenant. "My sights just locked in. They're in range."

Chris looked through his red dot and nodded in agreement. Then he tapped his forearm and opened the tactical channel. "Alright, let's light 'em up."

Chris put the red dot right on the chest of one of the soldiers moving in the stack on the west side of the boulevard. The ballistic computer in the sight had him tilt the muzzle upward slightly and then it locked on. He slowly squeezed the trigger almost at the same time Private First Class Mallet did. Two of the soldiers went down. There were several other shots from across the rooftops and the Ueys started scattering for cover.

"Keep the fire on them, Loonies!" he shouted over the net. "That's slowing them down a bit."

"Got one of 'em!" he heard someone announce.

"Take that, you sonsabitches!"

"Cernan Dome!"

"I'm out. Reloading," Mallet said.

"Covering." Chris fired until he felt the click and then he noted the counter on his sight showed he was empty. He was beginning to think they needed larger magazines. Mallet started firing again quickly.

"I'm out. Reloading." He depressed the lever under the

trigger guard, ejecting the magazine. Without missing a beat, he rolled onto his back and slipped a second one from his belt, snapping in the housing. "Firing."

For about the next ten to twelve minutes the snipers on the rooftops of the Main Street and Dish Boulevard crossing held their ground. But then something big started rolling down the street in the distance.

"What the Hell is that?" somebody shouted over the net.

"Armored vehicle," somebody else responded.

Chris looked at it carefully through his telescopic sight and didn't like what he saw. Almost as soon as he zoomed in on it there was a glint of a fifty-caliber turret-mounted machine gun pointed in their general direction. Then all Hell broke loose. Muzzle flashes appeared from the weapon and suddenly bricks, concrete, and other debris started flying up from the edge of the rooftop in front of him. A small piece of stone ricocheted off of his mask, leaving a scratch in the visor, and the HUD went crazy for a brief instant.

"Shit, move!" Chris pushed backward, slapping his rifle against the concrete roof and using it to push him in the other direction as he scooted in a prone position. "Fall back! Fall back!"

The fifty-caliber rounds chewed through the walls like they weren't even there. Chris knew that they were going to have to get several layers of building between them and that damned armored vehicle or they were toast.

"Terrence is down!" he heard and then, "Fuck, I'm hit!" There was a lot of chatter on the channel. He tuned it out.

"Follow me, sir!" PFC Mallet dove headfirst off the

second-story clothing shop and judo-rolled onto the top of the single-story building connected to it. "Two buildings up, there's a hole in the roof. We can drop to ground level and get under cover."

They raced as fast as they could, bouncing many meters at time until they reached the alleyway between the next set of buildings. The private didn't stop and leaped midair across the road below onto the rooftop of the Ice-Cream Shoppe. The building was torn to Hell and gone but the kid was right. There was a hole in the top of the building allowing them to drop to ground level.

Chris dropped through the hole and then bounded over the glass on the southside wall of the shop and started running as fast as he could manage. In two leaps they were over the concrete barricades at the end of the street and then they were past the fountain and the park.

"Head count of my snipers!" Lieutenant Gray ordered.

"Marcus, I'm hit, but here."

"Tailor here."

"Samuels here."

"Mallet here."

And that was it. Out of ten of the snipers, five of them counting himself were accounted for. He hadn't counted on the armored vehicle and the heavy caliber, but he should have.

"Okay, get back to your squads and spread out. Sergeants Ames and Moralles, are you ready?" he radioed. "We're coming in with heavy artillery right on our heels."

"Moralles here, LT."

"Go, Moralles."

"We have the buses lined up for cover and if they try

to break through them that's where they'll hit the booby traps. We can lay into them from inside the school."

"Good. On our way."

"General Jones, Meeks."

"Go, Sergeant."

"The UNE Companies from the south have completely entered the North Dome. Our militia has engaged and are pretty much on the run."

"I'm watching the tacnet feeds, Shawn," Tamika told him.

"Yes, ma'am. But they're all inside on the South. And they are split from the troops to the North."

"We don't want to get surrounded, though. Tell the South Burrow Militia to keep retreating past Aldrinville Elementary right up to the West Dome tunnel." She pulled up the battle map and could see where the North Burrow Militia had engaged with the two companies to the north. They were retreating in the exact opposite direction and the two groups would soon be crossing each other's paths, drawing both General McMillis from the north and Colonel Suarez from the south right into each other. As far as they thought they were about to surround and capture the Aldrinville militia. Tami grinned knowingly.

"Keep coming. Keep coming," she said to herself. And then thought to warn the sergeant. "Shawn, get the word to the North and South Burrow militias to watch out for cross fire and blue on blue as they start retreating into each other."

"Yes, ma'am."

"Ten more minutes. Jones out." She changed the

channel over to the external wide-area feed. It was encrypted but the Ueys might have broken it so she used code. "Gravelpit, Gravelpit, this is Dogleg, copy?"

"Go, Dogleg."

"Ten minutes and counting."

"Understood, Dogleg. We'll make it. Any word from Schooner?"

"Not yet."

"Schooner here and in place. Do you copy?"

"Good copy, Schooner. Dogleg copies."

"Gravelpit copies."

"Dogleg out." Tami looked at the battlescape map as the red dots and blue dots were moved about by intel inputs, computer updates, and troop-suit coordinate updates. "Ten minutes . . ."

Major Teri Carboni had been the ranking officer in the North Burrow Militia for almost three minutes now since Colonel Jonathan Gurley was torn in half by that damned fifty cal those Uey bastards had brought with them. Teri had grown up in Aldrinville and knew the northern burrows like they were the back of her hand. The five squads of the North Burrow Militia had been whittled down to two full squads of five. A few isolated others were moving and still fighting but they were wounded. Teri had finally realized that staying and fighting the overwhelming and overpowering force was suicide. She sounded the retreat, telling the militia just to get away and not even consider fighting back unless that was the only way they had of escaping. The order given was "Run! And don't look back!"

The northern end of the dome was mostly residential—housing units and apartment habitats that were stacked in tight against each other lining the outer walls of the dome and in straight lines running along the streets east and west. The volcanic dome top was a bit lower here and was only a good thirty meters overhead. The tallest of the residential buildings were apartment rises that went up to about ten stories. There were only a handful of those. The rest of the buildings were single- to three-story private homes. This was the oldest section of Aldrinville and it looked like any city that had been around for a couple decades and was still growing. Or it had. Now it looked war-torn as the UNE forces marched through, chewing up the buildings with automatic-weapons fire.

Teri led the two remaining squads through habitats across the streets and inward to the central nexus of downtown as fast as she could. All the while the damned Ueys were heavy on their heels. She wished she had a truckload of claymores she could leave behind, but the militia only ever had a handful of those and they'd used them up at the start of the skirmish.

"Stay between the dwellings. They'll be too close together for that damned armored vehicle to get through," she ordered her troops. "Don't look back, just run!"

"Major, we can take cover near the transport tube for West Dome and make a stand!" Sergeant Orville Burns told her audibly with his visor up. She'd lifted hers as well as it was fogging up something terribly. The atmosphere in the dome was still holding, and Teri would have taken her helmet off had she not been worried about getting shot in the head—not that the helmet would really offer much protection anyway.

"No way we can stand against that army," Teri replied. She was panting hard, barely able to catch her breath. Her heartrate had to be over two hundred beats per minute. "As soon as we get there and holed-up, they'll be on top of us. And worse, the South Burrow squads are running right at us with an equally sized army on their heels."

"Jesus, we're so screwed."

"We have to make it to the West Dome tunnel," she told the sergeant.

"Then what?"

"Then, we hope General Jones will be there." She connected to the net. "Listen up, everyone! No firing to the south. We're expecting to see friendlies running right for us any second. Pay attention to your blue force trackers. Our goal is the West Dome tunnel. Get there! Get there as fast as you can and don't look back. Don't stop to fight. Don't stop to set traps. Don't stop until you get to safety."

"Lie still," Tami said softly over the tactical-net channel. "Nobody fires until I do. Nobody moves until I do. Hold still. Patience . . ."

Tami held position in the window of the five-story office building about seven blocks north of the elementary school and one block east of the West Dome tunnel entrance. She'd moved her company underground using the alien transport system and then moved them through the sewer and up into the buildings along the western wall of the dome just outside of downtown. She could see City Hall and the mayoral office about three blocks down to her right. She watched north then turned to the south and could see the signs of the militias' retreat and the UNE Forces' advance. As long as they held still, the Ueys would never know they were there, at least not until the Loonie Volunteers showed them they were there.

The sound of rifle fire got closer and then all Hell seemed to break loose at Aldrinville Elementary School. Tami was pretty sure the school had just exploded. Fifty-cal fire rattled the street just to the north and Tami could now see the North Burrow Militia squads running for their lives for the tunnel with what had to be more than a hundred Ueys hot behind them. Several armored vehicles followed, tearing through buildings and down the street. Heavy-caliber rounds chipped up concrete all around them and they were only barely managing to stay out of the line of fire.

"Shawn, have your rocket teams lock in on those armored trucks. Take them out first." She looked down below as the two and a half some-odd squads from the north continued their panicked run. "Engage! I repeat, all teams attack!"

The windows and rooftops along the western wall of the North Dome suddenly sprang to life with automatic-rifle fire and a barrage of rocket-propelled grenades careening downward into the sea of United Nations of Earth Armored Forces, leaving sinewing trails of smoke in their wakes. Several of the RPGs hit home, throwing jets of orange-white flame in every direction. The debris from blasted vehicles splattered about, raining down in the low lunar gravity.

Tami took aim with her rifle at the driver of one of the

trucks that hadn't been hit by the first barrage of RPGs. She aimed carefully through the windshield of the vehicle and adjusted the ballistic computer until the dot locked on red. She squeezed and held the trigger and watched as the windshield was chewed away with multiple hits. The bulletproof glass protected the soldier from being shot but it startled him to the point that he lost control of the vehicle and slammed it headlong into a streetlamp that in turn crashed onto the fifty-cal gunner, killing him instantly.

"Damn, that worked better than I thought it would." Tami swept her rifle to the south, looking for targets putting the most pressure on her retreating volunteers. Then she caught a glimpse of a school bus barreling down a sidestreet two blocks west of Main Street. There were several soldiers on top of the bus in prone position, firing behind them and doing their level best to hang on. "School bus to the south! Give it cover fire!"

"Hang on, Lieutenant!" Sergeant Moralles shouted over the net to them. PFC Mallet was wondering who had taught the sergeant how to drive.

"There!" Mallet shifted his grip on the bus with his left hand and did his best to fire his rifle with his right. "Sergeant! Turn left! NO! My left! Right! Turn to your RIGHT!"

The bus lurched to the left and then right, almost rocking up on two sets of wheels. Mallet was thrown off his feet and across the back of the bus. As the bus fell back down onto all wheels he managed to reach into and through the glass of one of the rear windows on the driver's side. He gripped with all his strength, knowing that if he got thrown from the bus the Ueys would have him for certain. Just as he lost his grip Lieutenant Gray's hand grasped him about the wrist of his left hand.

"Hang on, Mallet!" Lieutenant Gray shouted. Several rounds zipped through the side of the bus centimeters from Kevin's helmet, scaring the shit out of him.

"Jesus!" Kevin placed his boots against the bus and kicked upward, tossing him in an arc away from the bus. Had the lieutenant not had a good grip on him he'd have flung himself out across the sidewalk to the west of the sidestreet. But as it was, he came back down on top of the lieutenant with a *thud!* "Shit! Shit! Shit! Thank you, sir!"

"Get off me, Private! And keep goddamned firing!"

Suddenly as if from nowhere a rocket crossed right over the top of the bus in a twisting and spiraling path right into the pursuing vehicle. The Uey truck exploded in a fireball with pieces flung asunder in every direction. The wheel on the front was blown completely clear and continued to roll off in the opposite direction still aflame.

"What the Hell?" Kevin shouted.

"That'll be General Jones!" Lieutenant Gray said. Several more rockets zipped into the line of the UNE forces in pursuit. Then a hail of gunfire rained down onto them, dropping the UNE troops in their tracks. "Moralles! Get us to the tunnel entrance!"

"There, LT!" Mallet pointed about three blocks up. There was a squad of North Burrow Vols running right for them and with heavy pursuit from the Ueys. The general was covering them well but it didn't look good. Kevin started picking out targets to shoot at. "They ain't gonna make it, sir!"

"Moralles, eleven o'clock! See them?" Lieutenant Gray radioed over the net.

"I got 'em."

The bus swerved right then left again; but at least this time Kevin was able to hold on. He crawled forward on top of the bus to get a better line of sight on a squad of Uey bastards chasing his comrades. He drew down and locked the dot red just as his magazine ran dry.

"Shit! I'm out!" Kevin shouted. He fumbled about his body for another clip but had nothing but a grenade left attached at his molle straps near his left shoulder. He pulled it loose and popped the pin. "Well, here goes nothing."

Kevin pulled himself up to his knees and flung the grenade as hard as he could. He dove back to the bus for cover but looked back. The grenade took a fast arc across the street just to the other side of where the volunteers were retreating. He wished he'd have gotten a few more meters on the throw, but it was just enough. The grenade detonated, throwing glass and concrete from the side of an office building's first-floor windows. The blast wave of debris cut across and between the rushing squad of Ueys and stalled them long enough that Moralles could slide the bus just to the other side of the North Burrow squad.

"Get it!" Sergeant Moralles worked the door open for them. Rifle fire continued to pour down from the office buildings, chewing up the streets between them and the Earthers and giving them enough cover to load the bus and get the Hell out of there.

"The tunnel, Moralles!" Lieutenant Gray shouted.

"Where the Hell is all this resistance coming from?"

Colonel Suarez of the United Nations of Earth Forces kept enough distance from the front lines that she could direct Bravo and Charlie companies from near the southern wall of the dome where they had entered. "We had them on the run and wiped out."

"Ma'am, forward lines of Bravo are reporting so much resistance that they are slowed to a stop. They are dug in and can probably hold off any advances, but we got stopped cold just shy of the West Dome Tunnel. General McMillis was stopped too, but look at this, ma'am." Master Gunnery Sergeant Kelly Vors pulled the three-dimensional map of the battlescape up in front of them and started making marks. "We have them surrounded from the north and the south. And it looks like we have twice the force level, maybe three times. They can't hold that position in front of the tunnel."

"They could retreat back through the tunnel, though, Gunny." Suarez looked at the layout of the battle. The initial attacks had started to wind down and the lines had stabilized over the better part of the last hour. "They hold this wedge here at the tunnel and at the west wall. Mac is pushing in from the top and we're holding from the bottom."

"Yes ma'am. We could do an orchestrated push and take them out. We might push them into the tunnel but then we just follow them right in and mop them up. This revolution could be over by nightfall."

"Any word on Nathaniel Ray's volunteers from the west?"

"Last intel we had still seems good. They were a good hundred kilometers or more from Aldrinville on the other side of the Dish Crater. It would take him at least a day to move his troops here," Vors explained.

"That's what we thought about Jones' troops. How the Hell did they get here so damned unexpectedly?" Suarez was perplexed. "The last intel we had showed them fifty or more kilometers to the south. What about Hamilton?"

"Captain Blalock from the blockade command just detected Hamilton moving a group of about forty soldiers with a few vehicles coming from way out west," Vors said.

"Where's he going?"

"Looks like he's coming here."

"Too little, too late. Let's mop up General Jones before he can get here."

"Yes, ma'am."

"Suarez to General McMillis."

"Go, Marissa."

"Sir, you ready to make a final push and end this nonsense with these Loonies?"

"Damned right."

"Lieutenant Chris Gray, at your service, General Jones." The young South Burrow militiaman stood in front of a good fifteen or so tattered men and women.

"Major Teri Carboni, ma'am. We can rearm and reload and jump back in the fight."

"I appreciate that, I certainly do. Get your wounded out. You all have seen some serious fighting and more is coming," General Jones told them. "If any of your volunteers want to stay and fight, I won't stop them. But know this, what's left of four full companies of the UNE's

finest are about to press against us any moment now. It
will get rough."

"Yes ma'am. Can't be much rougher than what we just
saw," a private first class standing behind the lieutenant
said out of turn. One of the first sergeants looked as if he
were going to strangle the private.

"Very well," Tami told them. "Your mission is to hold
the entrance to the tunnel in case we have to make a run
for it. But I hope it never comes to that."

"Ma'am. Yes, ma'am!"

Tami turned back out to the edge of the tunnel and
jumped in the back of a LoonieCart II that was waiting
for her. The drive quickly accelerated the car down the
back alleyways of the office district about three blocks to
the rearward-operating base they'd set up. The lines had
stabilized, but she knew that wasn't going to last very long
at all. In fact, she was expecting to see the Ueys attack
with all four companies momentarily. The forward recon
units had all reported back that the Earthers were getting
ready to march. The car came to a screeching stop just in
front of First Sergeant Meeks.

"Shawn, status?"

"As you can see, we lost about eleven percent in the
first wave. We're down to about seventy troops. We just
got a resupply from the West Dome, so ammo and rockets
are good," First Sergeant Meeks said. "I think we don't
have enough to hold the line this far from the wall."

"Well, we can add seventeen soldiers from the militia
that just reupped, That probably still ain't enough. What
do you suggest?"

"Retreat back closer to the West Dome Tunnel

entrance. There, we can increase our troop density and we can hold that longer. Plus, the damned Ueys will get overconfident and bring everything in close trying to take us out with one push."

"I like it. Sound the retreat now. Be expecting it to trigger an attack."

"Yes, ma'am."

"Schooner, this is Dogleg. Do you copy?"

"Schooner here. You ready, Dogleg?"

"No better time like the present. Start a ten-minute countdown. We're going to retreat westward," Tami said over the long-range "encrypted" channel. She assumed the Ueys had hacked it.

"Understood, Dogleg. Godspeed. Schooner out."

"McMillis to Suarez."

"Go, General."

"Intel just hacked a long-range communication that had to be between the King and Queen of Spades. Jones is retreating westward to the tunnel. Attack now!"

"Roger that, General! Commencing attack."

Lieutenant Chris Gray leaned into his rifle stock, squinting at the ballistic computer–driven red dot sights. He could see the motion in the distance as one big flurry and the occasional skittering of a few individuals, but it was too much all at once to truly choose a target. He knew that would change very soon, though. They'd lined up several street barricades, an excavator, and a line of blocks and sandbags across the main loading ramp for the tunnel. The makeshift barrier and foxholes stretched in either direction about thirty meters. They'd parked the school bus at one end, wedged in the middle of the street so it would make it difficult for the Ueys to drive their armored trucks into the tunnel without some doing.

"They're coming, LT," PFC Mallet said nervously. "At least this time we've got an escape route that ain't on top of a damned bus."

"We hold our ground until the general tells us otherwise, PFC Mallet." Staff Sergeant Moralles dropped in the line between them and made himself comfortable. "We're better fortified. They have to attack us. As long as we keep the fire on them hot and heavy, they won't be able to take us. They're gonna use big numbers and push in single points. We'll have to concentrate our fire there."

"And watch our flanks, because if they get in behind us, we're sunk," the lieutenant added, "But we're close enough to the wall, I think they'd have to go outside the dome to do that. Major Carboni's squads are around the corner. I think they'll have our south flank covered. The general's men have us to the north."

Several rounds fired a couple hundred meters to the south and then more to the north. There were several explosions and the firefight moved closer. Lieutenant Gray let out a breath and watched through his sights until he could make out several targets moving in cover formation along one of the sidestreets. The battle for North Dome was about to begin.

"Alright, here we go. Pick your targets. Fire when ready!" he ordered.

"I'm out! Reloading!" Chris ducked back down behind

the sandbags and switched out a magazine. He looked to the south and could see Carboni's squads firing just as heatedly. The general's troops were about thirty meters out in front and more to the north, fighting house to house, building to building, and street to street. "Northeast, Moralles! Armored truck!"

"Got it!" Moralles leaned up over the barricade, propping a grenade launcher on his shoulder. "Fire in the hole!"

The orange exhaust sprayed out of the rear end of the launch tube while a path of smoke streaked out in front of them. The rocket-propelled grenade twisted over twice and just missed the armored vehicle.

"Shit! Missed!" Moralles shouted as he ducked back down behind the barricade.

"Just keep pouring rounds on their location!" Lieutenant Gray replied. "Mallet, get us another rocket!"

"On it, sir!" Mallet scooted down and crawled toward the stockpile they'd made in the mouth of the tunnel. Chris hoped the PFC didn't take too long because the little nine-millimeter rifle rounds didn't do enough damage to stop the armored trucks unless they got lucky and the driver panicked. And it didn't look like this driver had any intentions of panicking. In fact, he was heading right down the street for the barricades. His fifty-cal gunner in the back of the vehicle was firing molten rounds that glowed hot as they ricocheted about, chewing up the blocks and sandbags the Loonies were hiding behind.

Chris had just about had enough of those damned armored trucks. The heavy-caliber weapons had torn his squad up earlier and they'd been running from the damned things for the better part of the day. Something in him just snapped. He couldn't, no, he *wouldn't* take any more of it. He was going to stop that goddamned truck!

Lieutenant Chris Gray jumped over the sandbags in a single leap and immediately bounced with all his strength as soon as he hit the ground onto the top of a plastic green awning leaning out over the entrance to one of the office buildings along the sidewalk. In a single spinning motion he came to the ground about ten meters in front of the armored truck, off balance, and sliding belly-first toward the vehicle. The gunner had tracked him but somehow Chris had managed to stay just ahead of the barrage of gunfire. Once his belly-slide came to a stop he began to realize what he'd done and that he was fucked—or so he thought. Then an RPG hit the side of the truck, knocking it over sideways. The explosion pushed him backward and took the wind out of him. His ears rang violently. He tried crawling on all fours and shaking his head, but that didn't help.

Sergeant Moralles landed next to the lieutenant on a knee, firing another rocket down the street. PFC Mallet grabbed the back buddy-carry handle on the lieutenant's suit and yanked him to his feet.

"Crazy shit, LT!" PFC Mallet said. "Let's get to cover!"

"Uh, right." Chris shook his head, still trying to regain his senses, and out of the corner of his eye saw a couple of Ueys stacked up and moving around the corner, getting the drop on them. "Look out!"

Chris pushed the private down to the sidewalk and the two of them bear-crawled to the doorway of the office building hoping to find cover against its outer wall. Then the wall exploded all around. Chips of debris flew into them, stinging like bees. He was certain the integrity of his suit had been compromised. Chris and Mallet belly-crawled through the door and to the first-floor stairwell.

"Up?" Mallet asked.

"Up," Chris ordered. The two of them bounced at full speed up the steps, skipping several steps with each bounce. Coming to stop at the second-floor landing he shouldered through the door and dove to cover behind a wooden desk in a small office across the hallway from the stairwell overlooking the street below. "Keep an eye on the stairwell, Kevin!"

Chris flipped the desk over next to the all-glass wall and hunkered down behind it. He could see the barricades about thirty meters down the street. He couldn't believe he'd managed to get them pulled so far away from their cover position. An explosion rocked the building and smoke and dust blew in from around the stairwell door. Several seconds later the door kicked open and Staff Sergeant Moralles stuck his head around the corner.

"LT?"

"Moralles!" Chris was happy to see him. "We need to get back to the barricades."

"Worse than that, sir." Moralles said, pointing his rifle barrel in a general northerly direction. "So many damned Ueys just rushed by, we ain't going nowhere soon."

"He's right, sir. Look." Mallet crawled over to the window ledge and watched as at least two dozen of the UNE forces filtered by beneath them. Somehow, they had broken through the line and were coming right down the street toward the tunnel onramp. "What do we do?"

"Hold on." Lieutenant Gray opened the command channel on the net. "General Jones, Lieutenant Gray here. The Ueys have broken through at the tunnel onramp. More than a couple dozen are about to jump the barricades."

"Gray! Do not pursue! I repeat! Do not pursue! And take cover!" General Jones replied.

"Attack!" Nathaniel Ray shouted as all one hundred thirty of group A from his company ran out the West Dome Tunnel, firing their automatic rifles at the unexpecting Uey soldiers from General McMillis's Alpha Company. "Don't let up until they're begging for mercy!"

Nathaniel passed out of the tunnel and down to the onramp, leaping over the fortified line that the militia had done their best to hold. The wave of Schooner's A Group washed over the barricade and out into the streets so quickly that the initial onslaught to McMillis's Alpha Company decimated them in their tracks. The Luna 11 Volunteers split out of the mouth of the tunnel in a classic pincer movement, spreading in two lines. One line took a southerly route while the other northerly, and between them they trapped all of McMillis's western-most troops.

"We're pushing them out, Tami!" Nate announced over the tactical net. "Pushing them right back by you."

"Fish in a barrel, Nate!" Tami replied. "Bring in B Group from the east before they try to get back out of the dome on the North side."

"Schooner's B Group! Attack!" Nathaniel ordered on an open channel. At that point the wall opened up from an explosion on the east side of the dome between the tunnel to the Dish Crater Observatory and the North

Dome. The rest of the Revolutionary Volunteer army, all one hundred seventy of them, flooded into the North Dome, wading through both McMillis's and Suarez's soldiers. "Free Luna!"

"We have to move quickly before they figure out what we're doing!" Mayor Hamilton hung onto the edge of the flatbed truck as it bounded down the gravel road at a top speed of about seventy kilometers per hour. "Here!"

"Hold on!" the driver warned. The truck came to a screeching halt, slinging the loose gravel and lunar regolith up into a glimmering dust cloud with the occasional rainbow of light peeking through. Hamilton went right to work pulling the large cylinders out and off the back of the flatbed. He popped the release handle on the ratchet strap and kicked one of the tubes off the side.

"They're numbered!" he instructed. "Put them together by the numbers!"

Alton bounced down from the flatbed to the side of the long lightweight metal cylinder he'd just kicked off the truck and started propping it up as best he could over one knee. "Here! This is number one. There's two." He pointed. Two of the soldiers grabbed it and twisted it into place until the cylinders were adjoined into a single longer one.

"What next, sir?"

"That one is number three. And there's four!" Alton helped the rest of the squad grab the parts and fashion them together quickly. Then he jumped back up onto the back of the truck and worked a pile of girder work free that was strapped down there. "Help me with this!"

They stacked the girders together over the side of the truck until they formed a small tower about ten meters tall. The bottom of the makeshift tower rested against the lunar regolith and midway up the tower two of the men worked strapping material around the tower and ratcheting it tightly to the stanchions of the flatbed truck.

"Alright! Extend it up now!" he told his team. Several of them managed to get underneath the nose of the long cylinder and started walking it into position. The base of the cylinder slid across the regolith until it *clank*ed against the tower and then they walked their hands down the tube, raising it upward, reminiscent of the Marines raising the flag at Iwo Jima in World War II.

Five more minutes and there was a twelve-meter-long rocket standing upright and locked onto a launchrail that was ratchet-strapped to a flatbed LoonieCartII. Hamilton looked a hundred meters down the road in front and a hundred meters behind them and there were two similar sights. That made him smile. The plan was coming into place. They just had to get the job done before the Ueys figured out what they were doing.

"Make sure the launch lugs are tightened down on the rocket, but not too tight on the rail. They have to slide!" Alton ordered them. "David, you watching all this?"

"Yes, Mr. Mayor, it looks like all is going together as planned," David's voice sounded back to him through his suit speakers. "And you should know that Schooners A and B have attacked and it looks like all of the UNE Forces are being surrounded in North Dome as we speak."

"Great news!"

✦ ✦ ✦

"Captain Blalock!" The young lieutenant commander turned from his station. "The convoy moving westward on the old gravel road has stopped."

"We have current eyes on them, yes?" Blalock asked.

"Sir."

"Bring up the latest video we have," he ordered and sat still in his command chair waiting patiently. Blalock had been ordered to keep an eye on them, but intel reports suggested they were headed to North Dome to join in the fight. Blalock hadn't figured they'd make it before the fighting was over.

"Here, sir." The reconnaissance video popped up on the screen in front of them and they could see the old gravel road that ran from Luna City to Aldrinville that nobody used any longer. The convoy of three flatbed trucks and several LoonieCarts had spread out and there were troops scurrying about.

"What are you up to?" Blalock said to no one in particular. "Zoom in on that central truck."

"Yes, sir." The video zoomed in, revealing several of the soldiers lifting a long tube upright nearest some type of construction they'd put together on the side of the larger flatbed truck. "Hold one second, sir. Video is transferring to the next orbital platform in three, two, one."

The video went black for a few seconds and then reappeared. Blalock knew it was from the lack of complete lunar surface coverage from the constellation. The blockade had a good seventy space vehicles at a one-hundred-kilometer orbital altitude spread over most of the entire sphere of the orbital inclinations. But there were some gaps in the recon view here and there. The gaps were short lived and the system handed off from one spacecraft to the next as one passed by and another moved into place.

"There! Look at that." Blalock pointed at the screen. "Zoom in there to max view."

"Sir."

"Well, looky here. The Loonies have built themselves a rocket. I think they're gonna try and shoot us down with that thing." Blalock laughed out loud. It wasn't quite a guffaw, but rather a laugh of disbelief.

"Is that even possible, Captain?"

"Well, yes, I suppose it's possible. But three rockets against over seventy ships? Sounds like some symbolic gesture or stunt if you asked me." Blalock thought about it for a second and couldn't get any ideas as to why the Loonies would waste such an effort. "Well, we can't let them just take potshots at us, can we? Helm, locate the nearest three birds in the constellation that can deorbit and strafe that location."

"Got it, sir."

"Dispatch them."

"Sir."

"Mr. Mayor! We've got ship movement in the constellation!" David's voice came over the long-range net-encrypted channel. They didn't trust those channels hadn't been hacked by the Ueys but communications had to happen even if the enemy might be listening. "The radar system at Luna Thirteen and at the Aldrinville Dish site detected three of the blockade ships in the constellation applied delta-vee burns and are deorbiting.

The radar guys at Aldrinville said they ran a filter on their tracks. They'll be in firing range of you within the next twenty-two minutes. You can probably see them already."

Alton turned and could see one of the men pointing upward at the blockade ships. There were two of them that appeared to be breaking from their orbit and headed their way.

"Alright. We have about twenty minutes before they can deorbit enough to be in range to fire on us! We have to keep moving and get the flight computers set up and ready for launch." Alton looked at the timer in the upper-right corner of his visor and started it. "We were expecting this."

"Sarah." Alton changed channels. "How's rocket two coming?"

"Rocket two is almost locked to the rail. Starting the electronics initialization now," Sarah replied.

"Rocket three is almost ready, Mr. Mayor," Carla said over the net. "Ready to synchronize the launch computers when you are."

"Be advised that the Ueys have dispatched some ships. They're on their way for us," Alton warned the rest of the teams.

"I'm sending you the updated radar tracks, continuously," David added.

"We see them. There's time," Sarah replied.

"He's holed-up in the City Hall building, generals." First Sergeant Meeks stood at ease in front of Nate and Tami, pointing down Dish Boulevard in the general direction of the town's center. "We captured Suarez fifteen minutes ago. They're rolling her in as we speak."

"Great news, Shawn. Is McMillis still fighting back or just holding us off?" Tami asked her NCO. Nathaniel just listened and observed the battlescape map changing dynamically in front of them. The entire red color-designated forces were surrounded by blue lines, very thick blue lines, and there were just a few red-on-blue skirmishes scattered about.

"He's fighting back from his cover point, but he's trapped," Meeks explained. "We also have some mopping up taking place here, here, and down here by Fountain Park."

"I see." Tami looked to Nathaniel as if he had answers. Nate shrugged.

"Hey, you and Alton are the masterminds of all this. But if you ask me, we need to capture McMillis alive. We need to have him surrender on video," Nate said. "And Alton better come through for us on the blockade or none of this will mean anything."

"I agree. Alright, then. Shawn, take the militia squads, and whoever else you need, and shut McMillis down. Once you get him to cease firing, call us." Tami looked over at Nate and nodded approvingly. "I think we should also get teams to all the openings that were blown in the dome walls and start on repairs."

"That makes a lot of sense to me," Nate agreed. "I'll get some engineers on that right now."

"Major Carboni." Lieutenant Gray shook the North Burrow militia leader's hand. "There's got to be seventy or more troops dug in down there. Any thoughts on getting them to throw their hands up and just quit?"

"Ha-ha-ha," Carboni laughed. "Maybe we need to start playing old fashioned heavy metal over the city sound system."

"Nah, they'd probably just like that." Gray chuckled. "I suspect McMillis won't quit as long as he thinks the blockade can swoop down and back him up at any time. We might be here at a standoff for days."

"Well, then, Lieutenant, we'll starve the bastards out," Carboni replied. "I guess we need to be prepared for an overnight stay."

"Moralles!" Lieutenant Gray called out to his staff sergeant. "You and Mallet get over here."

"Yes, sir?" PFC Mallet was quick on the lieutenant's heels.

"We might be here awhile," Gray told them. "Isn't there a pizza place about six blocks east of here?"

"Uh, yes sir, but I'm sure it's shut down," Mallet said.

"No shit, Private," Moralles said with a raised eyebrow. "Chow duty, sir?"

"Chow duty," Gray told the staff sergeant. "Pizza, sandwiches, whatever. Take a car if you need it."

"On it." Moralles turned to PFC Mallet. "Private, on me. We've got pizzas to cook. Ever turned on a pizza oven before?"

"What? Uh, no."

"General, your Bravo and Charlie companies have been either wiped out or captured. Colonel Suarez is in our custody, currently receiving medical treatment for wounds she received during the battle. You are surrounded and if we make a push you have nowhere else to go." General Tamika Jones spoke to the UNE Forces' leader over an open video link. He sat with a scowl on his face and appeared to be chewing at his lower lip as his jaw tensed.

"What? Are you asking me to surrender?" McMillis literally spat to the side. "You don't have me trapped. You are trapped. Here on the Moon, you *are trapped*! You can't resupply. Your logistics lines depend on the kindness of Earth and unless we let anything through the orbital blockade you are at our mercy."

"Be that as it may be," Tami said slowly and methodically, parsing her words carefully so as not to lose her temper. "You *are* surrounded. And *you* cannot go anywhere. Please submit, General, so we don't have to have more loss of human life today."

"There will be more loss, Jones." McMillis was seething with anger. "I'm calling into the blockade to rain fire down on Aldrinville, Luna City, and all the other colonies until you surrender. This little revolution is over. The United Nations of the Earth will no longer tolerate the insolence."

"I'm sorry you feel that way, General McMillis. We'll talk again soon. And, who knows, maybe in a bit you'll have a change of heart." Tami frowned and cut the video, not giving McMillis time to get the last word in.

"Well, that could have gone better, I think," Nathaniel told her. "It's in Alton's hands now."

"Yes, he better get on with it too."

"Flight systems are synched up. Wi-fi signal between them is good," Sarah and Carla separately confirmed from their stations. "We're good to go, Mr. Mayor."

"Alright, my clock shows the Ueys will be in range any minute now. No better time than the present. Let's start the countdown on my mark. Five, four, three, two, one, mark!" Alton depressed the red button on the control panel and turned the key. The red button lit up and a green light on top of the panel turned yellow, then red. The clock on the panel started counting down from fifty-nine. "Fifty-seven, fifty-six, and counting."

"Counting down on Two!"

"Counting down on Three!"

"Alright, listen, we can't do anything more here. Everyone load up into the LoonieCarts and start heading back west toward the gravelpit entrance. We need to get clear before the Ueys start firing on this position." Alton looked around to make certain he hadn't forgotten anything. Hell, he wasn't a rocket scientist. He was barely a good mayor, much less a mastermind revolutionary. But he knew to do a double check.

He motioned for the rest of the squads back and walked behind them as they boarded the vehicles. He stepped up on the back of the nearest cart and grabbed the cargo rack for a handhold. He tapped the top of the buggy with his right hand and the buggy started up. He watched the clock in his visor ticking down. The countdown for the rockets was at seventeen seconds. The countdown for the Ueys to be in range was at two minutes. The buggy jerked slightly as the high-torque motors turned the wheels against the soft lunar regolith. A bit of dust was kicked up but not enough to obscure his view of the rockets.

"Ten, nine, eight, seven, six, five, four, three, two, one . . ."

For a second Alton thought the rockets weren't going to launch but then white smoke and orange sparks sprayed from the bottom and suddenly the rockets shot from the launch towers at extremely high accelerations. All three of them tore into the lunar sky, leaving behind a twisting trail. The smaller rockets along the base of them were canted at just the right angle to induce a spin on the rockets so they would be stabilized in the lack of aerodynamic forces from an atmosphere. The rockets flew beautifully.

"Stage separation should be any second," Sarah said over the net. "Come on . . . come on . . ."

The buggy continued to accelerate westward as the rockets careened through the sky. The second-stage pyrotechnics fired, dropping the first-stage solid motors. A couple of seconds later the second-stage solid motors fired, pushing the rockets farther up and up. The trails of the three rockets spun apart from each other and appeared to be travelling in different directions. As they climbed Alton kept a watch on the telemetry feed coming back from them in his visor.

"Seventy kilometers and climbing," he said. "Looks like velocity is currently at seventeen hundred meters per second and holding steady. Roll maneuver is about to go, right?"

"Roll maneuver any second," Carla said.

"Mr. Mayor, the radar has the Ueys in range. Take cover," David warned them.

"Altitude ninety-seven kilometers, ninety-eight, ninety-nine, engine burn out and . . ." Alton watched hopefully. The brightness of the engine burns was all he could see, but they were so far away now he wasn't sure if he was seeing them still. Then a bright flash. "Telemetry reports detonation!"

"Detonation on all three rockets at altitude and velocity!" Sarah agreed jubilantly.

"Let's get the Hell out of here!" Alton held on tighter and hoped the buggies could outmaneuver the orbital ships. "Take off road to the craters if we need to. Scatter and don't give them any collective targets."

"Captain Blalock!"

"What is it, Lieutenant Commander?"

"Sir, we just detected three explosions at one-hundred-kilometer altitude!"

"The stunt the Loonies were pulling," Blalock said nonchalantly. "Have we got reports back on the mop up actions there yet?"

"Sir. Uh, no sir. B-but . . ." the lieutenant stuttered annoyingly. Blalock was going to have to have a talk with him about how officers carry themselves.

"Spit it out, Commander," Blalock said impatiently.

"Sir, radar is detecting three very large expanding clouds of orbital debris. They are moving very rapidly over several inclinations!"

"Sir! UNE *Rochester* is taking on major damage and reports casualties," the communications officer announced. "The *Jiang Xhi* reports catastrophic failure in life support."

"What the . . . ?"

"We just lost the inspection station . . ."

"You clever sonsofbitches." Blalock rubbed his chin,

not believing what the Loonies had managed. "Call off the attack on the Loonies and evacuate all vessels from the blockade out past the two-thousand-kilometer mark."

"Sir, at that altitude we can't maintain stable orbits around the Moon."

"I'm aware of that, nav. And I suspect the Loonies were quite aware of that too."

Once the three rockets had reached one hundred kilometers' altitude and an orbital velocity of over seventeen hundred meters per second, whatever was there when the engines cut off would be there in a stable orbit—just like the blockade ships. The nose cone of each of the rockets was filled with hundreds of thousands of millimeter-diameter iron pellets. Once the explosive charge in the nose cone detonated, the pellets were scattered into a debris cloud that would have relative velocities with any oncoming vehicles of at least a thousand meters per second. Every pellet was then a high-velocity rifle round. And most spaceships weren't designed to take multiple impacts from that type of bombardment. Typical spaceship safety protocol was to detect debris fields and move out of the way of them before they hit and did any damage. If they didn't move, the ships were destroyed and even more debris was spread about. Over time the debris clouds would spread uniformly about the orbital altitude creating a shell of nearly impenetrable debris. With no atmosphere on the Moon the debris field would be there pretty much forever. This would make maintaining any orbital blockade of the Moon almost impossible. It would also make cargo and tourist trips to the Moon much more hazardous and would require calculated windows of takeoffs and landings. This way, nobody could come and go from the Moon without the help of global lunar radar debris tracking stations. What it meant was that there would be no more attacks from space. The Ueys and the Loonies would have to work together to maintain the Moon.

"Keep it moving, you Uey bastard." PFC Mallet held a piece of pizza in his left hand as he nudged the line of surrendering UNE troops with the rifle in his right. "All weapons placed here in the pile. Explosives there. Nothing but suits. All visors are up."

"Hands on your heads," Moralles warned them.

Lieutenant Gray and Major Carboni stood behind their squads, watching them line the UNE soldiers up as they marched out of the City Hall building and surrendered. Several minutes passed and a car pulled up. Generals Ray and Jones got out of it flanked by First Sergeant Meeks.

"Has he come out yet?" General Jones asked Major Carboni.

"Not yet, ma'am." Carboni replied. "But he can't go anywhere."

"Maybe he's waiting to go last?" Nate asked with a shrug.

"No, he's waiting on Hamilton," Tami said. "The mayor is inbound. Any minute he should be here."

"We'll wait, then."

Several minutes passed as the soldiers from Earth continued to file out into custody. The stacks of firearms piled up several meters high. Then a LoonieCart II rolled up beside them. It stopped, backed up and repositioned itself into a parking spot with a sign posted THIS SPOT RESERVED FOR MAYOR HAMILTON.

"Nice," Tami laughed. "Mr. Mayor, it is great to see you."

"You too! Tami! Nate!" The mayor hugged his friends and shook their hands.

"He's waiting for you, Alton," Nate said.

"Well, let's not keep him waiting any longer."

The three of them, flanked by the ranking NCOs and by the militia officers, marched to the top of the City Hall steps. Seconds later the doors opened and United Nations of the Earth Commanding General McMillis stepped through the revolving doorway of the Aldrinville Mayor's Office Complex.

"General McMillis, I am Mayor Alton Hamilton. I would very much like to accept your unconditional surrender at this point." Hamilton held out his right hand.

"Well played, Mr. Mayor. The UNE forces under my command surrender."

"Thank you, General. We'll discuss conditions."

"First, Mr. Mayor, can I at least get a look at this alien artifact?"

"Well, that is what this was all about, isn't it?" Hamilton nodded. "Let's see if we can work *together*, this time."